SPLINTERS

A SAGA OF THE NINE WORLDS BOOK ONE

MARK EVERETT STORE

CAMEL
PRESS

KENMORE, WA

CAMEL PRESS

A Camel Press book published by Epicenter Press

Epicenter Press
6524 NE 181st St.
Suite 2
Kenmore, WA 98028

For more information go to:
www.Camelpress.com
www.Coffeetownpress.com
www.Epicenterpress.com
www.Markeverettstone1.com

This is a work of fiction. Names, characters, places, brands, media, and incidents are either the product of the author's imagination or are used fictitiously.

Cover design by Scott Book
Design by Melissa Vail Coffman

Splinters
Copyright © 2024 by Mark Everett Stone

Library of Congress Control Number:

ISBN: 978-1-68492-193-5 (Trade Paper)
ISBN: 978-1-68492-194-2 (eBook)

To my best friend Muad'Dave. *waves*

ACKNOWLEDGMENTS

I'D LIKE TO ACKNOWLEDGE the fine folk at Camel Press, to my publisher Jennifer who has always been supportive and puts up with my BS. Thanks.

THE TREE

THE TRIC

ONE

Life, or something like it

I USED TO THINK THAT MONDAYS AND THE LACK of good coffee were the things that sucked most in life, standard rules of the universe and all that. Turns out that was the arrogant thinking of the young, of which I no longer partake. Thoughts and age alike.

Monday morning came alive with A Flock of Seagull's *Space Age Love Song* on my cell's alarm and a good cup of joe courtesy of the finest espresso machine money could buy, a ginormous steely affair the size of a ten-year-old that brewed coffee like Adele could sing. Aaaaand . . . everything kinda went downhill after that.

Back to the coffee. Smooth, slightly bitter and warm as a prom date, it slid down my throat and set up shop in my tummy as the caffeine went to work dispersing the morning haze that clouded what was left of my mind. It's sweet nectar of life clashed a bit with the chemical burn that was my emotional state, something that even stimulants couldn't quite ease, and I marveled that I wasn't crazier than a shithouse rat. But, then again, if I was . . . would I know it?

Never had I thought I would see fifty-five. Seemed like every day new pops and cracks made an appearance as I stretched the sleep from my bones. I was in pretty good shape, still keeping the comfort padding away with regular exercise, but the cost of age and my previous lifestyle meant that recovering took days instead of hours. I'd slowed noticeably and when injured, hurt more.

Clad in my teal boxers and a blue, ratty bathrobe that was new back when the first Bush was president, I sipped my coffee and read the paper, not really wanting to watch a talking head on the television give me the day's bad news. There's such a thing as too much information. What I read in black and white didn't ease my mind either, though, because its news was *all* bad, graduating to worse. Terrorist bombing there, a highjack over here, and a stock tumble that had people panicking, which seemed to be the usual crap I read every morning. Maybe I should've dispensed with the news altogether and lived like a hermit. Nah, I needed to keep tabs on the outside world or the emptiness of my life would swallow me whole.

Back in the day as the former director of the Bureau of Supernatural Investigations, I ate, slept and drank the news because I needed to *know*, to keep my fingers on the pulse of the world, so to speak. These days the only pulse I had to worry about was my own, and the lack of constant stress was amazing. And annoying. Sometimes, if you've been at the job long enough you become the stress, it defines you. Now, I'm defined by the lack.

After the second cup, I placed the paper into the recycle bin and dressed for the day: faded jeans, an old Nine Inch Nails T-shirt that had more holes than a politician's promise, and sturdy Timberland work boots. I checked my uGlass and saw that a small stretch of warding on the east fenceline was down, which meant that it needed some quick attention or there'd be a cascade failure and the whole warded perimeter would fail. Most likely a break in the silver and copper wiring that transmitted magical energy to the fence, but I reckoned a little elbow grease would keep my mind off of Desmond, my boy.

Not so much a boy these days, though. Twelve going on thirty, he was spending the next few weeks of summer vacation with his grandparents visiting his gaggle of cousins in Finland, and the hole his absence left in my heart hurt worse than a pulled tooth. This was my first time alone in more than a decade, and the ache of it ran deep and long in my soul, reminding me again of my status as a widower. He was the only reason I didn't spew hot, molten crazy all over the place.

Truth be told, since his mother died, I think he viewed me less a dad and more an obstacle, a fleshy wall that kept him from acting on all the bizarre and destructive impulses that hit kids when they became half an orphan. It had grown so damn hard talking to the kid without him throwing up a serious wall of attitude to bloody my nose on, even though I tried like the devil to be the kind of understanding father that could reach through and *communicate*, an honest-to-God Phil Dunpy or Howard Cunningham type. I even went as far as to read a few parenting books written for such circumstances, but that proved to be money flushed down the Amazon Prime toilet, so I did the next best thing and sent him abroad to people who wouldn't put up with his hurting, petulant, adolescent bullshit. Sure, my mom and dad would spoil him rotten, but they were tough as nails and wouldn't allow backtalk or such.

So I hoped.

The kid was sharp as a tack and sure knew how to press my buttons. I can't tell you how many times he made me see red just by tossing me a condescending smirk or a casual barbed comment. Too much like me by far.

Dressed and pressed, I looked under the kitchen sink at the little toy Winnebago I'd purchased years ago, the home of my little Brownie friends I'd rescued during a time when I was merely a field agent. Brownies were shy Faerie creatures (so shy I still didn't know what they looked like), a class of Supernaturals that didn't bother anyone and could do you a good turn if you treated them well enough. I traded cookies and milk for housekeeping and minor repairs, which suited my lazy streak just fine. I'd tried to give them their freedom several times, but they kept coming back like the proverbial cat, and so to be an accommodating landlord I'd purchased an old uPhone for them a couple of weeks ago so they could have some entertainment. They'd been binge-watching *Game of Thrones* and *Stranger Things* ever since.

"Hi guys," I said to the little toy RV, interrupting a spiel by Tyrion Lannister about how he drinks and knows things. "Sorry to bother you, but the bathroom sink keeps dripping. Can you help me out?" In exchange, I placed a malomar on the floor next to a saucer of milk.

The *GoT* soundtrack cut off and was replaced by REO Speedwagon's *Keep on Lovin' You*, which I took as an affirmative. I headed toward the back door, snagging a roll of duct tape from the junk drawer near the pantry, and put the uGlass tablet into sleep mode.

My spread lay outside of Silver Bay, Minnesota, a hop-skip-and-jump from Lake Superior. Far enough from town that I felt the need to drive for groceries, but close enough that I could jog there and back most mornings and keep my wind. With a population shy of a couple grand, it was the perfect out-the-way retirement spot for a celebrity such as myself so as to avoid those that came looking. The people of Silver Bay were fiercely proud of their Scandinavian heritage, being a rather reserved bunch, that is until the beer and vodka flowed freely, and they became just like any other bunch of drunken idiots who needed to blow off steam. Good neighbors, they didn't care much about bothering their famous neighbor, or expressing that fact with great emphasis when necessary. All in all, it kept my private life private, which was the whole point anyway.

Bright sunlight hit my baby blues and I blinked a few times to let them adjust as I stood outside my white, three bedroom two-story. A modest place for a man of my means, but why would I need bigger? Me and the kid already rolled around like BBs in a boxcar in the eighteen hundred square feet plus basement. Seemed kind of stupid to waste money on room you didn't need, and any vanity I used to have died a couple of years ago with the wife.

Tamarack and hemlock bordered a backyard that needed mowing, and in its center a goodly sized burr oak stood lone sentinel, the home of a tree house I built Des a few years ago as a cool place he could hang with his friends. Since his mom died, however, the little place suffered from a lack of maintenance and visitation, its yellow paint peeling and stained. It looked like the Keebler elves' ghost house.

Thrusting maudlin thoughts aside, I went for a hike through pine, birch and cottonwood with my dog, a Staffordshire Bull Terrier named Darby at my side. At fifty pounds flat, Darby sported steel trap jaws that could break a grown man's femur with one snap, constituting my second line of defense against unwanted visitors.

The first was the fence.

As I walked through the trees, I played fetch with Darby, the warm air of summer caressing my skin. A few fluffy clouds dotted the crystal blue sky and I could easily smell the lake on the breeze, which gave me a sense of peace, that everything was all right in the world as long as I was in it, even though that was a damn far sight from true. I bent and picked up a foot long stick and hurled it with as much gusto as I could muster just as I exited the tree line. Darby took off like a brindle blur, his brick-like body moving with surprising speed. He never barked, choosing instead to be a silent attacker.

A small steel windmill, eight feet tall or so, spun lazily ten feet from the fence and I looked to the left and right, noting that its brothers spun as well. Set at one-hundred-foot intervals, the windmills were the primary power source for the warded barrier that rode the fence line like a tick on a dog. Five years ago, a rather clever Magician figured out that wind power could be used to augment spell power, which gave a near unlimited supply of magical energy (measured in units called merlins) to the wards which bordered my large property. The tricky bit of all the magical mathematical equations was the electro-magical conversion process, which I knew nothing about and didn't want to. I mean, I could pop off a spell or two, but this techo-magic crap was so far above my head that I could develop a severe crick in my neck just thinking about it.

The whole thing, windmills and all, cost more than GDP of Bolivia, but I had the money to burn coupled with a gutful of paranoia that necessitated I owned a state-of-the-art magical defense system. After that, I didn't need to know much except how to maintain the bloody thing. Usually I'd toss money at the problem until a savvy Magician-cum-handyman fixed it up right (trust me, this suited my lazy just fine), but I needed to shake some purpose into my life now that the kid was gone for the summer, and this was a good start, my lazy be damned. At my age, a good day's work would lube the joints just fine.

I followed the power conduit from windmill to the conversion box to the secondary conduit to the fence, examining each foot carefully while taking time out to throw the stick for Darby to fetch. I separated the wire from the conduit to check the integrity and the sheathed silver wire from the conversion box looked undamaged, so I began to inspect the fence.

Truth be told, it didn't look like much, seemingly a common split rail that ran for a couple of miles around my spread. What made it special lay along the inside of the top rail, the long line of silver and copper wire set a half-inch into the weathered pine. Twisting around each other, the wires represented the transmission vector for the spell that warded the property, and at each post the wires formed an intricate knot half the size of a quarter coated in clear polymer. In the heart of that knot lay a garnet attached to an equally small transmitter that sent data to the uGlass by some sort of technomagicbabble that left my understanding in the dust.

Quick lecture for the newbies: precious metals can absorb and transmit magical energy while gemstones, even semi-precious ones, can store that magical energy and hold complex spells set there by a Magician, which was the true reason mankind had always valued them so. Spells, even the simple ones, are merely magical energy that is given shape by a Magician, which can be placed into gemstone and also physically represented by molding precious metals into the appropriate form, such as Celtic knot work, which were originally ancient spell shapes. Spell shapes, like the ones warding my property, first give trespassers the heebie-geebies and if ignored, do rather nasty things. Like turn them into puddles of glow-in-the-dark goo. I even had signs posted every hundred feet warning them of such things, but, as my dad always said, you can't cure stupid.

Each fencepost held a garnet in a wire spell knot and each garnet measured about a carat and a half. The sheathed copper wire leading from one particular knot looked to have damaged, severed about a foot along down the rail. The clear polymer sheathing seemed to have been . . . chewed off.

"Wonder how this happened, Darby," I muttered to my dog, who merely stared at me in adoration while waiting for me to hurl the stick, which I did if only to buy some time so I could mark the break with a strip of duct tape. "Squirrels? Oh well, one down and I have no clue as to how many to go." The problem with this ward fence was that it only deterred those creatures larger than Darby and if I'd gone for the itty bittier critters, the whole fence line would be littered three feet deep with tiny, gelatinized, corpses.

Twenty feet on came another break, the sheathing around the wires also looking like it had been gnawed, and I figured I had me an enterprising varmint who couldn't leave well enough alone, which kind of made me the Elmer Fudd of this story. I marked the spot with duct tape as well and continued, the sun baking my neck as Darby fetched as fast as his brick-like body was capable of. Time passed in sort of a pleasant haze and I briefly forgot about my broken little family and the shit that was my life without my wife.

Jeanie and I had been married for over a decade and being with her was right, had provided a sense of order and calm that my turbulent life had lacked. Working for the BSI, killing those beasties from the World Under (the congruent dimension that was the origin of our myths and nightmares that leaked like a sieve, which allowed them slip into our reality) gave me a sense of purpose and focus in my strange life. Back then I was half crazy, and the BSI used my crazy to their advantage and as long as I proved useful, hunky-dory with whatever nutso shit I got into. That all changed when I met Jeanie. She didn't put with my bullshit or my tenuous hold on morality, but took me to task and made me a better man, made me *want* to be a better man.

Now she was gone. Needless to say, my sanity was swiftly becoming smaller and smaller in my rear view.

I traversed ten posts and spotted seven breaks, but after a while I spotted no more. Stretching, feeling the muscles in my shoulders protest, I threw the stick again for Darby to chase and went back to the house to retrieve my repair kit, which consisted of several spools of silver and copper wire as well as a few dozen small, plastic wire connectors. This would be a temp fix until I could get a proper Magician up to the house to do the job right.

From the garage I could hear the *GoT* theme music again as my little tenants continued to binge watch. Really, those dudes needed a hobby, too much television rots the brain.

Back at the fence I disconnected the wires from the nearest conversion generator and set out on a makeshift repair, enjoying the summer sun on my fairer than fair hide and the feel of the slightly warm breeze ruffling my graying blond hair.

Darby kept at my heels, slobbering on my shoes and licking my hands when they came within range, but that was all right because Darby was family, a constant for the past five years that had warmed this widower's heart somewhat.

"Will you look at this, Darb," I said over the third break. "This squirrel has serious hate going for these wires." Good thing it wasn't the gemstones, they were becoming more and more expensive to replace as demand soared. A decade ago, the various governments on the planet decided to spill the beans about magic and the Supernaturals that plagued us, not because they wanted to, but because it was necessary. The truth could no longer be hidden, there were too many cameras, too many cell phones and satellites and keeping a lid on the situation was becoming more and more untenable every day. Nothing to see here, folks, don't mind the evidence right before your eyes, continue watching reality television. When the news broke about the World Under and all that other fun stuff, humanity lost its collective shit.

At least for a while. Eventually the mass hysteria faded, the religious wingnuts who prophesied the apocalypse were proven wrong, and all that was left was a trail of corpses from the aforementioned hysteria and the shattered remains of lives for those who couldn't cope. There was only so much strange a person could stomach before finally throwing up their hands and saying, "Fuck it, I need a beer."

So what was the next thing? Try to make money off of magic, of course. Capitalism will have its day and all that and every corporation, company, and conglomerate on the planet wanted in on the future cash cow. They sought out Magicians and gemstones, one to cast the spells, the other to store them. These days even semi-precious stones like tanzanite and topaz sold at hugely inflated prices that would make a millionaire gasp.

Sighing, I picked up the slobber-soaked stick and tossed it, watching Darby take off like a four-legged missile. Time for the fourth repair. I strolled over to the next strip of duct tape that marked the break and examined the wires set into the wood, squinting. My eyes weren't as sharp as they used to be, but I could still see enough to set me back on my heels a bit as I noticed something that had me scratching my head. Where the first three wires looked chewed by varmints, the plastic sheathing gnawed, this break looked clean, precisely cut without damaging wood.

"Darby, you think we have more than squirrels running around?" I asked the dog, waiting for him to slobber on the hand I stretched out.

The sharp snap of a twig pulled my head around.

Instead of my dog, a man stood a dozen feet away, hunched and ragged. For a second inane words were about to spill from my lips, something to the effect of 'Oh, can I help you?' when I finally *looked* at the guy.

Cataract white eyes glared from beneath mottled brows while cyanotic lips split in a jagged, split-lipped grin, exposing teeth gray as tombstones made larger by receding, black gums. Strips of flesh hung from his cheeks, exposing the bone beneath and I could see he was missing a couple of molars. Ragged and tattered sweats hung from a reeking, skeletal frame and it goes a long way to show how lax I'd become that for a split second, I was frozen in shock.

That's all the time the guy needed. In an instant he went from *there* to *here* and swung a stick thin arm that caught me in the chest like Paul Bunyan chopping at a tree he hated big time. Ribs creaked as the force of the blow lifted me clean out of my boots and my butt hit the top rail of the fence at speed, pinwheeling me over and over, the pain not even registering because it was too big. I was too busy being in shock and trying to get some air in my lungs when the ground decided hit my spine like an out of control semi.

Pain at the back of my throat. An aching hurt that felt like an ember of coal behind my heart seizing my lungs. The world was a wash of black spots that swam across my vision as I tried draw breath, but my diaphragm wouldn't cooperate. I rolled over to face the fence from the outside.

The raggedy corpse in his raggedy clothes and decaying sneakers vaulted effortlessly to the top rail, balancing on the pine crossbar like a crow, crouching and grinning with his slate teeth. "The Tree is dying, Kalevi Hakala," he said in a voice like obsidian chips rattling around a tin cup. "And that means the world will start to shatter and fall apart." He tilted his head to the side. "Did you know that? Were you the one that poisoned the Tree? Are you the reason the sap is corrupted and shards are flying? It is a terrible thing." *Clack, clack, clack* went his teeth as gnashed them, whether in anger or frustration I didn't know. "Either way, I must kill you before you get to the Yaga and muck things up further."

There, sweet breath, a cool sip that eased the hot ache in my chest. "Wha-" I coughed. "What the living hell are you talking about?" My limbs were still on vacation, so my best bet was to stall. "Tell me what this tree thing is about."

Shaking his head, the corpse said, "Nope." It lightly hopped off the rail, small bits of rotted flesh falling to the ground from his ragged clothes, and he began to slowly stride my way with almost delicate, mincing steps.

Oh, damn.

Getting to my feet was more an act of will than strength, but will was something I could spare. "This tree thing," I gasped, slipping a hand to my belt. "Did it look like this?" A red glitter flew as I performed a soft lob.

The corpse grabbed the shining bauble I'd launched and held it up for inspection.

"FLIPWOZZLE," I said.

You might think that's an odd thing to say when an undead menace is bearing down on you ready to rip your favorite head from its moorings, but you'd be wrong. Gems not only store warding spells, but those spells that go boom, and I mean a big baddaboom. All that's needed is an activation word not in common usage (it would be so sad if you blew half the boardroom to hell because you chose the word 'douchebag') and you have instant, crystalline mayhem. Trust me, some of the words the BSI use sound like they came from an episode of Fraggle Rock.

The dead guy barely had time to register what I'd just done when the gem cooked off, a blossom of fire erupting from his hand to engulf his face, and a concussive wave re-introduced me to launch speeds as I found myself tumbling ass over teakettle across nettles and wildflowers, the former scraping my skin through my T-shirt, the latter offering up pollen and a pleasant smell I had no time to enjoy. This time, however, I was ready and performed a neat little tuck and roll so the only thing that really hurt was the fist-sized rock that punched a serious ouch to my left deltoid.

Aching and shaking, I rose to my feet and turned to see the corpse still standing, minus an arm and half a head, rotting brains dripping down onto the summer grass. If he was in pain, he sure didn't show it because the next thing I knew he came at me in a shambling run, malice dripping from one white glazed eye along with gray matter onto tall grass. This time, however, I was ready for a fight.

At five feet it lunged for me, hand outstretched, but I spun, lashing out with a leg so he went down with a thud, flattening grass and shedding putrid flesh and only then did the odor of rotting flesh hit my tender nasal passages. I did my own lunging and landed on his back, driving a knee between shoulder blades and snaking an arm around the remainder of his neck. With all the power in my back, I wrenched upward, ignoring a rotting hand that clamped down over my forearm until it began to *squeeze* and a diamond splinter of pain spun through my nerves as the bones began to grind together. But I didn't stop, because the corpse had the strength to turn my body into Kal goulash , so I braced both knees against his spine and pulled with every last fiber I possessed until, suddenly, I found myself on the back of my front with a head in my arms. Not my head, fortunately, but a half of one that stunk to high heaven. The dead don't wear cologne.

It'd been a long time since I pulled the old 'rip the head from the body' trick and it was nice to know that the old man still had it in him. Still as gross as I remembered, though.

"Ah, gack! That stinks." I threw the head to the side and made my way slowly to my feet, knees creaking like rusty door hinges. His glazed eye stared blankly up at the white fluffies buried in their nest of blue as I hobbled toward the fence, rubbing my aching forearm. A hand-shaped bruise was already starting to form and I knew it would hurt like a bitch soon. I'd need an ice pack and a cuddle with Darby to make me feel better.

My heart plummeted and my stomach performed a slow roll as dread hit me. Darby.

The top of the split rail flew under my heels as I landed back on my property running, calling out for my dog. He would've smelled the dead man in his raggedy clothes even with the breeze blowing the wrong way, would've come like a toothed bullet, and the thought that he didn't sent an icy spike of panic down my throat.

Into the trees I ran, eyes darting and peering through the undergrowth, my chest aching where the dead man clobbered me with his rotting, stick-thin arm. Another bruise to add to the collection, like the one on my ass from the split rail. I knew tomorrow the aching would cripple me up good and I'd have to resort to chemistry to function at a fraction of normal.

Head swimming, I felt battle fatigue setting in as well as the post-adrenaline let down had my body shaking as if palsied. I spit, tasting copper and stumbled back and forth, back and forth, mind racing.

Suddenly everything came into razor sharp focus as I spotted a mass of brindle fur hurled as if were garbage against the base of an aspen, dots of blood stippling the trunk.

I sank to my knees, not minding that it hurt like the blazes. "Aww, Darbs." I buried my face in bloody fur and wept. How the sonofabitch surprised my dog I didn't know, but he somehow managed and I didn't really care right then.

Motherfucker killed my dog.

TWO

A friend in tweed

"JESUS, KALEVI. SORRY ABOUT DARBY." Kenneth Sorensen held his wide-brimmed hat in his rough, large knuckled hands and slowly kneaded the brim as if it were bread dough. The badge on his short-sleeved blue shirt glinted in the afternoon sun like a promise of better things. Close cropped graying hair and a dark handlebar mustache gave Ken the quintessential small-town cop look I knew he aimed for. Despite looking like a backwoods hick sheriff, Ken handled my name a like a pro, not mangling it to unrecognizability like most Americans. *CALL-eh-vee.* Or Kal for short. Is that so hard?

Ken knew me before I became a widower, back when he was a sheriff's deputy and the head LEO was Nolan Bjornson, an affable, sturdy little man, slow to anger but a hellraiser when his temper flared. Nolan died peacefully in his cruiser of a heart-attack while eating his favorite quarter pounder with large fries, no doubt the cause of his early exit from this life. Now he could eat all the McFries and McDoubles he wanted in the McAfterlife.

I nodded, sipping a coffee and staring at the dining room table. Although Ken was a good sort who was always willing to do me a solid when able, I didn't feel much like talking. Putting words to how I was feeling was like licking a cheese grater . . . seemed too painful to try, but I did manage to explain that the spell within the gem I had used on the dead guy was like a line of computer code, an *if/then* statement. *If* the activation word was used, *then* boom happens. He seemed to think that was pretty cool.

Darby's body lay where I found it. Not that I wanted it that way, but because in the case of a Supernatural occurrence, all evidence needed to stay where it lay and I knew my status as the former head of the BSI wouldn't buy me a nickel's worth of leeway when it came to this kind of crime. And believe me, raising the dead was a serious crime, one that came with a one-way ticket to a Michigan supermax built specially to contain Magicians of all stripes, a spell warded concrete house for the magically foolish.

Another sip of coffee. I tossed Ken a thank you nod for the sympathy and we sat in an uncomfortable silence. that stretched out so far that I felt one of us must scream just to release the tension, but it kept on and I was oddly okay with that. I'd been in far worse situations.

Eventually the outside world came into my house in the form of Special Agent Arliss Frikes and the newest batch of hard-assed G-men produced by the BSI. He'd been the first one of the team I'd met, the point man, so to speak, but then the others had arrived and I wasn't too damn impressed . . . all of them cookie cutter agents built in the same government factory.

Fit, trim and all straight up and down, he looked fresh out of Naval Base Coronado (one of two islands where wannabe agents are trained) with hair shaved down to the skin and the kind of muscles only achieved through hard work and ass kicking. Tough and rugged, his package came complete with a pug nose that had been broken one time or ten, and an expression of mild distain carved in granite. I had never met the man before today, but had his measure . . . he was a man born woefully without a personality. Or a sense of humor. Outside, there were five other schoolboy

Johnnies at the scene of the attack collecting evidence, including one Magician who no doubt was using some ultra-cool spell to do . . . whatever the hell Magicians did. All I really cared about was the healing spell she laid on me to take away the bruises from my tender and aging body, or I would've been in crutches for a decade or two. Being a VIP did have some privileges besides hotel room discounts.

Back in my day we agents worked under the radar, federal ghosts who posed as anything else but the people tasked with eliminating Supernatural threats. In and out with no-one the wiser, and if someone did twig to what we were, a simple spell and Interdiction kept them from spilling the beans so we could disappear quietly into the mist. Nowadays, BSI agents were just like any other fed law enforcement types, just better trained.

"Mr. Hakala," Frikes began, immediately upon entering the kitchen. Not Director, or Former Director or any other honorific, just Mister. And he didn't do so well on my last name, putting all the emphasis on the middle syllable. In Finnish, the accent is always on the first, but I didn't expect him to know that. "You may take the remains of your pet at your convenience," he intoned gravely in a voice better suited to a cement mixer.

I guessed it was as close to empathy as the macho, musclebound bonehead could muster, but I kept my sarcasm reflex under control and merely nodded.

"I do have a couple of questions for you." An incredibly brief pause. "If you don't mind."

Of course I minded. Darby was dead and I felt like ten pounds of crap in a five-pound bag, but he was just doing his job. I waved at him and said, "Go ahead."

The agent pulled out a uGlass mini-tablet and started poking at the glowing icons on its transparent surface. "It says here you used a spell gem on the Supernatural. Is that true?"

Ken looked like he wanted to unload at the agent for being a world-class douchenozzle, but I laid a hand on his arm to calm him down. Agents are *paid* to be douchenozzles. "Of course it is, I'm pretty sure your Magician verified that fact."

"Where did you acquire the gem?"

Really? "Part and parcel of being the former director of the BSI means I receive a Class 1 Security Package, of which the security system on this house is one. Spell gems are another. I have the proper licenses to carry concealed magical weapons."

With a nod, the agent pocketed the uGlass, apparently satisfied. "We will find out what kind of undead variant intruded upon your property." Straight, deep monotone, Frikes sounded like someone inserted a Standard Speech audio chip in his brain and he couldn't vary the dialogue if he wanted to. He handed me a card. "Should you desire any relevant information to this case, feel free to contact me at your convenience."

I took the card and tossed it on the table. "Thanks. Have a cup." I indicated the pot resting on a doily.

"Sorry, sir. I don't drink coffee."

Heretic. Philistine. Men such as he shouldn't exist in my world, but I was a kind man and forgave him his trespasses. Besides, I didn't need him or the Bureau, I needed answers and those lay outside such auspices, which meant I needed this man to vacate forthwith.

"Don't need the card, Sonny Jim," I drawled, turning back to my coffee. "I know what attacked me."

That captured his attention quick. Both eyebrows began their glacial climb to his hairline. "Sir?"

I hid a grin with my coffee cup. "It was a Sending."

"Sir?"

Sigh. "Don't you study at all?" I asked. A blank look answered me. "Ask your Magician, a Sending is a spell given form to deliver a message or to kill, perhaps both if the Magician is feeling their oats. In this case, the spell animated the corpse of the recently deceased." I thought for a moment. "Best guess, the Magician spelled some varmints to chew through my ward wires at the fence then sent the corpse to do me dirty. Quite ingenious, if you think about it."

My words bounced off of Frikes' thick skull before settling down in his frontal lobe for a think. "I will take that theory under advisement."

"You do that. For now, though, finish up and head out."

He did so without a backward glance, and I escorted Ken to his cruiser. Deep down in the ashes of my heart an ember began to glow, the barest warmth of excitement that presaged a blaze to come. Someone had tried to kill me, make me an ex-ex-Director of the BSI, and I wanted to know why. There was only one person I could think of who had the brainpower to offer some help.

FROM THIRTY-THOUSAND FEET THE EARTH LOOKED kind of unreal, like watching a sitcom or a political debate. It didn't much matter to me, though, because I preferred napping in my seat in first class, the sleep mask provided by the flight attendant keeping the sight of the passing earth from my tired eyes. One thing I learned in all my years as an agent was that if the opportunity arises for you to catch forty winks, take it. It also helped that the flight attendant, a young guy named Ashton, was a fan of mine who kept the other fanboys from bothering me for the price of a simple autograph. Fame hath its perks.

When the world learned of the existence of magic and the Supernaturals (those things that went bump in the night and often killed people in horrid ways), I was the guy tasked to be the public face of the BSI because I was its longest serving agent, putting a shiny spin on the ugliness of what we had to do. Heck, they even made a movie about one of my more sordid adventures, which bugged me to no end because they took some serious liberties with my back-story. At least I still receive a residual check every now and then. However, it meant that traveling risked fans and their need to adore someone they've never met, which while flattering, was also down-right annoying. The one good thing about being a genuine govern-ment type celebrity is that I'm allowed to travel heavily armed . . . just in case a fatal attraction fan has the desire to boil my bunny.

My flight was mercifully brief and the plane soon touched down at Eppley Airfield in Omaha, a place I'd run on op-in once before. I wasn't too thrilled at being back, lots of bad memories of bad behavior. When I exited the terminal, I did my best to pull the bill of my Twins baseball cap down to cover my face and slink off to where a rental was waiting for me, backpack over my shoulder and fatigue in my heart. Next stop, nowhere Iowa.

Well, actually . . . a little town called Minden, but it was as close to nowhere as you could get without falling off the map. Blink as you drive and you'll miss it. I took the Railroad Hwy north of Council Bluffs through another small blip called Neola, passing by more Iowa farmland that I cared to observe in the early afternoon sunlight, before exiting onto Tamarack Ave for the last couple of miles.

Minden, IA. Population: who gives a rat's ass? I managed to find the street that took me past the Minden Bowl (home of the deep-fried whatever you want) before I came to a quaint little Victorian, on the corner of who cares and what the fuck, painted a dark blue with a light cream trim.

According to the address, I was where I needed to be . . . the home of the geekiest, nerdiest, and downright cleverest scientist-Magician to have ever graced the halls of the BSI with the imprint of his shoes.

It didn't take long for the door to open and a set of wiry arms to encircle my freshly healed body. The BSI Magician had taken away most of the ache, but there was enough left over to have me feeling like a bowl of deep-fried horse shit with a side of gravy fries. "Goddamn, Kal, good to see you," said Alex Dumont from the vicinity of my neck. Not tall, not short, Alex was middle middle with a Peter Parker haircut and birth control inducing horn-rimmed glasses. He had a penchant for wearing sweater vests which completed the entire geek/nerd ensemble. Even in the summer he wore those hideous sweater vests. Except now, he was sporting a blah-colored tweed jacket with patches on the elbows like he was playing an English professor in a bad movie.

The former head of Special Branch, the R&D division of the BSI that designed new equipment and spells for us schlubs who had to put themselves in harm's way, Alex leaned back and look me dead in the eyes. "You look like shit," he said, smiling a wide smile before resuming the hug.

"Hiya, kid," I said through my own hug, which made his ribs creak.

Finally giving my sore muscles some much needed relief, he said, "When did you get old, Kal?" Fine lines radiated from the corners of his eyes and I realized with a start that Alex wasn't the geeky kid I knew from yesteryear, that time had caught up to us both with a vengeance. The person who stood blinking at me through his cheaters was a man, all grown up and everything. The disconnect from memory to reality knocked me on my mental ass. I told him he looked great as I viewed him through the haze of nostalgia that colored my vision.

In the family room sipping Kona coffee (did this kid know me or what?) we exchanged pleasantries. Once again, he commiserated with me on the loss of my wife and I gushed over the pictures of his kids: Donovan, Nathaniel, and Marlene, who were with their mother for the summer. It wasn't easy being married to a magical genius, but divorcing one was a piece of cake. I made sure not to mention his ex and by the guarded look in his hooded eyes, I could see he was grateful for the courtesy.

The living room looked tasteful, hardwood floors and just right amount of decoration not to seem overbearing, but if you looked closely, you'd notice everything was top-shelf. From the hideously expensive Persian rug to an original Chegal, it signaled wealth. I knew that he supplemented his ridiculous government pension by designing and creating new spells (nothing combat related) and selling them to highest bidder, which usually meant a corporation. Combat spells went to the BSI, illegal to sell on the open market, and if you broke that law, there was always room at the Michigan supermax.

Finally, we got down to tass bracks. He stared at me with a laser focus. "What can I do for you, Kal?" He knew I wasn't there for small talk or to borrow a cup of magic, so I let spill the whole gory incident at my place.

"Damn," he breathed when I finished. "I think you're right, I imagine it was a Sending. But why come see me personally? You could've called."

"True, but I needed to get out of the house and staying there would've meant the Magician who sent that corpse might've done it again. At least now they have to work at it. That being said kid, what's your take?"

He gave me the old hairy eyeball. "You didn't tell the Bureau all this." Not a question. Damn, I hated being predictable.

"Nope."

Laughter hit the air with a hard slap that carried less humor than it did sarcasm. "You've got the smell, don't you? There's finally some fire in those old veins of yours and an itch to get back into the thick of it."

"This Magician killed my dog, kid. That can't go unanswered." But he was right, I had the smell in my nostrils and the yen to hunt. Stalking a Magician didn't lend itself to longevity, but I didn't give a fuck. "And who you calling old, four eyes?"

"The Bureau can handle the op for you." Alex stood and poured two vodka rocks. I shook my head. "Yeah, you've the itch alright, or else you'd finish the coffee and grab the tumbler." He downed one, then the other, making a face. "Been a while for me, you know." Booze back in the cupboard, ice dumped into the kitchen sink, he returned in a moment wiping his hands on his chinos. "I love you, Kal, you know that. Hell, I'm Des' godfather, but we are both too damn wrong for this . . . me too divorced, you too widowed to go gallivanting on some foolish crusade. Those days are in the past. Stay retired in peace and find some solace in the arms of a willing woman, or travel to Finland and enjoy your family. Stay out of the danger business, and forget the itch that drives you to risk your neck again and again. You've got a son who needs you."

"Right now, if I stay put and let the Bureau handle it, I'll most likely to die, and possibly Des with me." An ample amount of contempt dripped from my words. In the days when the BSI was secretive, the mortality rate was greater than being a Sherpa leading entitled tourists up Everest, but now they had military and civilian assistance up the wazoo, so it seemed agents didn't have to try so hard anymore. The Bureau had gone from being a scalpel to becoming a broadsword. "It's not like the old days, kid. The Bureau has become just like every other fed agency, they've lost their edge."

Alex shook his head sadly. "It should be their problem, Kal, not yours."

I looked here and there as one of my oldest friends continued to implore me to hang up my guns. Alex lived a comfortable life among his treasures, earned righteously by a mind so sharp it could cut you to the bone. I understood his desire to crawl into the back ass end of nowhere and pull the hole in behind him, but I wasn't built that way. It wasn't *my* way. Call me eccentric, but I'd been resting on my laurels so long that moss had started growing on my north side and although I'd become come used to the sensation thanks to Desmond, he wasn't here this summer and I needed to *do* something. "I'm all alone in a big house in the wilds of Minnesota, kid, and this Sending killed my dog. What do you want me to do? Wait until the next one? Whoever this Magician is knew they that if the sending broke the ward line, I'd come out from my even heavier warded home to fix it, and that doesn't sit well at all."

"That means they're afraid to beard you in your lair. Only the Pentagon and the White House are more magically protected."

"And what if they try dropping a bomb from a helicopter or plane? My house reacts poorly to explosives."

"You really aren't going to listen to reason, are you?"

"Have I ever?"

He grimaced, then nodded in defeat. "Come," he urged and turned the front of his shoes toward the basement door. Down the stairs we went into darkness, the kind full of foreboding and musty smells that gave birth to the premonition of awaiting serial killers or demons hiding around corners. But no murderers or otherworldly menaces lurked, only a tingly sensation that slid across my skin like old cobwebs. My eyes did a sort of ocular dance in their sockets that had me reeling for support, which was kindly supplied by Alex, who reminded me again that there was some real muscle underneath his checkered tweed jacket. Even the Magicians in the Bureau underwent a shortened version of SEAL training.

When my peepers stopped their jig, I found myself in a spotless room filled with more techno-geek junk that you could shake an IT guy at. I'm pretty shrewd, but I couldn't figure out half of the geegaws littering that place, except that they looked like props from a sci-fi show.

Shiny.

Fortunately, Alex, proud as a father of a kid who just scored the winning run in Little League championship game, (okay, that was my kid five years ago, so sue me), began pointing out this and that. "Look, that one is used extrude wire in spell shapes designated by the Magician, and that one will laser encode a spell shape *inside* a gem, enhancing the spell threefold. Quite new, that one. Cost me more than I care to admit, but I had to have it."

Oh boy. "Right. Alex, how about we leave off the guided tour?" I sat on a padded stool and tried not to stare at machine that looked like a cross between an octopus and an orange juicer. "I appreciate your collection, including the marble tile floor, very nice, but what I need are answers."

Alex shook his head. "Don't rush a miracle man, Kal . . ."

". . . or you'll get rotten miracles," I finished with a grin. "I get it. Thanks for your help, though. It is appreciated." Yeah, I did. Appreciate it, that is. If not to find the Magician, at least to do something with my time and if I died . . . well, there were worse things. Like C-SPAN.

For a moment, just a tiny moment, I thirsted for an ice cold shot of vodka. The slightly metallic taste on the back of my tongue, the slow burn of it down my throat and the hot explosion in my stomach when it hit ground zero. Jeanie had kept me off the sauce and only inertia kept me on the wagon. Inertia and Desmond. A dad does for his kids, you know.

Before I could give into the thirst and the lonely thoughts of my boy far away who wouldn't understand why I needed to finish this , I shook my head and continued. "Anything you can tell me, kid. Anything to help me solve this thing."

Time ticked by, tick tick tick, as Alex and I stared at each other, me with a sort of tired Finnish stubbornness and him with a middle-aged, geeky sadness that would've been funny if it hadn't hit my heart like the stab of a dagger made of ice. It was then that I realized that the poor schlub was miserable. Almost as miserable as me, and wasn't that a bitch?

With a wave of a hand and what I could only assume was a small bit of magic, a drawer opened at Alex's elbow and he pulled out a thick, transparent uGlass laptop. "This has a database of Supernaturals," he said. "I can't find a Magician, even a lousy one, by if they don't want to be found, but maybe I can point you in the right direction." He powered up the laptop, which gave out a small, electric hum. "This is a compendium of anything and everything magical. Took me a while to put it together while in the Bureau, but I managed. Took a copy as part of my retirement."

I goggled. I wobbled. "They just *gave* you something CEOs would sell their grandmothers for?"

"Gave? Nope." He shook his head with a smile and said. "Not hardly. I said I took a copy as part of my retirement, not that they let me take it, but what the Bureau doesn't know lets me rest easy." Icons appeared on the laptop and he stabbed at them furiously. After a while he grunted in satisfaction. "The Sending mentioned that a tree is dying. Throughout mankind's history there have been many magical trees: the Norse Yggdrasil, the World Ash, the Bodhi Tree believed to be the Ficus religiosa under which the Buddha achieved enlightenment, the Kalpa, or wishing tree, the Thai Nariphon, the Whispering Oak of Dodona of Greek mythology, and the Tree of Zaqqum, mentioned in the Quran, which only exists in Hell." He grinned. "And last but not least, the Tree of Life which grows at the banks of the Fountain of Youth. Take your pick."

I rubbed my eyes. "There are so many. The only part of the Sending thing that makes sense is the mention of the Yaga, which I take to mean Baba Yaga." The ancient witch of Slavic folklore. Thanks to my years at the Bureau, I knew Baba Yaga was not only real, but lived somewhere in the Ukraine, hidden from the world of humans. But there hadn't been a sighting of Baba Yaga in over three decades, and people had been *looking*.

I shuddered as Alex gave forth a grin so evil it should've belonged on a televangelist. "Oh, Kal, this is the part you're going to *like*."

Oh . . . darn.

THREE

Even after all this time, magic is still a mystery

WHEN A CAR BRAKES ON THE HIGHWAY its tail lights flash, causing the tail lights of the car behind to flash, and so on and so forth. If the highway is busy enough, a wave of red light travels down the road, like the pulse of a living organism or the ripple in a pond, even long after the first car's lights have dimmed.

I don't know why that thought wheeled around my skull, perhaps because I was currently zooming down Hwy 80 heading west like a scalded cat, the drone of the tires a mesmerizing hum that somehow comforted me and sent my mind into a zen place, my eyes unfocusing slightly at the vanishing point. It was there I headed, to the horizon, speeding along the flat Nebraska countryside with the corn and cattle and flattened corpses of opossums decorating the shoulders. Too slow to dodge, too stupid to care. I'm pretty sure there was a lesson in there somewhere.

"This will get you where you need to go."
"It's a piece of shit. My eyeballs need a tetanus shot just looking at it."

Alex grinned. "It's what's under the hood that counts, Kal."

Corn a green and brown blur on either side, I pushed the old Ford pickup as hard as I could, its engine responding quickly with a deep rumble like boulders tumbling around at the bottom of a well. It sounded better than the rusted out shitbox looked.

Eighty mph and still climbing, I fervently hoped that when it hit eighty-eight I wouldn't go back in time, even though I didn't see a flux capacitor anywhere. The speedometer needle quivered and the truck decided to play along, giving me the feeling that I was on one of those old motel beds you popped a quarter into to receive a 'thousand finger' massage. I saw spots, but not enough to impede my vision as I juked around other vehicles, some speeding up like we were drag racing or something. I hit ninety and left those with poor impulse control behind.

Under the hood of the rusted-out hulk of a truck lay a conglomeration of silver wire the size of a pizza box that hovered over the engine like a protective mother. No visible means of support. The silver was a spell that had been given physical form in the metal, through what they called a spell shape, or what a Magician sees before casting it out into the real world.

"Holy crap, Alex!" I almost shouted.

"Holy crap, Kal." My friend laid a hand on my shoulder. "Even after all this time studying magic, I still haven't been able to figure it out. Magic, for all intents, is ineffable. I just can't seem to eff it."

He took a deep breath. "Magic can't create objects, at least no Magician I've ever heard of has been able to, but that doesn't mean we can't do some really cool shit."

One-hundred, and flashing blue lights passed by in streaks of cyan and cobalt that hurt when I stared directly at them, so I didn't bother. Something under the hood rattled and growled, sounding like hate or fury, and for a moment I felt something I thought lost long ago. Fear. Intoxicating, that rush that raced along my nerves like an electric current. I smiled . . . all teeth that had nothing to do with mirth.

The sky darkened between the blue flashes, turning to a mauve that shouldn't have anything to do with a decent sky, but even as my stomach went flippty flop, I chewed back the nausea and kept the pedal to the metal. One-hundred ten and the cars I passed started to look ghostly, like see-though holograms. I felt the hair on my head reach for the sky. Bet I looked like Billy Idol in that moment.

The colors of the sky gave way to a steel gray as the corn disappeared, replaced by miles of ashen flat as far as the eye could see, with only the interstate zipping right through.

"Let me get this straight: this rust bucket will travel on a ley line and get me where I need to go in a matter of minutes." I almost leaned against the truck, but I didn't want stains on my jeans. "And it works? I mean, people have survived this?"

Alex grinned even wider and ran a hand over the beautiful silver spell shape. "Major roads were built on ley lines and no one knew why except for those at the pinnacle of power. Those lines of geomagical force actually aid in travel" He shrugged. "Why? No clue. Yet. And yes, all of our test subjects survived."

That raised the hairs on the nape of my neck. "Test subjects?"

"Mice, cats, dogs and, even a baboon. All survived and showed no trauma, not even the larger primates. I remote controlled the car on dozens of occasions and each test was a resounding success until I shut the program down."

I gave the little skink the old raised eyebrow treatment.

It bounced off his armor of indifference. "I shut it down because it was government funded research. I told them it was a massive failure, that at this juncture it couldn't be done. I didn't want to give them the golden ticket." He chewed at his lower lip for a moment as if considering some dire consequence.

"Meaning what, Mr. Wonka?"

Haunted eyes met mine. "*Would you give an existing govern-ment the ability to put a weapon of mass destruction anywhere on the planet in a matter of minutes without detection?*"

Steel gray lightened at the horizon, taking on a pearlescent sheen that crept up and up and up. The flat vista slowly morphed into jagged mountains that poked upward with no snow line, only hard, black rock that looked as unforgiving as a mother-in-law.

"*Jesus wept, Alex,*" *I sighed, head in hands.* "*This is the best way?*"
"*Only if you want to get where you need to go. The Sending men-tioned Yaga, who is now the next link in our chain. Only problem is that Baba Yaga lives on another continent, and one that will not will-ingly let in the former director of the Bureau without keeping an eye and a few minders on. In fact, its government agents that will stick to you like glue. You'd never get close, assuming you could even find a mythical, near all goddamn powerful Eastern European spell slinger who no one's seen in decades.*"
I tapped a fender on the truck with a nail. It made a hollow, clunking sound. "*But you know how to find her. Him . . . it, whatever.*"
"*That I do.*"

Trees that looked like fractal designs dotted the landscape, their edges hazy, as if a clumsy artist made a poor attempt at eras-ing them from reality. Soon a forest of these strange trees bor-dered the road, which kept its straight course through eternity. Now mine was the only vehicle gliding along its even concrete, the tires a steady hum and the engine a deep roar that shook the floorboards.

My teeth ached from the vibration and splinters of pain punched through my smiling cheeks, but I couldn't relax the mus-cles to save my life. Terror washed through me as the landscape changed once again. I was in no-man's land. Or no humans' land if the centaur like creatures with the fernlike antennae were any indication. They stared at me with luminous yellow eyes, their antennae waving softly in my direction, and I felt a hot tightness in the region of my bladder.

Suddenly, I realized the road wasn't a road anymore, but a softly glowing line that ran ahead, regularly intersecting other glowing lines at right angles. Ley lines, the lines of magical power that crisscrossed the earth, on which I was zipping along, more scared that I'd been in years. Damn, but it felt good.

Alex showed me a plain circle of silver. Unremarkable in every way. It glinted in the sun, untarnished and bright. "And?"

"This is the artifact that will power the . . . ah . . . ley line GPS." Alex placed the ring in the middle of the spell shape where it stuck fast with a solid sounding clink. *For some reason it seemed to attain a greater solidity, as if it was more real than the reality that surrounded it. I shivered. "It belonged to Josef Stalin. When worn, it instills an unreasoning fear in others."*

"How in the name of the Father, Son and Holy Ghost did you get that?" I asked. In my career I'd come across many artifacts and honestly I wasn't a fan. Not a bit. Some artifacts did very little or had beneficial effects, but some were more like a magical version of mustard gas or a fuel-air bomb. Many were even worse.

"The government gives me all the toys I want as long as I produce." He shrugged. "Told them it was destroyed on the second run on the ley line. I've been holding on to it for a special occasion. This fits the bill, considering Baba Yaga is a Supernatural from Slavic legend who often regarded as a boogey man. Coupled with an artifact belonging to a Soviet dictator who was a very real boogey man for millions, the two should share a kind of . . . affinity. Give me an hour and I'll have it tweaked right."

The fractal trees gave way to nothing, a vast empty completely unaffected by the light of the ley line. As for the truck, it took on a glasslike quality, the rusting colors fading from clarity, and I realized with a shock to the core that I was becoming as transparent as the vehicle. I could still feel the cold hardness of the steering wheel against my transparent palms, and I figured that if I could still feel, I was still there, despite my attempt at becoming spectral.

No sky shown, only the empty and the line and the steady roar of the engine. And the fear. The same fear that always ate at my heart, but you can only feel fear for so long before your soul becomes numb to the sensation, and all that's left is a tired apathy and inertia that keeps you moving when that wee part of you wants to chuck it all down the crapper and flush. It would be so easy, giving up. Just let your hands drift off the wheel and ease back on the throttle. To see what Alex meant by keep the speed up or else, because you want to see the else, to feel for the split second before your body becomes random atoms on the ley line express. No coming back from disintegration, or whatever the hell happens when you take your eye off the ball one last time.

But we Finns are a stubborn lot. *Sisu*, the Finnish word for *chutzpah* or dauntless. Shameless audacity and guts, hardness and grit, resilience, all those words rolled into one. Trust Finns to condense such concepts, to boil it down into the bare essence of four letters that and say so much in one syllable.

I had *sisu* plenty. You have to when you work for the Bureau, and do the hard-knock job of policing the Supernatural world and facing down creatures that would make normal folk shit their pants for a year. So it was *sisu* that kept the pedal to the metal long after many would have given up, just like it was *sisu* that kept me going after my wife, Jeanie, clutched her head in agony one day, collapsing dead to the floor before I could react.

They called it a CVA, a cerebrovascular accident. Like her brain had slipped on a banana peel or something. The doctors told me that aneurysms were virtually undetectable unless you were looking for it, and even Alex couldn't find one without conducting an exhausting magical scan (and why would he?), so it was really just a matter of time. So, when I held her lifeless body, and fought hard against putting a 9mm round into my brain pan and turning all that gray matter red, it was my *sisu*, that damn stubborn Finnish resilience, that wouldn't let me.

I'd like to think it was the idea of raising my boy Des, of not leaving him fatherless that kept me going, but I knew deep down that he'd be fine as houses without me, which was my secret shame. You'd think that being a father would be enough, but I was none too sane to begin with, and so the love for my son became eclipsed by my *sisu*. I knew our little family was broken without Jeanie, because nothing worked without her. But I had to make it work somehow.

My thoughts spooled along these lines as the ley line disappeared from my sight, and, speaking of lines, I couldn't see it anymore, too far gone in my head while my foot stayed firmly stomped on the accelerator like it was welded there.

Iowa sunshine washed over me as I stared at the piece of crap magic truck and tried to think of a reason not to go on this harebrained adventure. "Why did you and Dove get divorced, Alex?" The question broke free of its own volition, as if the pressure of keeping it bottled up allowed it to burst forth. It was out now, no taking it back, so I cocked an eyebrow at my friend and waited for an answer, an apology on my lips in case I crossed a line.

It took a while of him hemming and hawing, staring this way and that, before he finally answered. "Magic and the Bureau, Kal. When Dove retired from the Bureau and we had kids, I kept doing private magical research for the government while she wanted me to quit. She wanted a clean break from such entanglements. Said we sacrificed enough for king and country, and didn't want our family tainted by it." He sighed, a broken sound that told me more that the words that tumbled from his lips. "She figured I could do research and sell my findings to the private sector, make money that way if I really wanted continue mucking about in magic, but I felt an obligation to the Bureau, to the agents who put themselves in harm's way.

"*Six months before she filed the papers, I developed the magical equivalent of a targeted laser strike, a spell that could pinpoint a Supernatural from orbit and take it out. The spell gem, a diamond the size of your thumb, could be recharged using solar energy*" *Then Alex did something that floored me . . . he removed a pack of smokes from his back pocket and lit up. I didn't bother scolding him with the whole cancer and emphysema thing. He was a big boy now.* "*Anyway, thanks to my clearance level, I found out that the government was using it to take out high-value military targets.*"

"*Like people?*"

He gave a hard laugh that had to have scored his throat. "*Exactly like people. When I told Dove she freaked out. Left me right then and there.*" *Puff, puff, puff. The cig smelled like stale ass.* "*Shoulda kept to the private sector. Now I work on the jobs I want to, tell the government what will and won't work, and cash the checks.*" *Puff, puff.* "*What will and won't work,*" *he repeated hollowly.* "*The government trusts me enough that they believe me when lie to them. My penance for shitty judgement.*"

We stood there in companionable silence letting the warm breeze wash over us. Me lost in morbid thoughts, my normal for the past couple of years and Alex smoking his lungs out, coating them in a fine layer of cancerous tar. Perhaps he was committing slow suicide.

Now everything blended into smears of white and blue. I couldn't see my hands or the truck as everything that existed turned into those smears, but I could feel them, so I closed my eyes and let the sensation of motion course around and through me, surrendering myself to the ley line, to the sensation of actually going somewhere.

Reality's a bitch and it came at me swinging. Cool air rushed into the cab and my eyes snapped opened as my breath left my chest in a *whoosh!* My foot slammed on the brakes and the tires on the old truck locked up like a miser's purse, shedding rubber across pavement as squeals of protest reached my ears and the smell of the smoking tires assailed my nose like an uppercut.

The truck slewed one way then the other as I desperately tried to adjust, finally coming to a shuddering standstill, somewhere dark and lonely.

Outside a gazillion stars shone down through the leafy fingers of trees tall, enough to put everything at eye level into the near pitch-black zone. It was only by the grace of the meager starlight that I could see that the small, two-land road I now occupied.

Side view mirror adjusted and seat belt on, I checked the rear view. Not a lot of good considering the crud smeared on the back glass. Oh well, what was behind me didn't matter. Only the road in front and under counted.

Alex rested his arms on door as he leaned in. "Keep the speed over a hundred. You'll know when you get there." He grinned, and for a moment he was that eager kid I'd met all those year ago, discussing how magic was really dark energy and such. I felt the soft pangs of nostalgia. "Remember, head west. I don't know why, but ley line travel only works if you head west and remember, it's pretty safe. Every test subject came back A-OK, buddy."

I shook his hand. The hard calluses of yesteryear had given way to the soft hands of a man who hadn't kept up his training. "Thanks, kid. I appreciate it." A pause. "Would you do it differently? If you knew that Dove would take the kids and leave, would you have stayed out of the government's reach?"

Without hesitation he replied, "No doubt. Biggest mistake of my life."

I nodded and fired the truck up.

"Kal?"

"Yeah, kid?"

"How did you get over Jeanie's death?"

"I didn't."

FOUR

Into a fairy tale

W HAT ELSE COULD I DO BUT TURN ON the headlight (the only one that worked) and head off down the road, leaving skid marks behind like dirty laundry. A small bulb taped to the radio, its plastic-coated wire slid into a hole drilled in the dash, began to glow a feeble red. My magical witch hunting GPS, placed there by Alex and powered by Stalin's ring, still affixed to the spell shape under the hood. An indication that I was headed toward Baba Yaga. I prayed she wouldn't turn me into a newt before I got some answers.

Sweat poured down my face despite the cool night air that whistled into the truck. Probably an aftereffect of a massive adrenaline rush. Nothing gets the juices flowing more than traveling to a different continent in less than five minutes. Beam me up, Scotty.

Wherever this jaunt left me, I sure didn't recognize the constellations through the leafy canopy above, and the road didn't offer up any clues, either. I puttered along in the piece of shit truck, surprised it didn't break down on me like I had expected it to, considering we had been converted to magical energy and then somehow re-integrated. There had been a fear that I'd be reassembled inside out . . . don't laugh, it happened before, check the BSI files.

Perhaps a half hour passed with not another headlight in sight and the fuel gauge barely moving a tick, before the little red bulb on the dash began to glow brighter and brighter, its scarlet light becoming distracting as I tooled down the highway. When a cold, sharp light appeared through the trees, the little red bulb gave one last heroic flash and burned out, the illumination fading like a politician's promise.

"Sonofa—" I began, as the truck neared the bright point among the trees and I saw something that stopped the words in my mouth.

Coming into view was a long, single-story building with walls made of silvery metal and large windows letting loose a large amount of bright, fluorescent light out onto a small parking lot. No cars inhabited the tidy little lot, only a couple of parking signs in what I took to be Cyrillic, the same as the sign over the main entrance. I couldn't read the language worth beans, but the picture of a cartoon bear holding a spoon over a plate of steaming food wasn't hard to decipher. Right in the middle of a big black empty forest . . . an American fifties-style boxcar diner complete with classic rock-n-roll blaring through bullhorn speakers mounted on a light pole that threw a bright halogen cone onto asphalt.

What. The. Actual. Fuck?

Truck parked and backpack in hand, I stood, knees and back protesting mightily. The front door swung in at a touch and I entered the brightness of the diner, my eyes assaulted by the black and white checkered linoleum, neon red booths and tables and the smell of French fry grease. Bill Hailey and the Comets were rocking around the clock, the joyous guitar solo stunning the air. Somebody had turned the volume to eleven and broke off the knob, but I didn't mind, as it seemed to clear my head, the last of the mental cobwebs drifting away in the musical assault. I looked around for a place to park the back of my lap.

"(Something Something)," said a voice in a rich contralto in what I took to be Russian. I could recognize the language, but couldn't speak it to save my life, which was unfortunate considering my current situation. Then again, I did speak a few languages besides English. Like Spanish and bad French and . . .

"Puhutko suomea? (*Do you speak Finnish?*)" I asked, turning to the speaker with a hopeful grin on my face.

Holy Crapballs, Batman!

Standing no more than a dozen feet from me was the most beautiful woman I'd ever seen and, brother let me tell you, I'd seen my fair share. Eyes blacker than the sin in a murderer's heart stared from a long face framed by equally black hair that hung in curls to strong shoulders. Red, red, *red* lips, so succulent I wanted to nibble on them for few centuries, were curled upward in a smile so sexy I felt the desire to rear back on my hind legs and howl. A straight, thin nose and cheekbones so sharp you could shave your legs with them finished off the face, and I allowed my eyes to continue to a body so voluptuous that my glands kicked into hyperdrive. Said body was clad in a fifties-style bright red waitress uniform, so tight that the buttons were obviously in peril of failing to contain this epitome of female pulchritude.

Those soulful dark eyes sparkled. "Tietysti!" she exclaimed. "Puhun hyvin ja rakastan kieltä. Vaikka aksentti ei ole hyvä. Olipa istuin ja tilata ruokaa. Borski on erittäin hyvä kuin hampurilainen. (*Yes!*)"

Before my knees could buckle completely, I manfully stumbled into a booth and sat, keeping the weak smile on my weary face. "Thank goodness." I took a deep breath. "Place doesn't look too busy today." Those lips, those nibbly lips . . . so soft, so red . . . *stop it*! Grabbing my libido by the scruff of the neck, I shook it into submission and tried to watch impassively as her smile did things to my hindbrain I'd rather not mention.

"You caught me at the end of the day." Like everything about her,

her Finnish was *flawless*. "The Hungry Bear is ready for closing."

I stood. "Sorry, I'll leave."

The woman held up a perfect hand, long fingers topped with blood red nails. "Stay. You look tired and I have plenty of food left." Her eyes sparkled. "Tell me what you want."

I wasn't going to touch a straight line like that for a weekend romp with Jane Seymour, so I settled for asking for a burger.

"Coming right up." She gave another seductive smile and a sashay that put every other sashays in the world to shame as she disappeared through a swinging steel door into what I assumed was the kitchen.

Girding my runaway glands so my brain could function hormone free, I pulled a small, hinged case from my backpack and opened it to reveal a pair of gold, wire rimmed reading glasses. A gift from Alex and not one for reading, but for *seeing*. I fit them snugly over my baby blues and peered around the diner.

It still looked like a 50s style soda joint complete with jukebox (currently belting out *Chantilly Lace*) and a series of round stools attached to pedestals bolted to the floor. Everything gleamed as if my little Brownie buddies had taken Scrubbing Bubbles to the place. When the waitress sauntered back through the kitchen doors, she was as she appeared, although her too-tight waitress uniform had disappeared, replaced by a too-tight floral peasant dress, the bodice laces straining to hold in her bouncing bosom. I removed the specs and the scarlet uniform returned to my amazed eyes.

She held a plate in one hand and an icy beverage in the other, a foamy brown head dripping off the side of the glass dewy with condensation. Plate and drink were laid with loving care in front of me, along with a real linen napkin and silvery flatware.

It looked like a cheeseburger on a sesame seed loaded bun, and it sure as God made little green apples smell like the juiciest, most lavish sandwich to ever grace a plate, but when I put the specs back on, a different situation was revealed.

Instead of a burger running with juices and thick, white melted cheddar, in its place lay an old chipped china plate covered in nettle greens and mealy, brown apple slices. The glass of root beer morphed into a tin cup filled with what looked like dirty water, which gave a firm answer to my growing suspicion.

"Baba Yaga," Alex had said, pointing at the laptop down in his little Batcave basement. He leaned back with a smile, crossing his arms. "What do you know about her?"

I scratched my head. The basement didn't smell musty like most basements, but it did have an earthy odor, like a heater turned on for the first time during winter. It made my nose itch. "Well, most think she's an evil old witch who'll do you dirty for no reason at all. Flies around a forest in a mortar and wields a pestle like a club so as to introduce your favorite brains to the forest floor. Has a hut that walks around on giant chicken legs, which is an image I don't want in my mind at all, and while most think she's the Slavic boogeyman, she's more amoral rather than evil. She does do a good turn every now and then, but it's rare."

"Like huts with chicken legs."

Laughter bubbled up. "Yeah. There are stories, but nothing concrete. First mention was in 1755, in Mikhail Lemonosov's *Rossiiskaia Grammatika.* A few other stories, but nothing much to pin her down." I leaned back in my chair. "How's that?"

Alex kept the grin on his face. "Still well read, but two years ago a Russian bibliophile, an oligarch named Smironov, discovered a manuscript older than the *Rossiiskaia Grammatika,* written in 1487 by a Greek scholar by the name of Aristidis Kontas. It's this ancient text that contains the very first mention of Baba Yaga."

I leaned forward. A text over two hundred years before Lemonosov about Baba Yaga written by a Greek? That was akin to finding biblical writing in India. My palms itched and I motioned for Alex to continue.

Continue he did. "In this work, it said that Baba Yaga trapped men, not women, but men, by serving them with poisonous food enchanted to appear a great feast. Once the man eats the food, he is compelled to serve Baba Yaga for as long as she wills it to be because of her great hatred for," his finger touched the laptop screen, highlighting a section of what looked to be Greek, "'The arrogance of venal men' It's all here. I'll download a translated section to your phone."

And there it was, a plate of crap disguised as the best burger a man could stuff into his pie hole and a sultry waitriess-witch looking at me with a seductive, anxious look on her perfect face. Baba Yaga.

"Is something wrong?" she asked.

I shook my head. "Sorry. It's been a while and the road is long. Just need a moment to collect myself."

For a second, a fickler so brief that I couldn't be sure it really happened, a look of anger and disgust fled across her features, but the happy, smiling waitress was back in a jiff, standing there at my elbow waiting for me to take a big, juicy bite. "Well, my dear," she purred. "Take your time, Mr . . ."

"Toivonen," I offered, holding out a hand. "Pekka Toivonen."

She grasped my mitt and I clenched hard. A sizzling sound came from our joined paws and a wisp of greenish smoke drooled from between my fingers as she drew in a startled hiss.

Before she could try to pull away, I leaned up into her pained face and grated, "Baba Yaga, by silver, hawthorn, and rose I bind you and constrain you. One time, twice and three, Baba Yaga, so it is done." The words slipped easily through my lips, but I enunciated the Finnish carefully because if I flubbed a single word, she'd most likely turn me into something she could squish under foot.

The wind seemed to leave her sails as her shoulders slumped in defeat. "You great douchebag," she sighed and took a seat opposite me in the booth, elbows thumping down on the table top. "You've read Kontas, big deal. I should have never slept with that sneaky Greek." She pouted and I instantly became distracted by the shape of her lips. "Now fucking what?"

I slipped the silver Franklin half dollar and the rose petal and hawthorn leaf I'd palmed earlier back into my pocket and breathed great sigh of relief. Truth be told, I wasn't too sure this would work and my plan B was to resort to good, old-fashioned non-lethal violence before she could cast a spell. "You tried to enslave me, so consider this tit for tat, so to speak." I tried not to stare at her bosom while leaning back and shoving the plate of weeds across the table. I didn't bother to remove the glasses. "Funny, I thought you'd be older."

Baba Yaga actually spat on the floor, her gorgeous face twisted ugly by hate. "Misogynistic misinformation spread by insecure males who could not stomach the thought of a strong, independent woman who did not answer to them." She flung me a savage look which I easily dodged. "Those stories! They made me a *crone*! Those filthy man-children! For hundreds of years they told tales of me riding around in a damned mortar and wielding a pestle, for God's sake! As if kitchenware were acceptable weapons." A long pause as we regarded each other, her breathing like she'd just finished a sprint. "Who are you, old man."

Well, that hurt. True, I was no spring chicken, but mid-fifties wasn't really *that* old, was it? I mean, on the inside I still felt like that piss-and-vinegar thirty-year-old in the middle of his Bureau career, shooting ogres and killing insects the size of Buicks. Though the outside has sported some country miles and I knew I couldn't hold up like I used to.

"My real name is Kalevi Hakala," I stated flatly, giving her a level stare.

That produced a result. Her creamy complexion paled further and her ruby lips parted in surprise. "I am a dead woman!" She exclaimed, throwing her hands up into the air.

"Get over yourself and dismount the drama llama," I replied. "I'm here for information only."

Lightning quick, she switched to English, albeit with a slick of a Russian accent. "You're the real boogeyman, Hakala, the one who kills those who are different, the one who murders those with magical abilities."

It seemed my reputation as a world class killer of Bad Things proceeded me. My laughter rang across the diner. "Now that is misinformation spread by those who don't know me. I kill Supernaturals who kill or enslave the innocent. Or I did when I was in service. Now I'm retired. I have no interest in your death, I only want to ask a few questions, be answered truthfully, and then I'll be out of your hair."

The squinty look she laid on me spoke volumes about her doubt.

"Listen," I said, easing back and spreading my hands. "If I wanted you dead, you'd be dead, so consider my magically neutring you as a sign of good faith that I will leave you be and head on out once my questions have been answered." A pause. "Truthfully," I added.

It didn't take a world-class poker player to see the wheels turning behind her eyes as she considered the situation in which she found herself mired.

"Don't think about it." My voice fell like iron ingots. "You're stuck and you know it. Anything you can think of, I've thought first. You obviously know me, know my reputation, so don't insult my intelligence."

"As if a no-good *zhopa* like you has intelligence worth insulting."

"You wound me to bone with the keen edge of your wit."

"I should trust a killer like you? One who destroys magical creatures and witches as casually as cats kill pigeons?"

Enough of this happy horseshit. "Listen lady," I snarled, losing my cool. A vein began to throb on my temple and I admit I saw red for a bit. "When a Supernatural comes to my attention it is because they did something to warrant a bullet in the brainpan, nothing more, nothing less. I don't kill unless there's a deserving reason, so don't go about giving me one."

Babs was smart enough not to push me further. She shrugged, trying to hide the sudden flicker of fear in her eyes and said, "What do you want, Hakala?"

It took a sec, but I calmed my happy ass down, reining in my admitttedly short temper. Last thing I needed was to blow my stack and spatter Babs across the diner, which seemed unnecessary considering everything Kontas wrote about binding Baba Yaga to obdience seems to have worked. "I need you to talk to me about a tree . . ."

FIVE

Tree in need

LONG STORY SHORT, I TOLD BABA about the whole sorry mess, starting with the Sending and ending with me sitting in an enchanted diner, holding her down thanks to a magic ritual found in a centuries old Greek text. Of course, I left out the part about traveling the ley line and using the Law of Sympathy to locate her (okay, Alex used it, I was just the test pilot).

The look she gave me could've fried eggs. "What do you know of the Tree, Hakala?" Baba asked me in her thickly accented English.

I heard the capital T. "Which Tree, Babs? The Tree of Life, Yggdrasil? Which?"

"Ach, you are more ignorant than a blind mouse."

Perhaps that was an insult, but I really didn't care. "So?"

Baba Yaga rolled her eyes so hard I thought they'd pop from their sockets. "The Tree, imbecile! The Tree is everything! It is everywhere. It is all. Do you understand now?"

A deep breath didn't help. "What was that middle thing?"

"(Russian expletives, most likely concerning my father and a scrofulous sheep)," she said, with a wildly waving hand and a face so beet red you could've cooked it and made borscht. I fantasized about face/borscht soup for a while as Babs vented, hurling insults I didn't understand. It sure beat television. Eventually, she calmed down.

"All right," she muttered, taking in a deep breath. "I should know better than to let a man get to me like that." Another breath before continuing, "Everything you know, this world, this universe, this *reality*, is the Tree. There is ever only one Tree across multiple dimensions, all the others are merely pale reflections of it, echoes that press upon the world as we perceive it. Yggdrasil, the Tree of Life, the Gaokerena, are all the Tree, but only the tiny bits that you can understand because it is too big for mortal minds to comprehend. All realities, this one and the other eighty-nine, are all part of the Tree. They *are* the Tree."

Okay, mind wobbling time. "What?" I said. "Eighty-nine? You mean dimensions, a multiverse?"

That garnered me an almost pitying smile. "Ninety, yes. The theory of an infinite number of realities is dead wrong, there are only a finite number and that number is ninety. There are nine Prime realities, or worlds of the Tree, of which we inhabit one, and each one of the nine casts shadows, or sub-realities that mirror dimensions linked inexorably to the Prime. The Prime realities are the anchors which ground the mirror realities."

"Mirror realities from the Primes? Like nine other Earths with nine other Hakalas and Baba Yagas?" I asked. A small flare of hope ignited in my chest. Nine other versions of *Jeanie*.

Babs shrugged, then popped the balloon of my growing hope almost casually. "The mirror realities differ farther the distance from the Prime. Mirror Earths one and two might resemble this one, but three onward might be wildly different. Like realities where the Nazis won, or America stayed a colony of Great Britain. Remember, small changes in the past could have devastating effects on the present."

I snapped my fingers. "You're describing the Butterfly Effect, just with a tree analogy. The more the branches split, the more different they become from the main."

"Even a blind squirrel finds a nut," Babs declared in some satisfaction, rising from the booth. "Don't worry, little man, I will return." With that she sauntered off through the kitchen door before I could think of a response or compel her to stay. She did have a world-class saunter, though.

A feeling I'd learned to rely on during my years in the world's most dangerous job niggled at the back of my mind. Babs had gone from terrified to confident, perhaps even fearless, in a just a few heartbeats, and this worried me a bit. Then came to my olfactory senses the odor of piscine decay emanating from the vicinity of Scandinavia.

But true to her word, Babs returned, this time carrying what looked to be a glass sphere the size of one of those Magic 8-Balls that the gullible rely on to foretell the future. "Here," she said, placing it gingerly into my hands. "Look."

On closer examination the sphere appeared to be hollow, the walls almost eggshell thin. Inside the sphere lay . . . nothing. At least nothing that I could see, but something tugged my eyes and I gave a good squint to try and pierce the thing's heart.

My brain skittered away even though my eyes had locked on . . . whatever it was. It was as if I was focusing on answering a question, yet unavoidable distractions kept my brain from concentrating, ping-ponging on various tangents that didn't allow for full engagement with the object at hand.

"Focus, Hakala." Baba's voice carried along by her breath caressed my ear. "It's right there in the middle. Focus."

Right. Focus. My eyes didn't want to, though. In fact, they wanted to look anywhere but the inside of that strange glass ball, but we Finns are a stubborn lot, so I put the full force of my considerable will into gazing deep and long.

There . . . a sliver, a slice of, of, something, or nothing. Whatever it was seemed triangular in shape and small, perhaps half the size of a grain of rice. A triangular nothing which I could feel trying to force my eyes to regard anything else. That put my blood up more than anything, because if there's anything a Finn hates, it's being told what to do.

Gritting my teeth, I bore down on the floating triangle of nothing with every ounce of energy left in my tired, old mind. I'd been attacked, disintegrated, reintegrated, traveled thousands of miles in minutes, and faced off against a legend of witchery. By all the angels above and devils below, I was drained and almost empty, but I persisted until eventually, that sliver of whatever came into sharper view.

A few years ago scientists had managed to photograph a black hole. Not a picture of the hole itself because no light emanated from it . . . no, they photographed the area *around* the black hole. They were able to capture its shape of the material and energies affected by the event horizon of the singularity. That's what I saw in that glass globe: the area, the reality, around the sliver. But my mind still couldn't grasp the fragment itself.

"What the everlovin' hell?" I whispered, my chest a cavity where my heart used to be.

Babs answered, "That is a fragment of broken reality that cuts and destroys the realities it touches. I have . . . neutralized it for the time being because it is so small, but it will eventually shave away at my magic and be free. There are more, smaller pieces. Not many now, but they are multiplying."

My guts became a block of ice. "What?"

"You heard me, Hakala. I can sense more of these . . . absences of reality growing in number and size, and when they grow large enough, they will rip our reality to shreds and destroy a Prime world of the Tree. This slice of not-reality means that the Tree, reality itself, is dying. And it is up to you to save it."

Realization hit, but before I could move I found myself floating a few inches in the air, toes dangling over linoleum. Baba's face was lit in a horrific smile that made me want to lose forty pounds, all brown, as her grip around my throat threatened to knock me unconscious.

"A setup," I breathed. "You set me up."

More smiling. A very toothy one, and I noticed that while Babs remained a hot number, her teeth had grown longer. And sharper. "Like I could be incapacitated by a simple ritual!" She said with a heaping spoonful of scorn. "Me, Baba Yaga. Puh-leeze!"

"It was you," I squeaked through her grip, loosing man points. "The Sending, the message." Of course, it made sense, but . . . "Why? Why the charade? Why go through the bother?"

Babs shrugged. "I wanted to see if you had the balls to come yourself. For thirty years I've heard about the fearsome slayer named Hakala, the man who destroys magical creatures. A fierce human monster who could not be stopped, could not be reasoned with or run from. Vodyanoy, Leshy, Kikimora . . . creatures that caused fear in humans for millennia all are afraid of the legendary human named Hakala. I thought you a myth, something the spirits of the world talked about to entertain, but when the public was made aware of the existence of magic and magical creatures, I learned the truth."

"Mind. Enlightening. Me?" The combination of magic and brute strength held me high and Baba's arm, which felt like it was made of iron.

The next words came as a snarl of anger and hatred. "You are just a man. A weak, loathsome worm of a man who used the assets of his government to kill." She shrugged and I bobbed up and down for a moment, my neck creaking. "But I gave you no more thought because, like all men, you will grow old and die. I was content to wait you out, Hakala, but the shards," in her other hand she held up the glass sphere, "The shards are slowly multiplying and slicing reality to ribbons. The Tree is dying, and I need someone heal the Tree, to undertake a mission to find out how."

"I'd. Be. Pleased. If. You'd. Do. It."

That toothy smile widened, the corners of her mouth touching her earlobes. I was seriously creeped out. "I cannot, bound as I am to this world by vows so terrible that to even contemplate breaking them causes pain. This is a job not for a group of macho heroes who would fumble about shooting everything in sight. That would be like using a broadsword to remove an appendix. No, I need a scalpel, a champion, and my magic tells me you may have the wherewithal to succeed. It must be you because I wish it to be so."

Thrillsville.

"Mind. Not. Choking. Your. Champion?"

Alone, sitting in the booth, the diner quiet, my breathing heavy, sweat staining my face and hands. I looked around, no one in sight. "Jesus," I whispered. One second I was dangling like a tree ornament, the next sitting in the booth. Fuck me, I felt trapped.

Babs came sashaying back through the kitchen door, plate in one hand and a chocolate shake in the other, complete with whipped cream and a cherry on top. Her face was back to normal, no more creepy smiles that seemed to wrap around her head. How the fuck did she get from here to there and back again without me seeing.

Duh . . . magic.

"You'll need strength," she said, plopping the plate down. A cheese burger and curly fires. The shake hit the table top a second later. "It's real food. If you had eaten the spell food earlier, I would have known you to be weak. I still would have used you, but your will would have belonged to me, and I probably would have kept you as a janitor to sweep up the place every now and then or change the fryer oil."

"Animate a bunch of brooms to do your dirty work." I looked at the burger and decided to throw caution to the wind. Obviously, the incantation in the Kontas text had amounted to diddly squat, and if she wanted to do me wrong she would've, although she could be playing with me. Hell, I didn't really give a fuck anymore. I dove in with a will and damn if that burger wasn't cooked to a perfect medium, the cheddar an earthy, nutty counterpoint to the juices that ran down my chin, the sesame seed bun soft with just the right amount of moisture. Lettuce, pickles and tomatoes crunched between my teeth as I chewed, my mouth flooding with saliva as I wolfed down the sandwich. The shake wasn't half bad, either. Though I wasn't going to tell Babs that.

The glint in her eyes told me she wasn't fooled for a second. "If you rely on magic to do everything for you," she said primly. "Then you'll become a fat, lazy, idiot. Like most Americans."

I raised an eyebrow as I finished the last bite of the cheeseburger.

"But you are not yet fat, merely old, and still not too old to do what needs to be done. You proved that by passing my test. I thought time might have passed you by, but you are far more resourceful than I had credited."

"And what if I say no?" Not that I would. Who else would I trust to save the world. Hell, to save *reality*? Said reality happened to include my favorite, and only, son. The current crop of bozos at the Bureau couldn't handle Supernaturals without backup and a complimentary hand job.

"You will not say no. I have seen you, Hakala, and know of your pain, the loss of your wife, the Magician Jeanie. I know that you think yourself a shitty father now that she is gone and never to return, which is the true reason you sent young Desmond to stay with his grandparents for the summer. You don't know how to handle a pubescent son with budding emotional issues, and you need the distance to deal with your own problems. And I know you are a Magician, your powers stunted by trauma in your past, but a Magician nonetheless and not to be underestimated." Babs shook her head. "This mission is tailor made for you."

She shrugged. "Besides, time is the main factor here, and the world will start unraveling faster and faster. Imagine these shards floating all around the universes, dissolving the realities of everything they touch, growing larger and larger over time. Small scale effects like loss of all power on Earth, machines failing, planes falling out of the sky will be forgotten as entire solar systems, even galaxies, will cease to exist, just before the universe melts away like snow in the sun. All reality will disintegrate, matter and energy ceasing to exist despite Einstein's assertions. Everything that was, everything that is, will end. You and I, everyone, *will never have existed at all."*

If I didn't know fear before, I sure felt bucketloads now. Not death, but negation. Not to have existed, undone. Unmade. Unreality. My stomach roiled with acid and a spike of nausea threatened to reintroduce the burger to the outside world. "Can't some, I dunno, some Purple Sidewinding Snorkasaur from Arcturus III heal the Tree or something? Am I really the only one?" I had a feeling I wouldn't like the answer.

Of course I was proved correct. "The damage started on our world, Hakala," said Babs, pulling a smoke from between her cleavage. The end lit up and a gray curl wafted toward the ceiling. Perhaps she could magic away lung cancer and emphysema. "When our solar system goes, it will start a cascade effect that will shortly destroy the galaxy. And because time and distance mean nothing to the unraveling, the universe will follow faster than you can possibly imagine. Even a male mind like yours can grasp that, yes?"

Gulp.

Before I could frame a suitably witty reply that would burn her to the core with my caustic intelligence, she held up a hand palm outward, cigarette between first and second fingers. "No, I do not know what caused it, so do not ask. Just trust that there are but two outcomes: you succeed and life goes on, or you fail, and I will not be around long enough to regret sending you on this mission."

"You say I have the balls to get the job done, but you're no fan of my gender." I shook my head, feeling oddly tongue tied. "I guess what I'm trying to say is, why me?"

For the first time Babs looked . . . sad? Confused? Troubled? I couldn't put my finger on the gamut of emotions knotting her face. "I am no great seer, Hakala, but what I can tell is that you are the best hope to save us all."

Well, wasn't that a kick in the ass? "What do you need me to do?"

Babs smiled sadly. "Possibly the smartest words to exit from your mouth since you arrived. The answer is I do not know, but what I can do is set your feet on the correct path. From there, you must walk it to where it leads. I hope and pray, for all our sakes that it leads to success because my magic tells me that you have a very good chance at healing this world."

Her hopes, her prayers, my ass on the line. Truth be told, all our asses on the line. I was still grappling with the idea of a universal Extinction Level Event of uncreation, a concept too big for my head to wrap around, and the day was starting to hit me. I stifled a yawn and asked, "What is this path and what will I do when I get to where I'm going? Somehow, I didn't think it was a matter of simply finding and opening a universal breaker box and replacing a fuse or two."

The ancient witch of the Ukraine slid a card in front of my face. The writing on it was German. "Here. Go see Dr. Helmut Ostergard in Munich. My magic tells me he can assist you. After that, it's up to you."

"What are—"

"No more questions. You must leave. I had disabled the cellular phone in your backpack, but it will work now."

"This is a shitty way to start saving the world."

Her glare could've cracked stone. "There are people you know who will aid you. I would give you a lift, but my house doesn't like you." Before I could process the thought of architecture holding a grudge, she said, "You will have a chance, as long as the forces arrayed against you do not succeed."

"What? What forces?"

"I don't know everything. I am not *that* powerful."

Life sure can kick you in the balls and it looked like it was hauling back to put me right through the goalposts. Impossible odds, strange quests, deadly peril leading to almost certain death . . . or worse. It was almost like being back on the job. Is that why my heart was racing like a Kentucky Derby thoroughbred? God help me, it wasn't fear, but excitement flushing through my veins, igniting my skin, charging my mind up to almost computer speeds.

The diner swirled around me, colors running every which way into muddy brown blend of light that resolved into the nighttime world. I blinked, realizing I was standing next to the rusty, shit-pile truck parked under a halogen light. In front of me was the diner, the metal plates of its walls shining starkly in the hard light, Babs standing just inside the door offering a sardonic wave. Before I could give her a one-fingered salute, the entire diner shuddered, then began rise in the air, supported by a pair of chicken legs thicker than a sumo wrestler. Wicked looking yellow claws tipped each toe, tearing at the earth with every step, clods raining down. My last sight of Baba Yaga was of her at a window, nodding slightly as the diner moved with deceptive speed down the road under the light of the stars, leaving me standing on asphalt.

SIX

The good doctor and the bad guys

DR. HELMUT OSTERGARD STARED UP AT ME through a pair of coke bottle wire rims, dark eyes enlarging to anime proportions.

"As I live and breathe," he said in wonder, shaking my hand. "*The* Kalevi Hakala!"

The Kalevi Hakala. Whoop-de-fucking-do.

Turned out Alex's magic truck had landed me in the middle of Ukraine's Podilski Tovtry National Park, not too far from the Romanian Border. Since my contacts in the Ukraine died or disappeared years ago, I called up an old Romanian buddy of mine, Ionut Popescu. As the former head of Romania's version of the BSI, we had met several times at summits to discuss rising Supernatural threats, and struck an unlikely friendship that transcended geopolitical issues. As any good agent will tell you, if you hire a political hack to lead an agency for taking on Supernaturals, you'll wind up with the bodies of fellow agents to clean up. This often led to said hacks disappearing or retiring rather sharpish. Ionut was one of the good eggs who despised political chicanery, which put him high on my list of sharp cookies.

I drove the truck to a little town called Chernivtsi to meet Ionut, stripping the spell shape from the engine block before he drove me across the border to his place in Cluj-Napoca. Alex wasn't getting the truck back, but at least he'd have his spell shape once Ionut sent it through FedEx. That much silver at six-hundred an ounce was a fortune, and who knows, perhaps he'd have a chance to use it again.

Cluj-Napoca is the unofficial capitol of the Transylvanian region of Romania and home to many gothic style buildings that looked right out of Stoker's wet dreams and a few Black Sabbath album covers. Modern and thriving, I had no problems making like a tourist, especially as many of the establishments didn't mind American dollars one bit. I shopped for necessaries while Ionut set up a flight to Munich, no questions asked. One look at my face and he had known the game was afoot.

Google searching found me a couple of articles about Dr. Helmut Ostergard of the Ludwig Maximillian University of Munich, the Dean of the Faculty for the Study of Culture (think archeological, historico-philological, anthropological, ethnological and sociological studies all rolled up into one, big, greasy ball). His responsibility was prehistoric and early archeology. Once I knew where to go, all it took was Ionut flexing some political clout at the airport for my backpack to go through unsearched, and I was gone, gone, gonesville.

As for the professor, finding him in LMU Munich took more elbow grease than I expected. The university looked like a god-damn city in and of itself and the only German I knew would get me face-slapped by a pretty *fräulein* in a heartbeat. Another issue was where to find the Faculty for the Study of Culture since the university has buildings all over the city and I had to find the correct one, but the English-speaking cabbie spoke perfect American dollar and was willing to help me with legwork as long as his palms were sufficiently greased in greenbacks. By midday I stood in front of an oak desk of biblical proportions covered in enough loose papers to completely obscure what they lay upon.

Ostergard looked to be a trim man in his early forties, with dimpled cheeks, an impeccably groomed mustache and goatee, and short hair on the auburn side of brown. Although a head shorter than I, he radiated enough confidence and strength that I assumed he could hold his own when push came to shove. He wore an expensive tan suit and a tennis ball green tie that made my retinas ache.

I let him have his fanboy moment, even signing a research notebook and a posing for a couple of selfies. His offer of lunch was gladly accepted, considering my last full meal was a roast ham hock with rustic cabbage prepared by Ionut's wife Juliani. The ham hock hadn't been bad, but the cabbage had tasted like refried assholes (before you ask . . . please don't). He led me to a little place not far from campus where we sat at a patio table, a plate of schnitzel weiner art (deep fried pork cutlet) with potatoes in front of me, and a cold mug of beer at my elbow. This food wasn't bad, but was greasy enough to make a Taco Bell value meal seem healthy.

I ate slowly as the events of the past couple of days caught up with me. Every muscle in my body wanted to turn into Jell-O, and as tension bled away, I was so fucking tired that even a beautiful, modern city like Munich had lost some of its luster. Frankly, at that point my give-a-shitter was well and truly broken, but at least I was drinking some damn fine beer, chowing on fried food, and nobody was trying to kill me. Talk about a win-win.

During our lunch I hit the highlights of my mission, trusting the good doctor would see the necessity of helping out, but Ostergard grew more and more fascinated as I talked, finally throwing up his hands in glee when my narration came to a close. Not the reaction I had expected from telling the man that the entire universe was about to be un-created.

"The Tree as a manifestation of reality!" he exploded, drawing stares. I sipped at my beer. Much better than Miller time. "I knew the legends held the kernel of truth!"

"You're not worried about reality shredding apart?" I asked, more than a little confused. "I mean, the situation is rather grim."

"Ach, why worry?" he asked, also sipping his beer. "You are famous for saving the world many times over, *ja*? I trust you will do it again, so there is no worry." The professor waved his hand. "Besides, if I will never have existed, then all regret, sadness, hope, death will begone. Who will know, *ja*? What makes me happy now is that the legends concerning the Tree are founded in reality, not fantasy."

Was this guy for real? A sane person would be gulping down Tums like Pez. "Which legends?"

"All of them! Every single religion has a sacred tree in their catechism, from the Tree of Knowledge that bore the Forbidden Fruit, to the Aztec culture whose artists painted the world with trees at the four corners holding up the sky. I could go on and on, but the gist of it is that we humans have always held certain trees to be holy, or sacred. If what you're telling me is from a source like Baba Yaga herself, a witch who legend says lives in a forest, this is an incredible vindication of every theory I've written about the relationship between the divine and sacred trees."

"Now hold on, Dr. Ostergard—" I was about to chill him out a bit because the last thing I needed was an archeology professor working himself in to a lather, but before I could, I was interrupted.

"Excuse me." The man who suddenly appeared at our table and sat without a 'by your leave' looked to be the type whose job was to stay in shape. Dark hair, a hint of five o'clock shadow on his moderately handsome face, and an impeccable black suit that drank the light. was all that I noticed before he took an empty chair, legs crossed casually. He proceeded to toss a beatific smile my way. "It is truly a pleasure to meet you, Mr. Hakala." His pronunciation of my name was flawless, despite the fact he looked more Middle Eastern than Finnish. "Sorry for the interruption, but I have some information about your current . . . ah . . . assignment, so to speak." Eyes like dark brown marbles dipped in liquid nitrogen regarded me, as I noted the fain acne scars on his cheeks.

The hairs on the back of my neck stood at attention, and my hand slid slowly into my backpack, which rested next to my chair.

In a voice smooth as freshly polished steel, the man began. "I wish to start this conversation with an expression of my utter admiration for you, Mr. Hakala." His English was salted with an accent I couldn't quite place. He put a hand to his chest. "You are, without a doubt, one of my heroes, and my companions, it is safe for me to say, would say the same."

The professor was about to protest, but I lifted a finger and he settled down. My curiosity button was well and truly pushed and I wanted this wiggler to elaborate. "Your companions, Mister . . .?"

"Rafa," he supplied with a shit-eating grin. "Rafa Sari of the *Tempora Apostolorum Vestrorum Praeceptorum Finis.*" The words hit the air as if I should be well and truly gobsmacked, but I remained resolutely gobsmack-free.

Beside me, however, the professor paled, large eyes widening behind the thick lenses of his gold wire rims, and I knew he was gobsmacked enough for the both of us. "What gives, Helmut?" I asked, keen to find out what he knew.

"*Tempora Apostolorum Vestrorum Praeceptorum Finis* is Latin for Apostles of the End Times," he said, each word seemingly wrenched from his mouth like fish hooks. "I—I thought them an urban legend. A myth."

Rafa spread his hands, his smile unfaltering. "Obviously not." I noticed the callouses on his fingers and palms. Callouses that came from long hours of knife fighting practice. I knew those callouses well, my friend Canton, a former member of the BSI, bore the same. At my look he said, "Our order was created in the 1800s by Pope Pius VII, blessed be his name, after his restoration of the Society of Jesus. In his blessed wisdom, he created our order to watch for the coming of the Anti-Christ and to facilitate the End Times, which we have been doing ever since."

"By whatever foul means necessary," blurted Helmut, disgust overriding his fear. "It is said you *aided* Hitler in the Final Solution."

"We thought he was the Anti-Christ." Rafa studied his nails, trying to appear nonchalant, but I could see the tension in his shoulders. "A mistake, of course, but the Kingdom of Christ must come to be, no matter the sacrifice. The reign of the Lord will give this world to the faithful. I must say, Professor Ostergard, the fact that you know this much about us is remarkable. We have worked hard to keep secret our existence."

I was starting to feel rather like a third wheel, something that didn't sit too well, and I leaned toward Rafa, struggling to control my temper. "Do you understand that all of *reality* is coming apart?"

"Of course, as God wills."

"How do you know all this? I just learned about it from an immortal witch who found out only recently."

Again with the shitty smile. "You must mean Baba Yaga. Not surprising she would know." His eyes bored into mine. "The Apostles have our ways, Kalevi Hakala, ways provided by God Himself."

Wonderful. Mystical mumbo jumbo mixed with idiotic fanaticism. I should've stayed in bed. "When reality fades into nothing, only the Holy Trinity will remain and God will recreate all, setting his chosen Son upon the new Earth to rule for a thousand years." Rafa's voice took on a singsong cadence and he raised his hands in the air, as if a little café in Munich was a church. "And the newly recreated mankind will bask in the glory of His presence, His divine rule. Do you know what that means?"

"That you need psychiatric help?"

Smack! A heavy iron ring on Rafa's middle finger connected with the table top. It seemed I had managed to eat away at his patience, a practice on which I prided myself. The patrons all around us looked over for a moment, then went back to their lunches. Polite Germans, who woulda thought? "I am deadly serious, Kalevi Hakala," hissed Rafa. "Our God wishes to unmake the world and you need to let it happen. Even now, it begins." He pulled out a uPhone and held it up.

My eyes grew wide as multiple news headlines scrolled across the clear plate of the cell: PLANE CRASH CAUSED BY SMALL HOLES IN ENGINE. THOUSANDS DEAD AS MYSTERY VIRUS TUNNELS THROUGH TISSUES, DISRUPTS BODILY FUNCTIONS. SERIVNYA NUCLEAR PLANT FACES CRITICAL MELTDOWN. SCIENTISTS ALARMED AT SPIKE IN TECTONIC ACTIVITY.

"See?" he said. "It will only grow. Soon God's plan will unfold and the universe will be reborn."

"For you and your holy roller boys club? Or can anyone join?"

"Not just a boys club, Mr. Hakala. Women of true faith already belong . . . just like the one who has you and the good professor in her sights." Rafa's grin widened. "Don't bother looking for red dots. Shiana doesn't need laser sights, I assure you. Check over my left shoulder, Look up."

My eyes climbed a four story some thirty yards behind the fanatic, and sure enough, I spotted the dark form on the roof, perfect positioning for a sniper. The muscles at the corner of my jaw tightened.

"Stand down, Mr. Hakala. You have already lost, but in doing so, have also won. Join us in rebirth for the thousand-year reign of Christ."

"How did you find me?" I asked, trying for nonchalance and failing miserably.

A small shrug. "I can find anything and anyone. We are all blessed with particular gifts, that is mine."

While he was talking, my other had hand slipped out of sight, and before anyone could react, I jumped to my feet, flipping the heavy table into the air toward Rafa, and grabbed Ostergard by the arm. In midair the table *spang*-ed, a nickel-sized hole appearing in the iron, and I beat feet, dragging the professor and my backpack toward the cafe. Behind me, I heard cursing in a language I didn't understand and sure didn't want to. Another round from the sniper took a patron who was beginning to stand, punching a hole through her cheek and spraying blood and brains onto my left arm as I ran past. Damn, that sniper could shoot. That victim was less than a foot away when she was hit, and I knew the next would find me. Center mass. Screams began to erupt as the other diners started to realize that people shouldn't be suddenly sprouting bloody holes.

I ducked, dragging the professor down to my level behind a chair filled with a fat man, whose stomach exploded in red. We crawled, using the large corpse as cover, and slid through the front door as glass shattered and brick façade blew apart from repeated shots, the sounds of which never reached my ears. Whoever the sniper was, they either had a world-class suppressor, or the rifle had been magically silenced, which meant there could be a Magician among the Apostles of the End Times. A pretty shitty name if you asked me. Funny, but I didn't think the bad guys really wanted my opinion on nomenclature at this moment.

"Ach!" gagged Helmut. I realized I'd had him in a death grip.

"Sorry," I said, not letting go, but easing up some.

With a violent wrench, Helmut pulled his arm away and grabbed mine. "You come with me!" he urged, beginning to crawl his way through the restaurant as bullets continued to pepper innocent bystanders.

We belly crawled our way as fast as we could and made it to the dubious safety of the kitchen, all stainless steel and fryer oil smells. "I know the owner," yelled Helmut over the hysterical screams of cowering cooks. One enormous lady with tight blond ringlets was curled in the fetal position and babbling in rapid fire German. It sounded like a prayer. "This way!" He surged to his feet and I followed, sneakers slapping against tile. As we ran down the pass, I snagged something brown and deep fried that smelled too good to pass up. I took a huge bite, not minding the scalding heat of the thing. Hmmm . . . veal unless I missed my guess.

"You're *eating*?" Helmut exclaimed, looking back and seeing my cheeks smeared in grease. "At a time like this?"

"Muh lunch wad interrupthed," I murbled around a mouthful of meat. Swallowing noisily, I said, "Eat when you can, don't turn away vittles. You never know when your next meal will be."

Shaking his head, he led me to a small storeroom with a steel trapdoor in the middle of the floor. "This takes us to the sewer," Helmut said, closing the door. A light flickered to life overhead. He leaned over and hooked two fingers through a large steel ring affixed to the trap door and heaved, lifting it easily until it was upright. Darkness yawned at our toes, a steel ladder running down into the black, and without further ado, he swung down the ladder like an academic monkey. A smell hit me then, an all too familiar one, and I nearly gagged, my half-digested veal hitting the back of my throat. Holding my nose, I stuffed the rest of meat into my mouth and chewed quickly, the threat of immanent death stoking my appetite despite the nauseating odors. I shrugged, and followed the disappearing professor.

SEVEN

Allies

"WHERE ARE WE?"

The room crowded in, the walls too close for comfort. A small rack to catch a few winks, clean but ratty covers, a kitchenette that was little more than a sink, and a hot plate and a small oven barely big enough to cook a bagel pizza. A door at the far end of the little place led to the bathroom that made a commercial airplane's lavatory look spacious.

"It's a friend's apartment." Helmut tapped on his uPhone. "I have use of it when necessary."

Translation: It was his little love bolt hole (no pun intended) for those grad and undergrads who really wanted to connect with the dapper prof. I wondered what kind of Jackson Pollock painting would appear if I flashed a UV light around. Considering my hedonistic past, who was I to judge? I briefly reminisced on how we arrived at Chateau Ostergard.

My feet had hit water at the end of the ladder, entering the city's sewer system and the smell grew more intense. Shit, piss and other unsavory aromas had assaulted my nose with nuclear force and I did my best not to gag, or think of what the squishy things beneath my boots were.

The trapdoor had cut off the sound of gunfire, leaving us with the smell, the sound of gurgling water, and the light of our uPhones.

Bad guys with automatic weapons were hunting us, but all I wanted to know was, "Hope you know where you're going, Helmut."

The dapper professor nodded. "*Ja*. I worked for the city to pay bills while I attended university. Have no fear, *Herr* Hakala, I will lead us away from danger."

Through a sewer infested with things that would make the average Supernatural gag? Sure . . . but I was clean out of ideas, so I had to trust the prof and hope he didn't expose me to hepatitis.

Our footsteps echoed weirdly as we made our way along the tunnel, hunching slightly. The walls were a mixture of newer concrete and decades-old red brick, as if the German government couldn't wrap its mind around the concept of modernization, and the result was a slapdash of new juxtaposed with the old. Thankfully, there was enough new that we soon came to a section of tunnel where the sides were raised, and we could walk next to and above the center channel filled with disgusting effluent.

I'm not sure how far we walked, only that my feet were tired and the power on my uPhone had dropped to forty-three percent when we came upon another section of tunnel that didn't have any runoff whatsoever. In fact, the smell had become a distant, if unpleasant memory, for which my nose thanked God. Shortly thereafter we heard voices and stepped into warm puddles of yellow light provided by widely spaced bulbs. I slipped my hand into my backpack, but Helmut merely grinned and urged me on.

Voices became people, a group led by a flashlight wielding, bored looking elderly man with thinning hair and far too many years eating *sauerrbraten* under his belt.

"Just join the back of the tour group, *Herr* Hakala," the professor whispered. "We will be out of here in no time."

No time sounded like the right time to me, and we exited the Munich underground with a gaggle of Swedish and Danish tourists none the wiser, although a certain amount of stink still clung to my boots.

"I just retrieved my research from the uCloud," Helmut said, taking a seat on a raggedy chair that was the only other stick of furniture in the place. "Let me link it to your cell." He held out the small sheet of transparent ironglass and I did the same. He swiped on an icon and it appeared on my cell.

"Thanks, Prof," I acknowledged. "What can you tell me about the Apostles? You seemed to know something about it that got that Rafa guy hot and bothered."

"I know rumors, writings of either a madman or one filled with remorse," said Helmut, still tapping on his uPhone. "In 1879 a man named Victor Brott wrote in his diary about the Apostle's efforts to aid the Confederacy against the Union, an attempt to fuel global conflict, the price of which would be a war against England. Now, I'm not sure if Brott was a member of the Apostles, someone in their employ, or a complete nutter, but I am absolutely certain that mentioning them in his journal was considered a breach of practice, not to mention trust. Who or what he was is not important, only that his journal was donated by his family to Bavarian State Library, where I happened upon it by mere happenstance. It is, to my knowledge, the only written account of the Apostles in existence." He paused. "There have been other rumors. I have a friend who belongs to Opus Dei, the prelature within the Catholic Church that many believe has masonic ties. During a long weekend that involved a great amount of ale and bratwurst, mind you while he was in his cups, he hinted about 'a secret, small organization within the Church whose purpose was to 'ensure the End of Days,' as well as his belief that they had encouraged the Final Solution during WWII. I had, up until a few hours ago, thought them to be fanciful tales."

"That's all well and good, Helmut, but Baba Yaga said you could set me on the path, so madman or sadman aside, can you help?"

Ostergard stroked his bottom lip. "Besides the relevant research on trees and their religious significance, I have in my possession a translation of the Bjornson Travels." Helmut tossed me a knowing look, as if I should find that information incredibly important and be suitably impressed by it. I met his look with a blank expression that I had practiced throughout my years of marriage.

He sighed. "The Bjornson Travels are the most significant, but most overlooked and ignored stories in the last thousand years. While most scholars attribute Leif Erikson as one of the greatest explorers of all time, the lesser known Hogrim Bjornson actually *predated* Erikson by a hundred years."

I slowly counted to ten, reigning in my temper. Really, why couldn't academics just come to the fucking *point*?

Sensing my slowly mounting anger, Helmut decided to hurry things along. "These stories, translated from oral history, tell of Bjornson's travel to find the legendary Yggdrasil. *And he said he found it!*"

"That's more like it!" I exclaimed, clapping him on the shoulder, very much relieved. "Do these stories tell you where to find it?"

He nodded. "*Ja*, in a manner of speaking. I have gathered enough clues that I think I can pinpoint its location."

"Tell me."

Standing, Helmut gave me a grin, his eyes sparkling madly behind his wire rims. "I will show you. This is a trip we will take together."

Oh, brother.

GREENLAND.

Yeah. Fucking Greenland. Plenty of land, not so much green.

Helmut didn't have the pull to arrange quick travel under the radar, but I sure did, and finangled a private flight from Copenhagen to Nord with four phone calls (one to the Finnish Embassy in Denmark) and some liberal palm greasing to the tune of a fuckload of money. Not that I cared about the cost, I was bucks up with more money than I could count in a lifetime, but it was the principle of the thing, you know? Once the Ambassador, a kindly, bookish lady named Ulla Taarkinen found out what I needed, she delivered in spades. A day later, after some much needed sleep, we were airborne.

I'm kind of a rock star in Finland.

Hopefully, that Rafa character's particular gift of finding shit out wasn't that amazing so as to give Helmut and I enough of a head start, because I really didn't need Shiana the sidekick sniper here to open a few holes in my favorite body (that would be mine, in case you were wondering).

The Jannik Svendsen, Chief of the Royal Danish Army, proved more than happy to fly two adventurers out to Nord on the QT as a favor to Taarkinen. The man was Top Secret and made sure no one guessed our identities, providing enough cover to hide us . . . and all at the cost of dinner with his slightly chubby blonde wife, Amanda, and his grown children Connie and Else. We exchanged dinner and selfies and stories about my time in the BSI, including the one about Denver, the op that nearly turned me into a charcoal briquette. That same op that Michael Bay turned into a movie complete with over-the-top explosions and gratuitous violence, you know . . . a summer blockbuster. It turned out that it was the Svendsen family's favorite movie. You find fanboys in the oddest places.

All that attention made me uncomfortable, and I hid it well enough that the Svendsens didn't twig to it, but Helmut could tell, and by the third shot of akavit and a glass of absinthe he was chuckling into his soup at my predicament. Snarky bastard.

The end result is that we landed in the coldest ass end of nowhere you could find outside of MacMurdo Station in Antarctica. Station Nord lies a little over five hundred miles from the geographic North Pole, a military and scientific outpost where no sane person would want to live, so of course it was chalk full of Scandinavians.

The station commander, Leahey, welcomed us with open arms and something called aebleflæsk, which turned out to be salted pork belly fried with apples and sugar. I swear I could hear my arteries hardening with every bite. Needless to say, Helmut put to with such gusto that he became a Bavarian garbage disposal. How he wasn't dead from heart disease I'll never know.

Leahey, along with various military and scientific personnel at Nord, piled me with questions about my life as an agent and the Supernaturals I'd put down: which were the toughest, which were the nastiest, and which ones I hated the most. The answer to all three was vampires. If my hatred for those fang fuckers could be bottled, it would be considered a WMD.

Helmut asked for a map of the area and a person who knew their way around better than most. That turned out to be a rail-thin, tall pilot by the name of Madsen, with a shockingly black mop of hair and the air of a mortician. The professor pulled out his uPhone and tapped a few icons. "We wish to scout the northern region," he began. "South of the fjords, but north of the main glacial mass." His finger stabbed a section of rocky terrain not far from the station. "Around here."

"That's a lot of ground to cover," Madsen said dolefully. I found out later that Madsen did and said *everything* dolefully. The more I hung with him, the more I wanted to put a round through my frontal lobes. "Ravines full of ankle-breaking rocks with boulders rolling down to kill the unwary. If the cold doesn't get you, a misstep will." He scratched his long nose and sighed. "There are a lot of strange things out there. This land was considered haunted long before we knew about magic and monsters. Frankly, I'd rather tap dance on a glacier than travel that area by foot."

Helmut was undeterred. "Fortunately, we have some clues that can narrow down our search." He held up the uPhone. "Bjornson said the waters where . . . ah . . . we are going run black. Are there black lakes or streams in this region you know of?"

If you'd shot ten-thousand volts up Madsen's ass at that moment the effect would have been the same. His entire body stiffened, his eyes grew wide, and I swore his black hair did a jiggly little dance.

"No. No fucking way," he stated flatly. "If this region is haunted, the place you want to go is fucking *cursed*." He turned a hot-eyed glare my way. "You may be a famous monster hunter and killer, a big deal in the world, but that won't save my life in a place that hates man like the devil hates Heaven."

"A place that hates man." The words echoed evilly in my mind. I couldn't feel angry at the guy because most Supernaturals seemed to exist to cause as much horror as possible, and their favorite victims walked on two legs. Whatever put that kind of fear into Madsen would not take kindly to a couple of tourists.

"We have to go there," Helmut insisted, looking a little pale. "*Herr* Hakala and I have an important mission and if we fail . . ." he licked his lips. "We all die."

Madsen crossed his arms. "So you die."

"You don't get it," I cut in. "*We all* die. You. Me. Everybody."

"Bullshit."

I shook my head.

"How is that possible? How is getting you into the cursed zone going to save us all? Do you mind telling me that?" There was an edge of panic in Madsen's voice.

My eyes flicked to Leahey, who listened intently but kept his mouth shut, inscrutable as a statue. Sighing, I laid out an edited version of what we were up against, and it didn't hurt my case at all when Helmut pulled up the daily news on a laptop, showing more mysterious deaths, and more vehicles and machinery malfunctioning. Talking heads blamed the Sidhe, rogue Magicians, and the Taliban or some such shit, but the conclusion was inescapable . . . the clock on reality was about to strike midnight.

And that's how we found ourselves in a lightweight Fennec Eurocopter, hovering forty feet over a treacherous, rocky ravine filled, with hard edges ready to tenderize the hide of a middle-aged Finn. The ground looked like God had taken a mountain, stuffed it into the world's biggest blender and hit *frappe*. Time and weather smoothed some of the rocks into soft-looking humps and bumps, but there were plenty that reached up with points and basaltic blades ready to maim.

We were outfitted in the best cold weather gear money could buy, including goggles, real fur trimmed parkas and balaclavas, but the wind still slid through the cracks to chill our flesh, stinging like ice wasps.

Madsen, frowning and scowling like it was his job, held the helo steady at the forty-foot mark slightly above the lip of the ravine while we unspooled our lines, ready to rappel. Helmut and I lowered our backpacks on one thin rope before we took the leap. The wind ripped through the open door, chewing and stinging more and more, and I knew it was time. Flashing back to my training days in Coronado, I grasped the rope, braved the icy air and descended, the professor following close behind.

My booted feet hit hard stone and I scrambled for traction, not wanting to twist or break an ankle, a near death sentence thirty miles from Nord. When I was sure of my footing, I let go of the rope, untied our backpacks from the third line and grabbed Helmut, steadying the professor before he fell and broke his ass. When he was situated, I waved at the helo and it buzzed off, returning to the cold comforts of the station.

"I know the waters you are looking for," Madsen had said after I convinced him of the urgency. Even faced with an abundance of evidence, Leahey still had to order him to fly us close to our destination. Madsen stabbed the map. "Right here. A series of small streams that flow from beneath the ice cap. Not big, and hard to spot, but it's there if you know where to look. We had a scientist named Kloop who wanted to check the mineral content of the water, because most glacial outflows are whitish in color due to a high content of pulverized rock ground down by glacial movement. The dark color of this water was a mystery he wanted to solve."

"And?" I urged.

"Nothing. When he didn't check in, me and the other lads looked, but there was no sign of Kloop or his gear." Something in his voice told me it wasn't all, but it didn't seem like a good time to press.

Those words echoed in my mind as I observed the waste in which I found myself. Cracked and crumbled stones littered the ground near a foot-wide stream that glistened blackly under the cloudy sky. I bit my glove and pulled it off, crouching by the inky water and plunging my hand in. Cold. Cold so deep it felt like heat an instant before my hand became numb, the demarcation between the air and water a fiery battle between temperatures, and although the air was cold, the water made it feel like a Hawaiian breeze. I quickly removed my hand and slipped the glove back on before my skin turned black as well.

"Does your research tell you why the water is black, Professor?" I asked, rising.

"Bjornson only said to look for black water, not why it was so." Helmut pulled an energy bar from a pocket and began to chew noisily. This man ate more than any three men I knew. If I tucked in with his enthusiasm I'd be eight-hundred pounds, at least.

"Where to?"

"Follow the water to the throat of Jörmungandr."

"The Midgard Serpent? The one that's supposed to circle the world and kill Thor during Ragnarok?" Not Marvel Thor, but Thor Thor, the biggest and baddest of all the Norse gods, who could shatter mountains with his short-handled hammer Mjolnir. Back in Munich, Helmut refused to offer me any of this information, insisting that if he did hand over the Bjornson saga, I'd leave him high and dry back in Munich. He was right, of course.

"None other," came the reply. I lifted the black balaclava and spat, offering a curse to the frigid air, the spit freezing almost instantly. Helmut chose to ignore the profanity and began to step carefully upon the rocky ground.

The walls of the ravine were as rock studded as the floor, and shone in the gray light of day with frost. Each booted foot had to be carefully placed as one slip would leave you with a turned or broken ankle, the frost offering little traction. I had half a mind to wade through the dark waters of the stream to find better purchase, but even my oil-soaked leather boots wouldn't resist the icy flow for long before becoming soaked, leaving me with dead clubs for feet.

Crack! I stopped, crouching, and whipped my head around. Forty feet away, a rock the size of my skull fell down the steep wall, bouncing once, twice, three times, shedding sharp chips with each impact until, with a tremendous splash, it landed in the stream.

"We should be quiet," Helmut whispered, staring up at the lip over our heads. "Even our voices can trigger a fall."

Okay, good pro tip. I tossed him a nod and continued walking, slowly, high stepping across rocks that wanted to hurt me, patient sadists waiting for me to hurry a little too much, or to fail to test my footing. They'd have me then, breaking bone and mortifying tissue, leaving me a cold mess at the bottom of a rocky ravine. Beside me, Helmut held his arms out, balancing and nimbling his way across the rocks, practically doubling my speed. I guessed being lower to the ground allowed him to see the safe spots.

My ankle turned suddenly, forcing my knees to give way and I dropped, hands outstretched. Pain lanced up my right wrist as it scraped across cold stone, blood christening the ground. I grunted, biting my lip.

"Are you all right?" Helmut must've heard my gasp or my boot slide off of rock.

"Been hurt worse," I grunted, examining my damaged wrist. Ragged and jagged, it bled like a right bastard, the sharp stone having razored through the insulated leather glove as if it were thin cotton. Within moments the glove was soaked in red. "Another scar."

"I saw the movie they made about your time in Colorado. Is it true you picked up a lot of scars there? The ones around your body." Helmut licked his lips. "If you don't mind my asking, *Herr* Hakala."

"No, I don't mind." I wanted to caress the faint, corkscrewing ridges around my torso, a physical reminder of the heat that once seared my skin. "My life is full of scars." A long pause as I tended to the wound with a medkit from a thigh pocket. "It's all gnarled tissue." With that Helmut kept his questions to himself and we continued on our way, heads down against the wind, the burbling of black water at our heels.

Night came quickly, slowing us further until every tenth of a mile took a century to cross, and the air became a brittle thing with sharp edges that forced our breaths into plumes in the light of our flashlights. The black stream began to develop a thin skin of ice, the dense mineral-y water below resisting the freezing temperature. Helmut took a sample of the black water, placing the metal vial carefully into his backpack.

Eventually we were obliged to stop, or fatigue would see us with broken bones or worse. We sat on time-smoothed boulders and warmed ourselves by the heat of a tanzanite spell gem the size of my pinky nail, supplied to us by the well-meaning Leahey. The little bluish purple gem shone with cold intensity at odds with the heat it radiated, heat that had the rock it rested upon steaming and giving off the musty smell of a sauna. The ground proved too uneven, too rocky, to pitch a tent, so we had to make do with curling up in our sleeping bags beneath Mylar blankets and taking power naps while the ferocious warmth of the gem lasted.

Light began to give a little color to the world when I awoke, alert and ready, the tanzanite now a fading warm spot on a rock between us, Helmut snoring like misfiring V8. I tried to stand, but the hard ground and advancing age had put some kink into my muscles, forcing me to stop and go several times before I could make it to my feet. Joints popped and cracked, and my muscles protested mightily that I was seven kinds of fool for napping on stony ground. At least I had managed some Zs. That thought didn't provide much comfort to my old, aching bod, though.

Helmut awoke and grumbled, pulling out a protein bar and munching noisily. I grimaced. "You snore like constipated bear."

He grinned around a mouthful of nuts and honey. "You're not the first to say that."

After taking care of the necessaries, which included taking ibuprophen, we once again began our torturous trek through the ravine, stepping carefully and minding the sharp edges.

A couple of hours later, calves aching, we came to the end of the ravine. The V-shaped depression in the earth terminated into a cave, the roof of which was hardpacked glacial ice so crystalline blue it hurt my eyes. The stream disappeared into the dark, cold depths, its gurgling bouncing off ice and stone, the sound as frigid as the air.

"Is this the Midgard Serpent's throat?" I said, eyeing the cave entrance dubiously. Water dripped slowly from the roof, adding to the dark stream that bled from the black heart of the cave. Dread leeched into my bones like the cold air into my skin, and my palms itched for my grandfather's pistol, the Lahti L-35 that I'd carried for my entire career in the BSI. The only thing besides me that survived.

Before I could take a step, Helmut dashed inside, skipping across the stones like a mountain goat on speed.

"Shit," I muttered, charging after, trying not to twist an ankle or fall on my face. Early morning frost made the rocks even more treacherous, and I slipped a couple of times, having to save myself from falling with quick reflexes and muscle pulling gymnastics. The cave with its roof of ice swallowed me whole, along with the multitude of curses flowing from my mouth.

The light of a small flashlight illuminated my path, water dripping onto the hood of my heavy, black parka. The stream burbled at my feet as I passed the demarcation between an icy ceiling and black rock, plunging me further into Greenland's bowels, the black pierced only by the thin beam from the flashlight.

Up ahead I heard nothing, everything lay still, with not even a whisper of air. The bubbling of the stream seemed muted, distant, and a thought suddenly hit me: why couldn't I hear Helmut?

I angled the flashlight down so I could see where to put my boots, adding a little urgency to my steps.

"Dammit," I growled to myself, the words scarcely stirring the air. "Dammit, dammit, dammit, Helmut." Fucking Professor, getting all twitterpated by the thought of coming close to the Yggdrasil and leaving yours truly in the rear.

My steps were swallowed by the dark and the stony walls that refused to echo my footfalls, soaking up all sound contrary to what perfectly good stone walls should do, elevating the creep factor up to eleven. Sweat steamed from the exposed patches of my skin and plumes of my breath floated in the flashlight's beam. Sweat ran into my eyes and I blinked rapidly, keeping them on the floor of the cave so I didn't trip. My nerves were piano wire taut. So when Helmut suddenly appeared in the flashlight beam, I just about peed my thermal underwear. I skidded to a stop, small rocks scattering before me.

Helmut was standing with his back to me, flashlight forgotten in his hand, the beam focused to a narrow point far ahead.

"Jesus, Helmut!" I whispered fiercely. "What the fuck? Don't run off like that!"

He continued to stare off into the cave and lifted on hand to point. I followed his flashlight beam, that thin light guiding my eyes to what they illuminated. I swore under my breath in awe.

A snake. No, make that a snake's *head*.

Helmut's flashlight bounced off fangs of ice at least three feet long, the beams fracturing into rainbows that hurt my eyes. The black stream bubbled past what I could only assume was an ice sculpture attached to the tunnel wall, almost organically thrusting from the dark stone, moisture dripping from its translucent skull. Jaws open wide, the serpent's twinned tongue twisted out of its yawning mouth to terminate into the stream, as if licking the dark water. The damn thing must've been nine feet tall from bottom jaw to the top of its snout, which nearly brushed the ceiling.

"Ice," Helmut murmured. "A snake's head made of ice." He turned to me. "Who would carve something like this from ice?"

Rainbows. The light split into rainbows. My heart near froze in my chest, and I took a few stumbling steps forward, boots splashing through the icy water, kicking up spray. I pulled a glove off and placed a hand on one of the frozen fangs.

Smooth. Cold. And sharp. A line of red on my palm drooled blood.

"Jesus," I said, staring at the skull looming over me. The gullet was a tunnel that faded deep into the rock until swallowed by darkness. "Not ice, Helmut. I think this is a diamond. That's why it hasn't melted or broken since Bjornson's time."

"That's not possible!"

I showed him my bleeding palm. "Ice doesn't refract light like this. This is hard. This is a diamond. Trust me, I know. I've used spell gems for decades." I couldn't begin to calculate the value of the snake's head. Safe to say that this much diamond dropped onto the market at once, it would probably send Antwerp into seizures.

My voice fell into the darkness with hushed astonishment as I gave voice to my thoughts. "Wonder what the street value of two-ton diamond would be?

EIGHT

Nothing is easy, but I wish it were.

S TARING INTO THE SNAKE'S GULLET, I SHIVERED, noting that the
diamond head ended at the tunnel wall. Not that I had expected
a gemstone Midgard Serpent to extend deep into the bowels of the
earth, but in this business you never know.

Looking closely at the skull, I was amazed at the intricacy of
the design, the thousands of tiny facets and larger ones that made
up the whole, splitting the light from my flashlight into razor rainbows. "This isn't possible," I said. "No one has the skill to cut a diamond like this, it should have shattered to dust during the process
as the natural occlusions fractured the stone, but instead it's all in
one piece. It's impossible."

Helmut swallowed, the sound loud in the dark. "What's possible or impossible any more, *Herr* Hakala? We live in a world of
magic and monsters, so who's to say, *ja*?"

My eyes went to the tunnel of the snake's mouth. "Whatever.
All I know now is that this must be the serpent's throat and that
the Tree lies beyond. According to Bjornson, that is." I waved at the
darkness. The tunnel looked to be three feet in diameter. "Time to
make like Indiana Jones and go in."

Silence.

"Helmut?"

No answer.

"Helmut?" I turned to see the professor staring at the snake, eyes behind his wire rims saucer wide, terror sweat on his exposed skin. "What's wrong?"

"I cannot, *Herr* Hakala." The tunnel pulled at his gaze as if there was a physical connection. "This was to be a great adventure, *ja*? But this . . . this is too much. It's too real. I am terrified by what I may find because I have a feeling that if I do go down the throat of Jörmungadr I will never return. I am no Indiana Jones, no matter that I may have thought otherwise. I will stay behind, document the find, and summon the helicopter to pick me up."

My mind harkened back to Babs and what she told me. "This is my adventure, Helmut, and mine alone. I think you're right not to come." I laid a hand on his shoulder. "It's okay, really. People tend to die around me. You don't need to be the latest in a long string of bodies that lie in my wake." I paused. "But keep this discovery quiet, okay?"

That put the wind up his trousers. "But why?" he wailed as if I told him his first born would be sacrificed to Cthulu.

"Think about it, Helmut. A diamond the size of a Volkswagon that could lead to the Yggdrasil, a manifestation of our reality? Do you really trust government halfwits not to start a war over it? Or fuck it up five ways to Sunday?" I stared into his shocked eyes. "Do you really trust any bureaucratic system with poor interdepartmental abilities and a penchant for corruption to safeguard *the* greatest archeological discovery of the modern age? Honestly?"

"But we Germans—"

"Will probably face a crisis of biblical proportions if they somehow wrest control over a site belonging to a constituent country of the Kingdom of Denmark. If the rest of the world realizes this could be the path to the Yggdrasil, then things really will go pear-shaped."

Helmut slowly deflated, looking like a sack of dirty laundry stuffed into a dark parka. "*Ja*, I see your point. If the path through Jörmungadr's throat truly leads to the legendary Yggdrasil, this should be kept a secret."

I looked down the throat and leaned into the diamond maw, careful of the razor fangs that hung within inches of the tunnel floor. "Get thee back to Nord, Helmut." I held up my uPhone and tapped it to his. "There, I just downloaded the contact information you'll need if I don't succeed and things become worse."

"Who?"

"My best friend and the best agent the BSI has ever produced. Canton Alsate. If I fail, maybe he'll succeed."

A strong hand clasped mine, then released me into the throat of the serpent. "You will never get a job writing greeting cards."

My laughter bounced off a diamond palate as I crawled inside.

THE COLD BIT AT MY FACE, TEARING AWAY at the skin around my eyes and back of my throat with every breath. I crawled on hands and knees, the tunnel too small to walk upright, but large enough that I had no worries about bonking my head against the ceiling. Speaking of my tender brain housing, I pulled out a thick elastic band affixed on a LED light from a thigh pocket (who said cargo pants suck?) and slipped it over the balaclava, nestling the light on the center of my forehead, switching it on, and pocketing my flashlight. Now I had two free hands, in case I ran into some Yggdrasil sized termites or something.

Or Ratatoskr, the squirrel that ran up and down the Yggdrasil delivering messages. I imagined a rodent the size of a train car, with buck teeth that could pierce armor plating, as well as middle-aged Finns, and grimaced. There were other creatures besides giant squirrels too, such as the eagle perched atop the Yggdrasil and Níðhöggr, or the serpent who dwelled beneath one of the three roots of the tree. Hmm, maybe it wasn't the Midgard serpent I was climbing through after all. Didn't do anything for my nerves . . .

one giant mythological serpent couldn't kill me any deader than the next.

This was the point where knowing too much folklore becomes a giant pain in the ass.

I couldn't say how long I crawled along, except that I stopped three or four times to drink some water from a canteen and eat a couple of protein bars that tasted like sawdust held together with pulped cardboard. I soon realized after eating that I could see more than the light the headlamp was providing, and as the tunnel becoming clearer and clearer I turned the lamp off.

Instead of stone, I soon found myself crawling on some sort of dark brown glassine substance with several inches of depth, and when I leaned in close, thousands of striations came in view, imbedded deep in the glasslike rock. They were the source of the illumination, each one of the striations glistening with pinpoints of light. I looked harder.

There were hundreds, no, thousands of tiny, tiny glowing dots of all different colors, swirling strands of pinprick lights that stretched into and around and all over. The brown striations were not only dotted with these vast swatches of minute lights, but larger black dots as well, black so deep I could lose myself staring at them, they tugged at me so. The brown striations outnumbered the glowing pinpoints and the black dots provided a warm, almost chocolate light to the tunnel, which was now, I realized, almost perfectly cylindrical.

"I'm not in Kansas anymore." Shaking my head, I continued by the light coming from strange depths of the tunnel walls, which grew brighter as I crawled. You'd figure I'd have been terrified at the change, but I'd been in worse places. Like Staten Island.

Stopping a few times to rest my aching knees (getting old is a bitch) and change the bandage on my hand, I finally saw that the tunnel was becoming larger and larger, and I was soon able to stand upright. After working the deep kinks and aches out of my back and shoulders, I continued, and began unzipping my heavy parka and removing my gloves when I realized it was warmer. Much warmer.

With almost no transition I found myself in a . . . cave? A kidney-shaped space about thirty by fifteen feet, lit by the same, eerie invasive light that cast no shadows. Almost directly opposite the tunnel continued. The floor looked to be flat as week old soda-pop, shining with a kind of polished brilliance, and I would've studied the grand swath of pinpoint lights in their thousands, but I saw a man stood in the middle of the room, and immediately my hackles rose.

Back in WWII Germany there was a group of *uber*-assholes who called themselves the VGG. *Verteidiger gegen Geister*. Means 'Defenders against Ghosts.' The equivalent of the Bureau, but all Nazified and shit, which meant that they were complete and utter bastards of the highest order who tortured and killed more people than the Tonton Macoute (look it up if you've got the belly). Long story short, I fought a few of the scumbags during an op, and did them the kind of dirty found only in a *Friday the 13th* movie.

The man stood in the center of the cave with hands clasped behind his back, rocking back and forth on the heels of his shiny, knee-high, black boots, a sickly smile on his pasty face under a short, blond buzz cut. The rank insignia on his uniform labeled him as an *Oberstleutnant*, or lieutenant Colonel, which made him a big bad wig in the olden days. Too bad for him this wasn't the olden days.

"You must turn back," he said in thickly accented English. He sounded bored, as if tall Finnish-Americans wandered into his slice of life every day.

I noticed how threadbare his gray uniform looked. There was a hole in one knee. "Can't do that," I replied. "Don't suppose you'd be willing to stand aside for a few?"

He shook his head. I slipped my hand inside my parka.

Quick as a snake he brought out a Mauser C96 pistol, the ugly black weapon ready to spit 8mm Gasser rounds, but I was a little faster, already having pulled the Finnish Lahti M35. I filled the man's chest with seven 9mm bullets, a few spraying out the back of his shitty gray uniform.

A look of almost childlike surprise crossed the German's face, and he fell on his face with a muffled thump.

"Well, that was easier than I expected." There were always obstacles in the path of an adventure. I had expected better.

The Lahti flew from my fingertips as pain racked my hand, which had suddenly sprouted a throwing knife that pierced the palm. Blood began to flow.

Hollywood and fantasy novels always have heroes and heroines, who somehow through cool training or discipline, ignore pain and surge forward against the odds. That's horseshit. It's experience, hard won, fought for, and bitterly earned that allows a person to ride across a wave agony, to become almost used to it. The world is cruel and its lessons are writ large on my skin, so I managed to stuff the explosive anguish into the back corners of my mind. Still, it stung like a right bastard.

I turned, drawing the blade free with a hiss, and there he was, Mr. Nazi VGG sonofabitch himself, a big, pale, shit-eating smile on his pasty face and bullet holes from his chest leaking black blood. He beckoned. I decided to take him up on his invitation.

My first punch broke his nose clean and sprayed his blood across his cheeks and mouth. He countered with a hammering blow to my ribs, moving so fast I didn't even see his fist travel from there to here, only felt the sudden, hot agony of ribs breaking beneath iron knuckles.

I backpedaled, wheezing, tasting blood in the back of my throat. Hoping that he wasn't a martial artist, I sucked up the diamond splinter of pain in my side and launched a wheel kick, which connected right above his ear. Molten agony flashed up my side, turning everything white, and I fell backward.

Crack! The Nazi's head crunched sideways and he dropped bonelessly to the floor. My butt hit an instant later, igniting more pain in my side. I inhaled deeply.

Oh, God. The world receded as my lungs expanded, fueling the fire in my chest. I felt my ribs slide like snakes under the skin and set, badly broken but good for now, and I tried not to puke. Red spots appeared in my eyes, almost obscuring the Nazi's sprawled body.

One breath, two, then three. Each one an exercise in grating pain, but as I gently eased the back of my lap across the cool, slick floor in an effort to regain my feet, the whirling sensation of oxygen deprivation began to recede, leaving behind sweet relief. Relief was tainted by a thick scrum of agony along my flank and my hand.

Then the Nazi's body twitched.

Fear provided adrenaline surged through me, and I lurched to my feet as German's head, canted oddly to the side, straightened abruptly, the bones of the neck popping into place like the sound of a Styrofoam cup being crushed in a fist.

I drew my foot back and kicked for the cheap seats, my boot slamming hard into bad guy's testicles, scooting the body three feet across the smooth floor and eliciting a painful groan from the both of us. I recovered slowly and smiled through bloody teeth, advancing on the writhing German.

A boot heel hit my knee, bending it painfully to the side, and I fell on my damaged ribs. For a moment my universe was black with sheets of red, my breath frozen shards of glass in my lungs. By the time I came to, the German had regained his feet and was drawing a long trench knife from his boot, its wooden handle discolored with age and skin oil. Once again that evil smile hit his pasty face, and for the first time I felt afraid, the kind of bone deep terror that makes you want to dive under Mama's skirts for a few years.

And that pissed me off to no end.

Wheezing to my feet and nearly passing out from the pain in my chest and knee, I avoided the first slash ... but not by much. The tip of the trench knife slid across my parka with a zipping sound, opening a long, downy cut in the black material. I responded with a roundhouse left, but the German sidestepped quickly, leaving my knuckles to brush past an inch from his pearlies. He followed with an obvious feint to my eyes, then stabbed low toward my groin. I blocked and hit him square in the jaw, bruising my fist.

The Nazi asshole shook his head and spit out a tooth, jabbing for my eyes with forked fingers. I grabbed the offending digits in both hands and made a wish.

Snap!

One finger twisted the wrong way as the other, still gripped in my fist, tore clean off in a spray of putrid blood. For a second the German looked at the spurting stump, and that was all I needed. I put my full weight behind my punch and drove a fist into his throat, the larynx giving with a wet *crunch*. He gagged and dropped his knife, falling to the floor, writhing and twitching.

I limped over to the trench knife and set to cutting strips out of my shirt to form a makeshift bandage for my hand, which still hurt like a sonofabitch, but I was still kicking on adrenaline and managed to put the agony on the back burner. Once I had the cloth wrapped around my hand, I slipped the trench knife into a pocket and drew my own.

Fourteen inches long and razor sharp, the bowie was a present from my best friend and former BSI agent Canton Alsate, the best knife fighter I'd ever met. It was a replacement for the one dad had given me decades ago, which had been destroyed in St. Louis on one of my more horrific ops. With an edge so sharp it could cut your imagination, it was my go-to weapon for close quarters combat, but considering the sheath lay along my spine and under the parka, it was a bear to draw when push came to shove.

I set to work.

Later on, tired and bloody, I dragged my parka laden with: A) a single Nazi VGG torso, B) Two severed arms C) Two severed legs and D) A fine collection of internal organs now made external thanks to the bowie. I soldiered on, holding the head of said VGG asshole by hilt of my knife, which had been thrust through the bone of the temple to emerge from the other side. I could've left the guy chopped up into cutlets scattered on the floor behind me like Hansel and Gretel's breadcrumbs, but I wasn't sure how fast he could regenerate a whole body, and I sure didn't want to take time to find out. God, but my knee hurt from that Nazi boot, every step a spike of agony. Fucking Nazi dipshit.

The tunnel had grown taller and wider, still illuminated by the multitudes of pinpoint lights creating a pleasant, almost warm, whole. As I walked, taking shallow breaths because my ribs protested with every limping yard, I studied the pieces of the German for any signs of regeneration. While the arms, legs and torso remained unchanged, the skull's eyes stayed open, glaring. If hate were people, he'd be India, but I couldn't work up the energy to give a rusty fuck. Behind me the soaked parka left a red smear on the floor.

"You could've let me by," I told the head at the end of my knife. He blinked once and frowned. After a second he mouthed some words, which my rusty lip-reading skills told me was German. I only caught the cuss words.

"Same to you, Fritz. With special sauce," I replied.

Jagged razors of pain slid along my flank with every halting step, but despite the black spots dancing in front of my eyes and the rolling fatigue that near drove me to my knees, I kept going, one foot in front of the other. Sweat drooled down my face, the tunnel warm despite the Greenland cold outside. In fact, it was starting to get damn hot, but I couldn't rest. I had to see what was at the end.

"What do you say, Fritz? Am I gonna find roots or some gigantic pine beetles?"

Fritz chose not to respond.

"His name isn't Fritz." The words echoed off the walls and floor like they'd been bouncing around for a few years, blurring and jarring, but still understandable.

I looked around. Nothing but tunnel. "What?"

"His name isn't Fritz. It's Karl Von Andor."

Stopping was out of the question. The load of body parts was becoming heavier by the moment, and I knew if I stopped I wouldn't be able to continue. "Strange name," I replied as if mysterious voices were commonplace, the coppery taste of blood at the back of my throat.

"Strange man," said the voice. "Came in here back in '44 looking for the Yggdrasil, seeking the Well for his patron, that odd little man Hitler. He found what he was looking for. And then he didn't."

Another step and another. My head ached and sweat stung my eyes. "Riddles?"

"Life is the greatest riddle of all," the voice laughed. "What's existence without a few riddles, eh?"

"Simpler."

Laughter led me into a large, irregular cavern filled with the lights of a billion pinpoints. The floor sloped toward the center where a still, shallow pool of water shone, crystal in its purity. Despite being rather small in size, it dominated the room because of the warm glow that seemed to radiate from it, exuding peace and health, as if it was the very blood of existence. I wanted nothing more than to take a long, deep draught of that fluid. It called to me, sung to me of magic that wrapped around my bones and teased through my flesh, beckoning.

"Don't," said the voice, reading my mind.

I ripped my eyes away from the welcoming water and turned to see an old man in a light blue Brioni suit with a soft, pastel red tie.

"Tah-dah!" he grinned around a stogie. "Welcome to the Well of the Tree."

NINE

It's always something

I HAD TO GIVE FRITZ UP, OF COURSE. The old guy, sporting a neatly trimmed, gray beard below sparkling blue eyes the color of glacial ice, told me that the German was first guardian of the Tree, there to test the resolve of those seeking the Yggdrasil.

"Turns out, of course, you had means and ample reason to be here, not to mention the resolve," chortled the old man, whose named turned out to be Mimerandimus. Mimir for short, he informed me.

"Mimir? For real?" I asked. It felt good to lean against the wall, to slowly slide to the floor and sit there, and put down the body burden I'd dragged for who knows how long. My eyes wanted to close so damn bad, but I couldn't let that happen, so I settled for letting them rest at half-mast. I slapped my cheeks until they burned.

"Would have picked Gandalf or Slartibartfast, but you run into copyright violations," he said with a genuine smile.

"Mimir, the Aesir who guarded Mimisbrunnr, or the Well of Urd at the base of Yggdrasil. I thought you were beheaded during the Aesir/Vanir war." And there I was, showing off. It felt good, I rarely got the chance most days to use the knowledge I'd gleaned the last few decades.

The old being in his sharp suit pulled a Copperfield and materialized a sturdy wooden chair from nowhere and sat, producing and lighting up a fresh cigar. "You are well informed, but don't believe everything you read."

I shook my head. The motion hurt so I stopped. "Had to be well informed. Part of the job. Former job. In fact, I think in my time I was the world's foremost authority of all things Supernatural and mythological."

Mimir leaned back and the chair creaked. He puffed a smoke square, then some triangles. "Yes, you were. Kalevi Hakala. Finnish-American, father of Desmond Hakala and husband to the late Jeanie Hakala. BSI agent for fourteen years, then Director for near ten more before you retired, the genesis of which was the death of your wife. You decided to concentrate on being a father, but no matter what you do or who tells you otherwise, you think you are a failure."

Tired. So fucking tired. I blinked rapidly, but it didn't help and I was losing the energy to slap myself. I used to drink, fight and fuck all night and still face the morning bright-eyed and bushy-tailed, but those days were decades in the rear-view. Hell, I couldn't even summon the anger at how this old fart had summarized my life in a few short sentences.

"Ah, a touch of internal bleeding, broken bones, contusions and hematomas combined with a healthy dose of fatigue. We can't have that now. I need you at your best when you make your choice." A liver-spotted hand reached out and touched my chest.

Furious energy suddenly infused my body like a jolt of an electric current and I found myself on my feet, eyes wide and pulse pounding. I took the barest moment to marvel at how *healthy* I felt, that my ribs seemed fully healed and that the difficulty breathing I didn't even realize I suffered from made itself manifest by its absence. "Holy shit!"

Mimir raised a gray eyebrow. "Maybe too much."

I could only goggle. It took some considerable will not to break into jumping jacks right on the spot. "What did you do?" I walked in circles, trying to burn off the ferocious energy that sizzled through my tissues. I felt *good*. Real good, a kind of good I hadn't felt in years . . . not just vigor, but youth. Hot and pulsing through my veins . . . the strength and stamina of a kid fresh out of the University of Nebraska with a Masters and a future that stretched out long before him. "What in the name of the Holy Hand Grenade of Antioch did you *do*?"

"Magic, of course," came the reply. "I need you healthy." A chair hit me behind the knees, forcing me to sit. "You must have questions, but we don't have a lot of time, Mr. Hakala."

Right. Time. Everyone's always in a hurry. I gestured to the room. "Is this the Yggdrasil?"

He shook his head. "Not really. Think of this place as reality's antechamber, so to speak, an interface designed for those who wish to interact with the Tree." He grinned like weasel chewing on a chicken bone. "Here, let me show you the Tree." Mimir waved a hand.

The pinpoints of light that lay deep within the strangely transparent, striated stone flowed free, lifting from their resting places to coalesce in the center of the large cavern, hovering in the air like millions of tiny fireflies swirling in a geometric jig I couldn't begin to appreciate. They continued to dance for a few moments before slowly forming into a river of light, thick in the middle and tapering to multiple branches at one end, with the other end resembling a roughly spherical bulb. The pinpoints in their multitudes hovered there like a 3D abstract sculpture of light, or a . . .

"Tree," I whispered.

"Yes." Mimir's voice echoed strangely, as if he were speaking through a cracker box. "This is the Tree, or what your ancestors saw as the World Tree, the Yggdrasil when they were shown." The pinpoint sculpture of light spun slowly. "What you are seeing are most of the trillions of galaxies in the universe represented in three giant galactic drifts, with each mote of light representing a series of galaxies. The root ball is the Far Galactic Drift where all of creation took place. The body, or trunk, is the Core Galactic Drift where we reside, and the branches are the Outward Galactic Drift, which is in the slow process of reversing itself to rejoin the Core. Which will in turn rejoin the Far Drift and then compress back into what, in terms you can understand, is considered the singularity that began the universal cycle."

Too big. Each mote a series of galaxies? Looking at the millions of motes that encompassed the far reaches of the giant cavern, my mind refused to cope with the scale, so instead I had to compartmentalize my thoughts before the dizzying whole rendered me whackadoodle.

"How?" I stopped and shook my head. "Why us? Why Earth? What happened and how the flying frack do you fit into all this? Trillions of galaxies must mean billions of civilizations, so how come it comes down to us humans to fix this problem?" I put my head in my hands. To hear Babs talk about it, it didn't seem so real, but now that I had the barest, the tiniest inkling of the cosmic scale of things, it became so fucking hard to *cope*. I needed a drink. Or ten.

A smoke bullet hit me between the eyes and burst like my hope for a better future into dark gray vapor. "Listen close because I do hate repeating myself. Understand?"

I nodded, not trusting my voice.

"There is only one Tree, which exists in nine Prime realities. With their mirrors, there are a total of ninety dimensions, each a part of the Tree, but those nine are the anchors for their mirror realities. Call them what you will, but to me, realities are represented by nine worlds, which are Midgard, Alfheim, Niflheim, Muspelheim, Asgard, Jotunheim, Vanaheim, Svartalfheim and Hel. Travel between the worlds used to be impossible, and each world remained inviolate due to the dimensional barrier that comprised the bark of the Tree and all was as it should be."

"Before humanity began to walk upright on the surface of Midgard, there were in Hel the Old Ones, powerful beings of pure thought and immense energy, their world a paradise of beauty and balance. They could mold the matter of their realm to their will, as virtually nothing was beyond them, but their vast powers bred a vast arrogance, and led to two philosophies that were diametrically opposed. Domination and Service."

"Good and Evil," I said.

A slow nod. Mimir's voice grew sad, his cadence taking on a singsong quality of old memory. "Part and parcel of the diametrically opposed forces of Creation and Destruction. It led to a war that lasted uncounted millennia. My people devastated our world, ruining it in our need for the ascendancy of one school of thought over the other, and in that cataclysm we tore the Tree's bark. For a split second a portal we call the Breach was formed between all the worlds that led to Earth, pulling us into the world of men, Midgard, alongside creatures from the other Primes, inundating the land and seas with entities mankind would call monsters and legends. Along with these creatures came a great flood as the oceans of the other Primes entered Midgard, giving birth to the story of Noah, Gilgamesh, Deucalion, Väinämöinen and more." A heartbreaking sadness rose from Mimir like a cloud, and I felt my throat constrict. "But as Newton observed, for every action there is an equal and opposite reaction."

"The Third Law," I said, suddenly intuiting what he was going to say. "Beings from Earth were moved to the other Primes, weren't they? And some of our oceans, and the organisms within, were pulled into the Breach as well."

"Yes. It was a great cataclysm," the old man affirmed. "Like a vacuum, much of mankind was sucked into the other Primes during the nanoseconds of the Breach. As for the Old Ones, once the Breach closed, we found we could not leave Midgard because much of our energy had been depleted during our struggle, although the Elves, whom legends referred to as the Sidhe, later discovered a way to travel the Primes that did not violate the Bark of the Tree. Trapped on Earth, weakened, forced to clothe ourselves in gross matter, and given form by the imagination of men, became the gods of this world. Olympians, Aesir, Vanir, Angels and Demons, Hindu and Egyptian gods." He laughed, a sound that near broke my heart. "It turns out that mankind had greater influence over reality than we could have dreamed. Their belief gave us purpose we could not deny. They gave us form, and we gave them stories of the Tree and of other worlds.

"So, we were forced to remain, cut off from the other Primes because we lacked the subtle magic of the Elves that allows them to travel back and forth. Don't ask me how they do it because that knowledge is hidden from me, but there are rips in the fabric of reality, whirlpools among the other eight Primes that, from time to time, draw creatures into this world"

"The monsters from the World Under," I said. Back in my agent days it was believed that the World Under was the source of the Supernaturals that infested our planet. Shows how much we knew; it should have been called the *Worlds* Under.

"Correct. The Breach was not only a hole in the bark, but it weakened the fabric reality enough to create those whirlpools, which eventually caused a slow unraveling and the formation of splinters of unmaking across this region of space/time. As reality slowly becomes unmade, more splinters form, propagating across the Primes. The reason it falls to humans to fix reality is because the unraveling began on Midgard, and it is here where it is the worst. Midgard and the other Primes share a rough equivalency in space/time to each other and thus parallel to each other across the dimensions."

"Are you saying that Earth is the linchpin to reality across the universe? That hardly makes sense considering the whole wide spectrum of the Tree,"

"Excellent point, Mr. Hakala, if the Breach had not happened, but when it did, it aligned all the Primes throughout the realities so they inhabit congruent areas of the multiverse. The war between us Old Ones fundamentally changed reality as we know it and altered the very nature of the Tree." He closed his eyes, his cigar momentarily forgotten. "For our crimes, the Tree tasked me, the wisest and oldest of the Old Ones, to tend to its needs, which I willingly do as my penance for my sins."

"You sound as if the Tree has a will and mind of its own."

"Doesn't it?"

How do you cope with the idea of an intelligent, self-aware universe? Short answer, you don't. I put the notion in my back pocket for a moment and concentrated on the matter at hand.

"Okay, I've been around long enough, seen enough, to believe you, but what about God? I believe in Him." Not that I had much *faith* lately. "What about Heaven and Hell? Are they part of the multiverse? Part of the Tree?"

Those glacial eyes regarded me for a moment with infinite patience. "The force of Creation you call God (such limiting term for a being, for all practical terms, without limits), or Jehovah, Elohim, Yahweh, Allah, Hayyi Rabbi, Jah, Buddha, Aten, Mukuru, Dyēus Ph$_2$ter, and Shangdi, are all reflections of that force. Limiting words so that humans could wrap their minds around a high concept. Heaven, Hell, Nirvana, Paradise, the Elysian Fields . . . they all exist outside the Tree, not as a part of it, and if reality is unmade and the universes revert to unfocused potential, then I guess that force will be created anew, as the Apostles of the End Times predict. Perhaps even create an identical Tree with all of us playing our parts once again, but I doubt it. The only constants are the two diametrically opposed forces. The force of Destruction, like that of Creation, has many names as well: Satan, Lucifer, Shaitan, Crnobog, Apep, Ahriman," He sighed. "All those concepts, Good, Evil, Heaven and Hell, are bounded by limiting words, and, to use a gardening metaphor, they exist as the nutrients for the Tree. They are the soil upon which the Tree is grounded. I know it sounds strange, but to explain that which is unexplainable invites paradox and confusion, which has plagued countless races across the Tree."

I muddled that over for a minute (I wasn't about to show him how confused I was but I had a feeling he knew quite well) before saying, "So you need me to fix this problem, but why put that Nazi asshole in my way?" Yeah, I ignored the whole religion thing. My mind was warped enough trying to understand the concept of a fucking Tree being reality to deal with the nature of God. Best to just ride with it.

"I had to know if you could persist against long odds. Call it a test."

A test. A fucking test. Jesus.

All through my career I'd been tested. The BSI believed in constant testing (both mental and physical) to keep us fit for combat and, for the most part I agreed, even administering a few tests of my own when training new agents. But after a while testing got old, wore on the nerves and caused a state of near constant paranoia . . . not necessarily a bad thing in a profession with a forty percent fatality rate. Still, it got old quick.

"Why me? Isn't there another Kalevi Hakala on a mirror world somewhere that you can recruit?" I sighed. "Not some middle-aged widower whose only drive is to actually get up in morning without feeling like the world is going to shit on me." Although, to be honest, I enjoyed getting back on the proverbial horse again. Second chances and all that.

"The Primes must be fixed and only a person born of a Prime can travel to a Prime. A denizens of the mirror realities cannot travel to a Prime, as the transition to a Prime reality destroys a mirror being. If a mirror succumbs to unraveling, then only that mirror reality is affected. Destroy a Prime, however, and you start a chain reaction that destroys all realities, because the Primes are linked. It has to be someone resourceful, capable, and proven. There are other people besides you who might be able to complete this mission, but I believe you are the Primes' best chance at survival."

"What do I have to do?"

And like *that*, I found myself on my feet, facing Mimir who had grown twelve feet tall and was now dressed in long cloak of midnight cloth. I preferred the suit, though.

"Kalevi Hakala, will you take upon yourself this quest?" he intoned, pointing at my chest with one long, gnarled finger. The old man had gone full Gandalf on me.

I nodded, too surprised to speak.

An axe with a half-moon blade and a long wooden handle appeared at my feet, its bottom third wrapped in dark, well-worn leather. I could somehow sense that this axe held an edge sharper than a mother-in-law's tongue. "You must sip from the Mimisbrunnr and receive such knowledge as is needed to complete your task. It will allow you to travel to another Prime, where you will have a chance to find another aspect of the Tree, heal that world, and travel to the next." His eyes began to glow a cold blue, the kind of blue found at the heart of glaciers or the hottest of stars. "But know this, to drink from Mimisbrunnr requires sacrifice, a price for knowledge received. Wotan plucked his eye out to drink deep from the Well, so you must sacrifice that which is precious to you to partake."

"Are you fucking crazy?" I yelled, suddenly sure what kind of sacrifice was needed, and scared down to my socks. I mean, I'm the kind of guy who will lay down on the barbed wire to let others pass, to make the sacrifice play, but self-mutilation? My balls threatened to head north.

Anger rolled off the old god. "Decide!" he thundered and the Tree shook, the floor quaking beneath my feet. I marveled at the power it took to shake the foundations of reality like that. And I think I peed myself a little. "If you do not, I will call upon another to take your place. There is very little time."

Shitfire. The old Finnish stubbornness came roaring back. Don't send others to do your job, it told me. I'd never given up on an op, never turned my back on my duty. I'd sacrificed so much in my life for the Bureau, both for revenge and to do what I thought was right. I'd never looked back, hadn't had a single regret when it came to my responsibilities and I wasn't going to start quitting now. Taking a shaky breath, I nodded and slowly knelt next to the axe, picking it up in my left hand and placing my right on the floor. Oh yeah, I knew exactly the kind of sacrifice was needed, right down to bone and balls, and it churned the acid in my stomach and sent fear sweat to my brow. Bile flooded the back of my throat.

Before I could change my mind I struck, the absurdly keen edge easily slicing through skin, tendon and bone as if they were hardly there.

Shock, a dumbfounded amazement that part of me lay where it shouldn't, fingers still twitching slightly. Then the red, gushing red which spurted across the floor, only to be absorbed into its depths like a sponge, disappearing into the strange striations. Above me the tree twinkled, revolving slowly.

Then the pain hit. A complete, raging, unstoppable freight train of agony as my nerves finally reacted to the brilliantly sharp edge of the ax. Black spots appeared in front of my eyes, and I may have whined like a whipped puppy, or mewled like a kitten. Unable to think, unable to do anything but stare at my spurting stump, I knelt on the floor and watched as my life's blood gushed. My stomach rebelled, spewing bile and the remains of a protein bar every which way, spattering my heavy pants and boots. I could barely see, could barely think, everything starting to go white and red as I began to shake and shudder uncontrollably.

A long finger touched my stump and suddenly the pain disappeared, the red rawness replaced by fresh-grown skin gleaming with health, pink and perfect as if from a newborn baby.

"Damn," I whispered, nearly passing out in relief, although the horror of the moment still echoed in the halls of my mind. My hand still lay on the ground, no longer twitching, but an ugly reminder of self-mutilation. Then, right before my eyes, the hand began to sink into the floor, the Tree taking its due.

Sacrifice. Wotan/Odin plucked his eye out, a symbol of clarity of vision for the knowledge of future events. What did that say about me that I had to cut my own hand off to achieve the knowledge needed to complete the task in front of me? I spat, trying the clear the vomit taste from my tongue.

Pride in Wotan's vision, pride in my physical prowess. Sacrifice what you're most proud of . . . who said the universe doesn't have a sense of humor?

Mimir cocked his head. "Why are you laughing?"

Was I? By damn, I was! Dry, brittle laughter fell from my lips like shards of glass, shattering against the walls. "I don't know," I wheezed. "Perhaps at the silliness of it all."

He frowned.

"I need to fix the universe and the knowledge I need is in the Well, but I must maim myself to get at it, which jeopardizes my chance to save everything. Just seems so fucking arbitrary."

"Not so." Mimir sighed and once again he was dressed in the spiffy suit and sat in an overstuffed recliner puffing on a Cuban, blowing smoke pentagrams. "There is balance to everything. For everything. Trust that the Tree knows what is needed. Besides," he shrugged. "You don't get something for nothing."

"So why didn't you do it? You're the Aesir of wisdom after all."

"I cannot leave this place. Besides, my task is to maintain and observe, not to effect change. I have very little power outside of this manifestation of the Tree, save for appointing a guardian and giving visions to witches and madmen."

My eyes widened. "*You* helped Baba Yaga? She said her magics told her about the coming Armageddon," I exclaimed. It took a second for the other shoe to drop. Didn't I say the same thing to Babs? Maybe I was slowing in my old age. Rust on the mental gears, you know. "You set me up."

"Oh, I wouldn't quite use that term, but yes. Babs, as you call her, is powerful, but doesn't have the wherewithal to see the Tree for what it is or what it needs. I simply gave her a push." His grin had more teeth than mouth should have. "The Tree needed an able hero and you answered the call. Very flattering, actually, that is why it holds you in such high esteem."

"Color me grateful," I said dryly, knowing that my choices were limited. My stump looked years healed, not seconds. "Now what?" I hated to hear the whine in my voice, but it'd been a day, you know?

The ancient god with the avuncular face and sad, glacial eyes held out a hand. Floating above his palm was an acorn shell filled with water. I blinked rapidly. No, more than water . . . the stuff from the well, all shiny and shit.

"Doesn't seem like much," I said, regarding the shell dubiously.

"Wotan took a god-sized drink from Mimisbrunnr, more than a quart, and it nearly killed him. Your mortal flesh cannot handle more than this, but there will be knowledge enough. And power to do what is necessary." He gestured with his other hand. "Drink, Mr. Hakala. Knowledge and the ability to do what is needed will come."

I screwed my courage to the sticking place and took the acorn shell. Closing my eyes, I drank.

INTERLUDE

The Healing of Midgard

SPACE AND TIME WERE NOT WHAT I THOUGHT they were. To even try to put it into layman's terms would be an effort of futility. Safe to say that if you ever drink from Mimisbrunnr, prepare for some serious mind fuckery.

Screaming would have been nice, if I had a mouth and voicebox to give vent to one, but I had no self, no identity, no body, only the constant flow of information downloading into my soul.

Stand under Niagara Falls and let the water pelt you while you focus on the sensation. Never mind, you'll be crushed and drowned . . . that's what the sip from Mimisbrunnr felt like. Without the instant death, of course.

The universe opened up to me, performing a strip tease reveal of secrets, but I couldn't see because of the flood of information was too much, too muchtoomuchtoomuch!

STOP!

Peace. Well, not quite . . . the clamor of knowledge eased, a buffer erected between my mind and the endless torrent of download, which now seemed to be less in my conscious mind than subconscious. I could *feel* the flow, still raging, but it seemed distant, confined to the back channels of my brain. But . . . peace of a sort. Blessed relief.

Closing my mental eyes, I slowly counted to ten, isolating a portion of the data rush I could still acutely feel . . . languages, customs, landscapes and more. At the periphery of my mind, I was aware of civilizations, billions of them, too many to contain. Most of them were sluicing away to be lost forever, but a few stuck with me:

A trilaterally symmetrical squid-like species on an ocean world, braving the intense thermal vents on the seabed to begin the foray into a bronze age.

Immense balls of sentient gas on a giant planet surrounding a hot blue sun in the Far Galactic Drift, whose language rang through the thick methane clouds like a Brahms symphony.

Four-legged, hairy crab-like beings with six claw-like hands at the end of their long, multi-jointed arms had built a city that covered their home world, and were flinging themselves outward to colonize far stars using ships that bent the fabric of space. They possessed technology I couldn't begin to understand.

Closer by, a manta-like species that floated on thermals, their cities web-like structures between the peaks of enormous mountains.

Concentrate. I pulled my mind back from the data-threads, knowing that I could get lost in an instant to the staggering view of the whole wide universe. *Concentrate.*

Earth.

Midgard.

Blue and white in my mind, perfect in its entirety and complexity of life. Superimposed on the planet were nine more, all different and unique, their mirror shadows trailing behind. Through them all was a shatter scar, like gnarled, keloid tissue that pinned them together in a locus point of dimensional tangents. Or whatever, because describing it sure didn't do the knowledge justice.

All along the dimensional surface of Midgard were smaller scars that radiated from the shatter scar that pierced the dimensions.

Weak points that were vortices which led to the other eight worlds like bathtub drains that emptied into our world, turning our perfect little planet into the roach motel of the nine realms. Smaller, neat holes in our reality cropped up here and there, and I realized they were the gates the Sidhe used to enter our world. Pronounced *Shee*, they were the faë, or elves if you were into all that Tolkien stuff. Either way they were right motherfuckers who had done me wrong a time or two, but their gates posed no threat to the Tree because somehow they were *grown* into the bark of the universes, rather than drilled. Thanks to the magic download of information, I could see that they ran through all nine realms and radiated out from the planet known as Alfheim. Faërie. I could also tell that because of their organic nature they would be harder to close, possibly beyond my capabilities even with the magic of Mimisbrunnr.

And across the face of Midgard were tiny contrails of unreality, thousands of them. Hidden from the naked eye they looked like teeny tiny bits of ravening splinters, but to my mind which had been opened up by Mimisbrunnr, they floated over, in and through our world, dangerously weakening the fabric of reality to the point that I knew Midgard would be destroyed a matter of weeks. And if it went unchecked, this Prime reality, this universe, would soon follow, because time was nothing to the ravaging forces of unreality. This part of the Tree would simply cease to exist, and within moments, the other eight would follow.

Shit.

Where did all those flakes, those shards of unreality come from? As soon as I thought of the question, the answer came to me. The vortices. They had grown larger and larger, sucking in more Supernaturals into our world stressing the glass of reality, which had begun to splinter and crack, sending out the shards of unmaking.

And just like *that*, I knew what needed to be done. The answer bored into my mind from the plethora of data I'd absorbed. It was within my grasp to save my world.

But only this world. The nine other Primes were suffering, too, and although not as far along as Midgard, they would soon see their fair share of unmaking and when one went, they all would.

It's always something.

A strange music caressed my soul, a symphony so deep and profound that if I could feel my bones they'd be vibrating, and if I had eyes, they'd be crying. It was sonorous, vast and total, as if all of existence was giving voice to an aria, and I understood with the knowledge downloaded into my mind that these were the thoughts of the universe. Mimir was right: the Tree, the manifestation of all realities, was a living thing given to thoughts so complex and convoluted that my mind would pop like of a soap bubble if I tried to concentrate on them. All I could sense was that the Tree was in pain and had tasked Mimir to find a way to heal the damage so it would not die, and that the liquid in the well, that strange glowing water, was its distilled knowledge. No wonder drinking more than a sip would kill me, in fact, that sip was almost too much. If I'd been a lesser man, Mimir would be going through my pockets for spare change. Instead, I had lived and received valuable knowledge instead of death. Knowledge and a whole shitload of magic to use. A one-time shot to heal Earth. Midgard. Whatever.

With the power of the Well thrumming through me, I flexed my magical muscles, my atrophied abilities given a temporary boost because of the water, the liquid essence of reality, provided all I needed to get the job done. It made me powerful. I reached out with senses beyond my normal ones and felt the torn edges of the vortices as they churned and spun, ripping at the jagged fabric of the universe. With slow, deliberate thoughts, I smoothed the edges of the vortices, feeling them pull at the other Primes, the draw that brought creatures into our world that BSI agents died to combat.

And I closed them all. Immediately, I felt a great portion of the magic given to me by Mimisbrunnr drain away, leaving me with a few dribs and drabs.

With a mental sigh I realized that I'd just rendered the Bureau of Supernatural Investigation virtually obsolete. Oh well, could be worse . . . I could've fucked the whole thing up and shattered reality for good.

With the knowledge still downloading, the next steps came to me fully formed. Now that the vortices were closed, I could still aid the other Primes by traveling to one after the other, healing their injuries, fixing each reality as I went by finding on them extensions of the Tree. My next destination sprang into mind along with a bright point of power that indicated the interface where the Tree touched the world, but differently than Mimisbrunnr. It was more focused, a raging torrent of magic and fire, and it was there I needed to go next because that world didn't have much time left before it popped like the universe's biggest soap bubble.

Still in that dark place, floating in an infinite void, I girded my magical loins and used the last of the power the Well had lent me to focus on the Sidhe tunnels, the organically grown magical egresses to and from Midgard and all the other Primes, and exited stage left.

MUSPELHEIM

ONE

The frying pan

LIGHT. A LOT OF LIGHT, BRIGHT AND SEARING through my eye-lids and burning my retinas. Too much, too fucking much! I grimaced and groaned and made mewling noises like a baby. A hungry, pissed off baby.

"Gee, clodder, don't you look comfy?" said a voice like leather sliding over rough stone. A woman's voice, hard, with an edge of sarcasm.

I think she was talking to me, but I was too busy squirming in the light. I put my hand over my eyes. Or tried to. Something hard kept my left hand at my side. I heard the rattle of metal.

What?

When I thought I could open my eyes without shrieking in pain, I did so. Sunlight, photonic sandpaper on my retinas, blotted nearly everything out except for the dark form standing over me, who slowly resolved like a developing photograph into a sneering young man.

Curly black hair, skin halfway between ebony and ivory, eyes as dark as a televangelist's soul above a straight, aquiline nose. He would've been handsome except for the sneer that marred his thin lips and a knotted ridge of scar tissue that ran along his jawline from chin to his left ear. "Hey, clodder, yer awake."

Thank you, Professor Obvious. I squinted and tried to sit up, but a rough hand the size of a dinner plate pushed me down. My eyes followed the tree trunk arm up to an enormous gray body barely covered in a linen tunic, muscle upon muscle piled up into one big mountain of ugly, topped with a face even a mother would think twice about loving, fronted on a head the size of a basketball. A lipless mouth barely contained twin tusks (one chipped) that curved up to touch cheeks like granite shelves. Piggy gray eyes stared at me from the caves of their sockets, revealing all the emotion of a chunk of basalt. The skull, devoid of even a memory of hair, had enough puckered scars to tell of a lifetime of rough trade, and I felt a cold chill take over my tummy as I recognized this particular breed of homely. An ogre.

"Feckin' Hel," I croaked. It took a second, but I recognized the language I was speaking, the same one the sneering kid and the lady with leather voice used. Drinking from the Well downloaded all the major languages from the Nine Worlds, and this one happened to be Dholesch.

I was in Muspelheim. Oh yeah, the next world to fall if it wasn't healed. I'd used the last of the magic given by the Well to get here, although I must have biffed the landing.

Muspelheim, the world of fire which, according to Norse mythology, was supposedly ruled over by the giant Surtur. *Not* the garden spot of the Nine Worlds.

"Water," I croaked, staring at the ogre and wondering if he was sizing me up for an entrée. Kal *tartare*. Ogres weren't known for kindness or table manners and they were about as cuddly as your average bale of rusty barbed wire.

"Ha!" said the young guy. His grin showed a gap in his front teeth. "Clodder thinks he gets water, eh? Waste liquid money on his feckin' ass? Ha!"

"Clodder's right, Shem. He gets a sip or he's worthless to us," said the woman with the leather voice, and by the way the ogre ducked his head, she was someone in authority. A form moved into my sight and I couldn't help but stare. Tall, skinny, and dressed in a white leather tunic, this woman looked to be related to the young man, only slightly older. It wasn't her striking looks or hyper muscled form that caught my eye, but the sheer volume of cutlery strapped to her body. There were three swords (two short, one long) and a dozen knives of various sizes from itty bitty to *godgetthatthingawayfromme* in sheathes, strapped around her lean and mean bod. Like the ogre, she sported nothing on her head but skin, and she wore it well. By the way she carried herself, she knew it too. "Thought you were safe in the Outs, didn't you, clodder?"

Outs? I searched my mind but apparently that tidbit hadn't downloaded with the rest of the language. I tried scratch an itch above my eye, but I found that the reason my hand didn't travel north of my navel was because it had been chained to a thick leather belt affixed to my waist. "What the fuck?" I grumbled, becoming alarmed. The chain looked to be made some sort of bluish metal and there was no way in hell I could break the belt it was attached to, not without a shitload of hacksaw blades. For reasons made obvious by the stump at my wrist, they didn't bother cuffing my right arm.

"Oh, look, he's finally realizing how shadowblind he's become," said the kid, Shem, grinning nastily. Seemed like nasty was all the little dickwad could do.

As I grew accustomed to the light, my situation resolved itself into focus and I felt my skin pebble. It was the word 'clodder,' you know. A uniquely Dholesch word that meant 'human property.' A slave.

"You captured me," I grated, and Shem must've seen some heat rising to my eyes because he almost flinched. The ogre loomed closer, and when an ogre looms, it's practically an Olympic event. This sucker would've taken a silver, at least. I met those small, slate eyes with my baby blues and didn't give an inch.

"That's right, clodder," said the woman. "You're ours now, so I suggest you give with some answers or I won't find it in my heart to toss a water skin your way."

Thirst will make a body bow to any circumstance and this was no exception. I cleared my throat and tried to rise, but the ogre pressed me gently and my spine met the ground at speed, the air almost driven from my lungs. "Don't know where I am," I finally said.

The woman signaled and the ogre went from pressing me down to helping me to my feet. The world swooned and swayed, not righting until the lightness in my skull decided to go somewhere else. By then I'd grown used to the harsh light and was able to take stock of my surroundings.

Flat. Not Death Valley flat, but more of Iowa farmland flat with some gentle dips and rises to the landscape. Heat blasted grass the color of faded jade stretched out as far as I could see, and under a sky so washed out it seemed white, were little clumps of light green fronds or ferns dotting the landscape at irregular intervals, blowing softly in a wind designed to bake the flesh from bones. Land of fire, indeed.

"You said 'Outs,'" I croaked. "What is that?"

The woman cocked her head. "You're in it, clodder." She waved a hand, taking in the landscape. "All this, the Outs."

"Feckin' clodder don't know where's he's at?" cackled Shem, drawing a wicked looking curved knife and paring a fingernail. "With the strange heavy clothing and that big knife of his, he's an outcast from the Southern Marches, if I had me a guess, Giliselle. Perhaps even a Twilighter seein' how his skin is so fair."

The woman, Giliselle, gave me the old stink eye for a moment before nodding. "People go missing in the Outs, clodder, unless you travel in a band, like us." She squinted and patted the ogre on the shoulder. He was a band all by his lonesome. "But you know that, if I'm not mistaken. What hangs your carcass in the middle of the Outs, Southlander?"

"Not a Southlander," I mumbled.

"What?"

Louder. "I'm not a Southlander. I'm on a quest of sorts. A really important quest to save the world."

"Ooo-eee, Giliselle," crooned Shem still grinning meanly as he pared his nails. "We gots a one-handed adventurer in our midst, don't we? My heart's all a-flutter, I feel like a little girl!"

Ignoring Shem, I took a deep breath stared at my stump. Still looked shiny and new, without a freckle or scar. In fact, it looked natural, as if I'd been born this way.

"Sell him short at your own peril, Shem," said Giliselle, crossing her arms. "Look at those shoulders, the way he stands. An old man, but one that's kept in shape for sure. He's been marking our positions since he stood and noted every weapon in sight. I'll wager a good gold scorch that he's figured out where our hidden ones are and is wondering where we put his things. No, this one's a fighter."

"You sundamaged, Gil?"

She shook her head. "You know I have an eye for these things, Shem. He's *dangerous*." She turned to the Shem and the ogre. "Only a few days on our raid and we catch a winner, boys. I have a feeling this one will fetch quite a few scorch, a Hel of a lot more than the usual clodders we find roaming the Outs."

I sighed. "Don't suppose you'll take me to your leader?" I cut in, half-afraid of the answer.

Turns out, I should have been all-afraid.

Faster than a blink, an iron hard fist met my stomach and I suddenly felt the need to throw up so much that my boots would come out of my mouth, socks and all if I had been wearing any. Fuckers must have taken them. As I lay writhing on the ground, smelling vomit and trying to get my diaphragm functioning again, Giliselle leaned over me and smiled with bright white teeth filed to points. "If you're lucky, you'll never meet him."

Safety tip: don't ask about the boss.

Sunlight near blinded me and heat burrowed under the remainder of my heavy clothes (the parka had been left by Mimisbrunnr, still heavy with Nazi parts), setting up shop, taking payment in sweat and salt. My boots and socks were nowhere to be seen, nor was my Lahti or bowie, but I had a good idea where they were . . . in the giant backpack that graced the ogre's shoulders. Looked like there was room in there to house a motorcycle with just enough space for the rider. It could be that one of the other two had my weapons, but that was unlikely considering they dressed in tight tunics and thin leggings that ended in thick leather sandals, concealing very little.

For the umpteenth time I rattled the chain that bound my left arm to the belt tight around my waist. Sweat made the skin chafe under the leather and I knew that if I wore it for much longer I'd start to develop sores. Somehow, I didn't think this trio of party pals would give a fuck.

Good thing my socks were thick, because the pale green grass tore at my feet as I found out early on why the other three walked around the little fern-like hillocks.

"Ow, goddamnit!" I swore as a hot pain lanced through the sole of my foot. I hopped on the other, swearing up a storm. On the heel was a single, small patch of some greasy substance about the size of a dime. Usually pain fades, but this kept growing and growing until my swearing became howling, my nerve endings simultaneously flayed by fire and shattered by ice.

"Oh, burn me," Giliselle grumbled. "Clodder doesn't have the sense of a shadowblind chogg. Duul."

"Yes, Giliselle?" rumbled the ogre.

"You got enough in your bladder?"

"Always."

"Well, get to it."

The big lug handled me easily, grabbing me by the calf and lifting me into the air, my agonized foot sticking out from his fist like a chicken bone, and for a moment I thought he'd grab the other leg and make a wish. Instead, while I screamed and writhed, my head banging against the unforgiving ground, he undid his loose canvas trousers and pulled out what he must've been pretty damn proud of.

The fuck?

He let loose a massive hot stream of urine that sprayed like water from a firehose (trust me, it looked like it, too), splashing my foot and his fist.

If I hadn't been screaming like a wounded rabbit, I would've gagged as the thick, acrid smell of ammonia and . . . other things that assaulted my nose, but the pain, the fire and ice had grown to levels I'd never imagined, and I'd been hurt by the best.

Cool, sweet relief began to flood from the epicenter of my agony, traveling through my toes and finally my entire foot, the pain draining away as if somebody pulled the handle and flushed. Duul kept pissing for a good minute, liberally soaking me from toe to crown before putting away the scariest part of himself.

"Jesus Christ!" I yelled, or tried to. My throat felt plenty raw from all the screaming.

Shem was beside himself laughing. "I sure love it when Duul does that! Shadowblind fool doesn't know to avoid the twilight trees." Still laughing, he pulled out a skin and drank.

Giliselle made a face and tossed me her own water skin. "Wash the piss off and any remnant of poison," she said. "Don't waste the water. Next time, clodder, watch where you step or I'll have Duul carry your screaming carcass all the way to Til Mathgen." The hard line of her mouth told me she wasn't in the vicinity of joking.

Apparently, the download from the Well hadn't included lessons in geography, but I reckoned since Giliselle meant it as a threat, this Til Mathgen place had to be far. I rubbed my foot, noting the small greasy patch had been efficiently pissed away. Hell of a defensive mechanism for those, what did Shem call them? Oh yeah, twilight trees, although they looked to be ferns rather than trees.

After tearing up a section of trousers to make a bandage, I limped on after the band, Duul following right behind so I wouldn't get all nervy and try something.

Smelly, damp, and uncomfortable as hell, I marched on. A slave.

TWO

Fight

I WAS SO CAUGHT UP IN MY MISERY, the epic sunburn forming on my tender skin, the thirst scratching my throat, my drying clothes that smelled like the wrong end of an aardvark with diarrhea, and the teasing phantom sensation of my missing hand which was bugging me no end, that I failed to notice that the sun was hardly moving. Maybe a bit, but not enough to be noticeable unless you squinted. It was only in one of those moments of silence, when the sound of your breathing dominates your thoughts, that I suddenly noticed the long noon.

Ask Giliselle? Not on your life. To her and the others I was just a clodder, a slave, and I knew they didn't give a good goddamn about me except for what I'd fetch at market, which was where I assumed we were headed.

So thirsty. My eyeballs felt scratchy and I was desperate for even a hint of saliva on my tongue, the last drop having disappeared hours ago.

I didn't let despair eat at me. I'd been in worse places, worse situations, and I kept an eye out for a chance, any chance at freedom, although I supposed Duul was big enough to outrun me. Still, my eyes, when they weren't focused on evading the nubs of twilight trees, examined my captors. It didn't take too long for me to see that each one of this merry band sported a tattoo on the back of their necks. A blue rectangle within a yellow circle within a larger blue triangle. The colors of the geometric shapes were brilliant, as if the dyes glowed beneath the skin. I asked Shem about it.

"It's a citizenship mark, clodder," he replied in a tone of voice that told me he thought my marbles were nowhere to be found. "You don't got one an' that makes you fair game." He showed me the gap in his smile.

Giliselle poked me. "If you're not from the Southern Marches, then where are you from? How come you don't know about citizenship marks? Everyone in civilized lands, excepting clodders, wears them."

"Far away," I mumbled. "Farther than you'd believe."

She gave me the old hairy eyeball, but didn't ask any more questions. Why waste words on property?

After a rest stop which was far too short for my aching muscles, we came upon a walled fortress consisting of a single, square tower some forty feet tall, surrounded by twenty-foot walls made of what looked to be pale, gray adobe mixed with straw. Inset into the adobe walls at regular intervals were pale green crystals the size of baseballs.

Shem grinned from ear to ear. "Good water now, thank Surt."

"Yes," the ogre rumbled from deep in his massive chest. "Thank Surt, Shem," he made a curious gesture with his right hand. Something to ward off evil?

"Our mounts, more importantly." Giliselle turned to me. "Listen, clodder, you don't seem to know our ways so what I'm about to say will save you a lot of pain: shut your fat gob and keep it shut. Clodders don't talk to freefolk unless spoken to. That's it." She turned to the building. "Hello the fort!" she yelled.

A head popped over the wall belonging to an old man with the salty remains of his hair cropped close to the scalp. "Giliselle. I thought I smelled Duul there." A pause. "Well, come on in, then."

Seams appeared in the wall and a hidden door swung open, a clever construction in the adobe surface. Duul had to enter sideways, but managed well enough. His hand on my shoulder pulled me in with him.

Within seconds I was chained to post in a sere courtyard, my back against the looming walls, the object of very little scrutiny. Feeling how tired my bones were, I planted the back of my lap on the dusty earth. There was stable, a couple of smaller buildings and the tower, all with some of those baseball-sized green stones planted hard in their walls. The post looked solid enough to resist any effort on my behalf for freedom, so I sat and waited to catch some Z's. Last time I had slept had been in a rocky ravine in Midgard, and that hadn't been what you'd call restful.

With an empty belly and parched lips, I slipped into blackness devoid of dreams.

Ow!

The fingers that twisted my ear were the size of bananas and I woke quick enough, alert and ready to dish out some dirt. But when I saw the ogre perched over me like an animate monolith, my temper cooled faster octogenarian's lust.

"Wake," came the bass rumbling from the cave of that slate mouth.

"Like I can sleep with your fingers jammed in my ears," I groused, trying and failing to break away.

"My fingers not in ears . . . they pull earlobes," he said, giving the aforementioned fleshy bits an extra twist.

"Fucking ow!"

That earned me a slow blink, but the fingers disappeared. "What is fuck?"

What is—? I shrugged, realizing I'd cussed in English. "Curse word. Bad word," I said. "Like when you're angry and such."

The slow light of comprehension shone from the brute's eyes. "Ahhh, like when Shem says Feck. Feck is fuck, then."

"I guess." Yeah, feck is fuck. For some reason that rolled around my skull like a mantra . . . feck is fuck, feck is fuck, feck is *stopitgoddamnit!* I shook my head, as the heat leeched all the energy from my body. I felt logy, my mind filled with cotton.

Giliselle sauntered into view. "Awake, clodder?"

"Kal."

A raised eyebrow. "What?"

"My name is Kal."

A women's size seven sandal put an impression into my thigh and I grunted in pain. "You're a clodder, I don't care about your name."

Right. Slave. I nodded. Some day . . .

"Anyway, *clodder*," she said. "Turns out we get a discount on stabling if you show us some mettle." Giliselle knelt and put her face close to mine. It took some discipline not to give with a head butt. She gave with a pointy smile. "You are about to fight, to show your worth, which I believe is considerable. I know the signs, you're a warrior, and a good one if you got to be as old as you are. Now, you may be thinking that you don't want to fight, but you will fight or you will die, and if you die, that will vex me no end because of the time I've already wasted searching the Outs. Almost half a day now, so do *not* vex me. Fight or die. Those are your choices. Your *only* choices. Got me?"

I nodded, which earned me a slap.

"I said, got me?"

"Yes, I understand," I grumbled, rubbing my stinging cheek with my stump.

"Good. Get up."

Shem took that moment to make an appearance. "Why do we have to risk this, Gil? He dies, we're out some scorch." By the look on his face his confidence in my martial prowess was less than high.

"He dies, so what?" she answered. "Better find out now if we have a fighting clodder, because no one will buy defective laborer.

Won't be worth two scorch at auction and say he does die, we're not far from the Outs anyway. We'll head on back out."

The kid looked to the ogre. "What about you, Duul?"

Watching the ogre's shoulders move up and down was like seeing one of the menhirs at Stonehenge shrug. "Don't care," he said.

Getting up had my joints kicking up a fuss, popping and cracking like gunshots . . . the loud results of advanced middle age. After I shook the sand out of all the bendy bits I noticed a short fella in the same kind of spare tunic and sandals my captors wore, one rough hand holding a thick blue metal chain like the one that shackled my left hand. At the other end was a runty, squat, long-limbed humanoid with warty, toad-like skin, large black eyes and an overlong, pointed noise over a mouthful of razor blades.

"Shit," I breathed. "A kobold."

A guy named Gary Gygax, one of the co-creators of Dungeons and Dragons, had made his idea of a kobold fairly stupid, weak little bipeds that could be knocked off by a syphilitic one-eyed Halfling with a pointed stick. In reality, the short little terrors were obscenely strong, like little monster pit bulls, had IQs close to the genius level, and hunted in packs. They also possessed a hankering for the flesh of anything that hopped, walked or crawled. A group of ten (called quarries) of kobolds could flense an elk's carcass to the bone in less than a minute.

Gygax would've had a shit hemorrhage.

If the little runts had a weakness, it would be their lack of discipline and a certain level of gullibility found only in four-year-olds.

The little skink spat and garbled in his kobold language, which sounded a lot like nails in a blender. It jumped up and down, filthy loincloth flapping in the harsh sun. The man holding the chain barked, "Down, Gortt, down." The little kobold calmed down a bit, but glared at me with its shark eyes, one long fingered hand splayed on the ground, the other picking his long, warty nose.

"You want me to fight that?" I asked, not taking my eyes off the little, green-gray monster who was examining a booger at the end of long finger.

"Feelin' fear, old man?" Shem's voice held so much contempt you could spread it on toast. In one hand he held my bowie, in the other some oval, purple fruit that he had cut sections out of with the knife.

I pointed to the bowie. "Then I'm gonna need that."

He pointed back. "You gonna die first, clodder."

"We'll see about that. But you're gonna give me back my knife, kid, or I'll take it off your corpse."

Apparently slavers didn't cotton to mouthy slaves, but his hot reply was cut off. "Your clodder doesn't look like much," said the short guy holding Gortt's chain. "Tall but old, and with only one hand."

Duul took my chain and belt off and I immediately felt like I could fly. Too bad I couldn't because I'd Superman clean the hell out of that place. The big, slate-colored brute put a short club in my hand; in his it looked like a toothpick. "Here," he rumbled. "Good killing stick."

Good killing stick. Right. I popped my neck and loosened my shoulders, feeling the rust flake away.

"Git 'em, Gortt!"

Holy shit! The little buzzsaw sped toward me at mach 10, teeth flashing and snapping, upon me almost before I could react, but I managed to stumble back, clumsily raising the club. Large, triangular teeth the color of aged ivory snapped shut on the club and it splintered like it was made of balsa. So much for a good killing stick, right?

My ass hit the dirt of the courtyard, trousers tearing as the ninja pipsqueak sunk its inch-long black talons into my tender bod, sending embers of pain as it shred my shirt and flesh. I threw an elbow and caught the runt in the nose, which bent like rubber without breaking. Teeth flashed, and a sharp pain at my elbow revealed it to be a bit chewed up. I hoped the fucker didn't have rabies.

Bunching up, I kicked the rat up and out, sending him flying across the courtyard, but not before his claws turned my trousers into rags. Bouncing to my feet, spurred by a rush of adrenaline, I faced off with the little toad as it shook its head like a dog, fixing on me with soulless eyes as it smiled.

A chill ran through my guts. So many teeth, such gleeful evil. It sprang with inhuman speed, and I clubbed it to the ground with my maimed arm . . . good for something, at least. It bounded up, teeth flashing, and I hit it again, bashing its hard and rubbery flesh to the ground. Like a tennis ball it came back up, so I kicked it across the courtyard, getting only a small chunk bitten out of the side of my foot. It landed deftly, giving me a leering, wet grin.

Already I was breathing like a broke ass bull, lungs heaving, chest burning for oxygen. Sucks getting old. I raised my hand. "Come on, pipsqueak," I huffed. "I can kick you around all day."

That spurred the skink on and it flew at me, mouth opening like a shark heading for a plump, tasty seal. I swung for the cheap seats, my fist meeting its right eye so hard it popped like cherry beneath a boot heel. Foul fluid spurted and coated my fist.

"Yeeeaaargle!" The runt squealed, its guttural voice spiraling up and up, like nails on a chalkboard spearing into my skull, but I clamped down on the desire to protect my ears and delivered a kick that would've made the Vikings head coach proud as the little toad jumped up and down in agony. My foot found little kobold balls beneath the filthy loincloth, and it sailed across the courtyard to slam into the wall, arms and legs splayed Wile E. Coyote style.

Before it could move, I hobbled as fast as my injured foot would allow and grabbed the kobold by the foot, lifting and swinging round and round as if I was competing for the hammer throw at the Olympics, letting go after a full ten seconds of rotation. The runt sailed away at speed and hit the adobe wall with its pointy little head less than a second later, cracking the mud and sending straw flying. It slid down and lay still.

I landed on the dirt a second later.

"Gortt!" the handler wailed, rushing forward to care for its pet. He knelt, checking its vitals before turning to me. "You maimed Gortt!" he accused, tears streaking down toward his beard.

"Ah, shit. It's still alive?" Apparently whatever misbegotten mongrel god kobolds worshipped made them tougher than tough. I got my feet under me. "Let me take care of that."

The man snarled and attacked, but I gave him the same old foot-to-the-nuts business that I had given the little skink, and he let out a 'oof,' folding in on himself, collapsing to the dirt, and whimpering softly.

No thoughts, just action. I whirled, the courtyard a blur as I searched for the door. Escape. There, a simple turn wheel of iron. My feet took me there of their own accord, my hand gripping the wheel and putting the full weight of my body behind it. The wheel turned easily as my mind calculated the positions of everyone I'd seen in the place and what they could do to stop me: Duul, still several feet away, Shem, raising my bowie to throw, Giliselle, feet pounding toward me. The little rat still rolled up in a ball next to its master. A stranger, face wrapped in a dun scarf, all white skin and lean muscle . . . just leaning against a wall, no threat. Now.

The concealed door opened . . . and I was through, feet flying, leaving a blood trail from where the kobold bit me, but it didn't hurt because the wide open was in front of me and the slavers behind. Take care of hurts later, first it was time for freedom.

I picked the same direction we had traveled in before, because I needed to get to civilization and I wasn't going to do it as a slave. Figure it out on the fly, no time to plan, only improvisation. Far ahead I saw ruts in the earth, wagon tracks leading off in the direction I wanted to go, and I angled toward them.

I hit a steady, ground eating jog as old training took place, and I thanked my lucky stars that I kept in shape after Jeanie died, even if it wasn't like in the old days when I could run for miles without wiping myself out. The poisonous ferns of the twilight trees sped by, the sage colored grass crunching underfoot pinching my soles. Steady . . . steady . . . don't burn out, just let the miles flow at an even pace. I knew I could outrun just about anything.

That confidence was misplaced. The only thing worse than being proved right is being proved wrong, which came home to my terrified brain when I looked behind.

Duul. There he was chewing up the landscape, long ogre legs pumping, moving like Secretariat on coke. Shem sat on his shoulders, leering and jeering as they quickly ate the distance that separated us.

Okay, time for a little panic. Pumping my legs for all they were worth, I set my head down and *ran*. The taste of blood flooded my mouth and a small stitch ran up my side, but I paid it no mind, there was an ogre coming up on my six.

My feet went out from underneath me, twin thumps of pain at my calves like I'd been punched with brass knuckles, and my body spun and hit the stubby grass hard, my spine connecting with something that bit as a familiar fiery pain started traveling across my back. Twilight tree. I knew what was coming and come it did, my world dissolving into an absolute universe of pain and I screamed and screamed and screamed before the world suddenly went away.

THREE

Til Mathgen or bust

PISS. THICK AND REEKY IN MY NOSE, it woke me from the dark, dreamless oblivion that sheltered me from the pain and torment that comprised my life. Musty, musky, the piss smell brought my head up and down, my nose landing on something warm and surprisingly soft. A crazy quilt of scaly flesh undulated beneath me to a relaxing rhythm.

What surprised me this time turned out to be the *lack* of pain, only a vague discomfort as I labored to breathe. The scales came into sharper focus as I woke and realized I lay on an animal of some sort, a soft and warm brindle-colored mount covered in scales like a snake. The color reminded me of Darby, and I let out soft groan of sorrow for my poor dog.

"He's awake." Shem, I recognized the contempt in his voice.

"I know." Giliselle.

Yeah, Duul had pissed on me again, and this time there had been no clean up. I could feel the lingering heat of the twilight tree poison and the crackling of my filthy, tattered shirt as I made an effort to sit up. My legs kicked a bit and I could feel my lack of trousers. After a second, I realized that my waist and hips were draped in a loincloth. I fervently hoped it hadn't belonged to Gortt.

A giant hand gently pushed me down. "Don't move." Duul. You don't argue with ogres when they have the upper hand, so I didn't.

With nothing to do bound to the backside of some mount, I resolved to enjoy the ride, staring as the sere grass passing below and appreciating the rest. I had a sneaking suspicion that there would be little time in the future for lollygagging.

Some hours later we stopped for supper and Duul set me to the ground, gentle as a babe in his great arms. All the ogres I'd battled over the years for the BSI were ornery fucks who didn't care if the people they snacked on were alive or dead at the time, but Duul seemed positively civilized, which begged the question: "How did he get that way?" A question for another day. I rolled my shoulders, working out the kinks, and stared at the blue steel chain that once again bound my good hand to the wide leather belt around my waist.

Taking stock of my bod, I was pleased to note that while I was a bit sore from riding belly down all day, I wasn't as sore as I should have been. My shirt looked to be held together by a few threads and the loincloth that hid my giblets was none too clean, so I hoped the cloth didn't house some tiny little friends that would give me the itchies. But beggars can't be choosers. I decided cop a squat.

As I sat on the flat of my ass, I examined the mount I'd been on all day. It looked like a horse, but with no ears, just thin membranes that quivered over small holes in the skull. Likewise, I couldn't see its eyes, as the pits where eyes should've been were filled with long, pale cilia that waved like a heat shimmer in the air. Instead of hooves there were three-toed claws that looked like they could tear steel.

"Strange beast," I said.

"No stranger than you," said deep, feminine voice that definitely didn't belong to the slavers. I looked over to see the stranger I'd noticed in the courtyard, the one that didn't bother to help or hinder my escape. The arms that stuck out from her tunic were white as bone and well-muscled, enough so that I figured she'd give me a run for my money in the arm-wrestling department.

My laughter was as brittle as matchsticks. "I guess we're all strange."

"True enough." I couldn't tell if the woman smiled behind the dun colored-scarf that wrapped her head, which left only green eyes exposed, but she did hand me a skin of water. "Good fight. Not one man in ten could've beat a kobold barehanded," she remarked as I greedily drank. My skin felt puffy and sore, and my lips cracked and bled. At that point even my blood tasted good. "Much less one-handed."

"Lucky, I guess." I wanted to spit, but even saliva was precious now. "How long was I out?" I asked, handing skin back. She made it disappear inside a small, leather backpack.

"A whole sleep cycle," came the reply. She pointed to the sun. "See?"

Where the sun once hung a little after noon o'clock when I arrived, it looked to be about four, possibly five.

"Long time?"

That earned me a green-eyed squint and a nod. "You're not from around here," she said softly. "Where?"

I wanted to trust her. Something about her voice lulled me, but I wasn't short on caution. "Far away. Farther than you can imagine."

"The others said you're shadowmad, that your brains are weak no matter how strong your arm."

Shem chose that time to saunter over. "So, clodder," he said with a grin, the jawline scar pulling at one side of his mouth. "Now ya know better than to run away. No one outruns Duul." He held up a bolo and twirled it a bit. The small sand-filled leather balls blurred. "Yer legs don't hurt none, do they? These things hit like Surt's own fists."

Now that he brought it up, my calves did feel a bit tender, no doubt sporting a couple of bruises, but a good few hours of sleep had done wonders so I gave the kid a shit-eating smile and shook my head. His grin decided to make a run for it, but before he could say anything, Giliselle came into the picture.

"Don't run again," she said with a ferocious scowl that made my testicles want to hide, like . . . forever. "You can still fetch a good price as a fighting clodder without a nose, understand?"

I made sure to give voice to my complete comprehension.

"Good." To the other woman. "Listen, Twilighter, you don't get too near the property unless you're fixing to buy him. Are you?"

"Maybe. You never know."

The slaver *hrumphed* and said, "Fifteen scorch and he's yours."

"Maybe."

Taking that with a grain of salt, Giliselle left with a sour look. "We break camp in little bit, get ready."

"Twilighter?" I asked.

"You never heard of the Twilight Realm?" she asked, holding up her pale, pale arm. Her cream-colored tunic stretched over her small breasts and I tried not to stare. Apparently Muspelheim hadn't invented the bra yet.

I shook my head.

"What's your name."

"Kal."

"Call?"

"Close enough." Then, "Why are you here?"

She shrugged. "On my way to Til Mathgen. Travelers need to stick together in case of kobolds, tusk goblins or raiders. I paid a burn mark for the privilege and the slavers let me come because no one's crazy enough to tangle ass with an ogre."

My chuckle fell out of my mouth and plopped to the grass like a dead thing. "They're not so tough if you know where to hit 'em. Killed one with my knife about twenty years ago." I didn't mention that luck played a big role and that the ogre was near blind drunk at the time, but hey, never hurts to embellish a little, does it?

You'd have thought that about a jillion volts passed through her considering the way she jumped and stared. "You're serious," she accused.

"Very."

A piece of jerky and some hardtack landed at my bare feet. "Here," Duul grumbled, tossing me an odd look as he unshackled my hand.

Mouth watering, I chowed down faster than I thought possible, not caring that the hardtack hurt my teeth and I had no water. I forced down whole chunks trying to fill the void that was my stomach.

After my lunch I examined my wounds. They'd been treated with some sort of grayish goo and bandaged with semi-clean rags, and as they didn't hurt any I figured I was safe from whatever kind of Muspelheim bacteria happened to be lurking around. Not long after that we were on our way, Shem and the Twilighter riding their lizard horses and me sitting pillion behind Giliselle, my arm once again shackled to my waist. Duul trundled behind, eating the distance with long, ogre-y strides, a large backpack bouncing against his spine.

The sun had hardly moved at all before we came to another fortress built along the same lines as the previous one: single tower, adobe walls, small adobe stables with more lizard horses. Giliselle bartered for water and food, Shem tried to scout out what women were available (very few), and I found myself poked and prodded as a possible sale to one of several merchant types in tunics of cloth of gold, vermillion, and amber sporting more jewelry than a runway model. They all wanted me to flex and show my teeth like a good boy. The entire process was carried out clinically, with no abuse, just the humiliation of being treated like a piece of furniture or livestock. No one seemed willing to pay the asking rate of fifteen scorch though, citing my age and the absence of my right hand.

"Tell me about Til Mathgen," I pleaded with the Twilighter during our third stop, another fortress identical to the last two. Shem had actually found some girl who was either desperate enough for action or had low enough standards for men, and he disappeared while Giliselle relaxed indoors. Duul sat nearby with me in the dust, snoring like a diesel engine, enough drool dropping from his lips to qualify as a waterfall.

The Twilighter nodded as she mended a bit of tack from her lizard horse and continued our conversation. "Til Mathgen is the largest city in the Empire. The capitol, actually, the seat of Surt's power."

"The Empire?"

She gave me a cool, green-eyed stare from behind her scarf. I still hadn't seen her face or hair, she even slept with it on. "Surete."

"Tell me about the Empire, then, please."

A long pause. "Where are you from?"

Caution glued my mouth shut. Slaves can't trust. I shook my head.

Sighing, the Twilighter stood. "Then rest. We'll be at the city before the sun touches the horizon."

The thing about long boring rides is you get tunnel vision, so when the landscape gradually changes, you hardly notice until something knocks you out of your ennui. That's what happened to me when we came upon the last fort before Til Mathgen.

If the other buildings we had seen were forts, this one was a goddamn castle. Four towers soaring over eighty feet in the air connected to a solid brick of a building slathered heavily in terra cotta colored stucco, reinforced with animal hair rather than straw, although the enormous forty-foot wall still looked to be simple adobe painted a mustard sort of yellow. It looked like the Bavarian castle Neuschwanstein had fucked a Mexican restaurant, and this conglomeration was the misbegotten result. Instead of a hidden entrance, there was an actual portcullis and two large gates made of some dark wood. For a second, I wished Des could see this odd-looking castle, and my burgeoning smile died on my face.

Was he okay? Did he miss me? The distance between us seemed longer than our dimensions apart. I'd tried, *really* tried, to connect with him after Jeanie died, even engaging the help of a therapist, but nothing had eased the dark hole that once housed the image of my wife, his mother. That hole divided us, set us on opposite sides where we could look but not touch. Whether it was because he refused and couldn't reach out or I was too afraid and hurt to try, I can't tell you, but all I knew was that we were broken and I hadn't been able to figure out how to fix things. Maybe some things can't be fixed, not by those of us on the inside of the problem. Too close, too wounded.

I hoped Mom and Dad could handle my boy. A long-time army man, Pekka Hakala knew how to combine discipline with caring, and Terhi, possibly the stubbornest woman in all of Finland and North America, could charm the ugly off a bulldog. Together I prayed they could reach through the armor of my son's trauma and bring him back.

To me.

I furiously blinked away tears, turning my head so the others couldn't see, but I caught sight of the Twilighter studying me from behind her dun scarf.

Fucking wonderful.

Not bothering to match her stare I looked around with some surprise at the landscape. Apparently while we traveled the endless flat had become gently rolling hills cultivated for farming. With the sun nearing the horizon, I beheld a sight that would have knocked me on my ass if I hadn't been sitting. The twilight trees that looked like ferns were visibly rising out of the ground, moving many centimeters per minute until they stood straight and tall like palm trees, their ferns filling out to umbrella-like leaves that provided plenty of shade for the leathery pods that clustered like grapes out of the middle of the trunk. People walking the rows provided perspective as they picked the pods that grew at eye level, depositing them into long cloth bags that dragged the ground behind them.

Later, I would find out that the twilight trees grew under-ground, and hid from the harsh heat of the long day only to emerge as the sun neared the horizon. The farmers would pick the leathery pods, which were in fact an oily fruit called *uwa*, a starchy staple that tasted like a cross between jicama and egg-plant. Mashed, fried and boiled, the fruit graced every table of society from the halls of the rich to the cells of the clodders. The oil of the uwa was used for a relatively clean burning fuel and the seeds were roasted and eaten like sunflower kernels or pepi-tas. Come sundown the trees would slide back down into their sheaths in the ground, their leaves folding in on themselves until they resembled ferns once again.

"Clodders?" I wondered aloud, looking at the workers in the fields.

"No farm work for you," Giliselle answered, confirming my hypothesis. The slaves looked healthy enough and the tunics, while Spartan, were well mended. "Even crippled as you are you're headed for the pits. If you're good enough, you'll get women and some burn marks to spend. Not so good, you get beat up enough till you find yourself as a drudge in some house." She waited for a moment, squinting. No doubt she expected me to object or say something stupid, and to follow with a quick fist to the gut, but I kept my trap shut for once. Mom would've been proud. As for Giliselle, she merely grunted and looked away, no doubt disappointed.

Although the building deserved the title of fortress, I didn't have too much time to appreciate it because Giliselle passed it right by, not bothering to barter with the locals for fresh water or food. As the fortress went into the rear view, the Twilighter asked if I could ride pillion on her horse and Giliselle gave her a dubious look, but conceded as long as Duul, walking behind our lizard horse, kept an eye on me in case I became nervy enough to try escaping again. The ogre gave me a toothy smile that turned my bowls to water and wagged a giant finger at me. I got the message real quick: try something, pay a heavy ogre-y consequence.

A few yards from the fortress we came upon a wide, well-maintained road that looked to be made of sturdy slabs of basalt fitted almost seamlessly together, sloped to either side so rainwater would sleet off to the gutters fitted along the edges. Every hundred yards or so there were breaks in the gutters, channels that led to cisterns with wooden covers, and I surmised that during the rainy season the covers were removed and water collected. Considering the triple digit heat at midday, it made sense, although I reckoned the temperature had now dropped to the high double digits. I asked the Twilighter about the cisterns.

"For the morning rains," she commented without turning around.

Morning rains. I sighed and regarded the yellow disc of the sun. Considering the lengths of the day, what would night be like? Cold, I guessed, cold and bitter. No reason to ask how long the days were, though, considering there existed no frame of reference between their world and mine when it came to such matters.

We came across some foot traffic, carts drawn by lizard horses and some people who looked to be slaves like me, but dressed clean and looking relatively healthy, every single one carrying a green tattoo on their chins. A simple dot the size of a dime. My future in green ink.

Fuck that noise.

Bold as brass, balls the size of church bells, cheeky, sarcastic- all those cute little metaphors and similes used to describe me over the decades seemed like empty words when the realization hits home that life would come to a painful, unpleasant chapter, and there's not a fucking thing you can do about it.

I needed to get out of this chickshit outfit. My mind spun, trying to come up with a scenario that would give me the largest chance for success, but I came up empty. Then I became distracted by a pair of men in light leather armor riding lizard horses so big it made the band's look like ponies. Pedestrians steered clear as they dominated the road, twenty-four hands tall at the withers (ninety-six inches, or eight feet), scales jet black and glinting in the sun with pinpoint brilliance, and three-toed claws looking sharp enough to slice through stone. Each rider held a six-foot barbed spear and carried short swords sheathed at their sides. The heat had kept them from wearing the full leather helmets with face-guards tied to their saddles, so we could see the grizzled, hard stares of the veteran soldiers.

I grabbed the Twilighter's attention and asked, "Who are they?"

She didn't bother to look at the pair who were passing us by on the left. They looked to be carved from granite with the icy stares of professional bad asses. "Soldiers, obviously." A pause. "See the lightgems on their spears?"

I said that I did see thumb-sized greenish gems affixed to each spear head.

"Shadowfighters. Elite. They patrol near the Southern Reaches beyond the Outs. You don't want to meet them without an army at your back."

"They catch slaves, I bet."

At that she turned her head and gave me a squint. "And you'd lose that bet. Giliselle and her band catch runaway clodders and those who nibble at the edges of the Empire. There's an entire cottage industry devoted to catching criminals and outlanders and selling them to the cloddermasters in Til Mathgen and Duris Midan. This group is pretty well known for their competency and ability to wrangle those they catch."

Of course they were. And there I was, fresh from another dimension, the next world over, so to speak, unconscious on the grass, ripe for the harvesting. They must have danced a jig at finding me practically gift-wrapped. Goddamnit.

Time on the road became a blur of boredom and stiffness from balancing on the saddle of a brindle-colored lizard-horse, which had started to give me sores in places better off not mentioned. People didn't bother to give our little band a second glance, even with an eight-foot slate gray ogre trundling along behind.

"Are ogres common here?" I asked, trying to stave off the tedium.

The Twilighter snorted. "They're citizens of the Empire just like all humans. All giantkin are citizens, they're beloved by the Immortal Surt. No giantkin will harm a human and no human will harm giantkin, save to defend themselves." She held up a slim, long fingered hand, the palm sheathed in callous. "Before you ask, clodders are fair game if they attempt violence or escape, so don't anger Duul. Ogres often find employment as personal bodyguards or slavers." One slim hand flicked back at the ogre. "They command high prices."

"Have . . . uh . . . giantkin and humans always lived in relative harmony?" In the distance I noted a range of mountains coming into view, hazy and far off, but the unmistakable conical shapes of volcanoes caught my eye. The smoke was a dead giveaway as to their nature as well. Five dark plumes staining the sky with gray haze,

The Twilighter paused for a moment. "In the earliest times, when humans first arrived to Surete, the giantkin welcomed humanity as allies against the old gods who waged war across the land." She sighed. "It is part of history called the Long Death, where a majority of giantkin fell to grave sorceries."

I pondered that for a while. Her story jibed with the information given by Mimir. Humans had been sucked back into the other eight realms by the Breach before it closed.

Before long, Duul had lengthened his stride so he paced next to the Twlighter's horse, clipping another chain to my manacle. It looked to be a good fifteen feet long. "So you don't run," he said in his basement rumble, before trailing behind again, long chain wrapped firmly in one meaty fist.

"You might run before we get to the city," she commented drily. "But once you're inside the walls, you're there until someone frees you."

A surge of hope, which died when she said, "It happens. Usually after a clodder serves a house for about . . . oh, twenty years or so. It all depends on two things."

"Which are?"

"If you're a criminal sentenced to be a clodder, or a debtor. A criminal serves a set amount of time for the crime committed, while the debtor serves until the debt is paid."

Twenty years! My heart did a little stuttery thing. No way. The world would end long before that. In fact by my estimation, the clock was set at a few months before the universe devaporated, and even if it wasn't going to pop I really didn't want to hit seventy-five before seeing freedom.

Once again with the mind reading thing, the Twilighter said in a voice low enough that only I could hear, "I need a strong arm at my side, someone used to violence and who has the experience and maturity to tilt the scales my way on a little problem I'm having. You seem to be made for the order despite being a hand short, so I offer you this: promise yourself to me so I can eliminate this problem, and I'll put your feet on freedom's path. All you have to say is 'I accept.'"

While green eyes bored into mine, I gave the offer a good think. It came down to trust, plain and simple. As I considered, the band crested a low hill, and my breath went bye-bye.

A couple of miles away lay a city so large it seemed to dominate the horizon of checkerboarded farmland. The road ran arrow straight to that city as if it had been made using God's own ruler, but that wasn't what took my breath away. Or the tall towers shining in the sun, the throng of people heading toward it as the sun made its first kiss upon the horizon, or its majesty of scope. No, it was the wall that encircled the entire city. Walls so tall they put the stories of Troy to shame, so massive that Tolkien might have passed out from envy. Trying to figure the scale from such a distance with the people entering through a massive gate, I reckoned they had to be, at the very least, a hundred feet tall of light gray architectural grandeur.

"Jesus," I breathed.

"Til Mathgen," affirmed the Twilighter, a hint of pride in her voice.

"So *big*." Such a small word to encompass what I saw.

"Two million souls, all within the walls."

"How many outside the walls?"

"Are you shadowmad?" she practically exploded, her green eyes flying wide. "Where are you *from*?"

"Nowhere you've heard of."

She stared so long that I grew uncomfortable, and I'd been stared at by the best. "Make your decision soon because once you've been auctioned off, there's little I can do legally to help."

"How about illegally?"

More staring. Oh well, joke 'em if they can't take a fuck. I put my eyes back to the city as the long and slow twilight fell, knowing that a decision had to be made. "Do I have to make my mind up now?"

She gave me a look that expressed her opinion about my intelligence, or lack thereof. "Before the auction is over," she grumbled.

"Got it."

Til Mathgen came closer, the towering walls of carefully fitted gray stone (no adobe or stucco here) joined almost seamlessly together, with giant green crystals taller than a man set in the face at regular intervals above. Lightgems, the Twilighter called them, giant versions of the smaller stones set into the walls of the forts we had passed by during this seemingly endless day. By the time we reached the gates, guarded by a half-dozen lizard horse riders with their long spears, my neck had grown a crick from staring up and up and up. Forty feet thick, these walls would be a herculean task even by my world's advanced standards, much less than the seemingly primitive abilities of this one, which gave me pause as to the age of the construction. Much of the stone looked worn smooth by time and weather, so polished by wind and sand it gleamed in the fading sunlight. I rubbernecked the entire forty feet, lost in a state of slack-jawed awe.

Brilliant light nearly blinded me as we entered the city. Every alley, every corner had a lightgem either hung on a pole or embedded into a wall, and they all glowed with a yellow, buttery radiance that denied any hint of shadow or darkness. In fact, the inside of the wall held lightgems that matched the ones on the exterior, except in that they glowed, casting warm light across the rooftops and on the soaring towers. Lightgems. Got it.

A throng of pedestrians choked the road, all dressed for the heat in light homespun and many not wearing tunics at all, preferring to travel bare-chested wearing only a breechclout. Many of them were women. The indifference to the sight of bare breasts told me of a society where practicality outweighed prudish considerations. Like the walls, the buildings were made of the same gray stone, and if I had a guess, I'd say they were quarried from the volcanic mountains I'd seen in the distance. Moving that quantity so far must have taken centuries, which begged the question . . .

"How old is the Empire?"

The Twilighter shrugged. "Old. Lifetimes upon lifetimes. I'm no scholar, but I'd hazard a guess at a few thousand generations."

A few thousand—? My mind boggled and wobbled. Instead of replying, I kept my eyes peeled for an opportunity to escape, although my chances of wresting the chain from Duul and disappearing into the crowd seemed to be slim to none, and slim left for the day.

Brightly painted shops and inns lined this section of the road, which had become a grand thoroughfare slicing clean into the city toward the soaring towers that dominated the center. Most buildings here stood at least two stories, some three with the occasional four. As I craned my head around, I realized that I could read the bold letters carefully painted on stone, glass and wood, which translated to: CHOGG'S HEAD TAVERN, MULISK FAMILY CLOTHIERS, THE WENCH AND THE CUP. Apparently, the Tree thought I should be able to read the Dholesch as well as speak it. The air carried a heavy rank odor of piss and shit, and the reason why became clear as I saw a chamber pot emptied into an alley way between two of the taller buildings. So this society could build giant walls, but an efficient sewer system was out of the question.

After a couple of blocks, I noticed that while many chamber pots were emptied in alleys, there were large orange-glazed urns on every street corner. I stared at a couple as we passed and saw a woman with a green tattoo on her chin empty a chamber pot of urine into one of the urns.

The history buff in me rejoiced at something so familiar. In ancient Rome they collected urine in much the same way, letting the pee decompose into ammonia which was used for whitening teeth, growing pomegranates, washing clothes, and tanning. I figured that the Empire had an efficient system of collection that allowed them to use as much as they needed. It made me wonder why they didn't pick up feces as well, but figured that only the ritzier parts of the city had that luxury.

I had attracted a lot of attention, but no one gave Duul a second glance. Those that bothered to look at me for a few seconds did so with a sort of clinical detachment you'd see in a customer examining a new car or a side of beef. Here I was furniture, albeit an antique. The thought started a slow burn of anger in my gut, and I resolved to teach Giliselle and the gang a lesson in manners and why they shouldn't fuck with me.

Should I trust the Twilighter? Could I afford to? This world was doomed if I didn't get on with getting on and, somehow, I wasn't too sure she'd believe my tall tale of the Tree and the Well and the impending unreality.

What's a boy to do?

FOUR

Lock up

MUCH OF THE CITY PASSED BY IN A BLUR as I weighed my options, heart plummeting as things looked grimmer and grimmer. It got worse when Duul took me off the Twilighter's lizard horse so I could ride pillion with Giliselle. As for the Twilighter, she gave me a slow nod and peeled away from our group, heading down another wide thoroughfare, this one peopled with occasional ogre and even taller beings who towered over their smaller cousins. Giants. Giankin. The two I saw had skin like dark volcanic rock and hair like lichen, with thick brows and noses so large it could shade a family of four on a hot day. The Twilighter rode past the giants, the wide road providing plenty of room for large and small traffic alike. Going, going, gone went my chances to agree to her terms. This wasn't the finest mess I'd ever been in, but it did rank in the top five.

I did notice that the buildings close to the walls were made of adobe, with straw mixed in to bind the clay, all painted bright, almost garish colors. As we moved toward the city center, more and more of the buildings became stucco. No straw was needed for the mixture of cement, hair, sand, and lime painted in variations of white, yellow, orange and taupe.

And they were bigger, too. Much bigger, the walls built nice and thick to fend off the brutal heat of the day. Another indication that we were headed into more affluent surroundings. The streets were nicer, made of thick cobble and wide as ever, but cleaner, with less of the shit and piss smell in the air. No chamber pots emptied in the alleys here, confirming my earlier suppositions.

Before too terrible long, our merry little band entered a courtyard of a large, squarish building, and it wasn't until I spotted the bars over the windows that I realized our destination.

Duul tugged me off the lizard horse, setting me gently to the ground and placing a hand firmly on my shoulder as Giliselle and Shem made their way inside the forbidding building.

"Stay," the ogre rumbled.

I stayed and eventually Shem and Giliselle returned with a short, powerful man running to fat wearing a soiled green tunic. His ebony skin looked to be buffed to a high shine and light glinted off his dome. "Here he is," said Shem with his shit-eating grin. The gnarled scar on his jaw turned his smile into something evil. He had Duul jingle my chain for effect.

The short man strode up and looked me up and down, inspecting me as if I were a particularly large booger he'd just fished out of his nostril. He touched my pecs, my stomach and back, and I took it stoically. Duul still had the chain in his big fist, so anything I tried would be stopped right quick.

"By Surt's hairy nut sack, Gil," said the short man spat. "You bring me a one-handed clodder? Is this a feckin' joke?"

"No joke, Kla, he's for real," Giliselle replied, crossing her arms under her small breasts. "Moves like greased murder and has a lot of skill in hand fighting. Took out a kobold with only a small bite to show for it."

"The feck you say!" Kla's eyes went wide and he proceeded to give me a second look. "The feck!"

Shem threw his two cents in. "No lie, Kla. I hate to say it, but he's good meat. Will do well in the pits."

"Too old," said Kla, shaking his head. "Too damn old. He'll probably tire out quick."

"Hasn't tired out yet from out trip from the Outs."

Kla took some time walking around me, looking me up and down, before saying, "All right, clodder, are you going to be trouble?"

I couldn't help myself, my mouth got in the way of my common sense. "What do you think?"

The smile left the short man's face, but before he could reply, Shem's fist lashed out, a meat missile heading toward my cheek.

Good thing I was expecting it. I ducked and head butted the kid hard enough that his nose made a satisfying *crack*. Then, while he was letting out a yell that would curl your hair, I hooked him with an ankle and dumped him on the ground.

The knife at my throat stopped me from stomping the kid into tomato paste. "Ah, ah, ah," said Kla with a wide grin. He held a hand out to stop Giliselle from piling on while Duul stood there, chain in hand and a look of placid surprise on his granite face. "Now while there are laws preventing cruelty to clodders, it does allow me to feckin' *force* you to comply to my commands without leaving permanent damage. You get me, clodder?"

I got him.

"Good." The knife moved, but not far. "You got spirit, you feckin' idiot, which by itself is not enough, but a blind man can see that you have some feckin' skill at hand fighting. Tell me, how are you with a knife?" Kla pointed to my stump. "I hope that wasn't your dominant hand."

"I'm good with either one," I said, keeping very still. Shem was frowning mightily and Giliselle looked like she wanted to take part in slicing me down to four-foot nothing, but wasn't about to ruin a lucrative deal.

"Excellent!" The knife disappeared. "Come with me and mind yourself. I am, by law, obliged to tell you with words small enough words for you to understand that you will be treated with respect and earn an honest burn mark. But, if you attempt escape or harm me or my employees, you feckin' moron, you will be subject to disciplinary action up to and including having shackles permanently attached to your limbs. You got that, or do I have to draw a picture?"

Wonderful. "I get you."

"Kla."

"Excuse me?"

"No, I don't think I feckin' will." All jovial aspect left his features and the worm of fear turned in my gut. "You call me Kla or you'll land squarely upon my bad side."

What was there to say except, "Yes, Kla."

My world became a ten-by-ten cell with wrist thick iron bars, a bucket, and a floor covered in straw. The bars kept me in, the straw was for sleeping on and as for the bucket, well, I think you don't need three guesses what that was for. If you did, the smell alone would drop the biggest hint.

Despite looking like a set from a gladiator movie, the place was warm and the straw was clean, no little four, six, or eight-legged friends to keep me company. Even if I did have a few hundred invertebrate roomies, fatigue washed over me so completely that I was asleep as soon as I hit horizontal.

Light roused me from my exhausted, dreamless slumber, so bright that it speared through my eyelids and into my brain so hard I think my optic nerves began to short out. Shielding my eyes with my hands, I made it to my feet, looking around at what the everloving fuck was going on.

It was those greenish crystals, you see. Their light had replaced those of the dozens of oil lamps tended by elderly clodders and they shone with the same buttery radiance of the great crystals on the walls of Til Mathgen. The light seemed to pervade everything, as if it shone through the stone and steel, flesh and bone, as if coarse matter meant nothing to these hyperenergized photons.

"What the Hel is going on here?" I hollered, hand over my gummy eyes.

Kla's familiar hard-edged voice cut the air. "It's feckin' night, isn't it? Quit your yelling at let others sleep, you feckin' moron."

"What's with the light show, Kla? How can I sleep when it's so bright?"

My jailor came into view. The warm light shone off his dark skull as if it was waxed. "You can get shadowbit if you want, but I think that might put a damper on, oh, the rest of your feckin' life."

Shadowbit, shadowblind, shadowmad. All terms . . . nouns, verbs, adjectives, and negative ones at that. It didn't take a genius to figure that these folks were scared shitless of shadows. Keeping to myself wasn't working, so I decided to take a chance. "Imagine I'm from so, ah, feckin' far away that I don't know shit about shadows. Care to fill me in?"

For a second there was silence, broken only by snores of my fellow clodders in their cells up and down the block. Kla's face became still as mountain pond, and I could tell that he was more than a little taken aback by the question. Finally, "Where are you from, clodder?" he breathed. "Are you shadowmad? Or stupid? Strike that, I know you're stupid, but you aren't the kind of fool to survive to middle age by being extra special stupid, which is what your question is." He examined a grimy nail while scratching a patch of rash right above his breechclout. "Shadows are the bane of Surt, clodder, and they come out at night . . . mostly. Night is when they *feed*. And if you get bit hard enough by a shadow to draw blood, well then, you might as well stretch your lips out long enough to kiss your ass goodbye." Kla leaned in close to the bars. "Don't ask such questions, clodder. It's enough to get you in serious trouble."

I let him know that I'd keep my mouth shut.

Sleep did come and when I woke it was with the kind of sore muscles you get from lying on a hard surface. My joints needed lubrication and every stretch was an exercise in pain as my body told me I wasn't twenty-five anymore. From up and down the hallway I could hear others yawning, farting, and pissing into their buckets. Wasn't too long before a pair of guards the size of refrigerators wrapped in leather armor came along and opened my cell door. "Out," the left-handed refrigerator commanded.

I was ushered into great hall, a cafeteria if the smell of food and the wet sounds of chewing were clues, where dozens of men and women sat on benches with wooden bowls and spoons in hand. The two refrigerators shoved me in and turned away, closing the door behind them.

The chewing noises didn't stop, but about a gazillion pairs of eyes settled on my skin, which gave me the squirmies but I deflected with my advanced age and my ability not to give a shit.

Imagine a group of extremely fit men and women of various sizes, colors and levels of hostility giving stares that could peel the paint off a Volvo while they slowly chewed their food. At the far end of the room was a thick wooden table, the only table in fact, upon which rested wooden bowls and a large metal pot, the smell of which cut through the odor of ripe humanity with precision.

My stomach rumbled and I strode confidently toward the table, past the stares that slid over my skin, noting the faces, the muscles, the clothing. Tunics and loose trousers, quite different from the breechclout that I wore, and it was with a bit of surprise that I realized that the temperature had dropped to comfortable levels. Night time, right. My guess was that I'd need to dress warmer and warmer if the night was as long as the day and the world began to get all Christmas-like and filled with white.

A skinny kid standing behind the table picked up a bowl and filled it from the pot, holding it out to me with large, scarred hands. I took it and slowly counted because I knew what was about to happen, and that the rich, meaty smell coming from the bowl would be gone in a few moments.

The bowl went flying, striking the wall and sending thick stew everywhere. I turned, flexing the sting out of my fingers from the blow that knocked the bowl away. A middling size guy with massive shoulders and nose that had seen more flying fists than a Mike Tyson fight grinned at me, revealing teeth that could use a good brushing.

A test, of course. Always another goddamn test. In over a decade of agency work I'd been tested more than any other agent in Bureau history, so believe me when say that I can spot a test from a mile away.

Such bullshit. Alpha male dominance stuff, chest beating, full eye contact, teeth bared all aggressive like, testosterone nonsense that you can find in any prison or football field. I knew what needed to be done.

He knew I'd go for the balls, because it's a man's weakest point, so I didn't. He moved quickly, presenting his side to me, protecting Big Jim and Twins just as I expected, and at the same time my heel took him in the side of the knee, not hard enough to break, but definitely hard enough to have him hit the floor and bounce. Not a single person moved to help him, which cemented the notion of this being an alpha male dominance thing. My guess was that this bozo wasn't one of the popular kids.

Quick as a wink he made it to his feet, hobbling slightly, and threw a punch which I deflected with my forearm, or tried to. Swollen knuckles smashed the meat of my arm and it went numb from stump to elbow. I reacted with stiffened fingers to the throat and he gagged, spitting and choking. Following up with a left hook that took him in the chin, I came about with a backhand to the nose, or a back stump to be more precise. It didn't break, but the spurting blood was pretty impressive and the nub where my hand used to be hurt like the blazes.

Roaring, the clodder bum rushed me, ripped arms like steel cables going for a clench so he could squeeze the stuffing out of me, but I juked aside and landed a left in the gut, which felt like punching a velvet covered brick wall. He screamed in anger and swung a haymaker that, if it connected, would've introduced my teeth to the floor, but my face wasn't there. Instead, his fist passed with a *whooshing* sound and I stepped in, aiming my stump for his cheekbone and, at the last instant, folding my forearm along my bicep, smashing my elbow into his face.

The muscular clodder's eyes rolled up until only the whites showed and he made like a cut tree, falling full on his back, head striking the stone floor with the sound of a watermelon hitting pavement.

I stood there, breathing shallowly through my nose and gave the rest of the room a squint. Not a man jack of them met my eyes. Nodding, I turned to the kid behind the pot and gestured toward another bowl. Butts left benches as I made my way and picked a spot, figuring out how to eat a full bowl of stew with one hand considering there wasn't a table to set it on. Putting the bowl on my lap, I let the feeling of victory give a savory spice to the already delicious and meaty meal.

"No more bullshit," I said to no one. Everyone. "Leave me be." Just leave me the fuck alone.

"YOU KNEW, WHICH SURPRISES THE HELL OUT OF ME because of how feckin' stupid you are." Kla eyed me as he handed a bundle of warm clothing through the bars. In the hours since the sun went down the temperature dropped significantly and my tattered and battered shirt I'd received from the Danes really wasn't cutting it anymore, considering it was more holes than fabric. The bundle included canvas trousers, a thick shirt made of a wool-like material and a pair of felt lined boots, although the callouses on my soles had developed to a point that I could safely walk on glass.

"Knew?" Of course I knew.

"That it was a test. That Vortik was going to start something."

I snorted. "Of course I knew. Some things never change."

Kla gave me a hard squint. "Where you from, clodder?"

"So far out of the Empire's limits that you've never heard of it."

He nodded dubiously. "You got clodders in this feckin' mysterious land you hail from?"

"No." I shrugged. "Well, we used to, but it's been outlawed for centuries."

Kla leaned in close. "Let me explain something to you then, and I hope you listen real good because I hate, and I mean hate with Surt's own passion, repeating myself. Only non-citizens, criminals, and debtors become clodders. The great Surt, in all his bountiful wisdom, has decided that you scum are deserving of rights and that being a clodder is not a lifetime sentence, so all owners are responsible for proper maintenance of their property. Your freedom comes at a monetary cost, which is earned every day while owned, so after a certain amount of time, you can earn freedom and renewal of your citizenship tattoo. For non-citizens, it allows them to become citizens of the greatest empire this tired old world has ever been blessed with. Any questions?"

"How long will it take to earn fifteen scorch?" That was my asking price which Kla paid Giliselle.

Another squint. Did he need glasses? "Good question, clodder. Considering food, lodging, medical attention, which I am by law obligated to provide, whores and libation, a good twenty-five years for the average clodder. Pit fighters can do it in ten if they cut a few corners. Sooner if they take the death matches."

"Death matches?" My stomach felt queasy.

"All pit fighting is voluntary, clodder, and it's the quickest route to freedom. Death matches pay far more. Six death matches earns a clodder freedom, but only a few have survived to do so. Less survive whole."

The world didn't have the time for me to fight death matches and I sure doubted if I had it in me to try for six in one of these ridiculously long days.

My new owner prodded me through the bars. "Dress up. In a few spans it's going to be colder than ogre's pecker.

"I am a rich man, a well-educated man whose family has been in the clodder trade for more generations than you have teeth. It has treated me well and as a result I treat my clodders well. Now, fighting is voluntary, so if you don't want to fight, tell me now and I will sell you to a harbeest ranch or a big farm and make my money back and maybe I'll see you in a generation or so." He stopped and waited, folding his arms. His biceps bunched impressively.

For a moment I felt the urge to reach through the bars and put my hand around Kla's thick neck, but I had the sneaking suspicion he hadn't lived this long without being prepared. That realization didn't reduce the urge, though. "I'll fight." I kept my tone level.

He wasn't fooled any, his smile told me that. "Good man, clodder. Any more questions?"

I had a few.

FIVE

Desperate alliances

FIVE DAYS. THAT'S HOW LONG THE DAYLIGHT hours were in Muspelheim. Five. Fucking. Days. The nights, too. Alternating hours of brutal heat and bitter cold. It took long conversations with Kla and a few of the other slaves, but I finally nailed down a sense of time. Not that it helped much, but one of the best things a person in a stressful situation can do to handle said stressful situation is to find a sense of continuity, something on which to hang a frame of reference, and for me it was time.

Time had always been my constant, my comfort. Time and history, which are intertwined like Hermes' caduceus. I don't know where I found my love of history and the mechanisms of time, but in the chaos of life and death, they were the north star guiding me through the shallows and shoals of pain and loss.

Five days of light, five of dark. Thirty-six days in a year if the planet had similar rotation around its sun to earth's. Not really important to my mission, my quest, but it provided a stable platform for my already fractured sanity.

I'd heard that Muspelheim was a world of fire, not fire *and* ice, and ruled by the Fire Giant Surtur, although the name Surt came close enough that I figured they were the same person. If all things were equal, then the worlds of myth probably had very little in common with the reality of the nine worlds. Made me wonder what the other seven were going to be like.

Assuming I survived this one, that is.

My fellow clodders warmed up to me once they realized I wasn't going to open a can of Finnish whoop-ass to enforce my elevated status. It was from them that I discovered that Kla wasn't our ultimate owner, but a trainer who would sell us at auction. His job was to whip us into shape and teach us how to survive in the pits. The fact that he bought me for fifteen scorch seemed unbelievable to the others as fifteen scorch seems to equate to roughly, oh, an assload of money.

"You're gonna fetch a high price, a warrior like you," said a big man named Tivva, all muscle but no grace. He spooned up his stew into a mouth that should've been continued on the next clodder. His lips near touched his ears. He volunteered for slavery to settle large debts "Never seen a man or woman move like you."

A petite woman with hair shorn short to a stubble, ripped from days of fight training held my bowl as I ate. Her hazel eyes contained a puppy dog kind of devotion. I tried not to stare at her small, but near perfect, breasts. "Thanks," I replied, swallowing the stew. Best food I'd had in a goodly while, much better than I could effort. I'm a terrible cook, the only person I know who can burn water.

A gathering of clodders (murder, clowder, herd, rookery, troop or cauldron . . . take your pick) sat around me, all waiting for some gem to drop from my mouth, some valuable piece of wisdom that could aid them at becoming more efficient fighters. I found out that those clodders who fought in the pits did earn freedom earlier, but by the time they saw the end of the tunnel, so to speak, they were too beat to hell to really give much of a rusty fuck. All tried to resume what passes for a normal life, but many resorted to drink, gambling, crime, or found themselves returning to slavery, not because they wanted to, but because deep down they were like ex-convicts who needed to return to the prisons from which they so eagerly exited. Institutionalized, mentally unable to rejoin civilized society, or call it whatever the fuck you will, these people were so scarred the only place they fit in was the one place that brutalized them in the first place.

No great gifts of wisdom were given to the group because I didn't feel much like talking and, frankly, didn't have any to give. I was too busy trying to figure out my next steps, although my options were limited considering I was feeling every one of my fifty-five years heavy on my skin, deep in my muscle and bone. My emotional fatigue weighed and there was nothing I wanted more than to lie down and forget all this shit, forget that in a few of these fucking long ass days this world would disappear like smoke in a hurricane as this plane of existence, this reality, disappeared as well, dragging all the rest into oblivion. Everything will never have existed and while that didn't sound too fucking bad, what gave me the drive to go on, the momentum if you will, was the thought of my late wife and my son. The thought of them never existing in the first place was intolerable because they had made everything better. Reality was a better place because of them, I felt that down deep, and no way was I going to let some punk-ass primordial force of uncreation win. No fucking way, not on my watch, soldier, so it was time to buck up and do the job. My job.

"What's your name?" I asked the woman holding my bowl.

Her eyes lit up. "Dessa, great Kal."

"Not great," I countered after spooning a large morsel of some slightly gamey meat into my mouth. Tasted like a combination of venison and beef. "Just a clodder like everyone else."

Tivva snorted. "Not the way you move, Kal. No one moves like that, 'specially one handed."

I shrugged. "I used to be faster." And stronger. And taller. I finished the stew, not acknowledging Dessa's worshipful gaze. Not that she wasn't a fine specimen of womanhood, but it'd been a long time and there hadn't been a woman since Jeanie died who could do it for me. It meant a lot of lonely nights with me and my right hand. Now that option wasn't available. I could use the left, but it wouldn't be the same. Felt a little like cheating.

After lunch, shit got real.

CRACK.

The wooden sword swung past my right shoulder, the tip impacting the black stone floor. I pivoted and unleashed a kick to my opponent's hip which sent her flying. She landed with a hard thump and a gush of air from her lungs. I rushed after and landed on top, pinning her shoulders with my knees as she lay gasping.

"Yield?" I asked, raising a leather wrapped fist.

She nodded, unable to speak.

Years of training had honed my senses, so I when I heard the faint scuff of leather on stone, I leapt away, bounding to my feet as the padded club whooshed through the space my head occupied a second before. The lean man, all hard angles and rope-like muscles, spun my way, expertly readjusting his balance. In the instant before he attacked, I judged him to be more than the normal clodder pit-fighter.

The club came down and my leather-sheathed stump batted it aside. I went for a left hook, but his jaw refused to meet my fist. Instead, my opponent ducked and kicked out toward my balls aiming for the cheap seats. I shifted and took the blow on my hip instead, grabbing his calf and lifting with all my might while punching upward with my stump, which connected hard with his calf as it shot upward. The man howled as he flew ass over teakettle and landed on his back and I placed a bare foot on his throat, pressing gently. "Yield?"

He nodded.

"Hold!" Kla's voice rang out like bell, bringing the training session to an abrupt end.

The short clodder trainer ambled up to me and I noticed for the first time that he was bowlegged, which gave him the kind of gait you'd see on a sailor who spent a lifetime at sea. Kla grabbed my stump and checked the bindings I'd covered it with. After a moment he began to unwrap the leather strips and I cursed inwardly as the small, flat iron plates I'd placed on my stump clattered to the stone. "Cheating!" hollered the man I'd just downed.

For what felt like hours we clodders had been sparring in a great hall lit bright by lightgems, sweating and grunting as we practiced with all manner of weapons from clubs to axes, all made from wood and padded with leather. There had been a few accidents and several people sat against the wall nursing bruises, one man wincing and moaning as what passed for a medic in this world bandaged a broken finger. All in all, there were about eighteen clodders in the big room.

"What are these?" asked Kla as he picked up the small iron plates. I shrugged. "From your weapons locker. Iron plates from a cestus." I held up my stump. "Seems I'm one hand short, so I figured that a little extra weight wouldn't hurt."

"Cheating!" screamed my opponent again as he stood, rubbing his throat. "He deserves punishment, Kla!"

The clodder trainer shrugged. "Smart is what I say, Sivven, although he owes me some repairs on a cestus, that's for feckin' sure."

Sivven grew red, veins standing out stark on his dark skin. "Kla—"

"Shut your feckin' mouth," Kla snapped. "It's only good for shoveling food in." To me, "You're going to fetch a good price, clodder. All I need is for you to provide a little demonstration of your skills at auction and you'll make me some good scorch."

Demonstration. Like a trained monkey. My stomach suddenly felt heavy and sour. "No."

The smile that hit Kla's face didn't reassure. "Wrong feckin' answer, clodder. Don't be stupider than you already are."

I shrugged, feeling sweat trickle down my back. Even though night gripped the world outside, the lightgems and the several hearths kept the large training area almost too warm for the breechclout around my waist.

"Do you know why I can walk into a large room filled with feckin' aggressive and mean clodders?" he asked, leaning in close enough that I could tell he had eggs for breakfast. "And not worry about being feckin' killed?"

"Because you have twelve guards with crossbows strategically placed around the hall," I replied, nodding toward said guards. I knew those heavy crossbows could shoot a bolt through heavy armor from a hundred feet away, so the body of one clodder would mean dick should they decided to perforate my pale, scarred hide.

"That's the main reason," he agreed. "But I'm also a warrior, clodder. I can break bones with the best of them." His impressive muscles bunched on his short frame. "So clodders know not to feck with me. Don't. Feck. With. Me." All the good humor had evaporated from his face like water droplets on a hotplate.

He spun and made the long walk to the end of the hall where a short bench waited with a comfy cushion for his butt. Once the back of his front was deposited on that comfy looking cushion, he raised his voice to an impressive roar. "The first one to knock Kal out will have one scorch removed from their debt."

Fuck!

I spun in time to take a wooden sword to the chest, the dull tip smashing into my pec with almost numbing force, knocking me back in time to avoid a foot to the balls. Said foot belonged to the once adoring Dessa, whose face was a rictus of anger and determination. Fan girl no more. A spinning back kick sent her flying to crash hard on to the flagstones.

Another clodder came at me with a padded club and I dodged, replying with an elbow that shattered teeth, but a fist hit my ribs and the air left my lungs in a rush. I responded with a knife strike to the throat and the man gagged, dropping while I spun with a backfist that took a pair behind me, forcing them back, giving me room to lash out with feet, fist and elbows, my mind retreating to old habits, muscle memory. I became a meat machine, striking and stomping, sending bodies flying, ignoring pain, ignoring the thud of wooden weapons, the adrenaline in my system working better than any anesthetic. A woman fell, her mouth a red ruin and a big, slow clodder with a prodigious gut fell after I swiped his feet out from under him, using the momentum to jump high and kick another in the chest hard enough to send him flying back fifteen feet. I landed, panting, covered in a greasy slick of sweat. Eight clodders lay on the ground at my feet, moaning and retching while the rest stared at me with eyes filled with wonder and fear.

"Feck me!" thundered Kla, striding toward me. "You want something done, you feckin' do it yourself." The short man, brow filled with thunder, attacked.

For such a muscular man, he was fast as blazes, ham fists flying, seemingly everywhere at once. It took a few moments for me to adjust to fighting style, to analyze his patterns, but once I did, I found the holes in his attacks and, dodging a blow that would have demolished my nose, and began to block and strike back.

My left hand struck his gut, which felt like hitting a fire hydrant, but I knew I had him, so I kept up the pressure, staring to unload with forearm and open palm strikes designed to incapacitate, not cause lasting harm, because I was very well aware of the guards with their crossbows and what they could do to me if I broke their boss.

I took a fist to the chest and nearly stumbled back, but I recovered enough to hammer my foot down on his instep. He retreated, snarling, "What are you waiting for?"

It was the eyes, you see, that alerted me. They flicked over my shoulder for just a fraction of a second and that was almost enough time.

I stepped back as a leather kosh slammed down on the crown of my head rather than the back, bringing a universe of stars into my field of vision. Reacting instinctively through the dizzying pain, I grabbed the arm and put my hips into a throw that launched my ambusher over my head, onto to the floor where he landed with a clatter muffled by his leather armor. That was no clodder, but one of the guards!

"Feckin' Hel," growled Kla, moving in.

The world tilted around me and gray started to leech color from my sight, adding about fifty pounds to my skull which felt like it wanted to topple off my neck. An iron fist took me in the gut and I felt my feet lift off the ground. I lashed out instinctively with my right and felt my stump connect with Kla's jaw, which didn't seem to bother him any, although the skin of my wrist tore, smearing blood across his cheek.

My left hook missed, but his straight jab didn't. It felt like someone hit me in the face with a rock. More world spinning and a wrecking ball folded me in half, the pain a bolt of fire from gut to the tippy top of my skull.

"Finish him," I heard Kla say from far away.

Fists and feet became my world. Then pain. Then nothing.

BUSINESS AT NIGHT WAS CONDUCTED INDOORS despite the light-gems that illuminated every corner of the city because the temperature continued to plummet, so when I stumbled naked up to the auction block, I didn't have to worry about freezing my balls off. There were plenty of braziers lit to keep the attendees' toasty.

Clodders for sale milled inside an enclosure against the long wall opposite the milling throng of buyers. Representatives of those buyers inspected the merchandise under the gaze of crossbow wielding guards and a lone ogre who carried with her a sword big enough that I knew I'd barely be able to swing it, much less lift it over my head, but which looked like a child's toy in her hands. For an hour various agents poked and prodded me with clinical detachment, very politely mind you, but coldly. Fortunately, not one of them asked to inspect my twig and berries, which saved me some indignation, I guess. From the way Kla talked me up while I obediently turned around, you would have thought the sun was about to arise from my clenched butt cheeks. Oddly enough, my teeth seemed to impress a lot of the reps, which goes to show that good dental hygiene is always a plus. Soon it was my turn on the block, and I reluctantly followed Kla's lead toward my doom.

Bruises on my bruises, my left eye was swollen shut and my lips felt as if someone had inflated them like balloons. My torso was riddled with black and blue and my ribs protested with every step as, once again, I wore a thick leather belt and short chain that held my left hand to my side. As for my right arm, long bandages held it to my side, a testament to Kla's estimation of my martial skills.

The slave trainer put one hand on my shoulder while speaking from the corner of his mouth. "Feckin' with me is never a good idea, you idiot." We slowly traversed the four steps leading up to the large wooden platform that stood above the crowd of prospective purchasers. "When I take your restraints off, you will demonstrate your hand fighting skills for this lovely crowd, won't you?"

The warehouse reeked of the stale fried chicken odor of old sweat . . . that and the resignation of hundreds of clodders. Built of the same gray stone as the city walls, it fended off the night chill and kept the heat of the braziers in so I didn't freeze my ya-yas off while I walked to the auction block At least a hundred people had attended the auction and already Kla had sold off six of his best clodders for what I assumed was a good price. But I was the one who was expected to fetch the highest price.

Whoop-de-fucking-do.

I declined to answer. It hurt to move, hurt to talk because of my swollen lips, and my pride was stinging like a bitch. A hard elbow nudged my bruised ribs and I grunted, which Kla seemed to take as assent, so I didn't bother to disabuse him of the notion.

"And here is the purchase of the night!" shouted the auctioneer in a voice that could pierce stone. "You all have seen fine pit fighters trained by the Vol Traver house, but I have the assurance of Kla Vol Traver himself that this next specimen, battered and bruised he may be, is the finest pit fighter he has ever had the pleasure of owning. A stranger from the Outs, a warrior without peer, who came to us fully trained and ready to fight. Don't let the apparent advanced age or the lack of a right hand fool you, good citizens of Surete, this clodder is the best of the best, who defeated the entire cream of the Vol Traver crop at once *by himself.*"

The auctioneer, a trim woman in a heavily brocaded burgundy robe, let that sink in for a moment and the audience made all the appropriate appreciative noises. I looked out over the crowd with my good eye and saw men and women in every shape, size, and color staring at me, some in appreciation, some in derision . . . I did look a mess, after all.

Down below, off to one side, an effete young man dressed in a sleeveless tunic worked with a cup of green ink and a needle placing clodder marks on the chins of those recently purchased. He looked up at me, tossing a smile and a wink.

A woman with skin the color of well-aged parchment slithered through the crowd to get a closer look. Pretty in a severe sort of way, her dark eyes burned with an intense light that made me want to squirm. She nodded once, giving a small smile that had nothing to do with humor and something about her caused my stomach to cramp. Dangerous . . . I could feel it. This woman carried no goodwill towards me in her heart. Don't ask me how I knew, it's something instinctual, part of my lizard brain that screams: "Danger, Will Robinson, danger!"

"I'm going to remove your restraints now, idiot." Kla's hands began to unwind the bandage that held my arm to my side.

"Twenty scorch!" a feminine voice carried above the milling crowd. It was the intense lady. She had a familiar accent that rounded the vowels nicely.

"Well now," Kla shouted over the auctioneer and the outburst from the crowd. "We haven't started yet, my good lady." All charm and smiles was Kla, very different than the hard taskmaster I knew. "This clodder needs to demonstrate his skill. Oh, yes he does!"

Intense lady frowned, but the excited chatter from the crowd held her tongue.

"No demonstration," I whispered for Kla's ears, suddenly filled with a terrible calm.

A dark face came close to mine and he snarled low and hard, "Listen to me, clodder, you do this or I'll sell you to the guild that gathers all the night soil in Merchant's row. How do you want to spend the next twenty years gathering shit and piss?" A grim smile crawled onto his face. "You'll be feckin' vomiting every day, sleeping the sleep of the utterly exhausted and never being able to smell anything but what your dick and ass lets go of in the morning. How does that sound?"

I gave with a jack-o-lantern grin made more horrible by the swelling. "Go fuck yourself, shorty." Sometimes my pride gets in the way of my good sense, but not this time. Kla's face paled and his hands balled into fists, but before he could say or do anything, I shouted, "I accept!" My voice rang out hard against the stone walls.

The Twilighter, whom I'd spotted a moment ago, stepped toward the platform removing her dun scarf. When her face was revealed, the crowed backed away as if she was radioactive. The word 'Rhone' dropped from peoples' mouths with a mixture of reverence and fear and Kla paled to gray, mouth becoming a tunnel of surprise.

"In Surt's name I hereby purchase this man for twenty scorch," she said calmly.

SIX

The Great and Powerful Surt

MADRIGAL RHONE. THAT WAS HER NAME. The Twilighter, that is. Apparently, she worked directly for Emperor Surt as his 'eyes and ears,' and more frequently his hands. She'd built up quite a reputation as the baddest of bad asses, a woman you'd better cross the street to avoid and do it sharpish. An agent of the Empire, one of several who had the big guy's own authority to do what it took to get the job done with only the boss to reign them in.

Sounded awfully familiar.

All this I learned while I was receiving my genuine, perfectly lawful governmental citizenship tattoo on the back of my left hand. No tattoos on the nape of the neck, if you please. Not that I wanted one, but Madrigal said that without one snatchers would grab me up in a wink to sell me to the nearest purveyor of clodders, and with my luck, it would be Kla. Time to toss away the pride and lose my skin virginity to a grimy old man on Government Row who occupied a small, but neat, little establishment. Government Row was the large street in the center of the city where the business of empire was conducted with remarkable efficiency and as little bureaucracy as possible. This I heartily approved of and I wondered how such a marvel could have been maintained for thousands of years. Maybe I could find out and bring it back to Midgard where it could be patented. Nah, soon as I tried some sleazy little official would mark me for death and disappear the idea down the dark hole of governmental history along with cold fusion and term limits for politicians.

As for the little old man, all he did was citizenship tattoos and he handled the task with the minimalistic efficiency of someone who's done it every day for decades, using government approved dyes in brilliant blues and yellows that, the little old dude informed me piously, were impossible to counterfeit.

Madrigal had provided a set of large, yet comfortable clothes just my size, claiming that she'd known that I'd agree to her proposition. While the heavy boots were slightly too large, I was grateful for the warmth against the chill in the air, but at the same time, a little miffed that she could anticipate my failure to successfully escape. Pride's a bitch, you know.

"Most people don't do the back of the hand," the wizened old tattoo artist said. "Hurts too much, it does. Most would flinch. Yer not a flincher, pain is no stranger, is it?"

"There are very few of us who don't know pain," I replied. "For me, it's an old friend." The old man jabbed the finishing touches into my skin, the tattoo's electric colors sizzling against my retinas.

Now that Madrigal had taken off her dun scarf, her hard beauty near stunned me. Lean, angular features, a sharpish nose and piercing green eyes set in skin white as cream, the kind of skin you'd expect to see wrapping an albino. Her hair, cut short to her skull, was white as well, but the fire in her emerald eyes belied her icy exterior. I'd seen that look before countless times in my life, the look of a government agent with the crushing weight of responsibilities on their shoulders and the iron will to get the job done. The same look I'd seen in the mirror.

"When we're done here the Emperor wishes to speak with you."

The little old man paused for the smallest moment.

"Don't suppose we can grab a bite before? I'm famished and I look like I've been stuffed up the wrong end of an elephant."

"What's an elephant?"

"Nevermind. I need food and rest."

"You'll have both aplenty," replied Madrigal. "But we don't keep the Emperor waiting. Don't they have emperors where you come from?"

"Not many, if any." I thought about it for a moment. "Our system of government is aided by a top-heavy bureaucracy whose main purpose is to keep itself alive."

"Hmmm. We have our own bureaucracy, but like I said before, the Emperor keeps it starved to the brink of death."

"Then he's wise indeed. But what if I say please to the food and rest?"

Madrigal gave my battered mug a good look and said, "You'll get both. *After* we meet with the Emperor."

"Pretty please?"

"Tough it out."

Sometimes it doesn't pay to get out of bed in the morning.

Outside in a cold that was a few degrees above freezing sat the carriage that had brought us to Government Row, looking for all the world as if a stagecoach fucked an Edsel, low and sleek with fat wheels rimmed by some thick, grayish rubber that Madrigal informed me was derived from the sap of the twilight trees.

A team of six large lizard horses pulled the low-slung carriage and I had to marvel that the rubber rimmed wheels managed to keep the ride smooth, although the contraption made godawful squeaking noises like a hundred rats being tortured by a hundred constipated cats.

Within minutes we came to the palace, which hardly seemed to deserve the moniker. Dark and squat, it seemed more like an oversized Viking longhouse made of that same dark stone as the city walls studded all over with lightgems so bright I had to squint. The driver, a cadaverous looking clodder in a black tunic and trousers, drove the carriage to one end of the palace and stopped in front of a pair of double doors made of some dark wood banded in iron. The place reeked of minimalist efficiency mixed with a pseudo-gothic sensibility. The tall towers I'd seen from the walls (which Madrigal informed me belonged to a variety of merchant, educational, and noble houses that graced the city) looked over the palace like disapproving aunts. Some the rectangular buildings seemed more solid, more real than the towers that surrounded it.

"No, this isn't creepy at all," I muttered.

Madrigal heard. "Surt doesn't care for opulence or flash. What concerns him is keeping Surete safe from the shadows."

"Mind filling me in. It sounds all mystifying and shit."

Cool green eyes washed over me. "Introductions first, history later."

The double doors opened and we entered a long hallway floored in white, red-veined marble that gleamed magnificently in the illuminations provided by the lightgems that shone from walls and ceiling. No lanterns, no torches, and only a few guards in steel studded leather armor carrying short swords and those lethal looking leaf bladed spears. Their leather helms fully concealed their features, giving them an almost insectile appearance.

"I thought there would be more guards," I remarked, the echoes of our footsteps following behind.

"The Great Surt needs few bodyguards," Madrigal said as we traversed the long hall. "Consider these men and women an early warning system."

I muddled that over as we made our way down the hall toward a brass covered door at least twenty feet high and braced by a pair of stern looking guards who, in addition to short swords and spears, carried wicked arbalests that looked like they could put a bolt clean through ten Kals with no bother at all. As we approached, one of the pair opened the large door easily, swinging it inward with one hand and tipping a nod to Madrigal who, for the first time since I met her, cracked a small smile. I shtumped along after, face throbbing and head aching, fatigue nipping at my heels. After I married Jeanie I gave up drinking (to excess) and kept my feet on the straight and narrow, but now I could've murdered a bottle of vodka.

Beyond the door lay a large, plain room adorned with a single desk the size of a luxury car and a chair of dark wood taller than my six-three, and sitting within it, feet planted firmly on the floor, was a giant.

No, not a big man. A *giant*. Close to twenty feet tall, his curly gray hair tumbled down past his shoulders to the middle of his back, mingling with the thick silver beard that fell from his face to his lap. Thunderous brows shaded eyes the color of rotten ice over a long blade of a nose, on which a pair of silver wire rims rested, making those ice rotten eyes as large as manhole covers.

"Madrigal," he boomed in a voice like the wind through a mountain pass. Those strange eyes looked me up and down. "Is this himself?"

"This is the man," she replied with a half bow.

The giant stood, head nearly brushing the roof. A vapor gray robe covered his body and snowy white sizes fifties adorned his feet. "Hellooo, young human." He bowed down to fetch a closer look. "I am Vestaverous, First Minister of the Empire." Humor danced in his eyes. "And what do they call you?"

Young. He called me young. I almost fell in love with him for that, although I wasn't sure whether to bow or grovel. I tipped a deep nod instead and said, "Kal."

"Yes, what do they call you."

"Kal."

"That's what I asked."

"And I answered." *Who's on first?* I tried not to giggle.

Bushy eyebrows that deserved their own ecosystems lowered and Madrigal chimed in, "That's his name, Minister . . . Kal."

"Call?"

"Close enough," I chuckled.

"You humans never cease to bewilder."

I shrugged. "One of our strengths."

"As well as sarcasm."

"Our greatest strength."

A storm front sigh blew my hair back. "It's a wonder you as a species haven't become extinct, a great wonder indeed."

Madrigal hid a smile. "Is the Emperor available?"

"Himself is tired, oh yes indeed. Tired from creating light-gems and tending to dire needs as always, but himself said to send beloved eyes and ears in if yourself were to appear, and so it has come to pass." With that he gestured toward another, more human-sized door on the opposite wall.

"Thank you, First Minister." Madrigal proffered another shallow bow and I followed suit.

The giant sat at his enormous desk and picked up a pen the size of a horse's leg. "Good luck with himself."

"Luck doesn't enter into it, First Minister." Madrigal took my hand, her skin cool and dry.

Thunderous chuckling followed us into the next room.

"Okay, I've met an ogre, now a giant," I said quietly. "Any more, ah, giantkin I should know about?"

"There are several: mountain, deep, crag, hill, fathom and forest. First Minister Vestaverous is the rarest giant of all, a Sky Giant. His people live among the lightning and storms and possess magic that is second only to the Fire Giants of olden times. You have beheld one of the great wonders of Surete, Kal. Savor this moment."

It took a second, but I noticed she didn't mention anything more about Fire Giants, but right then what I wanted to savor was some deep sleep, so I didn't mention the fact.

Heat washed over me as I entered the next room as if the threshold held some invisible membrane that held the extraordinary temperature inside, leaving the First Minister cool and comfy. My eyes immediately watered, then dried up so quick that I could hardly blink and my skin felt stretched tight over my bones, the sweat popping up and drying instantly.

"Holy fuck," I breathed, tongue feeling like old leather. Blinking rapidly, I looked around, or tried to through eyes dry and scratchy to see a column of yellow and orange fire in the immense circular room, a wide pillar that stretched from floor to ceiling. At least fifteen feet in diameter, the column burned with a quiet intensity, the flames virtually silent as they licked the marble.

"Your Majesty!" Madrigal's clarion voice bounced off the walls. "I think this is the man we've been waiting for."

What stepped out of the flames about bowled me over in shock. Looming over us was a giant with dark skin like the carapace of a black widow spider, shiny and hard with small, glowing red cracks running crazy all over as if a furnace burned beneath. Perfectly proportioned, muscled like a weightlifter, the giant stared at us with flaming fumaroles for eyes and a caldera for a mouth. He had to be at least fifteen feet tall.

The voice that emerged from the giant was surprisingly mellifluous, musical tones that resolved into words, "I see that it is indeed the one. Welcome," fiery eyes bored into mine, "Kalevi Hakala."

"How—"

"Did I know? You stand before Surt, lord of Muspelheim. Now, I know you have questions, but I must rest, so take a seat while I continue to bathe in the holy flame." He began to back slowly into the pillar of fire and I couldn't help noticing he was as sexless as a Ken doll. No giant dongle on the master of Muspelheim, which made me wonder how this kind of giant reproduced.

Holy flame? With dry eyes I stared at the column of near silent fire and knew, with a certainty provided by Mimisbrunnr, that this was the extension of the Tree I had felt after I healed Midgard, the hot, focused point that interfaced with Muspelheim. Saving this world was a few footsteps away, and although I knew all I had to do was leap into the fire, that put me back on my mental heels right quick. I wanted to say something, but my throat felt like heavy grit sandpaper, causing me to dry cough.

"Ah, how clumsy of me." Surt's musical voice sounded almost

contrite. Immediately cool air surrounded me and my skin goose pimpled. I dropped to one knee as every vein in my body contracted and a wave of dizziness flushed through my flesh.

A strong hand grabbed my arm and helped me to my feet. Madrigal flashed white, even teeth. "Takes some getting used to." She led me to a cushioned bench and I gratefully sat, sighing in relief. Madrigal handed me a silver flask and I took a deep drink, sputtering as the fiery liquid within seared my throat. It tasted like really shitty gin mixed with cloves and jalapeno peppers.

Patting my back as I gagged and choked, Madrigal said, "Takes some getting used to."

I gagged. I spat. "This is what evil tastes like."

"Right now you are trying to cope," said Surt, his voice more relaxed, yet doleful. "You wonder how I know what I know. The Heart Flame, the holy fire in which I bathe, is an extension of what you would call the Tree, as you surmised. It supplies me with the magic needed to carry on my work. You are within its heat, and therefore the radius of my magic. I have gleaned your surface thoughts, which allows me to see that you are the one I sent Madrigal, the wisest and most capable of my eyes and ears, to find."

I noted the capital letters. "What—"

"Please, Kalevi Hakala, allow me to inform you of the situation in which you find yourself and do not interrupt."

What could I do? I nodded and tried to relax as my skin cooled.

Surt continued, "The world you know as Muspelheim once belonged to the giantkin, and the greatest of all the giantkin were the Fire Giants, who ruled over the vast volcanic lands. Fire was like blood to us and our hearts beat with the heat of lava. All other giants bowed to us because of our wisdom and might, our ability to govern impartially, and for uncounted ages we ruled justly, kindly, with the other Great Giants: the Sky Giants (such as our First Minister) who enforced our will, and the placid Mountain Giants, whose deliberate and deep minds made them our arbiters of justice, and all the others. This entire world knew peace as no other, and from Hill Giant to deep, all giantkin lived in harmony until the coming of those beings you know as the Aesir and Vanir.

"Tearing through the barriers of the nine worlds, they introduced a new concept to the giantkin. War. With their war came death, which is the one thing all giantkin fear because there is no afterlife for us, Kalevi Hakala, no Heaven or Hell, merely oblivion. We giants are manifestations, personifications if you will, of this world. We are its thoughts and feelings and its voice and once a giant dies, they die forever. That is the horror the Aesir and Vanir brought, and with it they taught us a lesson, the most terrible lesson of them all.

"They taught us to hate."

With Surt's words came visions that swirled into my consciousness, scenes of giants fighting with fire and wind, holding rocks and clubs the size of telephone poles against grinning demons and cruel-faced humanoids bearing savage weapons that ripped and tore into flesh, severed limbs and pierced bowels. Nausea gripped me as I saw giants clothed in flame spurting fiery blood upon trampled earth. I saw humans, disoriented and bewildered at the land they now found themselves in, allying with the giants against the imperious Aesir who trampled them underfoot like insects, and the Vanir who ate the fallen with fangs the color of blood.

"Some of the humans were what you call Magicians," Surt said as I bent over my knees, room spinning around with images of the past while Madrigal continued to drink from the silver flask. How she didn't have an ulcer after a few swigs I'll never know. "They helped found Til Mathgen and gave their allegiance the greatest of all the Fire Giants, Surtur. The last Fire Giants gave their lives to construct a vessel to hold their power. They created me, a construct of their magic, a being that held the combined wisdom of their race and the puissance of their collective magic fused into a being of singular will. What you see as a golem is the essence of Surtur and the last Fire Giants. With magic focused into a single intelligence I drove the Aesir and Vanir from this world and healed the Breach. But not completely.

"The lands to the south and west, the Outs, are unsettled, wild because those giantkin and humans that inhabit this world think it to be haunted. Not so. The Outs are an area of this world where the Breach is not wholly sealed, where creatures can pass unwillingly from Muspelheim to Midgard, pulled in by the Breach. Those that do are never seen again."

In my mind a map of the planet unfolded, showing a world much like Earth, but where the three main continents were surrounded by oceans teeming with life, some great, some small and some grotesque. The largest continent spanned from the north pole to the south, the majority of its landmass given over to jagged mountain ranges, most of which housed dozens, hundreds of active volcanoes. There, Til Mathgen sat on in a valley the size of Alaska, in what was considered the breadbasket of Muspelheim.

Before I could open my trap and say something witty, Surt said, "We are now experiencing the beginning of unmaking of our universe. With my magic, I can stave off the impending doom of the unraveling for several months, although it would task me greatly. But I know what you are looking for, Kalevi Hakala, and I will help you with your quest to heal the nine worlds and stop the Tree from becoming unmade. However, before I can do this, you must agree to undertake a quest for me, one that threatens my existence." The almost musical voice trailed off and once again I was about to go for wit, but Madrigal's hand on my arm stopped me. Her eyes were sad and wet from drink. She shook her head slightly.

"If I die now, my people and this world will die. I cannot have this, so I need from you an oath that you will undertake this task. Do this, make this promise, and we can save this world together."

What could I say? It wasn't like my options were limitless. I looked to the woman sitting next to me, reeking of that foul brew she was swilling, and saw jade eyes staring into mine, her normally hard face ravaged by frightened hope. To her I had accepted the terms that bought my freedom, and I wasn't the kind of asshole that broke a promise without a damn good reason.

"I made a promise to Madrigal that I'd help her and I don't go back on my word." A massive yawn cracked my jaws. "So, sure. Why not?"

SEVEN

Muspelheim past and present

MY FACE THROBBED AND MUSCLES PROTESTED every little movement as I sat staring at a column of fire that contained a construct of giantkin magic, filling the room with a furnace heat. Madrigal sat beside me sipping a foul brew I wouldn't wish upon my enemies as my one unharmed eye watered as I stared at the inferno manyp feet away. According to the Well of Urd, Muspelheim was the next Prime world on the hit parade and there was nothing Surt, a creation of immense magic and intellect, could do to stop it. Something, however, itched at the back of my mind.

"I got a question."

Surt's enormous face emerged slightly from the flame. "Slavery."

"That's unsettling."

Was that a smile? I couldn't tell, it hurt to look at a light so bright. "You are within the seat of my power, your thoughts are obvious. Don't worry, the deepest parts of you, the secrets that you keep will remain so." The face retreated into the flame. "You want to know why, if I am so wise and powerful, this world has slavery, a practice Midgard has all but abolished."

"Got it in one."

"Your world keeps its criminals in tiny cages, subjecting them to brutality and indoctrinating them into a recidivist lifestyle that does your people no service. With my access to the Tree, I have peered into Midgard, seen its heart and divined its weaknesses, not for nefarious reasons, but to sate my curiosity. I have seen all manner of social injustices that rival that of slavery, so many so that I would grow weary listing them all."

As much as I hated to admit it, he wasn't wrong. "But slavery?"

"The Empire has created a small bureaucracy to ensure the proper treatment of clodders and the penalties for abuse are steep. Murderers and rapists are executed here, not set into prisons where they can kill and maim their fellow inmates. Your prisons are rife with corruption and the kind of brutality that would make an ogre vomit. Our system of justice is efficient and sometimes cruel, but it is fair and does not spare anyone: the wealthiest face the same laws as the weakest, most destitute members of our society."

"Except for you. That's why I don't like monarchs." Beside me, Madrigal hissed and grabbed my thigh, squeezing painfully with her long fingers. I gently, but firmly, extricated her hand and looked to the fire.

"I share your abhorrence of the rule of kings and believe that such power should not be in the hands of the corruptible." He chuckled, a sound like the peal of bells. "But as I have said, I am not a person, but a construct, created to protect and rule and to do so fairly. I cannot be corrupted; I cannot act counter to the strictures of my creation. In that I have no free will, and although I am sentient, I do not have the ability to do anything but what I was created for, which means I am a true servant of the Empire's citizens. There is freer will in a horse than what I possess. You may not approve of our ways, but I assure you, everything I do is for the good of the people, of the Empire. I have not the capability for capricious acts."

Somewhere along the middle of that soliloquy I began to drowse. The heat, the beating, too much had happened in too short a time, and it was all catching up to me as my bruised flesh began to rebel against my mind, eroding my will. Madrigal braced me as I began to list, eye closing and my mind wandering back to Des, how he might be doing with my folks, if he was having a good time with his cousins. Did he think of me? Did he miss me? The room blurred as tears began to form.

"Surt's talking to you." Madrigal's voice cut into me like a razor.

"Wha—?"

"Forgive him," Surt said. "He is not well. His injuries assail him."

"Yes, Your Majesty."

A few hearbeats passed before Surt said, "Do you know why the seat of the Empire is in Til Mathgen, Kalevi Hakala?"

"Sorry, your Surtliness," I slurred. "But I'm in no shape for riddles."

Another hiss from Madrigal, but it was drowned out by titanic laughter. "Fair play, fair play." There came a pause long enough that I began to slip once again into unconsciousness, then Surt's musical voice came again. "It is the holy flame you see here. It is the source of my rejuvenation and, as you well know, it is the conduit through which you can stop the unraveling that threatens this world."

Come again? For some reason he wasn't making sense. "Excuse me?"

"As the Well of Mimisbrunnr in Midgard sustains Mimir, so the holy fire of Surturvadunir sustains Surt. The transformative flames will aid you, all you need to do is enter."

Houston, we have a fucking problem. Suddenly fatigue was in the rear view. "You want me to walk into *that*?" I pointed to the flame. I knew I had to, but walking into a furnace was last on my list of creative ways to die, right behind eaten by rats while being hosed down with lemon juice and vinegar.

Flying, leaving the protection of the cool zone, my skin instantly crisped as I stumbled toward the roaring flame. A black and red hand so hot it burned my skin before it even touched me. The searing pain as it clamped on and pulled me in.

What the fuck!?

FOR THE SECOND TIME A WORLD SPOOLED OUT in front of me, Muspelheim . . . a glory of blue and green spinning in the darkness around a sun that was blue rather than yellow, the fourth satellite in the system, right smack dab in the middle of the Goldilocks zone.

This is Muspelheim. The words flowed through me on musical thought.

I couldn't concentrate, my flesh was crisping, nerve endings frying, sending their last signals to my tortured brain right before they died, signals that overloaded rational thought. Blood boiled in my veins and the fat in my body ignited, charring down deep until the marrow in my bones exploded and my organs blackened and shriveled. Still the visions spooled into my mind, bypassing eyes that had burst from the fluid within turning to steam. Screaming didn't work, my vocal chords had become ash.

I saw Muspelheim turn into a war zone as the Aesir and Vanir, reduced from beings of sentient energy to creatures of flesh, lay waste to each other and the land, with the giantkin caught in the middle. Sky Giants, Hill Giants, and the giants of the deep places of the world were slaughtered in the millions, but no giantkin suffered more than the Fire Giants. They stood on the front lines and led the resistance against the alien beings. Against the forces of order and chaos who were indifferent to the damage they created as long as they could kill each other.

My people, my creators. They organized the giantkin after the first wave of warring beings swept the land, devastating everything in their path. The Fire Giants were the most respected, most powerful of all giantkin, and their magic was the blood of the earth. United in defense of Muspelheim, in great desperation they performed their penultimate feat of magic, creating the race of ogres, the smallest of the giantkin, but also the most warlike. The ogres became the shock troops of the giantkin army, wreaking havoc among the Aesir and the Vanir. It was not enough.

The pain receded as my body began to reknit itself, the fire reduced to a healing warmth that brought tears to eyes while the visions continued. A thousand Fire Giants, all that were left, swam in the heart of an active volcano, singing their magic to the magma, shaping it with rough, red hands, their flaming hair long and trailing down below their shoulders. The magma sculpture began to take shape, a nearly perfect humanoid one. The giants brought the sculpture to the surface where it began to darken and cool, singing their magic while all the while, infusing it with thousands of generations of power, even as the sculpture remained still and unmoving.

For a year those thousand giants forged the land's protector while their brethren died during the war. Millions of giankin, their bones littering the land and sea, snuffed out, their like never to be seen again. Remember, giants have no spirits, no soul, because they are part of the world they live in and are immortal because of that. Or nearly so. The grief felt with every giant death can crack the world.

Suddenly, without warning, the pain started again, the burning, the nerve frying agony of fire that boiled the flesh off my bones and I screamed, inhaling fire that seared my lungs to char. Fire clawed its way past my eyes, along my optic nerves and into my skull. While my mind froze in shock, I saw a thousand Fire Giants lining the lip of a caldera raise daggers of obsidian in their right hands and plunge them into their hearts. Fiery blood gushed from a thousand wounds, washing over the prone sculpture that lay below, and flowed *into* it, absorbed by the construct they had labored over for a year to form. A thousand bodies fell, rolling down the slope of the caldera to lie at the bottom. Fumarole eyes opened.

I was born fully formed and cognizant of the situation. A golem imbued with intelligence, magic and purpose. The might of a thousand giantkin and the magic of countless centuries of giantkin lore focused into a combined intellect, able use magic that they lacked the cohesion to perform themselves in unison. I strode out into the world knowing what had to be done. I am as they made me, a creature of unyielding purpose.

Sweet relief began anew as my flesh started to become whole, the damning fire once again becoming a pleasant warmth. I saw the newly created Surt, blackened skin blazing with the heat contained within, stride into battle against the Aesir and Vanir, wielding the combined might of the last and most powerful Fire Giants. In Surt they discovered a foe they weren't able stop, as he came to battle aided by human Magicians and warriors pulled into this world from Midgard through the Breach, striving to save a world not their own. The alien creatures of light and dark, of chaos and order, died by the thousands as they killed each other and were killed by humans and giantkin. Surt himself took a mighty toll on the would-be gods as his magic burned newly acquired flesh from bones. After several years, the aliens managed to flee beyond the Breach, forced through the vortices in the Outs to Midgard, leaving behind devastation, death, and hundreds of thousands of humans who had nowhere to go. Surt declared the Outs a no-man's land.

This world was wounded, scarred, and damaged almost beyond repair, but thanks to the alliance of our people, we began to rebuild. From humans we learned the concepts of cities and kingdoms, of class systems and industry. Beneath the ground, in a cave of violet crystal, burned the holy flame, an extension of the Tree, less powerful than Mimisbrunnr, but still powerful beyond description. From my creators I learned of the flame and dug down until it was exposed, utilizing this portion of the Tree to heal the land, to heal myself. It was the source of my rejuvenation, and I bent my will to create an empire for giantkin and humans with the flame as its heart. We created a cooperative that would elevate both races placing Til Mathgen (which means 'Shared Home' in the tongue of the Sky Giants) as the seat of government. Although humans bred faster than giantkin and grew in ever greater numbers, the alliance between our people held strong. We were at peace. For a while.

Back to the pain, to flesh eating flame that tore me down to the last atom before recreating me, an endless cycle of destruction and resurrection. I was the phoenix, immolating only to live again, to spring from the ashes. Pain and relief, destruction and creation. Like watching a movie, I saw the growth of Til Mathgen around the holy flame in the palace's heart. Sky, Mountain, Deep and Hill Giants porting great gray slabs of stone quarried from the mountains to the north while ogres and humans strived to design a city where both races could join together and thrive. No walls, though, only a grand metropolis with wide thoroughfares and a cycle of light and dark that lasted days. As the pain began recede, I felt a darkness begin, a pervasive evil that lurked just over the horizon.

What I did not know, what I failed to realize, was that the Breach not only drew in humans, but something else, a malignant force as well. Something from the world you would call Hel, the tattered and ruined homeworld of the Aesir and Vanir. Of Hel, yet not part of it, perhaps drawn from some distant void from beyond the Tree when the Aesir/Vanir war destroyed their home. A vast and hungry species that, like locusts, consumes everything in its path to leave nothing but devastation, all led by their ruler, the Queen of Shadows. Whether these creatures, the shadows, were created by Aesir, Vanir, or were born from the dark magics of their war, I don't know. All I do know is that their hunger is limitless.

I could feel the skin growing on my skull, an itchy feeling like insects skittering on my nerve endings. I saw the far continent, shaped like a three-fingered hand and covered with jagged mountains that reached so high that no human could reach the summit. It was there that the evil nested in the deep reaches beneath those

harsh ranges, hard-edged creatures both solid and shadow, unde-
fined in shape but of a singular purpose . . . to consume. Able to
create portals in darkness, they could travel large distances quickly,
spreading like lice. Once their numbers grew great enough, they
sought other prey outside their continent and found the giantkin.
They descended upon Til Mathgen.

*We suffered terrible losses in the first year of this new and terrible
war, a dozen centuries after the founding of Til Mathgen. Humans and
giantkin who weren't killed outright soon fell into madness, then became
blind. It only takes a small bite from a shadow to destroy a human.
Giantkin seemed to be immune to shadowblindness and madness, but
many were overwhelmed by the sheer number of the enemy. Only light
could kill a shadow, so I created the lightgems whose sole purpose is
to capture light during the day and shed it at night so shadows would
be foiled. Now we live in a state of constant warfare against the dark,
unable to expand the Empire during this time of strife because we lack
the advanced logistical and communication capabilities of Midgard.
Where your world relies on science, Muspelheim has magic.*

I saw men and women slashed by razor shadows slowly losing their minds, becoming slavering killing machines, devoid of
reason, as their eyes turned into black liquid that ran down their
cheeks. Yet somehow, they were able to sense their victims, and
bite and rend and tear until they were killed. There was no cure for
the shadowmadness that drove them. Surt created lightgems in the
heart of the Surturvandunir that expelled the razor darkness, gems
that soaked in the light of the long days and released it at night,
but it wasn't enough. More energy was needed to power the gems
through the long night.

*It takes the might of a volcano to add power to the lightgems,
the earth's rage and hot blood saving those that dwell upon the skin
of the world.*

I saw a smallish cinder cone mountain, barfing smoke into the sky, its belly a blister of heat and melted rock, and I recognized it as the same volcano the Fire Giants used to create Surt. That volcano, the southernmost in the range and closest to Til Mathgen, had been active for thousands of years and would be for far more. Mt. Idelhorde, the Knuckle of the World.

I could use the might of Surturvandunir to power the lightgems, but it would be as if I powered a 12-volt bulb with a 1000-volt power supply. The effects would be disastrous.

From the Harrowback Mountains to the Sea of Orlan, all who dwell in the Empire are safe as I can make them, but I lack the ability to heal Muspelheim of the unraveling that threatens it. The magic within me is not for healing, but for war. I can only delay the inevitable.

A shining, golden web stretched from the mountains to the north, connecting all the lightgems across the empire into an intricate glowing tapestry that thrummed with power. The gilded beauty of it dazzled my eyes, each juncture a pinpoint of light as the gems shone with an intensity of thousands of candles. Tears of fire bled from my newly healed eyes.

It takes a being who has drunk directly from Mimisbrunnr to survive Surturvandunir and to heal what is breaking. Through the magic of the Well that still resides within you and the magic of the holy flame that is the centerpoint of this reality, you will be able to save Muspelheim. No one from my world can do this, it must be you.

I saw it, the reasoning. Of the nine Prime worlds, only Midgard had Mimir's cave and the Well of Urd, which contained the knowledge needed to reverse the unraveling for each world. My sigh carried flame.

Here, in this holy place, you can do what is needed to stop the unraveling. I have brought you to this interface where you can save my world, Kalevi Hakala. Then aid Madrigal to save it again.

The magic. I could feel it as I stood in the flame, no longer burning because the cycle was complete, and I had made another sacrifice to the Tree for power, a sacrifice of pain and rebirth. The fire did not destroy, that wasn't its purpose, it was to *transform*. My mind flowed outward along the membrane of this dimension, feeling the wrongness of the splinters that chewed into Muspelheim, originating from ragged vortices that led nowhere because I'd repaired them on the Midgard side. With the same sweep of my will I used to heal Midgard, I felt along the splintery, crackly edges of the vortices and pinched them shut, feeling the glass shard edges against the fingers of my mind, infusing a kind of healing magic into the wounds to seal them permanently, and in doing so, those regions called the Outs became relatively safe for the first time since the Aesir and the Vanir had breached the dimensional barrier. Then, using the magic of the Tree, I destroyed the splinters of unraveling that still clouded Muspelheim, erasing them from this world forever.

Thank you, Kalevi Hakala. Surt's musical mental voice contained equal measures of joy and caution.

My mind warred with itself. Now that I resided in the crucible of the holy flame, a minor extension of the Tree, I knew I could slide right through the small Sidhe exits that punctured this reality like holes in Swiss cheese and get the fuck out of Dodge. The temptation was there, I knew what world was next on the hit parade and all it would take was the smallest nudge and I'd wake up on Svartalfheim, also known as Nidavellir, home of the Dwarves.

Just one prod. East peasy lemon squeezy. The flames, now cool caresses all over my body, were filled with magic potential . . . not as much as Mimisbrunnr, but still more than I needed. I thought back to Des and how much I wanted to see him again, knowing that if even one Prime unraveled, they all would. I *had* to go, promises be damned. Shit.

I felt you heal Midgard, Surt said, his voice oddly soft, a bare whisper against my thoughts. *And I knew you would be on Muspelheim soon, so I sent Madrigal to seek you in the Outs and bring you to me so you could save us. I thank you for your promise to aid us once again after the healing.*

Goddamnit! Why did he have to be so nice? Look at me, I'm a right asshole.

But not a fucking asshole.

"Yeah." I inhaled cool flames. "Let's go."

EIGHT

I want my knife

"**Y**OU PUSHED ME INTO THAT FUCKING FIRE." My voice came out surprisingly calm considering my fury.

Madrigal stared at me for a moment and I could feel those eyes all over my skin. My transformation by holy fire (which did not include a new hand, more's the pity) had also transformed my clothes . . . into ash. What was left was a balder than bald Kalevi Hakala. Not even the hair on my legs survived, but I didn't care because the memory of what happened was crystal clear in my mind. "Let's be clear about, Kal," she grunted. "I *threw* you into the fire."

"Why. The. Fuck. Did. You. Do. That?" Each word fell hard between us as I stood there trying not to feel self-conscious. My hands wanted to cover up the boys, but I wasn't about to give Madrigal the satisfaction, so she'd just have to bask in the reflected light of my naked glory.

She shrugged. "You were taking too long. I don't have the luxury of waiting for you to wake up or to find your courage to do what was needed."

"That was an asshole move." I sighed, rubbing my bald head.

One thing about being healed by the holy fire . . . I was perfectly manscaped now. A new sensation for me, but it did make me look proportionally . . . grander. "But I understand." Fuck me, but I did. Back in the day I'd done much worse for less reason and counted myself justified for doing so. Once, long ago, I got up the nose of new-ish agent, prodding him to see what he was made of, so much so in fact he screwed up royally. The result: half of Weed, California burned to the ground.

Yeah, I'm the king of taking it to the edge.

"Fine," I said, deflating a bit. "But I need some clothes, like *now*."

THE TAVERN LOOKED TO BE THE SORT where the owner has to sweep up the eyeballs after closing, where the beer is cheap and the women are cheaper, and if you don't watch yourself, you'll wind up with either a social disease or an empty purse. More often than not, both.

My kinda joint.

"They're in there?" I asked, pointing with my shiny new blade.

Madrigal nodded. "Their sort frequents this place almost exclusively. The keep makes sure clodder hunters get a discount."

I still wasn't used to how casual and common slavery was in Surete, but I had to admit his royal golemness did what he could to keep abuse to a minimum, setting up an entire system to oversee clodder affairs. Not my world, not my morals or ethics, even though it rankled.

Gleaming in the bright, yellow light of the gems that festooned near every possible surface, the blade at the end of my right arm looked sharp enough to slice three mothers-in-law in half with one blow. Called a scissor, it was a hardened steel tube that encased my entire forearm and capped off with a half-moon blade about six inches long. Often called a 'gladiator scissor,' they were used in Roman arenas during that empire's heyday. The blacksmith who constructed it for me many hours ago thought I was nuts, but conceded that the challenge of creating a weapon to compensate for a missing hand was intriguing. It didn't hurt any that Madrigal had provided the silver burn marks for the job.

The big blacksmith, with arms like tree trunks and a belly like a pony keg, didn't fancy me sticking my nose into his business, but once I used a bit of charcoal to draw out what I wanted and laid out the money for the job, he was more than excited to create the optional extras I ordered. I'd pick them up later, but for now I finally felt a little less naked. Having thick trousers of some soft wool-like fabric, a long coat, and a heavy tunic helped a ton, too, considering the temperature was approaching freezing. Madrigal told me that before the night was halfway through it would start to snow, which would turn to rain when the sun decided to peek up over the horizon.

My breath plumed out into the cold air as I stared at the grimy little tavern. Located near the walls, it had two stories and a large stable for lizard horses. Over the heavy wooden door was a sign depicting a man in chains crouching down looking for all the world like he was ready to take a dump.

"Please tell me that the name isn't the 'Crouching to Shit," I remarked.

Madrigals thin lips quirked up in a smile. "It's called the Squatting Clodder."

"That's worse. Much worse." I shook my head. Sounds of music played on some sort of stringed instrument and laughter hit the night air as a burly man in stained leathers entered. "Let's go see if they're in there."

Heat washed over me as I opened the door, far less than when I stood in the holy flame, but it immediately brought a thin sheen of sweat to my forehead. Thanks to the transformative powers of the holy fire (how I was transformed, I didn't know and was afraid to find out) I felt positively capital, aces, super-duper and ready to rock-n-roll daddy-o. Sure the holy fire hurt worse than watching C-Span, but on the plus side I had come out with all my owies healed, which beat my former health care provider cold. I'd bet my arteries had got a good scrubbing as well.

After the wave of heat, or more correctly, *with* the wave, came a good reason for someone on this world to invent deodorant. Crack an egg and pour it into a shoe, then bury that shoe in a compost pile of pig and horse shit for two weeks and you'd come close to the overwhelming acidic odor of unwashed bodies, old vomit, and spilled ale that the place had been collecting for about a thousand years. My nose wanted to wave a white flag and my eyes watered, but when they cleared enough to see the dozen or so tables chock-full of what gave off that smell, I managed to sight our prize.

Giliselle and Shem. The pair were hunched over cups of wine talking to three other disreputable types that had about a dozen teeth between them. Giliselle was all pointy-toothed smiles and Shem's scar bunched and humped as he laughed at some joke or such. I didn't care or bother to eavesdrop, I was too busy beating feet their way, happy to see that they weren't looking at me. I'd like to say that my heart was chockablock full of good intentions, but the worm of anger was turning in my belly and I was fresh out of happy thoughts.

A couple of the three noticed me heading over and stood up quick, which brought the raucous noise of conversation and bad string music to a stop. Good preservation instincts on these guys. Giliselle looked to see what everyone was staring at and her eyes had time to widen to the size of silver dollars before the half-moon blade of my scissor found the skin over Shem's throat. His eyes grew plenty scared when they met my baby blues.

"Told you I was gonna get my knife back, kid," I growled through gritted teeth at Shem, who looked like he was ready to soil his pants. "And my other possessions." I moved the scissor slightly and a trickle of blood flowed down his throat. His eyes didn't leave the blade.

He gabbled and gobbled, but stayed put. As for Giliselle, Madrigal made sure she stayed seated thanks to a blade that suddenly dimpled the skin under the slave catcher's left eye.

"Stay where you're at!" I barked at the barkeep who had a truncheon in one meaty hand and a mean look on his face. He pulled up short but didn't look scared. "I have business here and I'll leave peacefully once my possessions are returned to me." From all around, the customers, a motley a group of toughs as I'd ever seen, were giving us good glares while fingering some seriously sharp cutlery.

Mr. Barkeep cocked his head. "That true, Shem?" he asked. "You got this man's goods?"

The kid finally found his voice. "He's a clodder, Volk! I swear."

I held up my left hand. The freshly tattooed left hand.

"He's a citizen, Shem." The barkeep, who looked like he could bench press at least five of me, placed the head knocker on the bar and crossed his arms. "I run a legit business here, don't cozy to thieves."

Shem was too busy goggling at my new tattoo to say anything, and Giliselle looked like she wanted to remove my nuts with a rusty spoon, but the knife pressing her skin kept her sitting still. The customers disappeared their various pieces of hardware and sat back down, ready for a show. As for Madrigal, she looked bored.

On the floor under Shem's left boot lay a backpack, and I had me an idea. Keeping the scissor at his throat, I pulled it out and dumped the contents on the table, sending wine cups and wine flying. From the smell of the cheap stuff, it would've been better used as salad dressing. Amid some clothing, a small purse and foodstuffs lay my bowie, the Lahti, and a handful of clips.

Hot damn and pass the potatoes.

My heart did a little skip of joy and I had the bowie stuffed into one pocket and the Lahti in another after checking the clip. One round in the pipe . . . Shem was lucky he hadn't blown his dick off. "Okay, Shem," I said. "I'm going to back out of here. You try anything, you come after me, I'm going to make sure you pee sitting down for the rest of your short, miserable life."

Giliselle piped up. "Remember when you asked to see my leader."

I nodded.

"You remember my answer?"

"You said if I was lucky I'd never meet him." Oh. I'm slow, but I get there. As sneaky a sonofabitch as I am, I shoulda figured this out long ago. "Duul's right behind me, isn't he?"

Her smile and the hand the size of a catcher's mitt descending butterfly light on my shoulder gave me the answer.

"I think you should give the knife and the metal doodad back to Shem, right?" came the familiar rumble.

"My property," I answered. Out of the corner of my eye I saw Madrigal back away, blade held at the defensive.

"As long as you don't try anything, Madrigal Rhone," said the ogre, "you'll be fine. My business is with the, ah, *former* clodder."

Madrigal looked at me and shrugged as if to say, "This is your show now". Not that I could blame her, Duul's head nearly touched the rafters. How the hell had I missed him and how did he sneak up on me so quiet?

Before that big hand could clench and turn my shoulder to strawberry jam, I had the scissor back at Shem's throat. "Smart play, acting like the dumb brute while letting Giliselle act the brains." I turned slightly, keeping an eye on Shem. "Sneaky, even. I should've seen it."

A dip from that basketball sized head. Cavernous eyes bored into mine. "Yes, you should have. Now place the knife and the doodad back on the table and I let you go with a chiding."

A chiding? Who talks like that? Fear took a back seat as I found myself in the grip of stubborn Finnish pride. This was familiar territory. "No dice, big guy. These are *mine*."

Suddenly a grand smile split the ogre's granite mug. It was terrifying. "Good, then we'll duel for it, all legal like. I win, we keep it and give you a proper burial. You win, you get to leave here with the contested items."

"Sure." The word slipped out before I could stop it.

"Ahhh . . . *Kal*," Madrigal barked in exasperation. To Duul, in a voice like razor glass. "Take it back, Duul, Kal here is now one of Surt's eyes and ears and has a job to do."

The ogre never took his eyes from mine. "The law is the law, even for the eyes and ears of Surt and this citizen accepted. One thing about the Emperor, he is a stickler for the law and a dispute may be adjudicated by duel should the parties agree to one."

"Or an impartial judge."

Right. An impartial judge sounded all fine and dandy, but I knew one would rule in favor of the slavers. My possessions had been taken when I was a clodder, a slave with a few rights and I had a feeling that a judge would give me a thumbs down. By the smile on the ogre's face, his broken tusk gleaming in the gemlight, he knew he held all the cards.

Time to put up or shut up.

"It's all right, Madrigal. I'll fight the big lug."

Now it was her turn to get all round-eyed at me. "Kal, ogres are a warlike species whose magic is that of coordination. What happens to one, all will know."

"So, if I kill him every ogre on the planet will know who done it?"

"Yes, and they'll declare wargild on you!"

More smiling from Duul. Yeah, he held a pat hand, all right. "What does that mean and how long will it take?"

"It means that those of his clan will declare a legal vendetta against you, calling you out to duel one after the other until either you or the entire clan is dead." She shrugged. "Just guessing, not many of them in the city, but some will be here from the outlying territories in a day or two."

"Cool." I grinned and took the scissor from Shem's throat, backing out of Duul's reach. "Where and when, big boy?"

As if by magic, the entire crowd of lowlifes, who had been listening in rapt attention, backed away, taking the tables and benches with them. In seconds we had the center of the large room.

Duul spread his hands. "Whenever you are ready, little man."

The smile never strayed from his granite face. "I will be generous enough to give you the first shot."

Poor choice of words.

I'm not naturally ambidextrous, but I'd had enough practice so it didn't matter, and from ten feet away I couldn't miss. Lightning quick, my left arm rose with a fistful of Lahti and I fired two shots, both entering the deep socket of Duul's right eye. Because the rounds didn't exit his thick skull, I'd hazard a guess they ricocheted inside his brain pan chewing their way through his gray matter like Pac Man.

Everyone flinched or froze at the loud noise, but Duul merely stood there for a few moments, blood tricking down his cheek, before falling flat on his face with a mighty crash. I nimbly stepped out of his way before he could crush me.

"There you go, all legal like," I said, placing a hand on Madrigal's arm and leading out of the tavern.

NINE

This place is wierd

"THE SHADOW QUEEN SEEKS OUR DESTRUCTION," Madrigal had said after we took separate rooms in one of Til Mathgen's finer establishments. Apparently being an eyes and ears came with a hefty *per diem*. Madrigal sipped her wine, a much better brew than at the Squatting Clodder. "She has her own eyes and ears, assassins that travel in packs called Splinters."

I nodded, chowing down on a slab of the beefy venison that served as the primary source of protein for the Empire. It came from a herd animal called a loffa, which turned out to be Muspelheim's version of a cow, that is if a cow had six legs and looked a bit like an armadillo. "Go on," I said around a mouthful of loffa.

"A Splinter of shadows can track a singular target anywhere on the world without fail as long as they obtain, let's say, an article of clothing, or a single drop of blood."

Mmmm, whatever the veggies were, they sure went down fine, all slathered in butter and some semi-sweet pepper. "Sort of like bloodhounds." The wine was a little bitter and spiced with something I couldn't quite put my finger on, but it washed down the food well enough.

"What?"

"Never mind. Midgardian reference. Keep going."

"If a Splinter has your scent, you can't hide from them. As the most powerful of the Shadow Queen's creatures, they can endure the light for a short period of time, which means they can attack in broad daylight if needs be. No city, not Til Mathgan, nor Bor Haverse, nor Del Penetot can completely eradicate shadows, no matter how many lightgems they have."

A smiling, buxom server in a tight-fitting blouse and pants set a tray of pastries next to me, and I tucked in with a will, tossing her a wink for good measure. She blushed and chewed on her bottom lip before scarpering off. Maybe . . . nah. Not that I couldn't, but my gut told me my time in Muspelheim would be brief and I wasn't the hit-it-and-quit-it type. Not anymore, that is.

Before Madrigal could continue, I said, "Let me guess, some high muckety-muck knob got a Splinter on his ass," I chuckled around a baclava style yummy, "and we have to stop these critters from doing him no good. Close?"

Surt's agent leaned back and crossed her arms, green eyes narrowing. "Close. About seventy-five percent, actually. You're not as dumb as you make yourself out to be."

"Sweet of you to say. You're probably right. So, fill me in on the other twenty-five percent."

"You're right that Splinters are set on important people, just not important like you think."

That brought me upright. I gave her a good stare. Those angular features didn't move a single twitch. I reminded myself never to play poker with this lady. "They're after you," I blurted.

Finally, a reaction . . . her left eyebrow crawled up her forehead. "Maybe you *are* the one to help us out."

"Shucks, t'weren't nothin,'" I drawled. "From my understanding there aren't nobles, *per se*, in this burg, just the rich, the ordinary folk and the people who roam the halls of power. If a Splinter is not after someone rich, then it has to be someone important to the government, and considering how Surt was all full court press on signing me on, it had to be someone he relies on. His eyes and ears. You." I shrugged. "Seems reasonable."

"Not just me. All the eyes and ears. Six dead so far." Madrigal closed her eyes against remembered pain and said, "The people know about the shadowmad and the shadowblind, but what they don't know about, and the great Surt wants this kept quiet, are the shadowspies. Shadowbit, those infected by the Shadows, are people who look and carry on as normal, but do the Queen's bidding. Imagine the panic that would cause if news of such a thing were surface."

"Sellian Vry was one of the eyes and ears before he was shadowbit, one of our best, actually. Over a period of six months, he covertly gathered personal items, clothing, hair, whatnot, from the other eyes and ears and delivered it to a Splinter, who decimated our ranks. We caught him, discovered what he'd done and planned, but the damage was done. Now the same Splinter is out there and is going to kill us all, leaving Surt without his spies."

"Train some new ones."

Fury shone from Madrigal's long face. "It takes years to train a body in the way of the eyes and ears. There are more, but they're so green they wouldn't last a second against monsters that look like creatures of broken black glass who move like the wind and disappear like smoke. If all senior eyes and ears die, it will cripple a network it's taken generations to create."

"Leaving the Queen of shadows with room to maneuver."

She nodded. "Just so."

I sat back and patted my obscenely full tummy. I hadn't tucked in like that in over a decade and it felt wonderful. For a moment my thoughts drifted to Des, but I placed them away for another day. Nothing will get you killed like woolgathering. I picked my teeth with a finger nail and considered the situation. What would I do if I was a wee beastie of a Queen looking to take on an incredibly powerful golem with a host of giants and humans at his beck and call? The endgame was easy, a world where there was nothing to challenge her power. Surt and his eyes and ears were smart and capable, which begged the question, "How did Sellian get himself shadowbit?"

Madrigal's mouth opened, then closed with a snap.

SO NOW I FACED A WARGILD OF OGRES, a group of shadow assassins called the Splinters, and I had to survive long enough to get my happy ass out of this jam. And do it quick enough so I could head out to Svartalfheim before it unraveled. Man, I felt *alive*.

"Who did you say this skink was again?"

"Wendiver Halt."

The roof of Wendiver's residence lay some five feet below and fifteen feet away. Warm light bathed us as we lay on our bellies staring at the objective. The roof tiles pressing into me were cold, but I was dressed in enough layers that I didn't mind too much. Besides, I had a full tummy and felt wide awake; it would be hours yet before I'd start to yawn, but I wondered if I could find some sleep considering the soft, warm light that surrounded us.

"Don't you miss the night?" I asked.

Madrigal looked at me like I was crazy, and I cursed myself for being a damn idiot. Of course she didn't, the lightgems that protected the city had been there long before she was even a gleam in her ancestors' eyes.

Lightgems everywhere . . . on poles high overhead, on walls even on the roof emitting the butter light. "You can't get rid of all the shadows," I remarked.

"Living shadows need the dark," Madrigal replied, once again staring at the other roof. "Shadows that are dark and velvety so they can travel between their lair on the other side of the world to the Empire. Shadowdoors." A long pause. "What are we waiting for?"

"This is called surveillance. Trust me."

"Says the man stupid enough to kill an ogre."

"Not planning to stick around much, lady. Call it a motivation for success."

That earned me a green-eyed glance of disbelief.

"Look," I whispered, watching a medium-sized, non-descript man twenty feet below walk across the street toward the building we were casing. "Is that Wendy?"

"Yes, and have more respect. He's eyes and ears."

He was one of the surviving veteran agents of the spy network and the one most likely to fit the profile: single, a loner, no real friends and the most enigmatic of those that still breathed. Seemed custom fitted for the occasion. As smart as the golem was, he lacked in any sort of knowledge in behavioral science, which I had in spades. I shifted the small backpack on my shoulders to sit a little more comfortably. Time to teach the kids a thing or two. "Give him a minute."

"Why him?"

"Like I said, he's the type that no one remembers, has no attachments, no lovers," I explained for the umpteenth time. "A perfect target to become a shadowspy."

The sound of teeth slowly grinding was my only reply.

For several hours I had checked the records of the other living eyes and ears, men and women who kept Surt informed on the health of the Empire. Some were well known like Madrigal, while others moved in silence and stealth, phantoms that haunted the realm. Guess which category Wendy fit into?

Thankfully, First Minister Vestaverous' small bureaucracy thrived on record keeping, the kind that catalogued, in minute detail, all Surt's eyes and ears. With the Emperor's authority in my pocket, I had access to anything I needed and a host of giant and human scribes, scholars, and secretaries to aid in my research, research that led me to Wendy. This process, thanks to ample assistance, took a remarkably short time. Could my profile be wrong? Of course, but I was up shit creek for other leads so I went with my gut . . . the same gut that told me if best way to do dirt on someone or something was to be a sneaky fuck, and the eyes and ears were the sneakiest fucks around.

Next to me, natch.

Bells sounded across the city, bells that told the populace that it was the right time to catch some winks, and business would continue a few hours after shuteye. An efficient system for a culture whose day and night rhythms for a people (humans, that is) who developed on a world where the night lasted only twelve hours or less.

"Time to go," I muttered. The roof I found myself on was slanted slightly to shed rain and snow, but Wendy's was flat as a pancake, adding to its Southwester US flair with its tan adobe walls and wooden shutters. So many familiar things in an unfamiliar world.

I vaulted to my feet, backing up a bit before taking a run. I cleared the distance between buildings, tucking and rolling to reduce noise. A second later Madrigal landed next to me, light-footed, without a hardly a sound. Sarky youngster.

"Why don't we use the front door?" she asked, not even winded.

Kids today. "Trust me."

Crossing her arms, Madrigal gave with a skeptical look as a searched the roof. One of her objections was a lack of a door, but when it came to investigating fellow eyes and ears, all spycraft seemed to leak from her mind, which was not unusual. We like to believe that the person next to you sharing the danger is a decent sort, but I had my doubts.

You see, getting shadowbit was hard in places like Til Mathgen, and although the eyes and ears traveled the Empire, paranoia was their virtue so they carried with them sufficient lightgems just in case, which meant that Sellian Vry had to have been targeted, and successfully. How? It came to me that perhaps he wasn't the first. Perhaps he was the goat in case the Surt and the gang caught on faster than anticipated, which meant someone else on the inside was also a double agent, letting Vry take the fall and allowing them sufficient time to set up for a crippling blow.

It pays to think sneaky, and I'd had a lot of practice.

Eventually, with some judicious tapping and making my dice roll for Spot Secret Doors, I found one. Helps having some good old-fashioned D&D Thief skills.

In the corner where a five-inch hole in the foot high wall running around the roof allowed water runoff, I spotted a slightly raised section covered in what looked like normal dust and detritus. I wiped away the material to find a trap door only a couple of feet wide, the tar applied thick, overlapping the seam so water couldn't enter the building below. I turned to my companion with my best shit-eating grin, which, let me tell you, is world-class.

"Oh, shut up," she whispered. Her curiosity won out over her pride as I examined the door. "How did you know?"

"What do you do for Surt?" I asked. "I know you're eyes and ears, but what do you normally do?"

"What most of us do . . . travel to the various cities and gather intelligence on the state of the Empire and such. Fight shadows if the situation arises. Why?"

That didn't sound very secret agent at all and I said so.

"Nothing so secret about it. If we want to remain anonymous, we hide our faces, which is common practice in deep cold or in the heat of midday. We don't skulk, if that's what you mean."

Hmmm . . . odd. "On Midgard I used to hide my identity wherever I went. The organization I belonged to was a secret one, so thinking sideways was as natural as breathing. I figured that the Queen of Shadows is playing a long game, setting up a big fall for Surt, which is what I would do." I let loose with my scapegoat theory and Wendiver Halt, which until then I'd kept in my back pocket. "A good spy always has more than one exit from where they lay their head down. I just found Wendy's."

"I'm not sure I like the way you think."

"Most people don't, but I'm alive and my enemies aren't, so I'd call it a win for me."

The small space between the tarred roof and door was far too thin for the scissor blade, but underneath the thick tar lay wood, which was no real hindrance for the bowie. Working slowly and carefully, I sliced and peeled my way along the edge, widening the gap around the area where the bolt for the trap door should be. Ten long minutes of careful whittling and slicing, cutting away wood that had seen just enough water damage to make the job easier than expected, and the hole—roughly a half inch wide and four inches long— revealed an iron bolt which I teased back with the tip of the bowie. The door fell in and hit the opposite wall with a light thud. I winced at the noise, sure I'd alerted Wendy.

Darkness. Behind me, Madrigal hissed and pulled out a light-gem, thrusting the shining stone into the void below, illuminating a room the size of a broom closet containing nothing but a door.

"Traitor!" hissed the eyes and ears of Surt, her face a rictus of hate. "Darkness is the doorway for shadows." For a moment it looked as if she'd vomit.

"You need more proof?"

She shook her head.

I dropped into the room, landing light, with Madrigal close behind. The door led to a hallway floored with bare planks polished to a honey brown, the darkness running away from the lightgem in Madrigal's hand. The wide-eyed look of terror and the sweat beading her forehead in the cold air told me more about what lay in the shadows than any words could. I'd seen that look before on agents who fought giant insects and were-wolves. It was the same look I had on my face while I shot harpies out of the sky as they attacked, knowing that one scratch from a claw would slowly turn my flesh to jelly. One-hundred percent fatal, no cure, no hope. Madrigal feared the dark like dogs feared thunder.

"If you sense movement in the dark, Kal," she whispered. "Run."

"We can face it together," I replied in the same hushed tone.

"You're not equipped."

Of all the things she could have said, that unsettled me the most, that and her matter-of-fact tone of voice. They were the words and cadence of an agent who knows what the fuck they are talking about.

We continued, the light evaporating the darkness all around until we came to a set of stairs at the end. Down. I felt my hackles rise. My spidey-sense was starting to work overtime and I drew the Lahti. Guns don't solve all problems, but at that point it couldn't hurt.

Each step became a lesson in patience and caution as I tested each stair. If I was the type of paranoid asshole who planned dastardly deeds, here's where I'd plant a surprise. Said surprise came six stairs down as the plain wood planking I teased with the toe of my boot shifted suddenly.

Behind me Madrigal froze and I did my best to imitate a statue, one boot hovering in the air above the traitor stair. One second, two, then three passed in mayhem-less quiet. I let out a breath I didn't know I'd been holding and probed the next stair down, careful not to touch the previous one. Safe. I set my weight on that one and inspected the suspicious stair. The wooden plank lifted easily to reveal the darkness underneath. Madrigal shone a light and my eyes widened.

About ten inches down sat six iron spikes, all barbed, all rusty and wicked. Checking the plank in my hand, I found it had been sawed in several places so that anyone trundling up the stairs would find their foot suddenly busting through and impaling upon the spikes. The barbs would hold on to the flesh quite nicely, but that was merely cruel window dressing because I was pretty damn sure that wasn't rust on those iron spikes, but human excrement.

Nasty, nasty.

I grinned. "Now this is my kinda guy."

Once again Madrigal gave with the hairy green eyeball. Oh well, joke 'em if they can't take a fuck.

Down again, prodding, testing every step, my heart rate rose as a familiar tingle flushed through me. My palm grew sweaty around the Lahti and my right forearm almost felt as if it were on fire under the padding beneath the steel cup that held the scissor.

"Why are you smiling?" The air barely stirred as the words floated my way.

Why? Why was I smiling? Because I was enjoying this shit. For the first time I was proactive instead of reactive, in my element instead out of it, and I felt fucking alive and in control. This is what I trained for, the hunt, and I'd done it so many times in the past that it was like slipping on a nice pair of old slippers that fit *just right*. I recognized the feeling of life bubbling up inside, raging to come out and I would let it, oh yes, I sure would because there was nothing like facing down the Bad Things, the things that wanted to destroy and hurt, and kill them.

This is what I was born to do. Which goes to show how fucked up my life really was.

Best guess it took five minutes to traverse one flight of stairs to the first floor, but before my foot hit the ground level, voices drifted my way.

"Don't worry. Everything is proceeding as it should." A man's voice, velvety smooth.

The next voice came as a shock. "'Don't worry' he feckin' says, as if I'm a feckin' idiot." Kla sounded plenty pissed. "I feckin' told you this new clodder is trouble and these two confirm it. He's a feckin' eyes and ears on his world!"

"He old," said a third voice, female, her accent atrocious as was her Dholesch. The voice was familiar, however, but I couldn't quite place it. "One man, no hand. Is very possible to kill him."

"You're feckin' daft woman, you haven't seen him fight. He's a lightning storm with four limbs. Did you hear? He feckin' killed an ogre a cycle ago."

"My weapon will kill him. Will be dead in a few hours."

"She's correct, Kla. He's only one man," said the first speaker, a male voice. Wendy, perhaps? "It's Rhone we have to worry about."

"Another feckin' problem there, for sure. And what's with this feckin' fella here, hasn't said a feckin' word? You vouch for him, but I don't know him from a hole in the feckin' ground."

"He no speak Dholesh," said the woman. "I translate."

I passed the front door, a sturdy affair with a brace of bolt locks that looked like they could stop an elephant. A hallway ran for a good twenty feet before terminating at a door that had been left open a hair. A runner made of thick blue fabric with green diamonds traversed most of the way and I gingerly stepped on, still probing for traps. Call me paranoid.

"A wizard he be," continued the woman. "His magic found you so we offer help to kill one named Kal, keep him from making trouble. It make all happy extra, yes?"

Mr. Velvety Smooth Voice cut in before Kla could interject. "They came to me, Kla, and knew what was what. They have bold magic and fierce weapons that will kill this man you seem to hate so much." A short pause. "Their magic led them here and they could have killed me, but offered help instead. If they were in league with Surt, I would know. Now, we gather here because with our new intelligence supplied by Wendiver Halt, our allies will strike and we must be ready. Surete will fall soon, and be replaced, of course, by another ruled by our friends here."

All this went on whilst I tiptoed down the hall, boots silenced by the runner, Lahti and scissor forward, half-moon blade glinting wickedly.

The door opened, a slender man walking through looking over his shoulder and said, "If you will attend," he said in a rough voice like sandpaper on stone. "I'll—"

An 'oh shit' moment and I had to act, all stealth forgotten. No thought, just my fist full of pistol rising from the floor to smash the guy on the jaw. Two point seven five pounds of pistol broke bone and shattered teeth before dropping him to the floor and I was through the door in a flash, scissor raised, heart pounding in anticipation, Madrigal right behind.

Time slowed as if it were treacle, a thick liquid that hindered my body but not my mind, which shifted into overdrive. Nearly a dozen people dressed from simple to elegant, half of whom were seated at a long table, faces slack with shock, some with terror. Except for three. Wendy, the nondescript eyes and ears for whom it the word 'medium' was invented, behind him was a stout door and next to him were two people that just about made me lose my shit.

Now it was my turn for shock because I recognized one. Rafa Sari, the leader of the Apostles of the End Times.

What the fuck?

Next to him stood a woman I recognized as well, the hard, intense lady who jumped the gun at the auction. Her face was all business and frosted glass, cold and hard, and her eyes narrowed as if she had concentrated her whole being on me and only me. On the table next to her was a long, black case I instantly recognized as one from Midgard. A rifle case.

"Kill them!" yelled Wendiver Halt, drawing a long knife from his side. Next to him Kla snarled and leapt over the table at me, hands outstretched.

Suddenly time became real once more and things went to shit right quick.

Kla's hands came a kitty's whisker from encircling my throat, but I pulled back. But not quick enough to avoid his fingernails from scratching my throat. I swung the Lahti and smashed an eye, and he dropped on the table, howling.

A flash of silver. I jumped back, the knife in Wendy's hand scoring the back of mine and the Lahti fell to the carpet. A thrust with the scissor had him jumping back. Behind him a door opened and several of those in attendance beat feet out of there, having zero stomach for what was about to happen. One man, however, looked back at me with eyes entirely colored jet black, wisps of dark vapor floating from the ebon orbs. Looking at him made me want to puke day-glo. The man and the black eyes disappeared into the yellow light of the outdoors.

Wendy came at me again while the woman and Rafa waited for those fleeing to clear the doorway so they could light out as well, the woman grabbing a double fistful of rifle before she exited.

Fucking cowards, that shit wasn't going to stand even if I had to tear through the entire city to get to them.

A fist eclipsed my vision and pain blossomed on my cheek, the world going all red and wobbly as my head snapped back. My legs decided at that moment that working was a bad idea and I hit the floor hard, adding to the stars in my eyes. So many stars, in fact, I didn't see Kla wrap his hands around my throat and begin to *squeeze.*

I only caught a glimpse, but it was enough. Madrigal moved like a ballet dancer, almost inhuman grace coupled with precise, measured violence. Watching her spin, leap and stab was like watching a Da Vinci painting the Mona Lisa. Both hands were filled with knives that flashed in a whirling pattern dizzying to watch as she pressed Wendy, who frantically parried with his, ducking and weaving. Two thin, red lines decorated his shirt and the placid look on his face had transformed to worry. Madrigal bent over backward to avoid a thrust, then snapped back with blazing speed to take a slice out of Wendy's forearm.

That did it for the spy, who zipped out the door as fast as his legs could take him. As for me, things were getting hazy around the edges because Kla had his knees on my arms, preventing me from scissoring him up a treat, and both thumbs pressing hard against my windpipe.

"I got you now," he grated through a smile like a dog peanut butter from a steel brush.

I thrashed, my sight slowly fading, my lungs a burning mass of coals in my chest. This was it, the big sleep, and the only thing I could think of was Des, smiling down at me. He extended a hand, beckoning, and I raised mine to grasp it, to let him lead me to a special place where I didn't have to grieve for Jeanie any more.

For the first time in a very long while I felt peace.

TEN

Strange magic

AIR, ICY AND BRILLIANT, RUSHED INTO MY LUNGS, and for a long moment all I could do was inhale until they threatened to burst. Spots appeared in front of my eyes as I found myself sitting up, gasping, panting, the taste of blood on my tongue and the crisp, cold feeling of air in my chest that felt better than *anything*.

Kla stood, eyes wide and bugging, blood drooling from his mouth. He tried to reach the dagger that stood out from the middle of his back, but his muscular arms couldn't bend that far, and he dropped to his side before his eyes rolled up into the back of his head. A long, slow breath slithered past his lips before he stilled and the stench of voided bowels hit the air hard.

I got to my feet with a little help from Madrigal, who had a grip like a stevedore. We stood alone in the dining room now decorated with two corpses, one Kla, the other I had no clue. On the table lay the dark case the woman had opened and I sighed as I recognized the outline in the soft neoprene interior as that of a Barrett M98B, a sniper rifle that fires a .338 Lapua Magnum round.

"Not just a boys club, Mr. Hakala. Women of true faith already belong . . . just like the one who has you and the good professor in her sights." Rafa's grin widened. "Don't bother looking for red dots. Shiana doesn't need laser sights, I assure you."

I knew it in my gut, Shiana . . . the intense lady at the auction and a member of the Apostles. How the fuck did they . . . ?

Never mind. How wasn't the issue. The issue was what to do now.

"Are you well?" Madrigal was all business.

After my nod, she went for the door and the few gray cells I had left decided to kick in for a change, my hand latching on her shoulder and yanking her inside. A sharp crack and a hole appeared on the doorjamb where her head had been an instant before.

"We can't go outside," I said, pulling her toward the hallway. "That woman, the one we saw at the auction that bid on me . . . she has a weapon like a crossbow, but much more powerful and much quicker to reload. She'll kill us before we take two steps." My finger stabbed at the splintered hole in the jamb. I thought about matters for a second. "She probably has some vantage point on a rooftop with a clear line of sight down the street."

"Fecking Hel," muttered Madrigal. A thank you nod and she turned, heading toward the hallway. "Back upstairs, then, and out the trapdoor. We keep low, maybe we can surprise her."

Not like we had many choices. Stay inside and wait until something happened—or die of boredom.

The front door opened and closed quickly, followed by the sound of footsteps scrambling up the stairs two at a time. Anxious to catch whoever entered the house, cMadrigal and I raced to the staircase and I reached it a millisecond before her, turning and practically leaping over the first three steps in my rush. Fortunately, I remembered where the trap lay and pointed it out as I leaped over it.

"Kal—"

"Hurry!" I urged.

"Kal!" she yelled.

"What?" Top step, my eyes scanning the dark hallway for an ambush.

"You need light!"

The words had barely left her mouth when the sudden realization kicked in. The dim recesses of the hallway folded in on itself and I felt the hairs on the back of my arms rise.

When it struck not even reflexes honed after a lifetime of fighting could avoid the blow, a dagger sharp blade of night slid through the air silent and true, an ice-cold black slicing along my right side, parting flesh like silk. If I hadn't tried to dodge, it would've speared me through the sternum.

My left shoulder hit the wall with numbing force as the blood from the wound froze, sealing it shut, and my right arm flailed as another lance of darkness struck and deflected off the steel cup on my forearm. The cup shattered, icy shards raining down on the floor and my arm went numb.

I screamed in pain, in fury and denial as a thousand nebulous limbs thrashed in the darkness and a hard chittering met my ears. Just as another dark lance speared my way, Madrigal Rhone leapt forward, a dagger of blazing light in her hand pushing back the dark, and I could see the monster, see the shadow that hated the light so much, not a blob of softness, but a black, diamond edged creature that defied all definition because it sucked in the light and it *screamed*.

Iron nails jammed themselves in my eardrums as the high-pitched metallic wail flooded the hallway, bringing tears to my eyes and waves of agony to my skull. Madrigal leapt forward, brandishing the light dagger at the shadow, which cringed away from the harsh white, tentacles like black steel wire flailing. But rushing into the hall from a doorway to the right came the man with vaporous black eyes, his own dagger in hand, made not of a hard white light, but a cold, glowing black that ate the light as if he held the essence of shadow in one hand. Madrigal barely dodged his thrust, but his other hand grabbed hold of the wrist that held the burning knife the same moment her free hand grasped his hand, staying the black knife. Both snarled like wild dogs, muscles straining as dark as light strobed across the hallway, the shadow monster folding in upon itself while I gasped, trying to breathe as the blood remained frozen in my side, red crystals that burned my skin. I knew, down deep from balls to bone that I was shadowbit, that this was pretty much the end for me.

"Fuck that," I gasped as Madrigal and Black Eyes fell back through the doorway he came from, thrusting the hallway back into darkness.

My eyes hurt, a deep throbbing that felt like grit on the corneas and I blinked rapidly, sensing the shadow tensing in on itself to strike, to finish the job.

Anger washed over me in a crimson rush and I screamed *"Fuck you!"* in a voice so loud it hurt my ears, and I imagined a spell shape, the only one I knew, the Zippo spell that would bring a lick of flame into existence. Perhaps it would be enough to fight, to hurt the shadow but the spell shape didn't want to come, didn't want to be defined by this universe, so I cudgeled my will and my tiny spark of magical talent to bring the fire, fueled by my rage and hate, into existence and burn the shadow.

A dizzying rush flushed through my skin, as if suddenly all the blood in my body gushed out in a torrent like in a Tarantino movie, and the world went white, an intense white like the heart of a magnesium flare that ate everything around me, turning all into a maelstrom of heat and light.

The steam kettle at the end of the world sounded, a physical force that threw me rag doll like across the hall. My head hit something harder than it (surprising, I know) and the rest of me impacted on what felt like the entire planet. Something deep inside cracked and all desire to fight left in an instant of complete and total pain that ate up my existence.

Still conscious, I slid down, down, down, landing in a heap, eyes half-blinded as I stared up at nothing wondering if this was it. For a moment my life flashed before my eyes, but I didn't want to see it, didn't want to relive the pain of losing Jeanie and slowly losing

Des to the malaise of the spirit that formed between us. The white still shone, slowly morphing into yellow while the steam kettle that rattled the house faded to a high-pitched and rather sad whine that tugged at me.

Cold chewed at my soul, a spiritual frost that delved deep into my broken body. God, I needed a drink, something to save off the chill that slowly ate at me, but my arms and legs had decided to take a vacation, so I lay there, my sight dimming into dark.

Pieces of splintering wood fell on my face and plaster dust coated my scalp, but I didn't care anymore, caring was in a different zip code and I didn't have the address. Only the cold remained and that was eating at my lungs, freezing them so slowly that every breath I took felt like I had inhaled broken glass.

A sense of movement. Did I move? Doubtful considering the damage my body must've taken in the fight against the shadow. The chill crept further into my lungs and I felt my heart stutter in protest. No worries, in a few moments that wouldn't matter worth beans. Time to fucking die, right?

The cold called, a distant discordant tone that tugged at me as my spirit floated and bright light tapped at my closed eyes. I followed the tone, unheeding as to where it might take me because it was so insistent. *Come here, Kal,* it said. *Come. We welcome you.*

Isn't it nice to feel welcome? Across spans of time and space I followed the tone as it rang across the firmament of my soul, strong and inescapable. Something waited at the end of that tone, where the vibrations went to die. Something vast and patient, so patient it would wait for the stars to burn out if that's what it took to achieve its goals. I felt a mind as large as a continent and cold as the void of space, felt its indomitable will and power. This was an intellect so far advanced than my own that I felt like an ant in the presence of a colossus that had deigned to notice me.

Compared to the poisonous cold that flowed through my soul, this intellect fell to absolute zero, a chill that sucked me into a vortex of thought and icy emotion that flensed at my resistance. It wanted to dissect me, using its eon old experience and iron determination to lay my secrets bare like organs on a coroner's slab.

It didn't bother hiding from me, and I could see the vastness of its life, how it began in the void between dimensions and how it hungered to feed on the warmth of the worlds it found itself on, brought here by accident by warring beings of vast energy. I felt its delight as it sipped at the life forms it found here, the pulsing, sweet energy it consumed like a grain on the tongue and it wanted more, needed more, its hunger growing more and more persistent as if the lives it ate fed an addiction vaster than the oceans, more powerful than the tidal pull of the moon. It needed to eat life because it had become dependent on the lesser beings it ate, it had forgotten how to survive on its own and didn't want to stop, didn't want to turn back the clock to a time when it, by itself, was enough. It needed more and more and wouldn't stop until the world was cleansed of the millions upon millions of life sparks that roamed its surface and swam in the seas.

The alien mind narrowed to a needle point and tried to pierce mine, digging down into the center of me, of all that I was and could be. I think I screamed, but wasn't sure because I couldn't feel myself, couldn't see or hear anything. Everything belonged to the realm of the mind, to the country of pain and loss where I was the only inhabitant.

Perhaps the intelligence didn't consider me a threat because I could see what would normally be hidden, its intention and deliberate, slow purpose, its long and patient history.

The Queen of Shadows, indeed. Call it a she if you need to apply a personal pronoun, she was a creature that spawned intelligent drones every six months, all parts of her that were capable of independence yet dependent on her . . . energy, her shadow power to sustain them. Like ants serving their queen, they were completely and utterly devoted to her, their lives nothing in grand scale of things. She sent them traveling the shadow pathways that only her kind (if there were more of her I couldn't tell you) could use, to bedevil the people of this world, to harvest the bright light energy and return it to her, feeding her darkness so she could spawn more shadows.

At first, I was able to resist her probing while reading her cold intent, but the frozen steel of her intellect started to pierce the thin membrane of my defense, the pain of it a sheeting, icy spike into the center of my mind.

NO!

A voice like the skittering of spiders across a hotplate answered *–you cannot resist relax and you will die clean resist and only pain will be your reward.*

Fuck you, bitch!

A pause. Perhaps she didn't understand cursing. Suddenly, my mind reeled from an onslaught too great to put into words, the only feeling that the skin of my thoughts were slowly being peeled away from the muscle of my memories.

Okay, maybe she did understand cursing after all.

ELEVEN

Not dead yet

"H E LOOKS GOOD." A DEEP-ISH VOICE, one I didn't recognize. Ugh. Keep your voice down, why don't you?

"And he can hear us. He wakes."

That was Surt. Those musical tones flowed over me like butter.

"Can you hear me, Kal?" Madrigal. She sounded concerned. How sweet. "Wake."

Oh well, sleep looked to be in the rear view. "Yeah." Surprisingly, my lips worked just fine.

"You can open your eyes." Surt.

"Five more minutes, mom."

Madrigal. "Are you sure the shadow didn't damage his mind?"

Shadow? Oh, yeah, the black thingie that had looked like a sack of matte-black obsidian razor blades all jumbled together. Hey, why wasn't I taking the long dirt nap? I pried my gummy eyes open to see an ogre staring down at me from about a foot away. Adrenaline pumped through my body in an electric jolt and I sat up, raising the scissor, except there was no scissor. I think I may have peed myself a tiny bit.

"Not to worry," Surt soothed. The golem sat on a large stone block twenty feet away and I could feel the heat from his black and red magma skin as if it was a blast furnace. "This is Urgula, she is a medic and clodder working off a debt."

The ogre woman, Urgula, smiled around her shining tusks and the sight was *terrifying*. I noted the green clodder dot on her chin and the thick wrap around enormous breasts. Behind her stood Madrigal, weathering Surt's furnace heat like a pro.

"Medic?" I asked.

Urgula nodded. "As a clodder and a healer I am forbidden to wargild against you for Duul's death, although we are 6of the same clan."

"It was a duel."

A slow nod, the smile not moving a millimeter. I think she knew exactly how frightening it was. "Even so." With the last word under her belt (or blouse), she stood and exited quickly, closing the door behind her.

Soft sheets and an even softer pillow. A bed large enough for a small orgy and a room that rivaled my old office space back at the BSI, although it seemed smaller with Surt sitting against one wall, and I had to pull my sense of perspective back in line. I was in the castle and it had been built for giants, not men, so I needed to double, then triple, the scale of things.

"What happened?" I asked, running a hand along my side. No wound, no scar, just a small black patch the size of a dime. "I was shadowbit, so how come I'm still breathing?" Giddy laughter threatened to erupt. "Not that I'm complaining, mind you. Beats the alternative."

"The holy flame cleansed you of the shadowtaint," Surt said, fumarole eyes burning into mine. His magma lips slowly turned up at the corners, a geologic smile. "Shadow cannot defeat the flame. As you well know, you may enter the holy flame now without pain because you have weathered it once. You have been transformed, reborn, but not in any way, I believe, that is physically apparent."

Now that really creeped me the fuck out. I did a mental check of all my marbles and it appeared I hadn't lost any, so what the hell was he talking about? "What happened? How long?"

This time Madrigal spoke. "For two sleep spans you've laid here on this bed. You cast a spell and summoned a spray of white-hot fire, destroying the shadow. You failed to mention you're an Elemental Wizard."

Memory seeped back in. Heat. Light. The steam kettle scream. I rubbed my temples. "I remember . . . barely. But my magical ability is . . . atrophied. Has been since I was fifteen." I wasn't about to explain the trauma of my youth that culminated in the death of my sister and the stunting of whatever magical ability I once possessed. That's a story for another day.

"It seems," Surt mused in his musical voice, "that the holy flame healed your magical talent. You cast a fire spell so powerful it blasted the top off of Wendiver's home and caused a fire in neighboring structures, not to mention rendering Madrigal unconscious from the blast. It took two Hill Giant fireteams and their human aides to put paid to the flames. Quite impressive. It would be even more impressive had the shadowspy not escaped."

"What about Wendy?"

Surt shrugged massive shoulders. "Gone. I do not know where."

I shook my head. Blowing the top off buildings was never part of my resume. Sarcasm and mayhem, yes, but magical pandemonium, no. "But my only spell summons a small flame, not a conflagration!"

"In this universe, young man, spells are a matter of will, not of spell shapes." The golem held up a hand, the heat shimmer from the appendage confounding my eyes. "I know all about the magic of your world from the first wizards brought here through the Breach, but you are in my universe now. The laws of magic are a bit different here."

"Why didn't it heal my hand?" Speaking of which, where was the scissor? Oh . . . yeah. Shattered to itty bitty pieces back in

Wendy's house. Looked like I needed some more weaponry, but hopefully the smith who made the scissor would have the rest of my equipment ready.

"Sacrifice, Kalevi Hakala. You voluntarily sacrificed part of yourself to access the Well of Urd and what the Tree takes, what is willingly given, it does not return."

Sure, I figured that. I had just hoped . . .

Oh well. Feeling fit as a fiddle, I jumped out of bed only to realize, as the warm air from Surt's body hit my giblets, that I was naked as a baby. I wrapped myself in a sheet and cast about for some clothes.

With an arched brow, Madrigal handed me a bundle containing a new pair of pants and a heavy shirt. "Don't worry," she said drily. "I've seen better."

Face burning, I shucked the sheet and slid into the clothes. "In your dreams, blondie," I muttered, fastening a thick leather belt around my waist. "Those people we saw, the man and the woman. They're from my world." I gave the story about the Apostles while Surt listened intently.

"From Madrigal I knew these people were of Midgard," he fluted when I'd finished. "And I have formed a hypothesis as to their comings and goings."

It was my turn for a raised eyebrow.

"It seems to me that that the man is a wizard, what we call a Diviner, a sage with the spells to acquire knowledge and the ability to find that which may be hidden, which he used to find those that can aid him in the quest to kill you. As for the woman, I do not know how she learned Dholesch so quickly, as there is no magic that can speed the learning."

"Yeah, well, she's probably a polyglot, then," I replied, slipping the heavy wool shirt over my head. "Someone with a facility for languages. But that's neither here nor there, and we've got bigger problems."

Both the golem and Madrigal cocked their heads to the side like windup toys. I let them wait for a few seconds then, "You're not dealing with shadowspies," I stated flatly. "You're dealing with a *conspiracy*." I let that marinate for a few seconds. "Wendy isn't a shadowspy. At least, I don't think he is. Black Eyes is, obviously, but Wendy had ample opportunity to become all shadowy and shit and didn't, so I think he's normal. What we have here are a bunch of ordinary humans dealing with the shadows to advance their status, which means overthrowing the current government and installing a human emperor."

ONCE AGAIN SURT GAVE THE COCKED HEAD BIT, while Madrigal chewed on her lower lip a bit, sitting on the corner of the bed, eyes narrowed in furious thought as I sat next to her, putting on wool socks and a heavy set of leather boots. They were a little snug, but beggars can't be choosers. Complaining, however, everyone does *that*.

"Why?" Surt chimed. "Why would humans do that? It would mean their end. The end of all of us."

"Never underestimate the power of human stupidity and greed." If Surt had access to reality television, he'd understand. "Best guess, the human population is greater than ever and many feel resentment at being ruled by an undying giant." Something about the way Surt stood with head cocked just so itched at me and I realized with a start that he was holding something back. But what? What could an immortal genius golem be holding back from the guy who had recently arrived and was still adjusting? It took a minute of cudgeling my brain, but the answer came and I felt like three kinds of idiot for not thinking about it in the first place.

"You're not really surprised, are you?" I accused, staring at those fumarole eyes in that blazing black-and-red face. "This isn't the first time you've had to deal with human conspiracies, is it?"

Madrigal looked from me to her Emperor until, "Your Majesty?"

It was amazing how much a construct could project sadness and resignation. "No, it is not." he said, musical voice full of doleful tones like a funeral dirge. "Humans breed so much faster than giantkin, they outnumber us a thousand to one." He sat there on his stone bench radiating ferocious heat, but the words seemed to have drained him of the ability to stand. "Only the power and magic of the giantkin can balance the scales, but humans are clever, crafty. I have quashed innovations over the centuries that would have placed them as the dominant race on Muspelheim."

"But . . . but," Madrigal began. "We have advancements already. The printing press and the Elreghast separator for twillfiber bushes, both which make all lives easier."

The Emperor looked at her sadly. "Advances made centuries ago and suppressed until I deemed the proper time for them to come forward. Our society still relies on rough justice and clodders, vendettas and duels. Advancements in technology must come at times when a society matures enough to integrate them without dramatic, and often catastrophic change. Too much change can destroy a society as easily as it can enhance it."

For a brief moment I thought Madrigal might cry, but her long face closed suddenly, shuttering all emotions and she, too, sat as if her strings had been cut.

Surt continued, "It is my function to ensure that our society works smoothly and fairly as possible, to maintain the integrity of giantkin and humans alike. In this I have no free will, as it is part and parcel of my creation, but I can exercise some autonomy in the manner in which I maintain that integrity. Yes, it comes at a cost to human innovation, but the balance in the Empire is not human one, it revolves around all species. I do this without apology or remorse because protecting the Empire and its inhabitants is my primary purpose."

I cut in before he could continue, "My guess there are so many inventions you have suppressed over the centuries that if you introduced them all at once the citizenry would massively, and collectively, lose their minds." Like gunpowder and the assembly line to name two.

That earned me a nod. "Just so."

"And that suppression birthed more than one conspiracy to oust you in the past, but they all failed and they, too, were kept secret from the citizens of the Empire."

"Your sight is deep, Kalevi Hakala."

"No, I just know a lot of politicians." I scratched my dome, feeling a pang of loss for my unruly blond hair which hadn't survive the holy fire. "But you've missed the important question."

Madrigal didn't. "How do you know all this, about Wendiver and such?" She still sat there with strings cut, Surt's words the scissors that severed them. I briefly wondered if her loyalty had been shaken to its roots or if she would recover well enough to continue as his eyes and ears.

Not time to worry about Madrigal, though. "When I was shadowbit, I felt the Queen's thoughts began to invade mine and in turn, I had access to hers." I shuddered at the memory, the icy steel touch of her alien mind sliding across mine, bringing revulsion and terror, my mind screaming in horror at what I saw, what I felt. "The Shadow Queen isn't much on names, but Black Eyes is an important spy in her network, one she trusts and who is in constant contact with her." How that was possible, I don't know, but a pang of nausea pierced me at the thought, and just when I thought Madrigal couldn't get any whiter, she practically blended in with the sheets. "Thanks to Wendiver, the Shadow Queen now can successfully attack Til Mathgen . . ."

"That's not possible!" yelled Madrigal. "The lightgems will keep her at bay."

"Not really getting the whole conspiracy thing, are you?" I replied, feeling heartsick. "Somehow, the former eyes and ears learned about the vulnerability in the lightgem network." I turned to Madrigal. "Remember? Mr. Velvety Smooth Voice, the shadowspy I bet, said his allies will strike soon and that the only way they could have a hope for success is to take out the network. I saw it in the holy fire, the power of the lightgem network is dependent on the power from Mt. Ideldhorde. I'll bet you a bright scorch that the

Queen knows it now, too. It's only a matter of time before she musters the power to neutralize Mt. Idelhorde and I'm guessing soon after that the gems will run out of juice." I gave a mental shudder at the cold satisfaction of her intent and her icy resolve.

Surt stood suddenly and the heat of his anger that blazed from his red and black skin would've crisped my hair if I had any. The fiery pits of his eyes were focused on a point far, far away. "She must be stopped."

"How long will the lightgem network last without Idelhorde?" The golem's great head bowed. "Not long, a few hours at most."

I sighed. By my calculation, we had a couple days until dawn. It looked like it was time to earn some saddle sores.

TWELVE

Am I popular or what?

WHEN I WORKED FOR THE BSI, the most precious thing (other than my family) was time off. As an agent I was on call 24/7 to combat the monsters that lurk in our imaginations and under the bed, to keep them from eating John Q. Public as an *hors d'oeuvres*. Considering the forty percent mortality rate, it was a bloody miracle I lasted for ten years. Considering the bullshit I had to put up with as director from politicos after the governments of the world announced the existence of the supernatural, it was a greater miracle that I hadn't blown my fucking head off.

Thanks to Jeanie. And Des.

Nighttime is a shitty time to become maudlin and dwell on the glory days of youth, especially when your butt is planted on a great, big lizard horse in the middle of a battalion of men and giants doing their level best to hit the fifty-mile mark in less than nine hours.

One hundred elite Shadowfighters with lightgem spears and four-hundred giants of various types, predominately ogres with a few Hill, Mountain, and Deep Giants thrown in for good measure. The largest assemblage of giantkin that had been able to be fielded on short notice, and still enough to make my balls want to shrivel up and hide for a few years. The looks most of the ogres threw my way did nothing to ease the feeling.

If you want to terror to run up and own your back on little mousie feets, stare at a couple hundred ogres in heavy plate mail carrying clubs and swords the size of red oak saplings, all marching in formation and making the ground tremble under your feet. You get religious pretty fucking quick.

As for the rest of the giants, they also bore an assemblage of weapons ranging from clubs to maces to swords, but no armor. My guess was, since they towered over even the ogres, wearing plate or chain fit to their size reached a point of diminishing returns in the area of weight and cost.

The Shadowfighters' spears blazed in the dark, providing enough light to chase away the boldest of shadow monsters, but did little to alleviate the blistering cold the pierced my heavy leather and wool jacket. Hundreds of breath plumes dusted the air as we marched north at a lizard horse's (called choggs, but I liked lizard horse better) killing, butt bruising pace.

With such display of giantkin and human might, it was easy to see why there were so few enemies outside the Empire willing to take them on. The lands south of the Outs, creatively called the Southern Marches, or Southlands, was divided up into a few city states that were largely ignored by the shadows, as all their attention was saved for Surete. The Southlanders were too busy squabbling among themselves to bother the Empire much, and even further south of them was the Twilight Realm where only the hardiest lived, a small nation occupied with survival and keeping to themselves.

Gone was the worry about the Splinter of shadows coming for Madrigal, as now the threat was far graver than mere assassin monsters. Technically, my mission was over.

Before I left the enormous palace, Surt had looked at me with his fumarole eyes and said, "Events have overshadowed your oath to me, Kalevi Hakala. This is not your fight."

I shook my head and replied, "Maybe it's a matter of pride. Or maybe I feel a little guilty about Rafa. He came from Midgard chasing me, after all." Once I realized he was a Magician with some serious money and clout backing the Apostles, it was easy to figure that he could easily gain access to one or more of the known, closely guarded Sidhe pathways. The only thing that puzzled me was how he knew how to use them, because even Alex hadn't untangled that Gordian Knot of magic and he's practically the smartest person on the planet. "Either way, I promised to do a job and who knows, maybe the Splinter is still after Madrigal."

A musical 'hmm' was his only reply.

Making a show of checking the Lahti and my bowie, I said, "Answer me this: isn't there some way to, uh, rig up a capacitor or something to harness the power of the holy flame so it can power the lightgem network for . . . uh, ever."

An orchestra answered me, a deafening blast of music that almost blew me out of my socks. Surt was *laughing*. I waited patiently until he finished and my eardrums healed.

"Oh, I am so sorry," he chimed. "I mean no disrespect." The mirth devolved into wind chime chuckling. "The holy flame is not a true flame and the energies of the Tree are far too intense to harness in such a way. Imagine lighting a candle by throwing it into the heart of the sun. I do not have the knowledge or ability to create a buffering device to harness this power. Believe me, Kalevi Hakala, I have studied this riddle for centuries."

I had to ask.

Snow landed on my hand, a small flake the size of a pin head. I looked up, squinting against the lightgems all around.

"The snow is late," said Madrigal from where she sat astride her lizard horse a few feet away. Next to her marched an ogre woman named Elegat who stared at me like pit bull staring at filet mignon. Ten feet of gray muscle and enormous breasts enclosed in plate, she scared me more than Duul had, and even though Surt made the ogres foreswear the wargild against me until the threat had passed, I wasn't about to trust an ogre to not to 'accidently' bash my brains in.

Behind us a team of twenty lizard horses pulled a twenty-foot, lightgem studded, coffin-like wain made of thick wood and plated with iron, trundling the giant contraption along at a good clip. Great wheels a few inches taller than my own six-three held the slab-like box on axles that groaned alarmingly at every bump on the wide road. Every now and again, a Mountain Giant, a near twenty-foot monstrosity with pebbly skin and hair blacker than sin, would push the wain for a bit, giving the lizard horses a few minutes of respite. Whatever was in there obviously weighed a few tons and it itched my curiosity bump something fierce, but no matter how many times I asked Madrigal wouldn't spill with the info, merely saying that it was important for the mission and it was the only wagon allowed on the march. We traveled light, we traveled fast, and we traveled in hopes we could stop the Shadow Queen.

"Hey, Madrigal. We're heading to the mountain, right? The Knuckle of the World?"

Emerald eyes narrowed. "You know we are."

I flashed thumb at the wain. "How are we going to get that," then I pointed north, "up there?"

She nodded. "Ah. We won't have to. Just have to get close enough."

"Mind telling me—"

"No."

Ah. Okay.

I adjusted my wool cap that protected my chrome dome and pulled my eyes away from hers, pretending not to be disconcerted by Elegat's unnerving stare which was mirrored by the rest of the ogres. Eventually my peepers settled on the flanged mace that had replaced the scissor at the end of my steel forearm cap. While the scissor had been nice and slicey, walking around with a few inches of razor sharp blade like that invited accidents, so I had swapped it out for a three-pound mace head. Heavy and tiring to swing, it would give an ogre pause and that suited me fine.

A heavy, musky smell intruded and a voice deeper than the Mariana's Trench rumbled, "You killed Duul of the Val-Tuul giant-kin, yes?"

If I had hair it would've stood straight up as I turned to crane my head back to meet the eyes of the largest ogre I'd ever seen. Thirteen feet of steel-clad monstrosity stared at me with slate eyes. "Yes?" I replied, angry at myself that it came out a question rather than a bold statement, but the dude's tusks looked like they'd send Tars Tarkas into hysterics.

He pondered me for a moment, easily keeping pace with the lizard horse. "A duel, yes?"

I nodded. "Sure."

"Hmmm." A fingernail thick as a silver dollar ran up and down a tusk as he regarded me. "He die well?"

I will not freak out. I will not freak out. "Does anyone really die well?"

He waited.

And waited some more. Still staring. I grew uncomfortable enough to finally say, "He acquitted himself well."

"Hmmm." Then, "I am Xorix'c." He pronounced it as if the name had a few extra esses at the end. "Of the Val-Tuul giantkin."

Okay. I nodded. Same clan as Duul. I tensed.

"I will not hold wargild against you."

The breath I didn't know I'd been holding whooshed out. From behind Elegat guffawed, a deep basso belch of sound. "Thank you," I replied near breathlessly.

"I felt him die," Xorix'c continued. "I saw his last image of you through the bond all ogres share. You took no delight in killing him. There was very little expression on your face at all. It was as if you were completing a long labor you did not care for."

A little honesty was called for. "Some creatures I hate, some I don't. I didn't hate Duul, but he wanted to duel and I wasn't going to, ah, feck around with him about it." I pulled my eyes away from Xorix'c's and saw that at least ten ogres hand marched in close to listen to the conversation, expressions ranging from hate to thoughtful consideration. My digestive system suddenly felt like it wanted to run away screaming and my bladder felt hot and full. Ye gods!

It took a while, me on the lizard horse being stared at by a group of giantkin that could crush me without raising a sweat, but Xorix'c finally said, "As I thought. Great Surt said you were damaged, but honorable. A human of your word."

"Damaged?"

He tapped his temple. "Said you were torn from your clan, that your mate is dead after a life of war against the enemies of your people. Hmm." Xorix'c shook his head. "To lose one's clan is the worst pain of all and though you have killed one of ours, it was a duel. For these reasons the Val-Tuul giantkin will not hold wargild against you. I have said this, so it will be."

Xorix'c looked around and none of the other ogres would meet his gaze. I felt an enormous surge of relief. "Thank you. It's good to know I don't have to guard my back against ogres anymore."

"Oh, not so," came the rumbly reply. "Only the Val-Tuul. There are still several other clans that will call wargild on you. Especially the Lat-Korin clan. They are real assholes."

Fucking perfect.

I could feel Madrigal staring a hole in me, her, and Elegat, and it itched. "What?" I snapped.

Elegat continued the staring contest while Madrigal hid a smile. "Nothing," she said.

Great. Just fucking perfect.

"What exactly is a Twilighter?" I asked to carry the conversation in a different direction. I half knew the answer but I needed to be far away from things like wargilds and dead Kalevi Hakalas.

"A person from the Twilight Realm, which a mostly human kingdom to the far south," she replied, knowing exactly what I was trying to do. "Beyond the Southern Marches, at the bottom of the world where the sun barely peeks over the horizon. It never sets, but it is never full day. Hence the name, Twilight Realm. I called it home until ten years ago when I decided to travel to see what Surete could offer." A small sad smile lit her long face. "I do miss the lakes."

The sun never sets? That must mean that the planet did not experience seasons like Earth, that it didn't tilt much on its axis. If the sun was out, albeit barely, it must've provided pretty good protection from shadows. I asked her about it.

"Yes, it does," Madrigal affirmed. "Yet the Realm is not as . . . sophisticated as Surete. They have many beliefs that you would think barbaric."

"And they are?"

"Too long to list before we get to Idelhorde."

Her tone told me to shut the fuck up and spin, so I let an uncomfortable silence reign. That is until The Tilwhar rode up.

Of all the humans in the brigade, The Tilwhar (no, I don't know why she was called that, she didn't bother to tell me) scared me shitless. Tall and skinny, she had shaved head with a crazy collection of blue tattoos on her scalp that looked like they were designed by a spider on acid. Whorly and thin, the lines cross-crossed the top of her skull, dropped down her forehead and circled her left eye. Worked into the lines were tiny black runes of such complexity they hurt to look at and if I tried, I found my stomach fluttering with nausea. She nestled into the folds of a great brown robe that covered her from head to toe and added bulk to her tall form.

Apparently, wizards were as rare on Muspelheim as they were in Midgard, which is to say you have a better chance meeting an honest politician than a spell slinger, and this one had been attached to the battalion to assist.

"Is it me or am I just popular?" I pitched my voice enough carry over the clangor of marching bodies, but low enough that only Madrigal could hear.

"Your story has spread quickly," she replied. "Outlander, slave, savior, wizard. The last is what probably intrigues her."

I glanced over to where The Tilwhar was staring at me with her pale blue eyes. Lord save me from rumors.

"Wizard!" The Tilwhar cried suddenly. I tried not to jump out of my skin. "I would speak with you."

Good gravy. "So, speak," I hollered back.

"Come away. My words are not for the uninitiated."

You know, after the news broke about the supernatural world and magic and shit, Magicians on my world became a commodity, new celebrities for a jaded populace hungry for the unique and unusual. That inflated egos to Olympian proportions and looking at The Tilwhar, I could see the same careening arrogance that infected the magic users of Midgard. It pissed me off to no end back then and it sure as hell irritated me smooth the fuck out right now, I really wasn't in the goddamn mood. But it wouldn't do me any good to anger someone who could theoretically turn me into a newt if she had a mind to. How to find a happy middle here . . .

"Too bad."

Nailed it.

The Tilwhar flushed crimson in the yellow light of the gems, but she held her temper. "Is it your arrogance or your fear that drives you?" she asked tightly.

"Call it a bit of both." I kept my eyes straight ahead, although I could see Madrigal and Elegat suppressing grins. Popular lady was The Tilwhar.

"I see your power, which is considerable," she continued as if I'd never spoken. "But it's untrained, barely under your control. You're like a child playing with a sword, and you're going to get hurt." A significant pause. "Unless you find a master to apprentice to, and then you have a good chance to survive."

"Let me guess, you think I should apprentice to you?"

She spread her hands, her cloak fluttering in the wind. "Do you see any other wizards around?"

"No offense, Your The Tilwhar-ness," that nearly tripped up my tongue, "but once we're done doing what needs done, I am so far gone I'll be a distant memory before the new day dawns."

That set her back on her lizard horse and the look she gave me said volumes about my truthfulness. "Fine," she said stiffly. "Spurn me at your peril. You may think that living to your middle years lends you some discipline over your body, but magical talent isn't part of your body. The lust to use magic will seep through your mind like a pervasive rot until you start casting spells in your sleep." The Tilwhar let out a soft snort. "Then you will understand the true danger of magic and feel regretful for not accepting my generous offer."

That I could believe, but, "Sorry, but I won't be long enough on this world to suffer like that."

One last hard look and The Tilwhar sawed mercilessly at her lizard horse, drawing it through the crowd of marching bodies.

"Always making friends," Madrigal said wryly.

I nodded. "It's a skill."

"You shouldn't have told her you're leaving this world. She thinks you're lying, making sport of her and she won't take it well. Wizards don't like to look like fools."

"Oh, like I do?"

She snorted back laughter, but Elegat didn't bother, sounding like a tuba mating call. "Just don't get into a spell spitting contest with that one," Madrigal chuckled.

A cold knot slid down my throat. "I doubt she'll try anything before we get to the mountain. We're out here lighting up the night with a few hundred lightgems, a marching target the shadows can't miss or pass up." I nodded to the black beyond the light. "Every human and giantkin will be needed." After the Knuckle, however . . .

Madrigal tipped me a small nod in understanding.

"Elegat," I said. "Have you declared wargild on me?"

The ogre woman blinked. "Does it matter?"

"It matters to me."

A bark of laughter answered me, then, "I don't care for wargilds, or what you humans call vendettas. They waste time and lives." She shook her large, gray head. "I believe in the good fight, in revenge and a good fuck, in whatever order they may come or all at once."

Wasn't that a thought?

A long, warbly cry split the night, floating on the air, terror given sound.

THIRTEEN

Teeth . . . more than I can count

A S ONE, GIANTKIN AND HUMAN WARRIORS readied weapons, faces set into hard lines while I lifted my mace and wondered what fresh hell had decided to introduce itself into my life.

The warbling cry came again and someone shouted, "To the east!"

A giant cried, "No, to the west!"

They were both wrong and both right. "We're surrounded," I yelled, putting decades of authority into my voice. Elegat raised an eyebrow while Madrigal nodded. Glowing spears lowered and lizard horses champed and stamped their great claws. Once again wails sounded from all around.

Something about that caterwauling hit my memory bump and sheer horror flooded me. I'd heard that sound before about fifteen years ago on a spread outside Scottsbluff, Nebraska. Images came of teeth and flashing bodies, agents dying in gunfire, spells lighting up the night, illuminating scabrous toady bodies containing muscles like steel cables and eyes soulless as black holes. "Kobolds!"

Apparently, some sharp cookie among the humans had recognized the sounds as well, because an order rang out over the noise and the Shadowfighters dismounted as one, urging the lizard horses outside the protection of the battalion toward the midline between light and dark. All this happened as I rode to the wain and leapt out of the saddle, my good hand snagging the brake beam, and hauled myself up into the driver's box and from there to the roof. Whatever lay inside was large enough that I had plenty of room to maneuver and a hell of a view of what was going on. A moment later Madrigal joined me, her movements as graceful as a hummingbird in flight.

"Why are they shooing the . . . ah . . . chogg out into the open?" I asked of the wailing of kobolds that sounded like live cats being fed into a wood chipper. Commands were given and the lizard horses, trained to obedience, stayed in the no-man's land between the battalion and the darkness that hid the kobolds. They champed at their bits and pawed at the ground with taloned feet, but remained there.

The answer added to the leaden fear that lay heavy in my gut. "To slow them down."

A hundred feet out from where the light failed and the darkness emerged victorious, thousands of glowing green points of light came into view, hovering close to the ground from all sides of the battalion. They stayed there for a few moments suspended above the snow as flakes of white fell upon the giantkin and humans who waited with weapons ready. From what I understood about the shadows and all things shadowy, the Queen's servants could move from one darkness to the next, no matter where they were in the world. That give her one hell of a range for troop movement.

Nolis Tegg, commander of the 3rd Spear of the 5th Infantry, 2nd Army of Surete, a grizzled, hard man who held the rank Spear Leader Major (equivalent to Lt. Colonel as far as I could tell) shouted, "Hold!" in a whip-crack voice.

We waited. I noticed dozens upon dozens of crossbows at the ready. The giantkin held ballistae in their hands, bolt throwers so big I doubt I could have moved one, much less picked one up.

"Hold."

I could feel the terror lumping in my throat threatening to choke me.

"Hold."

More dots of light appeared until we were looking at thousands.

The noise suddenly died, and all I could hear was the sound of my heartbeat and the fearful whinnying of the lizard horses milling in the kill zone, between us and razor teeth. The moment stretched to its snapping point.

A wave of darkness swept forward, thousands of bodies leaping into the light that reflected off their dead black eyes. Kobolds of every size and shape, from teeny tiny ones the size of Pekinese to the size of my former adversary Gortt, which is to say about the size of a ten-year-old. Normal for a kobold.

Shark teeth flashed and lizard horses *screamed*. Not like horses, but like rabbits hit hard with a rock, a high-pitched wail that put to shame every scream queen every horror movie you'd care to name. Jamie Lee Curtis included.

Blood flew as toad-colored bodies covered the maddened lizard horses from sight and great big chunks of scaly meat flowed down thousands of throats. Soon there was a circle of churning, hungry bodies in the kill zone and not a lizard horse in sight, only the squirming kobolds as they all tried to feed, more and more flooding in to fight for scraps, building a circle of flesh taller than a man. Some lizard horses were able to fight back, crushing and slashing at the toady bodies, but soon even the largest of them were overwhelmed by the tide.

"Loose!"

Dozens of crossbows twanged, sending bolts flying into the press of kobold bodies, many passing straight through to pierce the ones beneath and behind, causing black blood to fly. Hundreds of kobolds died in the first few seconds, but thousands more kept joining the press of bodies, grabbing the newly dead and tearing out great hunks with their triangular, gleaming teeth.

Did I forget to mention that kobolds are cannibals as well? During this time the ogres had stepped in unison toward the circle of churning bodies, massive tower shields at the ready. More bolts flashed past the line of ogres, big ones the size of spears with wicked, chisel heads tearing through a dozen little skinks in one go, and drawing some attention. As one, the ring of ogres planted their shields and braced.

Suddenly, thousands of beady little eyes turned our way.

Oh shit.

Like a cresting wave, the horde of kobolds flowed toward us, a dark tide of knife-toothed death that sent icy dread down my spine. Each kobold jumped like their muscles were made of rubber bands, propelling them in great bounds as they ate up the distance between our forces.

"Jesus Christ!" I blasphemed, in awe and fear.

Then the ogres got into the fight.

With an ear-splitting *Ooo-uuungh!* and the discipline of Roman Legionnaires, they waited for impact, their six-foot shields a wall of steel and wood surrounding the battalion, the giants at their back and the Shadowfighters providing the core, protecting the wain.

The kobolds collided against the shield wall with a deafening clangor, the ogres setting shoulders firm and holding, not backing up a step. Legs braced, the great brutes held the line as the kobolds began to pile up higher and higher, climbing shields in an effort to sink their teeth into the gray flesh of the ogres, only to be met by the clubs, swords and spears wielded by enraged giant-kin, who set to their task with fierce determination and strength. I saw a Mountain Giant wielding a spear as large as a flagpole easily stab over the wall and pierce six kobolds at once. She shook the great spear and the bodies were flung off in a welter of black blood and gore.

One kobold flew through the air, bouncing over the bodies of its brethren only to be met with a giant's club that rendered it into dark paste. Another bounded over an ogre, pushing hard against a shield and slipping like a greased weasel past the giants, leaping toward Shadowfighters only to be impaled on a pair of glowing spears, leaf shaped blades sliding effortlessly into toady flesh.

A voice like a rumble at the end of the world yelled, "Back!"

As one, the ogres took a step back, the dead kobolds filling the space between the buildup of corpses and the shield wall met with more clubs and swords. Black blood flowed in rivers past the boots of the giantkin, slowly turning into dark slush on the freezing ground.

An ogre fell and a hundred screaming kobolds broke through the gap before a Hill Giant, gnarled bark-like skin almost impervious to the snapping teeth, could take the giantkin's place, smashing down with a club fashioned whole cloth from a good-sized tree.

Crossbows twanged and the kobolds that didn't die met the Shadowfighters, who slew the creatures with a smooth economy of motion and the same discipline as the ogres. That boggled my mind some because every ogre I'd met on Midgard was either drunk on slaughter or human blood, and had all the reasoning capability of a rabid pit bull. Now I looked at them and realized that what came to my world must've been damaged, driven mad by their unintended voyage from the Outs and separation from their clans. Here, they were magnificent soldiers wreaking death on creatures with the social skills of attacking piranha.

I spun around, looking at the battlefield, analyzing, assessing. I may be a sarcastic ass who has poor impulse control sometimes, but I'm also a veteran of the most brutal profession Midgard had ever produced and even survived the arena of politics relatively unscathed. This was my element, this was candy.

More kobolds came in, piling higher and higher, climbing over each other like army ants trying to breach the giantkin ranks. A thousand, two thousand, perhaps three thousand were dead, but the living outnumbered the corpses and they kept fucking coming.

"This isn't like kobolds." I hollered over the din of battle.

Madrigal turned my way. "What?"

I pointed at the press of little bodies. "Kobolds are smart, they attack when they have the advantage and do so with cunning. This is straight out slaughter, pitched battle with no thought of survival. Something is forcing them on." It clicked then. "They're not here to win, they're here to slow us down."

An ogre fell under the titanic weight of bodies and was covered, torn to the bone by teeth sharper than chefs' knives. Her place was taken by a Mountain Giant, basalt skin slick with kobold blood, a spar of stone in one massive hand flattening dozens with each blow, spattering offal high in the air.

"Back!"

The ring shrank once again, more kobolds falling from the heights of the new wall of bodies. Giant clubs smashed down over ogre shields, pasting the enemy.

"Too many," I said over the shrieks of enraged midgets. "There are just too many kobolds. The line's not going to hold if we keep fighting like this."

"Watch then, wizard. This is where I come in." The Tilwhar walked past me to face the roaring, seething mass of monstrous appetite.

I hadn't even seen her arrive, but I kept my eye on her now as she raised her hands, long wands of some dark colored wood held in each.

"This is why you need a master. I will show you how to win with a single spell." With that she began to scribble in the air, trailing light from each fingertip, creating looping whorls that confused my eyes and lit the air brighter than the gems that were mounted on the wain. I saw a Shadowfighter, a lean woman with large shoulders, look up and blanch, her face spasming in sudden nausea, fear of the wizard overcoming fear of the ravening horde a few yards away.

Those glowing patterns hung suspended in the air for a few moments, humming with dread potential before flying toward the kobold horde faster than my eyes could follow, disappearing into a pile of bodies ten yards from the shield wall.

White light so bright it burned red afterimages into my eyes flashed. There was no sound, no concussive detonation, just flesh and bone and blood exploding from the point of impact, the pressure wave lifting ten ogres from the shield wall and flinging them back a dozen feet, flinging the dead and living around like tenpins. Kobolds who'd been rushing the line were torn apart by the silent blast, rendered into chunks of meat no larger than my fist while the ogres not bowled over by the blast staggered back a few feet, boots scrambling for purchase on earth turned into bloody mud. Our circle of defense was now a C shaped mess as men, kobolds, and giantkin tried to absorb the enormity of what just happened. Silence and confusion reigned.

"Oh, no," I moaned in horror.

"See!" cried The Tilwhar in triumph. "See what a real wizard can do?"

"You idiot!" Madrigal raged, her lean, handsome face twisted in fury. "You bloody, thickheaded, stubborn idiot! The kobolds are more afraid of what's out there in the darkness than the power of your magic!"

It took a second, but The Tilwhar got it and her eyes widened in anger and alarm.

The moment on the battlefield stretched for an eternal second as the shocked combatants stared at the massive hole in the shield wall, until the kobolds rushed the breach, bounding like manic wolverines toward the soft, juicy center of our formation. Within moments they met the spears of the Shadowfighters, hundreds of kobolds chomping for the much weaker human center before the giantkin could seal the breach.

Spears flashed and kobolds died, pierced through while others piled on, until the leather clad defenders were nearly overwhelmed with bodies, spears fouled in the guts of their enemies. Swords were drawn as the Shadowfighters began to battle in earnest while a pair of Hill Giants waded in with their great clubs.

A little kobold the size of a five-year-old jumped up to wain as

The Tilwhar's eyes bugged out in disbelief, heedless of the frenzied engine of death that made to pounce on her back.

My mace hand whipped around and the flanged head smashed down, taking the skink between the eyes and sending a sharp ache up my arm. Not having a wrist meant that it couldn't mitigate some of the impact my arm felt and I knew this battle would render my arm a wreck, but better one limb than the rest of me. As for the kobold, he fared far worse, hitting the deck with a resounding thud.

By the time I tore my eyes away from the twitching wretch at my feet, the ogre line had retreated another step and more giant-kin had been put down, throats torn out and limbs bitten through. And still the kobolds came, like an army driven by one will, one desire . . . to consume everything in its path.

A thought teased at the back of my head, buffeted by the clamor of flesh on steel, the howls of the wounded and the gnash of teeth on bone. The rank smell of kobold blood, a mixture of turpentine and shit, threatened to drive all thought from my head, but I concentrated, separating, then dismissing everything irrelevant except the concept that struggled in my mental grasp.

What was it? What was I missing? The concept slowly resolved, too slow by half.

Almost absently I watched Madrigal impale a leaping kobold on a dagger glowing with yellow light, the gem in its pommel a radiant point that almost left me hypnotized.

Oh . . . *shit!*

"Stay clear!" I yelled to the two women. Madrigal tossed me a terse nod while The Tilwhar scowled.

Kobolds weren't army ants. Every single damn one of them I'd ever met were not only smart, but possessed the low cunning of a sewer rat. They didn't work in large mobs, they hunted in small packs.

What the fuck were so many doing here? Why were they attacking like this? I knew they were trying to slow us down, but what for? Who for? The answer lay bright in my mind and I felt a furious desire to do some harm.

"In this universe, young man, spells are a matter of will, not of spell shapes." Surt's words rang in my mind. Will, not shapes. Will I had plenty, so I decided to see what's what.

Focusing on a point beyond the light of the gems where the darkness reigned absolute, I *willed* power to come to me, willed it to be what I wanted, shaped as I wanted it to be shaped. The answering rush of power that flooded my consciousness swept through me sweeter than the relief of pain, more satisfying than an orgasm. I thrust my desire out into the dark, feeling the power drain from my body like water from a colander as it brought me to my knees, but the energy released came into being in form of a bolt of fire thirty feet long and a foot thick, that traveled from my hand to the darkness beyond the lightgems.

The bolt of blue/white fire fled into the night, slamming into the frozen earth with a clap of thunder and explosion that sent flames in all directions, illuminating a scene from my worst nightmares.

Packed thick in the light were shadows, razor-edged beings of every shape and size, obsidian creatures that oozed darkness. A thing like a black crab made entirely of right angles blew apart in the explosion, sending ebony shrapnel into other shadows packed cheek to jowl in the darkness, with hundreds of kobolds in-between. Little toady bodies were shredded by my bolt, blood spattering all around. In the aftermath of my magic, as the world swum in front of my eyes as if I'd had too many shots at a local bar, I saw a shadow larger than the others, twice the size of its brethren, a humanoid creature of black despair and cold void that stood tall like a colossus, a general on a battlefield.

Still on my knees I grabbed The Tilwhar's thick robe and pointed at the massive shadow looming over the others, unconcerned in the light of burning grass and bodies. "There!" I screamed. "Use your magic *there!*"

Arrogant as The Tilwhar might've been, she got moving when there was a fire under her butt, drawing runes of light in the air at dizzying speeds until you couldn't figure where the sigils began or ended.

"Volosh!" yelled The Tilwhar, spreading her arms wide.

The gaggle of runes, at least a dozen two-foot diameter eye bending cat's cradle of light, swirled toward the giant shadow at speed and hit it square in the chest, illuminating the black, jagged form for an instant before exploding like a grenade with a deafening roar. The shadow jerked, shuddered, and fell with a ground rattling thud I could feel all the way through the wheels of the wain.

A hot wind washed over the battlefield, wind and light like the burning of a thousand magnesium flares set the shadows screeching, a high-pitched sound like rusty nails scraping against a sheet metal roof. The sound entered my ear like an ice pick, stabbing deep and hard, bringing tears to my eyes and a clutch of pain to my chest that made me want to vomit my guts out.

The battalion cringed as the sound went on, humans putting their hands on their ears, giantkin shaking their heads madly as if trying to fling the noise out like droplets of water. It went on and on, and even the biggest hard asses in the group were crying out loud in pain and despair, because the sound carried with it a wealth of fear and anger and most of all hopelessness, that reached to such depths as to beggar the soul.

Despite the bone shattering howling, despite the pain that threatened the foundations of our minds, despite the horror of thousands of shadows still in dark, The Tilwhar still drew whorls of light in the air, sending those runes out into the dark in every direction. Explosions rocked the night, sending shadows flying, tearing them into shards and fragments of black that lay scattered across the frigid earth.

And then they were gone . . . the shadows melted into the dark as if dissipating into inky smoke, leaving nothing behind but mewling, milling kobolds who had enough sense to run now that their masters no longer prodded them into conflict. Like startled jack-rabbits they bounded away, not even giving voice to their horrid wailing until only the dead were left behind.

NOLIS TEGG WALKED AHEAD OF US, his spear held high with the lightgem dispelling the dark for many yards, encasing us in illuminated safety of a sort. I trailed a couple of yards behind with Madrigal by my side and a dozen Shadowfighters and ogres behind us, ready to do some pokey damage should any shadows choose to brave the light.

Far behind us the battalion bustled with activity as mountain and Hill Giants used their prodigious strength to tear at the frozen earth to bury the dead. Fifty-six ogres, fifteen humans and one Hill Giant lay at rest, victims of shining teeth backed by an insatiable appetite, the butcher's bill a high one considering the lack of reinforcements on our time-sensitive mission. There was talk about leaving the dead to rot despite the urgency. They deserved more respect than that.

"There," said Tegg, pointing with his spear at a large form lying all by its lonesome in the muddled snow. "The big shadow." He tossed me a look I couldn't quite identify. "Tell me again why we have to brave the night to find a dead shadow?"

My answer caused my companions to suck in a startled breath. "Since when do shadows leave behind bodies?"

Cold, alien memories slid through my mind like razors through flesh. Shadows only had substance when alive, and when dead, they faded like mist in the sunlight. Truth be told, not too many humans or giantkin fought shadows, but it was what these warriors were trained to do, their main purpose.

Tegg swore, "Damn me for a ball-less idiot, you're right."

We approached the large shadow slowly, carefully as if it were an IED ready to blow. Shadows reacted to light like skin reacted to acid, the stronger the light, the stronger the effect, and Tegg's lightgem was pretty fucking strong. But the black form remained still, the dark substance of it refusing to dissolve as it entered into the heart of the sphere of radiance.

It was a giant. Bald as a cue ball, skin drinking in the light so details were hard to see, but obvious nonetheless. Fifteen feet tall at least and muscled like a weightlifter, the giant's large features were unmistakable in the light, as were the voids where its eyes had once been.

One of the ogres, Elegat, tromped to the body. "Feck!" she swore. "This ain't possible! Giantkin don't become shadows!" There was an edge of ogre-y hysteria to her voice. "No matter how many times they get shadowbit, the infection never, *never*, spreads." She stepped back as if the shadowtaint was catching. "In all of time such a thing has never happened, so why does it happen now?"

An icy lump the size of a softball lodged in my throat and I couldn't reply, couldn't get the words past the obstruction because the fear wouldn't let me. Madrigal looked at me, *into* me, seeing the dread the crept through my bones, but she kept her trap shut as I stared at the tainted gaintkin.

"Mountain Giant, or I'm a chogg," said Commander Tegg as the rest of the Shadowfighters took position around the corpse. "Elegat's right, giantkin aren't susceptible to shadowpoison like us humans." He shook his head, turning to Madrigal. "This is wrong, Madrigal. Have you ever seen the like?"

"No." The word landed between us with an almost audible clank.

"Is this some sort of new weapon? Have the shadows developed a magic that can subdue giantkin?"

Part of me was praying that The Tilwhar wasn't unconscious back at the wain, being tended by a Shadowfighter medic after the amazing display of sorcery that left her drained and unconscious. I wished she was here with me, with us, to explain what was happening, but that duty now rested on my shoulders because I knew in my heart what had happened, what had tainted this Mountain Giant, and I didn't want to dirty my companions' ears with the knowledge.

Thanks to my glimpse into the mind of the Shadow Queen and the sip from Mimisbrunnr, I had a damn good idea of what had laid this giant low, and it scared me more than facing a rampaging troll because a troll can only kill you, squish you flat and snack on your bones. An easier death that what this giant faced.

"She's here," I said.

Madrigal blanched. Yeah, she got it right away. No doubt she was feeling the same nausea that clawed at my guts.

Tegg spun to me, eyes wide, falling back on a warrior's habitual anger at things he couldn't control. "Who? Who's here?"

"The only thing with venom strong enough to take down a giant," I replied woodenly. The lump in my throat hurt like the blazes, but I forced the words past. "It's the Shadow Queen. She did this. This is one of her elite shadow agents, one turned personally by her, which means she's close."

My eyes felt like they were filled with ashes. "We might be too late."

FOURTEEN

I really, really hate my job sometimes

THE TILWHAR'S SKIN LAY THIN ON HER BONES like a layer of wet paper that hid little underneath. Every line, every wrinkle stood out in stark relief within the buttery light of the gems carried by every warrior and decked on all the surfaces of the wain, including the roof. This was where I stood with Madrigal as the giantkin took turns pushing and the surviving twenty lizard horses strained mightily.

I could tell the Shadowfighters missed their mounts fiercely by the sullen faces they wore beneath their leather helms, the look of warriors adjusting to a situation completely out of their control. It was a face I'd worn more than once. Good thing the wide road still ran straight and true, allowing us to keep up the steady march without pause.

Madrigal told me that we were close to the Harrowbacks, a mountain range that, according the map she showed me, resembled the Cascades that ran from British Columbia to northern California. Most notably the High Cascades, the part of the range dotted with volcanoes, although where the Cascades ran north-south, the Harrowbacks ran east-west with the Knuckle in the middle.

Apparently, the Knuckle, like the sacred flame in Til Mathgen, carried a special significance to the giantkin (besides being home of the Fire Giants) and had been active for as long as anyone could remember, making it part of the bedrock of their society.

An hour or so ago, the flat valley floor had given way to gentle foothills which were home to the vintners and communities that had sprung up to support them. Lights in the distance marked the locations of the fort communities that shone bright enough to discourage shadows, but if the Shadow Queen had her way, those lights would dim soon enough and all life would be drained to dust.

Could the shadows really destroy the heart of Surete before the sun peeked over the horizon to chase them back into the dark? By the look on my companions' faces, that was a big, fat yes. That made my heart hurt because not only would the Empire fall soon after, but I wasn't too sure that I could make it back to the flame quick enough to use the Tree and get the Hel out of Muspelheim. Or if there would even be a Til Mathget to get back to. Then I couldn't travel to Svartalfheim and prevent that reality from unraveling, which meant the other eight would soon follow.

Wasn't that a fucking thought? Maybe I should've stayed in bed.

Back to my contemplation of The Tilwhar, the arrogant wizard who wanted me to hitch my wagon to hers. Except she wasn't so arrogant anymore lying there in a coma for God knows how long. Too much magic used too quickly had saved our asses but drained her like it had when I cast my first spell and no one, not man or wizard (or both in my case), could tell how long she'd be out. Or if she'd ever awake.

Arrogant, but powerful. She had saved us by killing the giant shadow, but at the cost of losing our only experienced magic slinger. Had to hand it to the Shadow Queen, she knew how to fuck up our day.

I ran a hand over her forehead. Cold, clammy and smooth as glass. It felt like touching a marble statue rather than living flesh and it gave me the creeps. Reflexively, I touched the Lahti tucked into my waistband and the bowie sheathed at my hip. I could cast a spell or two, but it would be wild, undisciplined and I'd probably drain myself quickly as I did before. As it was, I was pretty shagged out from that bolt of fire I'd thrown earlier, but at least I was conscious.

What awaited at the Knuckle? I wondered for the umpteenth time. How would the Shadow Queen cool the fiery heart of an active volcano, and do it in time before the lightgems would dim by sunrise?

"I don't know, Kal."

My head snapped up as I realized I must've spoken aloud. Madrigal stood next to me staring at The Tilwhar as if fascinated. She stroked her chin as she thought. "I have a sister," she said suddenly.

"Oh?"

A nod. "Yes. Younger by two years. Her name is Dolocine and she's beautiful." She took a deep breath through her nose. "The one good thing my pig parents ever produced lives still in the Twilight Realm, happy and safe. For now. She's the reason I fight for Surt, for the Empire. Not for duty or honor or any of a hundred different reasons the eyes and ears might name. For her."

This was getting intense, but I felt she was lancing a boil that had been festering far too long. "The Twilight Realm is beautiful and chilly and the people there are hearty and somber, that is until they start drinking. Before I left some fifteen years ago, my sister confided in me that our father had been . . ." she swallowed hard, "abusing her."

I couldn't speak, spellbound by the narrative that spilled from her lips. An old story, but one that never failed to make me sick to my stomach. After an op in St. Louis where my team each visited their own versions of Hell, Alex's ex, Dove Jacobs, noted in her ops report that she became lost in the intestines of some great beast that shat out a doppelganger of an uncle who had abused her when she was a child. It gutted me then as it gutted me now.

"It was hard for her to confess this to me," continued Madrigal. "Our father was a controlling fecker who ruled the family with vicious cruelty. I suffered the lash more times than I could count and when I reached my majority I left without looking back." She wiped away a tear. "I didn't think about Dolocine, which is a sin that still stains my soul. I was so happy to have escaped that house that I didn't think of anything else but freedom and to find a destiny that didn't include farming.

"A couple of years later, working as a chogg breaker for a drover in Honolgren, a port city on Trallic sea, Dolocine came to visit from the farm. I saw the bruises; I saw the hesitation and I could smell her fear. It must have taken everything she had to run away to find me, but she did. She wanted to escape like I did, but she was still shy of her majority. It didn't take long to winkle the story from her, of our father and his abuses, as Dolocine could never keep anything from me. She wanted me to hide her until her next birthday so legally she couldn't be forced to return to the farm and our father's evil."

I could see the end of this story clearly, as if it had been written down for me. "You killed him," I stated flatly.

"Yes. I rode a chogg nearly to death to reach the farm and confronted both of my parents. My father didn't bother to deny it, he seemed to think it was his prerogative, and my mother, weakling that she was, never tried to stop him."

Madrigal blasted me with green eyes given over to harrowing memories. "Breaking chogg is hard work, Kal, it builds muscle and as a single woman living in the city, I made it my business to find someone who would train me in knife work. To protect myself, you see? A woman needs an edge when on her own, even if it's the edge of a knife. I slit my father's throat before he could defend himself and then did the same to my mother for being a weakling, for not protecting her daughters when she should have." She shivered, but not from the chill in the air. "I set the farm alight, rode back to Honolgren and had my sister move in with me. The authorities chalked the incident up to thieves and I sold my family's land, waited a year for my sister's majority, and then headed for Surete, leaving her with good marriage prospects and the money from the farm. I haven't been back since."

"Why tell me this?" I felt brittle, as if my bones were made of glass. It's easy to blame evil on Supernatural threats, but humans had plenty of their own. A story as old as history.

"If we fail here, I promise to do everything in my power to return you to the holy flame so you can travel to the next world, and save all the worlds. But ours will be lost to shadows, which means giant-kin, humans, even the kobolds will all be dead. I need someone to remember Dolocine for me, to keep her alive in thought, even if it's just a story told on cold night near the Knuckle of the World. Something good must survive all this, and she is the best thing I can think of."

The wain rumbled uphill and the grunt of straining giants came from behind. We were ascending a steeper slope now, through a pass that would slice through the foothills. I rubbed my eyes. "Part of this dilemma is the fault of us Midgardians, you know. Rafa Sari is from my world and an enormous pain in the ass. That's on me, I should have found a way to stop or kill him. I need to finish this and take care of the bastard and his pet sniper Shiana."

We traveled in silence listening to the tramp of boots on stone and the creak of the great wheels on the wain. Above, the stars were blotted out by cloud cover and the light pollution from the gems, but I imagined how they must look up there. The stars, fragments of the Tree.

A little while later, Nolis Tegg boarded the wain, a severe look on his round face. "Wizard Kal," he began. "I think we come to trouble."

Both Madrigal and I looked up sharply. "What? How?" I asked.

The commander pointed north into the darkness. "At the base of Idelhorde is a Fort Devix, First Fort of the Empire. Not the biggest, but the one that guards the pass."

"And?"

"What do you see?"

Beside me Madrigal gasped. I squinted. "I see nothing."

No answer. The commander merely stared at me as if I were an idiot. I stared back until the revelation dawned. I'm slow, but I get there.

"No lightgems."

"No lightgems," he agreed. "The shadows have taken the fort."

FIFTEEN

Up

W HEN THE FORT CAME INTO THE LIGHT it was like looking at the shattered remains of hope. Adobe walls blasted
from their foundations, scattered in chunks for dozens of yards all
around. The central tower, once standing at least forty feet, lay col-
lapsed upon itself, architecture flattened by a vengeful child in fit
of anger. All that set a chill through my guts, but what set my heart
plummeting was the lack of corpses. Not one.

"Christ on a crutch," I breathed, my breath pluming into the air.

"Whatever that means," said Madrigal. "I agree."

We turned away, the sight of the ruined fort a painful one, and
trudged past, putting it in the rear view and contemplating the
mission at hand, dread lending speed to our feet.

The image of the shadowbit giant came to mind. A shadow
that size could take down the fort, but what of its defenders? I
asked Madrigal.

"Maybe they were part of the group that attacked us," she
replied. "Time constraints kept us from canvassing the area."

Time constraints. Right. A race to stop the shadows from doing
. . . what? I still had no clue as to how they would kill a volcano

that had been active for the entire history of the Empire. All I did know from touching the freezing, alien mind of the Queen, was that she'd do anything to make the lightgems fail, so that her forces could shadowtravel to every city and infect the inhabitants with shadowvenom. I touched the black dot at my side. The skin felt smooth and almost hard, as if it had been arrested in transition from normal epidermis to carapace.

"Wizard Kal," rumbled a voice so deep it made my bones ache.

I turned to see a Hill Giant, round face and shaggy hair that reminded me of dead grass, staring at me with loam brown eyes. "Yes?"

The giant pointed at a slew of giantkin that had approached the wain while I'd been woolgathering. "We carry this now. Please get off so you don't get hurt."

What? Oh. I scrambled down the wain, following the driver and followed by Madrigal. Elegat reached up and snagged The Tilwhar, who I hoped would wake soon, but my inner Eeyore told me that wouldn't be likely . . . *sorry, Pooh, I don't think the wizard will be of help* . . . After handing her over to me (she was surprisingly light), I gently set her on the ground.

Damn, Des sure used to love Winnie the Pooh. I blinked away tears.

The driver unhitched the lizard horses and led them off a few yards while four Mountain Giants lifted the wain and six Hill Giants detached its wheels and axles. Six iron rods thicker than my leg were placed in the sockets that held the axles, each much longer than the width of the wain. The Hill Giants knelt as ogres lashed thick hawsers of ropes around the rods and looped them around the giants' necks and shoulders. I knew what was about to happen, but the sight floored me.

The six Hill Giants stood, using their legs and backs to heave the wain from the Mountain Giants' grip, fully supporting the wain themselves. The weight of the wain made the iron rods and the giants groan.

"Madrigal Rhone, wizard Kal, let's go," Nolis Tegg motioned us to follow up the road a bit away from earshot. "The Emperor told me you used to be a military man."

I nodded.

"Good," he continued, staring into the dark toward Idelhorde. "Then you know the need for the chain of command. As a wizard and an agent of Surt I cannot command you, but I cannot have you giving orders during the combat which I know is soon to come."

The words, respectful and polite even, must have hurt to utter. Here was a man worried that his soldiers would suffer, possibly die, if I were to stick my nose into the business of war, and I couldn't blame him one bit. If I were him, I might not be so polite. Nah, I know I wouldn't.

"I have no desire to command a battalion, Nolis, so you don't have to worry." Damn, my thighs felt sore. It sucks getting old. "I'll take care of the magic and the people from my world and leave the rest of it to you."

He grunted and tipped me a nod before stalking off to check on his men.

Madrigal grinned. "I think he likes you."

"Not my type. Too hairy."

We were off the main road now and the footing had become rocky soil, frozen and hard against our boots. Strange fronds like truncated Venus Fly Traps, but blue and stubby, dotted the landscape.

"Funnel trees," said Madrigal when I pointed them out. "They sprout at sunrise and retreat at sundown. In the daylight the carpet the lower slope of Idelhorde in blue."

"Like the twilight trees."

She nodded. "Just so. Most of the trees emerge from the ground during the morning dusk and retreat when it becomes full dark." Her voice grew distant. "Not like the trees of the Twilight Realm that stand tall at all times."

Most of the surviving ogres, slightly less than two-hundred fifty, raised their shields and once again formed a line in front of the Shadowfighters, a wall of steel and muscle against whatever might come, and two lines of defense against anything that might attack from above. Here and there the other giants, Mountain, Hill and Deep, marched in time behind the ogres. None of the larger giantkin carried shields, just their enormous weapons, but their mass was shield enough, as were the several lightgems they carried to shine up the mountainside.

Normally the sight of so many armed ogres and giants would send a flood of yellow down my leg, but what lay ahead and above on Idelhorde was far worse. Like, 'get your soul taken over by an alien being from a dimension so far removed from ours it might as well not exist' kind of worse. I was sure glad the giantkin were on the side of the angels and that I had a wall of meat and metal between me and the shadows.

Behind the giantkin came the Shadowfighters, spears glowing so bright it hurt to look at, and behind them me and Madrigal, who trotted in front of the wain surrounded by the rest of the ogres, in case the shadows tried something sneaky.

I pointed to the wain. "Mind telling me what's in there?"

Was that a hint of smile on Madrigal's face? "This again? I told you, a state secret."

"Sooooo, you're not going to tell me?"

"You're pretty quick for an old guy."

I will not bash her head in, I will not bash her head in. That mantra kept my mind occupied while my thighs began to ache with the climb up Idelhorde. Each step started to hurt more and more, the fire burning deep in my quads, a reminder of my age and of the fact that, while I could jog all day, I hadn't trained for uphill climbing in quite a while. The deep cold of the night seemed to leech energy from my flesh as well, making the trek much harder. Note to self, get in better shape before I die.

Yeah, right. I somehow thought that old age wasn't going to be the death of me.

The burn traveled from my thighs to my chest as my lungs

began to labor. I tasted copper on the back of my tongue as my heart thudded with increasing rapidity. The sweat beading on my forehead almost immediately froze. I had to take three steps, wipe of the sweat slush from my face, take three steeps, pray for a merciful death, three more steps, and curse myself for not exiting this reality for Svartalfheim when I'd had the chance. Take three steps, rinse, repeat.

The way became steeper and the giants carrying the wain began grunt and strain, but they kept up the pace. A little while later they handed off their burden to four of the larger Mountain Giants. These mighty creatures hefted the wain as if it weighed no more than a bicycle and strode confidently up the slope behind us, serene looks on their craggy faces. I guess, being Mountain Giants, they were on their home turf. As for me, the slope was far steeper than I'd anticipated, and yet the footing was solid, as if Idelhorde welcomed visitors if they had the nerve to make the climb. My thighs were twin fires of agony now, my chest hot bellows that felt like they were about to burn to ash at any moment. I spit, my saliva coppery and rank, but I didn't see any blood when my spit hit the ground.

I remembered the day when this would've been an easy afternoon stroll. My legs would be warm and tingly instead of a burning mess of agony, all because the bitter gall of age churned in my stomach. It seemed that the power from Mimisbrunnr and the cleansing transformation of Surturvadunir hadn't been enough to turn back the hands of time and make this a picnic. It should belong to a younger man, one who wasn't huffing and puffing like he was ready blow down a little piggy's house of straw.

"Stop that," panted Madrigal.

I looked up. "What?"

"I can practically feel you feeling sorry for yourself."

"You have the comfort of youth."

"Blow it out your ass, old man."

My laughter startled the group and earned me more than one look that said I was a crazy person.

One foot in front of the other, Kal. You can do this, don't let this place beat you, no matter how tired or old you might be. *I think I can, I think I can, I think I can.* The mantra from *The Little Train That Could* provided enough comfort to keep me going while my body protested, wanting to lie down and nap for the next century or two. That and the fact I wasn't going to give up while Madrigal was watching. No way, no how.

Clangggg!

A rock the size of a basketball hit a shield and the ogre behind it barely lost a step, shrugging the missile off as if were a mosquito. Another bounced into the light, and a Mountain Giant choked up on her massive club and swung for the fences, transforming the rock into so much dust and shrapnel.

"I knew it," grunted Tegg as another, smaller, rock *spanged* of a shield.

Us humans couldn't do much besides march up the slope as more and more missiles bounded down the mountain, only to be deflected by our twin walls of giant muscle. Shields took a pounding, but the giantkin behind them were implacable, shrugging off blows that would have turned Mama Hakala's favorite son into strawberry jam.

We moved another hundred yards up the mountain, taking the brunt of falling rocks . . . some the size of wagon wheels which the larger giantkin took care of, knocking them aside with their great clubs. Before too long, the two lines wound up in a ragged V formation as a wave of boulders descended, thrown down by our enemies above. One ogre fell to a spar of rock that took her through the mouth, punching out the back of her head in a spray of gore. As the line tightened to fill the gap, I walked past her corpse and saw her gray eyes wide in the surprise she must have felt a split second before her death.

An ogre near tip of the V suddenly fell, his head turned into a canoe that spilled brains on the mountainside. The helmet bounced nearby, a hole embedded in the eighth-inch steel, and I couldn't comprehend what I saw until the sharp bark of a report hit my ears.

"Shit!" I swore. "Sniper!"

Commander Tegg looked at me. "What?"

"Stay behind the giantkin," I shouted to Madrigal and the Shadowfighters as another ogre fell shot through the throat. The blood looked impossibly red in the buttery light of the gems.

A small pinpoint of light in the darkness ahead and a Hill Giant fell, shot through the eye. An instant later the sharp crack of a report snapped through the night. We tramped around the body and I saw that the exit hole was as big as a softball.

Damn, a .50 caliber. We were walking straight into the line of fire of a weapon that could cut through armor like soft cheese.

"How many times can she do that?" Madrigal asked, ducking reflexively as another report sounded. She shouldn't have bothered, the bullet traveled faster than the gunshot.

"I have a feeling she came to this world pretty fucking well prepared."

Another ogre fell and more rocks boulders rolled down, only to be diverted or knocked aside. But the shots were coming steady now and almost every one took down a giantkin.

A hundred more yards and the boulders were flying fast, a few making it past the striding ogres, the V formations battered into letters that had no alphabetical equivalent. One of the smaller rocks, about the size of a plum, made it past the ogres and hit a Shadowfighter in her leather breastplate. She fell hard and slid a few feet.

"How much farther?" I asked Madrigal, looking for a flash from Shiana's sniper rifle.

"Idelhorde is not a big mountain, merely the most famous," she replied. "I guess in couple hundred feet, maybe, we'll reach the lip of the caldera."

A couple hundred feet. A lot more dead giantkin.

"Have you no magic to counter this?" Commander Tegg's face was inches from my own. "You're a wizard, right?"

Right. A wizard ... untrained, but still a wizard, an Elementalist. "Tell them to run!" I yelled.

Tegg didn't get it. "What?"

"At this pace we'll lose more than if we charge full out."

"If we run the ogres can't protect the Shadowfighters as well, and their shield wall will be sloppy and full of holes."

Another ogre at the wall fell, brains decorating the ground. I pointed. "That is magic from my world and if we walk, the giantkin will suffer more losses than we can stand. If we run, most of them will make the lip of the caldera alive."

He tossed me a look that told me I was a few fries short of a Happy Meal, but gave the command anyway, his voice whipcracking across the night. The mention of otherworldly magic had sealed my authority.

Immediately the giantkin burst into a fast trot, which for us humans was a pretty strong run that took a punishing toll on my thighs, but I set my will to the sticking place, remembering my nearly lost discipline, and carried on carrying on. Beside me Madrigal began to pant, as the Shadowfighters clattered on in their armor, taking the slope with ease. The real miracle came from behind.

The four Mountain Giants carrying the wain, those fifteen-foot tall behemoths, jogged gamely behind as their enormous burden creaked alarmingly, arms and legs straining, muscles bulging almost obscenely. A bullet hit one of the mountains giants a glancing blow on the arm and it ricocheted off, even the .50 cal not enough to penetrate their stony skin.

Another ogre fell, gurgling blood and letting in a slide of rocks that hit the Shadowfighters like bowling balls, knocking over several to the sound of snapping bones and pained cries. Before the line could close another ogre dropped silently, leaving his brains on the ground. More rocks, more screams, as the Shadowfighters took a pummeling.

The giantkin sped up and the ogres in front raised a bloodcurdling yell that shook the frozen earth, while the Mountain Giants at the wain heaved and bellowed their effort. My thighs were nothing but fire and misery, my old knees starting to splinter with pinpoints of agony while Madrigal puffed, still looking almost fresh compared to how I felt, which was like twenty pounds of dog shit stuffed in a ten-pound sack.

A punch to my chest sent me tumbling, my eyes suddenly watering, blurring, my arms trying to arrest my fall as my breath exploded from my lungs in a fiery rush. Head hit stone instead of earth, the force of it splitting my scalp, and I could feel the hot blood spurt as I bounced down the slope, howling, angry, *defiant*.

Before I could take more than two big bounces a hand the size of an overstuffed recliner plucked me out of the air and set me reeling on my feet, giving me a gentle shove up the hill. I looked up, eyes screwed nearly shut, to see one of the Mountain Giants hauling the wain place his enormous right hand back on the rod and flash me a quick smile. The basalt colored skin around his mouth seemed to fissure like rotten stone before becoming still once more.

"Careful, wizard Kal," he rumbled over the din.

Good advice. My chest felt like hot coals had been shoved under the skin and blood trickled down my scalp, my neck and my back, the wool cap gone. Madrigal reached me as another ogre died, the heavy round first penetrating shield, then skull.

I waved the woman off, trying to regain my stride and composure, but it was so fucking hard to breathe as I stumbled along, giantkin dying all around, shards of rock flying everywhere. The world swum all around and Madrigal's voice stretched low like a record played at slow speed.

Blood and brains splashed me as a Shadowfighter died, spattering Madrigal as well, and the salty, coppery taste hit my tongue. I spat out a shard of bone. But I kept going, still trotting that thigh-killing, chest heaving, sweaty trot that hurt more than it helped, because going back would mean the Shadow Queen would win. She'd rule this world, all life sucked into her greedy gut, and it still wouldn't be enough to satisfy her immense appetite. Going back and entering the holy flame to escape to Svartalfheim would mean I let a Supernatural win and that's something I never let happen in the past and I wouldn't in the future. I gave my word to an honorable person, someone who deserved my respect, someone who wanted to save his world from the darkness.

"Fuck her anyway," I panted, tasting salty sweat on my lips. The world slowly returned to focus, my breath, such as it was, returned.

"What?" Madrigal raised an eyebrow.

"Fuck the Shadow Queen. Fuck her and her entire fucking race." I touched the hot, painful spot on my chest. A rock. It must have been a rock that hit me and knocked me ass over heels down the slope. "Now I'm fucking *mad*."

"About feckin' time, Kal"

Into the light came shadows, a small wave that crashed into the line of ogres, stabbing for exposed flesh with ragged, jagged appendages, whips and claws and stingers of spikey darkness that bit deep into the flesh of the giantkin. Even as blood was drawn, the shadows started to bleed away into vapor in the intense radiance of the lightgems, a shadow kamikaze force of over a hundred that took down at least twenty ogres. One of Deep Giants, black skin rent by dozens of serrated claws, fell to her wounds, dark blood pumping fast, too fast, from a torn throat.

I swung my mace at a shadow that looked a like a cross between a spider and a bat and tore it from the sky. Its wings detached and turned to black mist before they hit the ground and chill swept through my weapon. I looked at my forearm to see the steel sheath covered in deep frost.

Click, click, click went my brain as several bits of data fell into place, echoing loudly in the corridors of my mind.

"Well . . . fuck a duck," I cursed.

Madrigal, still loping beside me, said, "What? What's wrong?"

"I know what she's up to."

And just like that, we made it to the top.

SIXTEEN

Suicide run

IDELHORDE WASN'T VERY BIG AS VOLCANOES WENT. Mt. Shasta is larger and so is Hood and St. Helens, but Idelhorde was an *old* volcano, worn down by rains, extremes of heat and cold and the meanest bastard of them all: time.

We stood on a semi-flat section of ground and by we, I mean what was left of the battalion: less than three hundred giantkin and seventy Shadowfighters, a horrific loss. Panting, my sweat freezing to my clothes, I barely had time to look around before another ogre died, the shot sounding an instant before his body thudded to the ground.

I'd half expected the shot, so my eyes were wide and expectant, and I saw far off to the right the muzzle flash that flared like a star in the night the instant before the giantkin was struck.

Gotcha!

On the trot up the mountain I'd kept thinking about magic, about the will and desire to cast a spell *just so*. A toll was taken whenever I cut loose, and the last time I had felt such a woozy drain that I had to fight to stay awake. Perhaps if I kept it simple, kept the energy output to manageable levels I wouldn't pass out after casting a spell. It seemed that the majority, if not all of Newton's Laws applied in this reality, and I wondered what new laws he would have discovered if he lived here a few years.

Probably all of them.

I made a gun out of my left hand, pointing to where I saw the flash and imagined my favorite scene from Star Trek (KHHHHHAAAAAANNN!!!), letting the rage build, but not too much. Set phasers to devaporate, Spock. I imagined it and it came to be, as a long, pencil thin line of blue/white fire emerged from my pointy finger and shot off into the night, cutting through the dark like a knife for only a second. In the distance I saw ragged, jagged forms scatter. A slight wave of dizziness washed through me. I waited a few more seconds but there were no more shots.

A thin voice filled with fatigue pierced the night. "Wizard Kal!"

My head whipped around and I saw The Tilwhar standing next to Elegat, the ogre supporting her weight. The woman looked wan and tired, but there was a fierce determination and hard resolve carved into her tattooed face.

"This is what a true Master Wizard can do!" she cried, staring hard at me. As Elegat held her under the armpits, she raised hands filled with wands and began to draw.

If the runes she carved into the night earlier had been brutal slashes of light, the new ones hanging in the air were the epitome of grace and beauty, soft lines of green light that made the heart ache to look at. As the seconds passed, the runes slowly revolved and split, multiplying by some magical mitosis into runes which in turn split into more, dancing in the air to some ethereal music only they could hear. In less than twenty seconds hundreds of runes revolved over her head, and with a final flourish she sent them out.

I had half expected explosions or some cool *Star Wars* special effect where the bad guys turn into balls of fire, but instead the runes flashed with unholy speed to each member of the battalion, sinking into their skin in an instant. I reflexively ducked as a rune streaked towards me, but it didn't do any good as it smacked me between the eyes. I felt nothing.

Then the world came alive around me.

Where there was once darkness there was light. Instead of the buttery light of the gems that reached a hundred feet or so before petering out, I could see *everything*. The Tilwhar gave us all the ability to see at night as if were day.

A kilometer away lay the other side of the massive, almost perfectly circular caldera, and it was swarming with shadows. Thousands and thousands of shadows, a horde of black razor beings of all shapes and sizes blotting out the ground, a living carpet of black that undulated weirdly as they streamed down the interior slope in what looked to be an unending tide a flood of cold, black death.

And then came the kobolds.

If I thought the little fuckers were tenacious and terrifying before, this time their single-minded, almost insane attack that came as we were trying to catch our breaths made me lose about twenty pounds of fear in sweat. They gave no thought to eating their dead as we punctured them, instead bounding along the rim of the caldera from both sides, a fleshy, toady carpet of teeth and dead, black eyes that saw us as something to snack upon before shitting us out. Within moments they were on us.

Like the disciplined soldiers they were, the ogres drew their weapons and set to work with a fierce unity and precision that set my hair on end. Before they had merely tried to hold the line against the horde of kobolds, to spare those behind and limit the loss of life. This time the giantkin came to play. The thirty-plus-foot-wide section of ground that was the lip of the caldera allowed three ogres to stand abreast and begin imitating a Cuisinart, their blades flashing almost too fast for me to follow. Dark blood sprayed from the collision of small bodies, drenching the great, musclebound humanoids with blood that flew far and wide. Imagine a few dozen hamsters being thrown into a spinning lawnmower blade and you'll get the idea.

While bits of kobold flesh rained down, I grabbed the mace on my right arm and twisted the head sharply, disconnecting it with a sharp click. With cold fingers I pulled a foot-long blade from a sheath on my thigh and jammed it onto the connecting port that was part of the forearm cup, a neat little design I offered the blacksmith who had made my accessory. Holding the blade by the ricasso, I twisted it to the sticking place. Now I had a dagger, probably a more effective tool against the kobolds than a mace, as long as I didn't slice my kibbles and bits off.

To the left and right the triple lines of ogres began to advance, the larger giants behind them throwing rocks that killed dozens of kobolds with each hit, but the little skinks kept coming, regardless of the consequences, just like the last time. They attacked like beasts instead of intelligent beings, maddened beasts with no desire to protect themselves, and you'd think that would be enough to win the day, to bulldoze past the giantkin, but it wasn't. Nowhere near close enough, and despite the fact that here and there an ogre fell under a mass of writhing bodies in their implacable advance, there was always someone else to take their place, to raise their blades against the tide.

I knew the kobolds were pushed by the shadows to slow us down and wanting to see if my guess about their plan was correct, I raced to the edge to look down the inner slope of the caldera. Much to my horror and dismay, I found my fears confirmed.

I hate being right all the time.

About six-hundred feet below lay a bubbling lake of lava that sent billows of smoke into the night sky, a lake larger than a football field that radiated a heat I could feel from the lip. The heat warmed my face pleasantly, but the smell of Sulphur and superheated stone made me sneeze explosively. The far side of the lake was dark with crusted rock cracked and splintered by the heat, rock that had formed because the shadows dove into the lava by the hundreds, by the thousands, in an effort to freeze the lake deep, to send bone chilling cold down into the heart of the mountain and kill it. The vast energies that powered the lightgems would fail and reduce the network into just some greenish rocks that did little to protect fragile humankind. The shadows were trying to kill the mountain.

"Jesus wept," I whispered. "It's a kamikaze raid."

Madrigal swept forward and looked at the seething mass of shadows committing suicide, throwing themselves into the lava to create that hard crust that immediately began to melt again. But as more and more shadows died, the crust became bigger, thicker, the cold energy of the shadows slowly overwhelming the lake. Smoke and steam blew crazily in the frigid wind of the heights, momentarily obscuring the scene. "Can they do it?" she asked.

"The Queen obviously thinks so," I replied. The thing was, I thought so too.

Commander Tegg chose that moment to snag us by the collars of our heavy coats and haul us away from the edge. "Just because you stopped one long range weapon doesn't mean they don't have another. We can't afford to lose a wizard!"

Stupid, stupid, stupid, stupid! What the hell was I thinking? I berated myself for becoming sloppy in my old age. If I was in Tegg's position, I probably would've kicked my ass for such an idiotic risk.

"They want us to split our forces." Tegg continued. "Hammer us from both sides, but I'm going to set up a rearguard action and advance to just one side." His fierce eyes bored into mine. "Which way do you recommend we go? To the left or right?"

"Well, the sniper was set up to the right, so let's go *toward* where the long-range weapon was set up." I looked to where I aimed the fire bolt. "If she has another weapon, we need to neutralize that one first. I suggest the bulk of the ogres advance to the right while a few ogres and the larger giantkin hold the rear, retreating slowly." I considered things for a moment. "And have the Shadowfighters keep a lookout for kobolds coming along the flanks. They may be fighting on the rim now, but I have a feeling that they might try descending and maneuvering to attack from below. Your crossbows will be most effective at that point."

That earned me a brief nod as the commander began shouting orders to carry the plan out, and with the precision of a Swiss watch, the battalion did exactly that. Almost as one, the rearguard began a slow retreat while shedding kobold blood in buckets, as the front line started to stamp their way forward, flinging kobolds bodies down the slopes of Idelhorde.

From my time in the flame, I knew that the lip of the caldera had been smoothed by thousands of giantkin and human feet over the centuries, the fissures and cracks filled in by those who came to marvel at the home of the long gone Fire Giants, and it was no surprise to see the remains of paving stones beneath our feet. Although said stones were liberally painted in kobold blood and decorated with bits of mashed flesh trampled flat. I kept my eyes up and forward so I didn't have to see what I stepped on, but every now and then something gave with a wet squish that had the gorge rising in my throat.

During our slow advance across the caldera, shadows continued to pour down into the lake below and more steam rose into the sky. I snuck a peek.

Halfway. Half of the lake was now a black crust of freezing rock. Shit.

I bet Alex would've found a way to hasten our advance against the seeming unending tide of kobolds, but I couldn't think of one that didn't drain me like a punctured water balloon. If I used too much magic my time on Muspelheim was over.

The crack of a rifle report sounded and an ogre staggered back, blood spurting from a hole in his shoulder. Another took his place in line quickly and efficiently, slicing a kobold in half with a hand axe, the head looked to be the size of a dinner plate.

"Wizard Kal!" Tegg shouted. "Can you do something about that?"

Shit. Either I missed with the last spell or Shiana had another rifle. Take your pick.

Another shot and this time an ogre's head snapped back. Blood gushed from a hole in his nose as he dropped. More of this and the advance would be stalled.

This was a holding action, I realized. They didn't need to beat us, they just needed time to blunt the energy from the volcano for a while, and then they could shadowtravel to every city and destroy entire populaces.

Madrigal grabbed my shoulder. "What's wrong?"

The slow, familiar burn of anger smoldered in my gut. "I've been thinking too much of the physical aspect of this battle," I said over the noise of the slaughter. "Not the magical one." There it was, the truth that slapped onto the ground between us. Too much time thinking like a fighter, not a wizard who could figure out how this magic shit actually works and use it to my best advantage. I used that anger to galvanize my thoughts, to actually use my brain for something other than the meat sponge that housed my mind. I used it to *think*.

Rafa can divine answers, find shit out quick. The Tilwhar slings runes that can explode and effect the mind. All this takes power, energy which seems to come from the wizard. Okay, Kal, it's pretty fucking obvious that the energy output of a fire spell is pretty severe, which, in turn, exhausts my happy ass, so what kind of spell can I cast that doesn't knock me butt over teakettle?

Will, not spell shapes. That meant that spells were linked to the imagination, what the wizard could conceive, which I proved with the fire bolt that looked to have burned with the heat of a magnesium flare.

Hmmm.

"I got it." My smile became a wicked thing. Madrigal looked at me doubtfully and I chuckled. "This should work."

Here's to hoping . . .

Instead of white-hot flame, I imagined the steady orange of a dry oak burning, the kind flame you'd see in a fireplace that keeps you all warm and toasty. I concentrated as another ogre fell, shot through the chest. A kobold arm fell at my feet, long fingers with sharp nails twitching. *Come on, Kal.*

Fifty feet of the caldera lip in front of us suddenly sprouted fire. Not the all-consuming blaze that turned flesh into charcoal briquettes in an instant, but the steady flames of a gasoline fire, liquid and pure. The battalion came to a halt, recoiling from the heat.

And I made it sticky, too.

Kobolds screamed in agony; harsh squeals of rabbits trapped by a predator. Flaming toadies bounded off the lip of the caldera, little skinky fireballs that bounced down the mountainside leaving behind their screams and the smell of burning frogs.

"What did you do?" screamed Tegg.

I looked down the slope. "Cleared the way." The effort hadn't drained me much, and I felt a slight grogginess but nothing too extreme, so I decided to do the same thing to the little bastards harassing our rear guard. The little bit of dizziness and savage cries of pain behind me let me know that it worked like a charm. Not willing to overdo it, I snuffed out the fires in front.

Charred bodies lined the way, smoking in the night air, but that didn't bother the giantkin any because they charged, clearing the fifty feet of corpses (flattening them nicely) to smash into the kobolds beyond. Toadies in a blender.

As for me, I still felt pretty good, so I decided to start the whole process again.

And again.

And again.

More ogres fell, but because of their height I couldn't get a bead on where the shots originated, and I sure as shit wasn't going to stick my head out to check. As it was, a wave of fatigue was washing over me like an incoming tide, but I soldiered on, bolstered by the fact that we were making good progress despite the cost in ogre lives. That's when the fecal matter truly impacted upon the rotary oscillator.

Even though we were making headway thanks to my carpet of fire, the shadows still appeared over the lip of the caldera in a surge that descended into the lake, which was now about two-thirds crusted over. By my calculations, we'd make it to the north end and the shadows in a couple of minutes to disrupt their self-sacrificing tide.

It was Madrigal who alerted me as to what was happening, pointing north and a little above the lip of the caldera. I followed that finger and about lost my lunch.

A horizontal slice of blackness a couple hundred feet across suddenly appeared a few feet above the lip, a thin line of darkness so black it not only sucked in all light, but seemed to tug at the soul as well, as if that darkness was the negation of everything. A thin thread of empty that slowly grew and grew until it resembled a rough oval of black that had my stomach rebelling in record time, like I'd eaten the breakfast special at Jack in the Box.

Something squeezed through that darkness, spilling from it like black blood from a gaping wound, a being of immense size and power and indefinable shape. I had the impression of a black octopus constructed of midnight glass and razor blades, an icy evil that reached down my throat to my heart and *squeezed*. I knew the being that appeared would never put herself in harm's way if she could avoid it, so the fact that she had showed herself told me how close the shadows were to completing their task, which added to the acid in my gut.

In my time Muspelhiem the giantkin had held themselves with aplomb and the cool dignity of diplomats, showing nothing but resolve and determination. Now I saw them react in fear.

The ogres howled, their voice an ululation of panic as they cowered, the kobolds taking heart and redoubling their efforts. The line faltered. As for the other giantkin, they gaped in shock at the black heart of the evil that slowly, with a spider's grace, descended to the caldera's northern lip as if stepping down from a carriage. Many of the Shadowfighters vomited in their tracks, and I couldn't blame them because my stomach wasn't too happy with what I saw, either.

Dripping from the immense black shadow were smaller shadows that joined the tide flowing down into the lava lake below, hastening the slow death of Idelhorde. Steam from the lake redoubled, partially blocking the view of the hideous creature constructed of shards of black glass and knives.

Yeah, we were fucked.

Madrigal, voice clotted with fear and puke, said, "Is that—?"

I nodded. "Yeah, the Shadow Queen."

SEVENTEEN

Things just got epic

IT WAS THE WAIN, YOU SEE. I'd forgotten all about it. Apparently, during all the fuss so had everyone else, except for the Mountain Giant minders who decided that now was a good time to put our secret weapon to use. Said secret weapon exploded out of the wain, sending wooden shards everywhere, a chunk of which lodged itself into my calf, a splinter five inches long and about one-half inch thick.

Surt. Goddamned Surt burst out of the wain which wasn't a wain at all, but a fucking insulated box designed to carry a seriously pissed off golem, who landed in a full run, vaulting over the front line like a kangaroo on steroids, landing amidst the seething kobolds who recoiled from the fiercely hot golem, flesh sizzling. Each running step killed dozens and the little skinks scattered, crying shrilly as Surt ran with alarming speed across the lip of the caldera. It didn't take more than a second for the giantkin to follow, their spirits soaring at the sight of their Emperor, roaring in defiance at the Shadow Queen as she belched more shadows into the lake below.

Grimacing, I yanked the splinter from my calf and with a flick of my mind set another fifty-foot wall of flame behind us.

I followed, eyes swimming with fatigue, trying to keep up with Madrigal who had slowed enough to grab my arm, urging me along at breakneck speed over remains of shattered paving stones, quite of bit of them covered in pulped kobold. At least the little bastards were good for something.

Another flash and report and Surt flinched slightly as a high-caliber round impacted on his forehead, but there didn't seem to be any damage, and all it did was to urge him to greater speeds. I saw through the press of ogres another flash before the golem swept out one great arm and swipe a tiny, humanoid shape down the mountainside. Scratch one sniper.

Sweat drooled into my eyes and dizziness threatened to shake me off my feet. The cost/benefit of the magic biz was tilting against me, so I flicked off the fire behind, which had the kobolds surging our rear guard again.

"I can't keep doing this!" I yelled to Commander Tegg.

Instead of answering, Tegg turned to the Shadowfighters supporting our rearguard, motioning to the swiftly advancing front line. "Go. We have this."

I gave the man a nod and stumbled after the line, putting my back to the sound of impacting bodies and the screams of the dying. Madrigal still had a killer grip on my shoulder, but I wasn't too proud to shake her off. At least the fatigue was starting to ebb slightly.

In front, advancing swiftly upon the Queen, Surt began to glow with a fiery intensity, light streaming from his body like the gems he had created to protect his people. Brighter and brighter he shone, until he looked like a star racing along Idelhorde at ever greater speeds, leaping over obstacles and shadows in his way, running with furious purpose and single-minded resolve.

Of course, the Queen noticed, and the giant, jagged beast shrunk from the light, flailing limbs trying to block out the radiance that burned her. Black steam erupted from her sharp-edged body and the shadow children that dripped from her like slime from a sewer bubbled and boiled into a dark mist as if they were droplets of water in a fire.

A noise hit us with sledgehammer force, bringing an intense keening of fear that we felt down into our guts. So much was conveyed in that rusty nail scraping against porcelain sound that I could hardly understand its entirety. Fear, sure . . . but rage as well, along with defiance and kind of shuddering negation as if such emotions were too alien for her to handle. Giantkin and humans alike screamed along with the Queen of Shadows as the sound tore at us, driving us to our knees, ears bleeding from the intensity.

That shadow ruler's vast bulk began to withdraw into the hole in the air, the shadow portal that I reckoned led back to her lair half a world away. But it wasn't fast enough, not by a long shot, because Surt was right there, a shooting star that flew across the ground to slam into her center mass with a sound like a boulder smashing into a well filled with volcanic glass and shards of old sheet metal, a sound so loud that the lot of us were swept off our knees.

I flew through the air, surprised and deafened, a tumbling mass of aged Finn that started to bounce down the mountainside until something hit my harder than usual skull and I decided it was time for a nap.

PAIN EVERYWHERE, DEEP AND POUNDING. Head splitting, a knot between my eyebrows so big it made the great pyramid at Giza look like a pimple. It hurt to move, so I didn't. Instead, I tried to open my eyes and was mildly surprised when I succeeded. Dark. Black with a hint of light came somewhere past the crown of my head, but that's not what really drew my eyes.

It was the stars, you see. A billion of them, more than I'd seen in a long, long while with a nice arc of a galactic arm eclipsing half the sky. The beauty of the unknown constellations would've knocked me on my ass if I hadn't been flat on my back.

Then there were the moons. Three of them, one large and dominant in the sky, and two tiny ones in orbit like eager puppies, visibly moving around their master. The big one looked bluish while the smaller moons were miniature versions of Midgard's orbiting satellites, pocked marked faces facing Muspelheim, leering down at the unconcerned earth as they hurled through space.

A few minutes of staring allowed me to come to full consciousness and to assess my condition. Bones broken: none, thank God. Contusions: too many to count, so don't bother. Head: still attached, if just barely, but no nausea, so probably no concussion. I decided to make an effort to sit up.

Yeeeargh!

Sweating heavily, the cold biting at my fevered skin, I swore a few dozen times as the pain radiating from my thigh slid right in my brain, setting up shop between my eyes and behind that ungodly knot that throbbed to beat of my pounding heart. I looked down. Something stuck up from the meat of my leg, an alien intrusion upon my tender bod. By the dim light I could see that it was the dagger portion of my forearm cup, which I noted was no longer attached. I guess during my tumble the weapon cup must've been knocked off, the dagger broken. Maybe I had landed on the dagger during a bounce, I don't know, but it sure as shit hurt like a bastard, deep and keen.

A little blood seeped around the blade that stuck out two inches from the heavy canvas trousers. Some it had frozen, but not a lot. I felt a near overwhelming desire just to flick the stub of blade, just to see what would happen, but I kept the morbid impulse in check. I'd seen grown men and women fiddle with wounds, with tears and punctures in their flesh, poking and prodding to the point where they start screaming in pain. It was the disconnect between the flesh before and after, the strange fascination about something that shouldn't be there, and I nearly fell for it like a goddamn newbie.

I looked back and saw a dim light coming from the top of the volcano, some lightgem on the lip of the caldera providing enough to see by, if just barely. The muscles of my leg were wrapped around that shard of dagger like a lover's embrace, and I figured if I tried pulling it free I'd start a gusher I might not be able to stop.

"Are you all right, Kal?" asked a high voice filled with gravel and grit.

The person limping toward me along the flank of Idelhorde was dappled in light and shadow, but I could see the thick bulk of Shadowfighter leathers hugging her curves.

"Depends on what you consider all right." I replied. "Been better."

"So you will live?" *Crunch, crunch,* the Shadowfighter moved closer.

"Yeah. A little beat up, but at my age that's to be expected."

I could say it was the glint of moonlight on metal that warned me, or some nifty sixth sense that told me she was about to drastically shorten my life span, but it was none of those. See . . . she spoke *English* and like a moron I didn't realize it until it was almost too late. Adrenaline surged and I rolled to the side as a short sword *chunked* into the ground where my heart was an instant before. Agony ripped across my leg, but survival is survival and pain takes a back seat to not becoming rather permanently dead.

My feet found themselves under me as the sword swept up, slicing along my coat, which parted to its keen edge. A hot sting told me the sword hadn't entirely missed. I stumbled back, eyes on the sword, hand slapping the empty spot on the small of my back where the Lahti once lay. Shit.

Another swing and I tried for a straight jab as and my leg buckled, but I managed to grab my attacker's sword arm. A knobby fist hit my nose and pain blossomed behind my eyes as it broke with a solid crunch. Blood gushed, slicking my teeth as I wheezed, turning my head as the hand came down again to smash against my cheek, my eyes watering some more. Desperately I grabbed at the arm, and managed to deflect the blow right to my ear, which became a hot ball of flame that joined all my other hurts. On one knee, I had both my attacker's arms, and was trying to keep the sword from my neck and the fist from my throbbing face when a knee introduced itself rudely to my chin.

I went down seeing only stars, but I knew the sword would soon find me and the fight would be over. Survival instincts kicked into overdrive, and I did the only thing to distance myself from the woman who was trying a thousand and one methods to drastically shorten the lifespan of a stubborn Finn. I threw myself down the mountainside.

Now, Idlelhorde looked to be composed of gently angled slopes that a person could almost leisurely climb in a day, which is deceptive as hell because there are plenty of places where a body could meet a messy end: crevasses, sharp drops, rock outcroppings eager to break the bones of the unwary. It had seemed like my goose was well and thoroughly cooked, but I somehow managed miss most of those things. Instead, I found myself shredding skin against much smaller rocks, leaving behind great swaths of clothing and small chunks of meat.

The world went all red and wobbly as the broken dagger was pounded harder and harder into my leg until it disappeared from sight, only the blood, black in the light of the moons, marking where it lay beneath the surface. Once again my skull hit a rock that refused to be soft and plushy, and things went white and red for a bit.

When I stopped, it was because of a low shrub with a thick trunk that knocked the breath from my lungs as I near tore it from the ground, my stomach the recipient of a vegetable gut punch.

Vomit splashed the ground, the jerky and dried fruit I'd eaten a few hours ago reintroducing themselves to the outside world. But I didn't care much about that because I couldn't catch a breath, it was like trying to breathe through a flattened straw.

The steady crunch of boots on shattered scree told me the woman was making her way down to me, fixing to finish me off. My diaphragm refused to cooperate, until suddenly, my chest expanded with sweet, cold air, and I almost cried with relief as I gasped buckets, lungs bellowing in and out.

"You lack the will for success," came the gravelly, high-pitched voice. "You can't do what's necessary. I can. That's why you'll die on this mountain and the worlds will evaporate to be made anew."

Ugh . . . monologue-ing. Why did they always have to do that? It was bad enough to want to kill me, but boring me to death? Then the realization of what she said sent fear icing up my spine. The worlds evaporating . . . it had to be that sniper, whatshername . . . Shiana.

These Apostles were really starting to chap my ass.

Favoring my right leg, I managed to regain my feet to see the shadowy form of the sniper approaching cautiously from upslope, wicked short sword in hand. I surmised she must've taken the armor from a dead Shadowfighter and slipped off to find yours truly when the world went all wonky after Surt had attacked the Queen.

"C'mon," I croaked, mouth filled with blood. "I ain't got all day."

"I am willing to die, Hakala, to achieve my goal. You cannot die to achieve yours. This is why I'll win."

It hurt to move. It hurt to fucking breathe, but knowing that my death was walking toward me carrying a sword provided motivation, and her cocksure attitude was pissing me off no end. What was I willing to do to win? If I died, then the Tree would have to find some other schlub to make the effort and while I wasn't afraid of dying, I was damn sure afraid of putting the existence of my son into some other person's hands. That I couldn't abide. Call it my control issues at play.

No, dying was out, but that didn't mean that I was going to roll over for this fucking asshole. "Come on then," I said, blood spilling down my chin. Something inside was broken, it hurt to breathe. My left hand rose, filled with fourteen inches of insanely sharp steel. The bowie felt good in my palm.

The last few steps Shiana took were at a clopping, plodding run, but it was a damn sight faster than I could've managed, the silver moonlight gleaming off her short sword as it came down in a savage arc. I juked left, taking all my weight on that leg, and slashed out with the bowie as the sword came a hairsbreath from editing my arm from my body. Shiana took the knife to her breast plate with no more damage than creased leather.

Anger slowly cut through pain and fatigue as I slapped her sword hand aside. She might have been a good sniper, but she was shit with a sword and I'd made it my business as a BSI agent to fight with any weapon I could lay my hands on. Hell, give me a paper clip and some duct tape and I'd MacGuyver up a neutron bomb. Keeping my distance from her now that I had my unsteady legs beneath me was almost easy peasy, despite the fact that I felt like ten miles of bad road.

Almost easy peasy. She still had me on speed because, in my current condition, I was moving with the swiftness of an aging, arthritic walrus. I stabbed with the bowie and Shiana parried my slow thrust easily. I wish I could say I was afraid, but everything I'd been through left nothing except the slow, simmering anger tempered with fatigue and pain.

A stinging slice landed across my right arm and slow warmth trickled down my forearm. She shifted her stance sideways and stared down at me with contempt, sure in the knowledge that she'd whittle me down to a bleeding, twitching wreck within a minute.

What was I willing to do to win? Short of dying, that is . . . the answer came to me quickly and I acted before reason could alter my plan. Shiana was a great sniper, but as a swordsman she'd make a better pastry chef, so when she thrust with the short sword, I did the one thing she didn't expect.

I impaled myself on her weapon.

Steel slid into my guts, hot and sharp through my left flank, stealing the strength from my legs, but I locked my knees and remained standing, the pain igniting the rage deep within into a bonfire that I used for strength. Shiana's mouth was a dark cavern of shock and I closed it with a head butt to her nose that broke it nicely, her dark blood smearing my face. Her hand loosened on the sword and I pried it from her grasp, dropping the bowie and leaving the short sword lodged in my side where it did nothing good to my guts.

A quick, hard punch in the throat destroyed her larynx, deforming it under my knuckles, and her eyes grew wide as she dropped to the ground, thrashing and making funny little gurgling noises. I watched impassively as she died, her face frozen in a rictus of surprise and pain soon she ceased moving on the frozen ground. Surprisingly, I felt no satisfaction, not even a twinge of pleasure at Shiana's death . . . not like in the past when I'd killed someone who'd tried to put me six feet under. There was always that little twinge that said I was alive and my enemy wasn't, a twinge that belonged to that little guilty part of me, the Neolithic grunter that beat his chest in victory like Tarzan.

Damn, I was tired. And my leg hurt so fucking much. More scars among the multitude. I looked down at the sword running front to back on my left side just under my ribs. Pretty certain something important was skewered and screwed.

One foot in front of the other, each step a lesson in agony as my limping right leg screamed at me, insisting I lie the fuck down and not move for about ten years. Strangely enough, there wasn't any pain in my side, but when I looked down, yep . . . the hilt of sword bobbed with every breath, the blade still buried somewhere in my gut. You'd think I'd be doubled up and vomiting blood.

Down deep I felt bones stir as I breathed, sharp pricks of pain that didn't hold a candle to what my leg was feeling, but I had to keep going, needing to find someone, needing to see what happened to the shadows, to Surt, to the Queen and soon those thoughts bled away from the wounds in my body. I was so tired but moving was the only thing keeping me alive, so I kept putting one heavy foot in front of the other, stubbornly refusing to quit until I fell dead.

Time turned out to be a fleeting concept as I kept my slow shamble upslope toward the light that shone upon the lip of the caldera. Everything had become a dreamlike haze of coppery blood and agony that drove away all reason and rationale. Only the walking mattered, not Des, not reality, not the Tree . . . nothing.

Hands the size of Nebraska grasped me, nudging the sword slightly and boy did I feel *that*. I screamed my way into unconsciousness.

EIGHTEEN

Aftermath

No pain. How novel. I blinked once, twice, three times before the world came into focus, and then wished I hadn't because the first thing that hit my baby blues was the sight of Elegat peering down at me, her upthrust tusks looking sharp enough to slice through reality.

What had roused me was a strange up and down motion that turned out to be Elegat herself, who was carrying me in her arms like a child. Light shone bright in my eyes from the gems fixed the spears that surrounded us.

Elegat snorted. "You are awake, Wizard Kal."

I heard the capital W. "Uh, yeah." Usually the wide open eyes was the first clue, but I wasn't about to pull snark on an ogre who could pull a Lenny from *Of Mice and Men* on me.

"You are gravely injured. Do not move, we return to Til Mathgen." She flicked her eyes to the side. "Madrigal Rhone, he is awake."

A moment later the top half of Madrigal's face came into view. "I'm glad you survived. So far."

That begged the question, "What?"

Her green eyes sharpened. "You took a lot of damage. How do you feel?"

Surprisingly well and I said so.

"That is the medicine we gave you, a powerful narcotic that dulls pain and instills a sense of euphoria."

Wow, so this world had Oxy, too. I giggled and felt a sharp twinge in my side.

"Careful," admonished Madrigal. "You still have a hole in you. The Tilwhar said you were not to move or the wound would bleed more."

One smart wizard lady who, it seemed, had survived her feat of magic on the volcano. I grinned at the thought of that sourpuss doling out medical advice like a medieval version of *Dr. Quinn, Medicine Woman*. "Dr. The Tilwhar," I giggled, feeling bones move with every twitch of my muscles. It hurt in a dim sort of way, not enough to raise a concern. Not that I could have lifted a concern to examine anyway, I was as weak as a little bitty kitty.

"I see we've given you too much," Madrigal said drily.

"Oh, you can't have too much medicine," I retorted with wide, sloppy grin. "Besides, I'm alive and that's pretty fucking good." I looked at my leg and would've gasped in horror if I wasn't doped to the gills. My thigh was nearly twice normal size, straining the fabric of the heavy trousers that had been loose before. Not good. Double plus ungood. I giggled.

Madrigal's upper lip twitched. "Yes, pretty fecking good indeed." Humor danced in her eyes, but it was mixed with a healthy dose of sadness.

"You mind telling me what happened?" I asked.

"What do you remember?"

"The caldera. Surt bursting from the wain. The Shadow Queen appearing. They went boom and that woman from my world, Shiana, tried to poke lots of holes in me." I examined my body and saw a red-soaked bandage wrapping my thigh. "Two holes at least. Oh, and my leg's all messed up, too."

"The Tilwhar removed a large splinter of metal from your leg. You're lucky it didn't hit the artery or we wouldn't be talking." She paused a moment. "And the sword in your side didn't help matters at all, either."

I'd given enough bad news in my life that I knew when someone was holding back. "And?" I prodded.

"And you're going to die. Soon."

"Oh." *Des* . . .

"But not if we can get you to the holy flame on time."

You'd figure I'd be angry, but the drugs they'd given me wouldn't let the fire burn. "You know you should really lead with that."

"I can't think of another who deserves it more with that mouth you have."

She wasn't wrong, my mouth has a mind of its own. "Good thing we're on the same side or you would've left me on that damn mountain."

"Don't think the thought didn't cross my mind." Her smile, a real honest-to-god smile, almost melted my heart.

We stared at each other for a while the tramping of boots held the rhythm of the pulse in my ears. It felt almost peaceful, in the cold and the soft yellow light of the gems mounted on spears and shields. I let it lull me into a fluid torpor that comforted me for a while before a thought finally floated to the surface of my mind.

"You gonna tell me or do I have to guess?"

A soft sigh that barely reached my ears. "You know."

I did. "Surt's dead. He went for a suicide run that did the Queen dirty and ended the threat. If I had to guess, the shadows aren't going to be a problem anymore."

"Well aren't you a bright burn mark? Got it in one, Kal. Surt knew the Queen would be at Idelhorde because only she had the power to freeze the heart of the volcano, so he hid in the wain so as not to be seen."

I tried to shrug and wound up sending a twinge of pain through my gut. "Wasn't that big of a secret if I figured it out. Hel, I think just about everyone knew. Everyone but the shadows. My guess is that the Queen's mind doesn't work in such a way that she'd reckon someone with Surt's might would deign to be enclosed in a well-insulated mobile coffin for a few hours."

"That was the Emperor's thought was as well."

Some pieces of the puzzle didn't quite fit and I tried to noodle on the problem for a bit, but in my drugged state thoughts were like greased eels, so I asked the obvious question, "What now?"

Madgrial sighed. "First Minister Vestaverous will assume the mantle of Emperor for a while until a peaceful transition of power can be accomplished. Emperor Surt left specific instructions on how to restructure the government in such a way for there to be adequate representation for all peoples of the Empire, a parliament."

That clever bastard. I laughed out loud, then winced in pain, but it didn't stop me from chuckling up a storm. Elegat and Madrigal both gave me the old hairy eyeball, but I didn't give with the humor, wanting to savor it for a while. They say laughter is the best medicine.

Time passed in a pleasant, narcotic haze in the arms of an ogress who could snap me in half with the ease of a child breaking a balsa wood toy. That drug they used should come in six-packs.

Despite my wounds the battalion rested, catching a couple of hours of much-needed sleep in the middle of the road, the camp ringed with lightgems to ward of shadows that were no longer there. A sour-faced The Tilwhar informed me that I could stand to use a few hours of rest, and was in no threat of dying just yet.

Campfires were lit, not for light but for heat and cooking. The darkness was kept at bay, but night's chill dominated the air. I sat next to the largest fire, just me and Elegat left to our devices. Out of respect or unease, I had no idea, but we bathed in the heat, luxuriating in it, and despite how warm my clothes became, the heat couldn't dispel the chill that had settled onto my bones like a cancer.

Elegat sat behind me, staring into the fire while my skin pleasantly tingled in the heat. Madrigal had disappeared somewhere but

I didn't much care because the cold that had settled deep inside took my thoughts. How much time? Would I make it to the holy flame? I knew the first stages of peritonitis were underway in my bowels, a long and gruesome death by fever and delirium, but I'd suffered other injuries as well. My leg, my skull. A deep ache lived behind my eyes, and I knew there was the real possibility of a concussion. The sum total of my hurts could do me in before too long, and that dominated my mind.

A big finger flicked my ear. I didn't have the energy to slap at the offending digit. "Someone comes," rumbled Elegat.

"You didn't have to smack me in the ear," I complained.

"Where's the fun in that?"

I grunted, eyes focusing on the person walking calmly toward the fire. Shadowfighter leathers, helm and spear adding its light to the glow all around. The man walked with a limp, and I saw a red-spotted linen bandage wrapped around his right ankle.

"Took you long enough," I drawled, hiding a yawn.

The man spoke softly from the shelter of his boiled leather helm. "You know me?"

"Been waiting for you."

Wendiver Halt removed his helmet and stared at me with eyes like painted marbles. "How?"

I gave a little shrug. It hurt. "Figured it out. Wasn't too hard once I knew how the pieces fit together."

The spy sat, wincing. "What pieces do you think you have?"

"There were no Splinters after Madrigal. It was a ruse. Surt set everything up. He used you to get close to the shadowspy and give him the information about Idelhorde. Once that was done, he sent soldiers from the fort to the caldera while the battalion marched to reinforce, but he still underestimated how quickly the Shadow Queen would act. He thought she would be more circumspect, less apt to take such a risk, and that he would have more time for the set-up before she appeared. She attacked the fortress, killed everyone inside, and had her shadows round up dozens of clans of kobolds to delay the march." I took a deep breath. "That was the big flaw in the Emperor's plan: the kobolds. He thought she would ignore them until she dealt with us, but what he didn't understand was that she allied herself with the kobolds instead of trying to kill them. My guess is that the kobolds had been on the shadow payroll for a long time, which is why they've survived so long in their warrens. They were already queen's subjects." I'd asked Madrigal about the kobolds once and she'd told me the little skinks could live virtually everywhere, although they preferred dark, dank places. "We were delayed on the road, attacked by the kobolds and the shadow giant. She almost won."

Wendy shrugged. "Almost, but didn't." He spat and the flames ate the moisture. "Do you know what we had to do to get as far as we did? The sacrifices made?" There was anger and sorrow coloring his voice, a husky regret. "Do you know, wizard from another world?"

"My guess is that people died to achieve the objective, but that's the way of things, isn't it? People die to thwart evil, or to bring victory that changes a world, that set history on a different course."

Agony like rusty nails thrusting through eyelids colored Wendy's voice and face as he said. "I played the traitor. Brought the shadowspy into my house, showed him my traps and my escape route through the roof, brought *darkness* into my home all in the effort to prove myself to him, to earn a measure of trust."

"It wasn't enough."

He shook his head. "Not near. He wanted victims, proof that I was the traitor I presented myself to be." A long pause. "The spy, Feadrix was his name, wanted me to bring eyes and ears to him to be killed."

Horror slid slimy feet across my spine. "What?"

"Surt asked for volunteers. Most did. Enough that Feadrix began to believe I could be used without being shadowbit. Then you came along, pursued by those wizards from your world you called the Apostles, and that gave us the impetus to hasten the plan. I had just given the information about Idelhorde to Feadrix when you attacked, and the ensuing fight proved to him that I was a traitor. I fought Madrigal and deliberately lost, although I had to make it look real."

"Madrigal laid down enough crumbs for me set up on your roof. I knew that information provided by the First Ministers and his scribes came a little too easily, a little too quickly. That was my first clue."

"I thought it rather ingenious, actually. We had to push things because of you. You weren't going to stay around for much longer, so we . . . ah . . . *forced* the issue."

While I digested all that, he continued. "We never worked that way before. Such methods aren't thought of. There's been peace in the Empire between the Southern Marches, the Twilight Realm, Cho-bodrur and Veladriec for a millennia, and no need for such subterfuge. The job of an eyes and ears is to assess the fitness of the Empire, to gather intelligence for reasonable governance, not to try to insinuate ourselves into the shadow world. It was strange that the Emperor would agree to such a thing."

I think I had an answer. "Because of me. He knew I was coming. He knew, or at least felt, that I could help tip the balance of the war." I smiled sadly. "Or maybe it was because he knew the world was coming to an end and he wanted to make sure the Shadow Queen died along with the rest of this reality. I was in her mind, at least part of it, while I was in the holy fire. The war between the Aesir and the Vanir brought her and her kind from beyond the reaches of space and time. She might have survived the world's unraveling. Either way, he took the greatest risk he could, rolled the dice and hoped for a seven." I shrugged. "It worked."

"It worked. And killed our Emperor."

"I think he expected to die. He's made provisions. This isn't the end."

"No," said Wendiver. "It isn't. And the idea for this charade wasn't the Emperor's. It was Madrigal's."

Well, fry me in oil and call me a donut. Turns out she had a lot sneakier in her than I had given her credit for.

That lay between us for a little while. Finally, I said, "Figures. This kind of duplicity is more human than that of an immortal golem." We smiled ruefully at each other. "Things are going to change rapidly now, you know. Before you were ruled by an incorruptible artifact, but now your fate will lie in the hands of mortal men and giants. Soon politics is going to become your new four letter word."

"I wish he didn't have to die."

No need to figure out who he was. "We all die. This world nearly died. Eventually all humans and giants will die, and this galaxy will either collide with another, effectively destroying this solar system, or your sun will grow into a red giant and fry this planet to a crisp. Perhaps a meteor will crack this world like an egg, who knows?" I reckoned he hadn't understood half of what I said, but Wendiver nodded nonetheless. "Everything ends, it's what makes life precious. It's what happens *now* that matters most. If I know anything, I know this: we don't end just because we die. We go on, there's something after. Even for giants, despite what they may think. They may be manifestations of this world, but their essence as such will live on, I'm sure of it." I took a drink of water from a leather flask. The cold liquid made my throat ache. "Even for Surt, there's an after. A thousand Fire Giants put their combined essence into his creation and the holy flame transformed him enough that he was able to reach a level of autonomy." That much I had gleaned during my time in Surturvadunir. Before he possessed a rudimentary sort of sentience, but the holy flame transformed him to be something more. "What happens to all that wisdom and such now that he's gone? It has to go somewhere. Take it from a guy who knows more than he cares to, that there's something beyond all this." I waved a hand, indicating the world. "Beyond anything we can dream of."

"What do we do? Now, that is."

"Well, I got me a hole in my gut and my leg feels like someone pumped a few liters of air in it." I looked at my swollen thigh where it strained against my once loose trousers. "You have anything to drink around this joint?"

EPILOGUE

Exit stage left

W ARMTH. NOT A BURNING HEAT, BUT A PLEASANT tingle that dispelled the chill in my bones. I could feel the flesh at my side and thigh beginning to knit, bringing about a furious itch I wanted to scratch.

Surturvadunir burned all around, clothing me in comforting flame. I guess I'd been transformed enough, the crucible having done its job, so now I was left with blessed healing and a slight lassitude. That and the world, like when I drunk from Mimisbrunnr, opened up all around me.

I had made it to Til Mathgen, of course. Thank goodness, or this narrative would be in the third person. No stopping to talk to First Minister Vestaverous (now Emperor Vestaverous, at least for a short while until an efficient transfer of power could be arranged) and only a brief goodbye to Wendy and Madrigal, both of whom looked like someone killed their dogs. Or whatever version of dogs existed in Muspelheim. They were tough, they'd get over the loss of Surt. I had sneaking suspicion the next few years were going to be so busy they weren't going to have a whole lot of time to grieve.

Mind wandering, I cast about for Rafi, the rat bastard who had caused me so much grief. Thoughts caressed Muspelheim, seeking, questing for some sign of the wizard from Midgard, but no matter how hard I searched, I couldn't find him. That left a cold sensation in my gut as I understood I'd probably run into that asshat again.

Well, revenge would have to wait, back to other business. *There* . . . the Sidhe tunnels burrowing through the bark of the Tree, uniform holes in space/time that didn't tear at the universe like the vortices of the Breach. Each one felt smooth as I traced a few, finding that some reached not only to the Primes, but to the mirror worlds as well. I concentrated harder, focusing my thoughts on those tunnels through reality and they became clearer, showing me a three-dimensional map that wobbled my mind.

Over a decade ago artists and entomologists made casts of anthills using dental plaster or liquid aluminum, digging the result up showing off the massive creative ability of the small insects. They looked like multi-branched works of organic art that resembled upside-down pine trees designed by M. Escher on acid. They branched all over the ninety layers of reality, a delicate lattice work of connections that pervaded the bark of the Tree like the holes created by pine beetles.

I blinked, dismissing the image before the complexity could overwhelm me, and I knew I had seriously underestimated the power of the Elves. If the two opposing branches of Sidhe (the Seelie, or kindly elves, and the Unseelie, those who would do us dirty) ever reconciled, they could very possibly take over a goodly portion of all ninety realities.

What a fucking thought.

That wasn't a problem I could dwell on, though. I had bigger fish to fry, so I cast my mind to Svartalfheim, or Nidavellir. Home of the dwarves, the next stop on the Hakala Express to save the nine worlds.

There. I saw it in my mind's eye clear as day, a world much like home . . . three quarters covered in water filled with enormous polar ice caps that at least doubled the size of Midgard's. There were four continents, the three of them at the Equator similar to Australia in size and shape, all separated and with vast swaths of desert in the interior, and the fourth just to the south, circling half the planet, the largest continent by far. Easily larger than Asia, most of it was mountainous and craggy, with enormous forests and a couple of great plains dotted with the corpses of vast volcanos the size of Oklahoma that nearly pierced the upper atmosphere. I knew a few geologists who would give their eyeteeth to study this world.

Once again, I concentrated, and felt a tug toward that great continent that I knew was my next port of call. Hopefully I could stick the landing this time and not wind up becoming someone's clodder. I've had enough of shackles, thank you very much.

I double checked my belongings, the bowie and the Lahti with its spare clips. Lucky Madrigal found it and returned it to me. I kept it safe from the whirling flames of the holy fire with a small piece of magic that flowed through me.

Time to go.

As I slid along the smooth tunnel through reality provided by the Sidhe, a construct that went beyond the physical and so had no real definition, I felt a sudden tickle at the back of my mind, and before everything went wobbly and dark, a familiar human mind touched me. Like mine it was filled with pain and loss and had been through the worst life could throw at it, and emerged hard and bitter, yet hopeful. I felt her purpose, a similar iron resolve to get the job done and do it right.

Before the darkness took me I smiled inwardly. I wasn't the only one trying to save the Tree. Looks like I had company.

To be continued in
THE DWARVES OF NIDAVELLIR

B ORN IN HELSINKI, FINLAND, I ARRIVED in the U.S. at a young age and promptly dove into the world of the fantastic. Starting at age seven with the Iliad and the Odyssey, I went on to consume every scrap of Norse Mythology I could get my grubby little paws on. At age thirteen I graduated to Tolkien and Heinlein, building up a book collection that soon rivaled the local public library's. In college I majored in Journalism and minored in English. Currently I have ten published works and I am feverishly working on my next book while my amazingly patient wife, Brandie, keeps me and our two sons, Aeden and Gabriel, in check.

I can be reached on Facebook at Author Mark Everett Stone
Twitter: @M3verettStone